APRIL SKIES

M.B. Lewis

*To Andrew and all my children, thank you
for all your love and support.*

PROLOGUE

ale yellow smudges of early morning light were beginning to seep over the horizon, lighting the cold and barren fields.

It was a good day to die. At least that's what Ellie kept telling herself as she pushed her old black Citroën down the winding country road. Her grip on the steering wheel was tight, her knuckles blanching with the pressure, her mind deliberately numb as she braked late into the corner on the icy surface, misjudging her speed.

The old car fishtailed as the tyres fought for grip on the slippery surface, and she only just managed to drag the car from a full skid as she tore over the stone bridge, her speedometer wobbling around fifty. She needed to get a grip and calm down. Losing control now would really screw with their plans.

She eased her foot off the accelerator and concentrated on slowing her breathing. As she rounded the second-to-last bend, doubts began to cloud her thoughts and chip at her resolve.

A single tear escaped, rolling aimlessly down her cheek and she flicked it away. She was about to break Finn's heart, but she was out of options. Accepting the inevitability of the situation did nothing to lessen the anguish tearing at her insides. Her only hope was that he would forgive her – in time.

It was too early to see any other cars on the seldom-used B-road, heightening her awful sense of isolation. She could have been driving on an uninhabited planet at the edge of time. But she was used to being alone. Ever since she was a child she had struggled through life by herself. Except for Harry, and now Finn – but look where trusting Finn and his empty promises of a happy, yet unobtainable future had led her.

The next bend was sharp with large red and white hazard signs – a well-known accident black spot. It was perfect for her needs. The winter-bare branches of the huge oak beckoned to her, sealing her fate. She pulled carefully into the layby opposite the tree, careful to avoid leaving any suspicious tyre marks.

She'd arrived early. The sudden quiet was unnerving and encouraged the growing void of despair inside her. It was all happening too fast. There had been so little time to think and no time to plan. She'd grown careless and made one mistake; one moment of misjudgement after years of vigilance. Being caught in the background of a photograph in a local newspaper had destroyed her life and her happiness – her almost-family.

With Finn, she had felt safe for the first time since that dreadful day she'd arrived at the children's home. His all-encompassing love and commitment had left her complacent, presumptuous even, believing she could live a normal life as a normal person. But she would never be safe.

He had found her. After all these years and all her precautions, he had found her. Cold fear filled her belly as she relived the nightmarish moment he had attacked her in the car park.

Older memories stirred – the things he did and the things he threatened, echoing from her childhood. The past and present collided in a jumble of dread as her heart quivered in her chest. No one was safe – not her, not Finn and definitely not the baby. Her hand fell instinctively to her stomach. She had to protect them, whatever the cost.

She forced a calming breath and then another, and with enormous effort she tried to push all thoughts of Finn from her mind. She needed to focus on the task at hand, or *he* would hurt them all.

Scraping her long blond hair into a high ponytail, she kept her mind purposely blank and pushed her fear downwards, deep inside her to the place it had lurked since she was a little girl. Resolve turned her heart cold. Her actions would slay Finn to the bone, but her priority had to be the baby growing inside her. She was determined that her child would never have to endure the hiding, the lies and the constant fear of her own miserable childhood. Her solution had to be final.

Harry's blue estate car pulled quietly into the layby behind her.

At less than five foot seven, Harry was lean with a runner's sinewy build. He stood for a moment rubbing his dark ginger hair vigorously, his breath fogging in the cold morning air. With his messy curls, he always reminded her a little of Ed Sheeran. He even had the same cheeky grin, but sadly not the voice. There was no smile this morning. Anxiety and sadness were etched on his face in equal measure.

Harry had taken some convincing to help. She hated involving him in this, but there was no one else she could turn to. Not Finn, not in a million years would he have agreed. Finn believed there was goodness in everyone, that anyone could change. Finn was wrong.

With a last rub of her pregnant belly, Ellie climbed reluctantly from the car, the cold wind whipping through her flimsy nurses' scrubs, making her tremble with cold – or was it fear?

Her car was too far forward in the layby. She would have to back it up if she were to have enough speed when she hit the tree.

Shivering, she waited as Harry unloaded the gruesome contents of his boot. Her thoughts kept drifting back to Finn – to how much she loved him and how much she'd miss him. How she wished she could explain, share her fears, help him understand that this was the only option. This was her predetermined destiny, put into play years before when her father was just a teenager.

Ellie took one last unhurried look around her at the idyllic country scene – at the bare trees and fields and the clear blue sky. She felt the cold air searing her lungs. It was a good day to die, but an even better day to be alive.

By now, Finn would be fast asleep on top of the covers at home, probably still dressed in his scrubs, exhausted after his busy night in the Emergency Department. In a few hours, the knock on the door would shatter his world.

She climbed back behind the wheel. It was time to end the madness.

'Vengeance is in my heart, death in my hand,

Blood and revenge are hammering in my head.'

TITUS ANDRONICUS ACT II SCENE III

WILLIAM SHAKESPEARE

CHAPTER 1

Finn

T hat fine line between being asleep and waking up – between dream and cold reality. The second before you return to conscious thought and remember. That glorious moment when hope flutters and you believe that all will be right with the world when you wake. But then you open your eyes and all hope withers and dies in the cruel morning light.

I remember everything with crystal clear agony. It runs on a perfect loop of recall, repeating in my head every morning as I wake in the loneliness of our bedroom.

The persistent knocking on the door, trudging down the stairs annoyed at the disturbance of my sleep. Police officers with sombre expressions, questions – my name, Ellie's name, the car registration.

And then the words that linger in my brain even three months later. They were sorry to inform me that nothing could be done. Dead at the scene.

The same well-worn words I used on occasion in A&E to shatter families, now used on me. I couldn't catch the details, only phrases that circulated my brain. Icy conditions. Lost control. Collision with a tree. No chance of survival. Fire. Dental records. Snippets of information as my world slipped off its axis. Ellie, my Ellie, was dead.

I shook off the memory and dragged myself downstairs to the kitchen. It was day 94, and still every morning, for a nanosecond, I imagined it wasn't true – that my beautiful wife and my unborn baby were still alive. But each morning I faced the reality of my heart-wrenching loss all over again.

I gazed at the collection of pills on the kitchen counter, a little surprised that they were still there. I'd collected them late last night and left them out, ready. The white ones were paracetamol, and there were a helluva lot of them – more than required. I identified a few sleeping pills in the assortment, and even a few grey and green capsules that could be Imodium. I didn't have the courage last night and I hoped I'd be braver this morning. A few swallows and it would all be over as my liver failed in days. But I was wavering again this morning.

This isn't what Ellie would want. She would expect me to be strong, to get on with my life and find happiness again – if that was even possible. I was failing miserably so far on all counts.

In the first few days, family and friends had rallied around. I had a thousand jobs to do and a hundred decisions to make. I had a funeral to organise, hymns to choose and a wake to plan.

94 days had passed since the accident and the knock on my door, and the reality of being alone without Ellie was biting hard. A weak March sun was fighting a losing battle against the growing collection of damp, drizzle-heavy morning clouds. The weather was adding to my sense of desolation. I was completely adrift without her, rudderless on an endless sea of despair and denial. The last three months had passed in a blur as the world continued to revolve around me, but now everyone else had gone back to living their lives. I had been left alone, standing in the kitchen in my boxers ready to eat a handful of pills and end it all.

I brushed the mound of pills into the bin and filled the kettle with a conviction I didn't feel, but the memories wouldn't leave my head. I'd self-medicated my way through the funeral and sobbed through a heart-crushing inquest where the coroner had ruled the crash an accident.

But how the fuck had I accidentally lost my wife and baby?

As days inevitably became weeks, I was simply expected to 'man up' and get on with my life. But I lived in the house Ellie and I had scraped together the deposit to buy. The house where we'd spent every free minute between our hospital shifts, the house that we had lovingly decorated, making it our home – a home we were planning to raise our child in.

Ellie's presence lingered everywhere, mocking my solitude. Most days I was convinced she would walk through the door, her nurse's uniform wrinkled after a long shift, her belly swelling protectively around our baby. Then I would find her muddy trainers in the utility room, and stand snivelling at the sink as I scrubbed them with infinite care.

My mum was one of the most caring people I knew, and she was desperate to help me through my loss. A retired midwife, she'd merely switched her focus from birthing mothers to her newly bereaved son. I appreciated my parent's support and knew they felt Ellie's loss too. Mum would tell me to focus on one task each day, insisting life would gradually get easier. What she didn't realise was that even getting out of bed was proving impossible, leaving me incapable of achieving anything more.

Ellie's toiletries still filled the bathroom shelves, and I had even ironed her nurse's tunics and hung them in her still-full cupboard. I missed her too damn much to eradicate all evidence of her existence from my life.

Now, day 94, I was supposed to return to work. The hospital had been very understanding following the accident, but my colleagues couldn't be expected to cover my shifts indefinitely. They wanted me back on a part-time basis, at least for the moment – but of course, they didn't realise how broken I was inside. How was I meant to manage patients and their families when I couldn't get through a single day without bursts of uncontrollable sobbing?

What the hell. Maybe if I could get through day 94 by blagging my way through work, then day 95 would be easier. I doubted it, but the alternative was swallowing the pills. Ellie would be so pissed at me for giving up.

As I poured the boiling water over my teabag my phone chirped with a text message. No doubt it was Mum with some well-intentioned words of wisdom; advice about how to cope on my first day back at work after my wife slammed her car into a tree.

A message flashed up on the screen from Anon@AnonTxt.com. Weird, and clearly not from my mother. I tapped to open it, grateful for the distraction.

Reading the message, my flimsy hold on reality shattered.

I know who murdered your wife.

I wasn't sure how long I sat on the kitchen floor staring incredulously at my phone, my knees having buckled as my legs turned to jelly. I kept refreshing the screen, re-reading the words as if they would unscramble, change to different ones and make sense.

CHAPTER 2

Dr Ravi Surdhar ignored the closed door and barged into my cupboard-sized office with its uninspiring view of the back of the busy hospital kitchens. A competent and caring junior doctor, he'd helped hold the fort for the last three months while I was 'in mourning' or whatever.
'You look like shit, Finn. What are you doing back so soon? And you're done for the day. Shift's over, go home already, we don't need you.' His slight Indian accent filtered through his awkwardness.

I looked up from my bottomless pile of paperwork, surprised to find that it was already twenty past seven. I'd inexplicably survived day 94 and my first shift back in the Emergency Department.

It had been a surreal day. None of my colleagues knew what to say or where to look. They'd all known and liked Ellie, and although medical staff are no strangers to death, this was personal for them.

The shift, as always, was busy. We had a warehouse fire, two cardiac arrests and an overdose – the irony of which was not lost on me. By lunchtime, the awkwardness was gone and it was business as usual, hence my mountain of paperwork. Inevitably, the more lives you save in the NHS, the more forms you fill in.

'I need to be back, take my mind off... things,' I repeated the mantra my mother kept using.

I was far from convinced I was fit to be anywhere right now, much less a hospital. I'd zoned out completely stitching Mr Harvey's head laceration, and even had a small panic attack when a young woman was brought in following an RTC. For a ridiculous moment, I imagined it was Ellie, and that this time I would save her. It turned out to be a cyclist with a broken wrist. I'd been so preoccupied after handing the patient over to my orthopaedic colleagues that I'd very nearly missed a potential meningitis case. Luckily, one of the nurses suggested I order a lumbar puncture on the miserable fourteen-month-old.

I almost didn't make it into work at all after receiving that malicious text. My thoughts returned to it every time I had five minutes to myself. The pills flashed through my mind again. If I'd only had the balls to carry out my fumbled suicide attempt I wouldn't need to care about the crazy message, and I definitely wouldn't need to be dealing with any of this shit right now.

'...think you're amazing, mate, but don't overdo it. Let's grab lunch later this week, ok?' I realised Ravi was still talking. Why did everyone feel the need to feed the grieving husband? Ellie was dead, but I was still capable of ordering a pizza. No, not just dead, *murdered* according to my new contact.

Ravi ran through some test results before finally leaving me alone, closing the door behind him – much to my relief.

I should have gone home then, but instead, I sat staring at the photo of me and Ellie paddleboarding in Thailand last summer. The thought of going back to the dark, cold house was filling me with dread.

Eventually I came to a decision and reached for my phone. I would delete the text message and block the number – presumably that was doable. Somewhere along the way my eyes lost focus and misted up. I'd kept scrolling on autopilot and opened Ellie's last text message.

What's your ETA?

Don't forget milk, we're out.

It was signed with a smiley face and a heart emoji.

Those were her last words to me, in a text, from only a few days before Christmas and the day before the crash. Seeing her words brought a familiar and crushing tightness to my chest as memories of our normal, happy life enveloped me. Despite her reminder, I'd stupidly forgotten to get the milk and Ellie had given me a right bollocking when I walked in the door. She'd been really grumpy and preoccupied in those last few weeks which I'd put down to her galloping pregnancy hormones. I would give anything to have her yell at me again.

Overwhelmed by memories and regrets, I grabbed my keys and escaped the hospital, leaving a good few hours of paperwork untouched on my desk. On the way home I stopped at Sainsbury's and bought some flowers and a microwavable lasagne.

I parked in the layby on the opposite side of the road from the big oak tree that killed my wife.

In the fading light, I walked over and carefully laid the bunch of yellow roses – Ellie's favourites – at the tree's broad, gnarled base. I slumped down on the damp soil and rested my back on the fire-blackened trunk. This tree and I were becoming firm friends.

Every day for the last 94 days I'd come here, refreshing the flowers when needed, sitting, thinking and doing a lot of crying. It was the only place where I could still feel Ellie's essence. Looking up into the tree's vast web of twisted limbs I spotted spring-green leaf buds emerging on the dormant branches, signalling the coming spring. A sure sign of rejuvenation and new life – just not for Ellie and not for our baby.

I looked back at the corner imagining Ellie at the wheel of her old black Citroën, racing down the road towards me, her beautiful face framed in the windscreen. As she took the bend, the car's wheels locked and the back fishtailed almost at right angles to the road. I saw her scream, her hands clasped on the steering wheel, desperately trying to pull the car back. And then the tree was dead ahead, speed pushing her towards it at a furious rate. Everything seemed to slow. Her face was etched with fear as her mouth opened and closed. Did she call my name in the moments before she died? At the last second her hands left the wheel and held her belly instead, offering our unborn baby what scant protection she could.

The bumper slammed into the tree, the bonnet concertina-ing as the car wrapped itself around the trunk. Ellie flew forward before being viciously yanked back by the seat belt with enough force to break her neck. Her face was lost to me as her hair fanned out around her.

The screech of collapsing metal hurt my ears and I saw sparks as the ancient tree held firm against the dreadful impact. The fuel cap had ripped off, and bright blue flames fluttered in the cold of the early morning, spreading out over the chassis with terrifying speed. I saw Ellie fighting the seat belt, screaming, blood streaming from a gash on her forehead across her terrified face. The flames danced around and flickered orange, yellow and fiery red as the fuel warmed, turning the car into a metal furnace. Ellie writhed and squirmed as the flames licked around her. I could hear her scream and smell her burning flesh...

I shook myself from my stupor, surprised to see the light dying over the fields and the quiet, still country road. My eyes ached as tears ran freely down my face. Like a video on a loop inside my head I watched her die over and over again each time I sat here. The details changed – sometimes she unbuckled the seat belt but couldn't get the door open in time. Sometimes she hit her head so hard she was unconscious as the flames roared through the car. But in none of my agonising visions did my beautiful wife escape.

Snatching at the tears I could no longer control, I felt my phone vibrate on the ground next to me, its screen glowing in the failing light. Another text from the anonymous sender. For a millisecond I considered deleting it unread, but who the hell was I kidding?

I know who murdered Ellie.

Who the fuck would do this? Who could be so cruel? Wasn't I suffering enough?

I was gripping the phone so tightly my knuckles were gleaming white. I fought the urge to fling the damn thing as far as I could into the field. My heart was pounding and my vision clouded as a deep headache grew behind my right eye. What I'd give for just two of the paracetamol I'd so rashly thrown away this morning.

As I sat trembling on the hard ground with my trousers growing soggy from the dampness, my phone beeped again four more times in quick succession. The bastard must really be enjoying himself.

I opened the messages and scrolled through them quickly, barely keeping focus on the words through my tears. I couldn't help it. I was like a moth to an agonising flame. Only my growing anger at being so easily manipulated kept me from losing it completely.

I know who murdered Ellie.

And again...

I know who murdered Ellie.

The onslaught was broken up with a text from my mother.

Hi Finlay darling. All the best for work today, I know it will be hard.

Dad and I are thinking of you.

How about coming to visit soon.

Love you Xx

And another...

Don't you want to know? Don't you care?

I ignored my mum's text and instead zoned in on the last message, the words swimming in my eyes as a gutting sense of powerlessness overwhelmed me. How could anyone even suggest I didn't care? Losing Ellie had torn my insides out, leaving me bereft, alone and suicidal. Anger and misery fought for control as I thumped the ground with my clenched fist.

It was an accident. The police, the insurance investigator, the coroner – everyone agreed. No one would murder my pregnant wife. Why would they?

I wanted to find the sender of those messages and pound him into the ground, but I couldn't move. A weight pushed down on me, keeping my body pinned to the earth at the base of the tree. The wind began to whip sharply across the flat fields, carrying with it the smell of rain.

On a whim, I scrolled through my contacts and dialled a number I'd never expected to use. My personal police liaison officer answered after the second ring. Less than five minutes later I'd already disconnected the call, feeling thoroughly reprimanded. All she'd done was confirm what I already knew, that Ellie's crash was an accident – there was absolutely no sign of foul play. I was only causing myself more anguish by questioning the coroner's verdict. I needed to stop rehashing the past and try to get on with life – her words not mine. I didn't mention the text messages. She already had me pegged for a wimpy idiot.

Sitting alone on the damp, cold ground I wished more than ever that I'd swallowed the damn pills that morning. Every last one. How could anyone accuse me of not caring?

CHAPTER 3

The knocking was loud, persistent and extremely annoying. As exhausted as I was I couldn't ignore it forever. Pulling on some shorts, I stumbled downstairs. If it was one of my over-caring, interfering neighbours with another casserole I was going to shove it down their bloody throat. My freezer was jam-packed with sympathy food.

The clock in the hall said half seven. Shit. I'd only gone up to bed at three, and only with the help of the better part of a bottle of Jack Daniels had I finally fallen asleep.

'Yes?' I meant it to come out all gruff and angry, but instead, a high-pitched, early morning whine was all I managed. Hopefully, my exasperated face would do the rest.

My heart stopped.

She was standing on my doorstep. I saw her incomparably beautiful eyes and her full lips with the dimple on the side. A nervous smile faded from her face as she took in my annoyed expression. Her hair was shorter, resting on her shoulders, but otherwise it was Ellie. My Ellie.

Only it wasn't.

The nose was wrong and the voice, when she spoke, wasn't hers at all. And there was no scar. Ellie had a keloid scar in the shape of an irregular four-point star covering her chin and cheek on the right side of her face. I jokingly referred to it as her perfect imperfection. Ellie had always been perfect to me. Pseudo Ellie had no such mark on her flawless pale skin, only a dusting of light freckles across her nose. She wasn't my Ellie at all, except the eyes...

'Oh... Erm, hi. Sorry to disturb you this early but I've come to see Eleanor. Is she at home?'

'No,' I stammered. 'Who the hell are you?' The look-alike was about the same age as Ellie. She was wearing a pair of designer jeans and a brown leather jacket. Now that I was looking closely I could see that she was a little taller than Ellie, with slightly narrower hips. I'd have preferred a casserole toting neighbour. The urge to slam the door shut and keep the world out was overpowering, but her eyes were too damn distracting.

'I beg your pardon, there's no need to be so rude. I've come a really long way. I know it's early, but Eleanor said to come as soon as possible. Now could you go and get her? Please?'

I let out a slow, calming breath, deliberately relaxed my bunched fists and fought the need to smash them into her irritatingly smug face. She edged one foot across the threshold, preventing me from closing the door without breaking a few of her toes. She stood there with her hands on her hips, her expression determined.

'No. Now take your fucking foot out of my doorway.'

'Wow. What's your problem? I guess you're not a morning person,' she added, only half under her breath. 'I'd like to see Eleanor, please. She's expecting me. Sort of.'

She hesitated, and a momentary wave of uncertainty softened her tone. 'Oh gosh, I'm sorry. This is the right house, isn't it? Eleanor Murray lives here, right?' She retrieved a crumpled piece of paper from her oversized handbag and quickly scanned the address, checking it against the brass number 22 on our blue door before repeating, 'This is Eleanor's house, right?'

'Yes,' I blurted out. 'I mean no. I mean you have to go away. She isn't here.' I felt completely tongue-tied, searching for an easy explanation. The last three months hadn't helped me to articulate the reality of Ellie's death at all – least of all to complete strangers.

The woman tilted her head to the side, regarding me as if I were the village idiot. I felt her eyes boring into me, and I shivered in the early morning chill, acutely aware that I was only wearing a pair of pyjama shorts.

'Well, which is it then? Is it her house or isn't it? I know I have the right address.' Her tone was incredibly condescending, and she waved her damning piece of paper in my face.

I was fast losing patience with this ridiculous conversation. The universe was conspiring to bring every moron to my door when all I wanted was to be left alone. I went for the jugular.

'Listen, whoever you are. This was her house, but it's not anymore because she's dead. Now please go away.' This time I was closing the door regardless of how many toes were in the way, but I hesitated a fraction too long, enjoying a certain macabre pleasure at seeing the stricken look on her face.

Her shock was tangible, her voice soft as a whisper. 'Dead? You're kidding, right? She can't be dead.' The blood drained from her face and she shook her head with frantic movements.

'I wish I was,' I mumbled nonsensically. This discussion was going nowhere. Ellie died three months ago. Why had this woman only come now? I'd posted a message on Ellie's Facebook page ensuring all her friends knew about her funeral.

'I'm sorry, I don't feel very well. I need to sit down,' she announced, shoving the door open and stepping past me into the small hallway. Feeling crowded, I took an involuntary step backwards. 'Did you say she's dead? Because that's not possible. She told me to come visit her as soon as I could.' Her voice cracked a little and she looked like she might faint.

Then my groggy, alcohol-soaked, sleep-deprived brain and I realised that she could be the one sending the text messages. I'd deal with the 'why' once I had control of my thundering headache. All I knew was that someone who looked a little like Ellie was standing in my hallway purporting to be visiting my dead wife.

Questions swam around my head and I tried to inject some strength into my voice, determined to get answers. Instead, my words came out in a rush, running together in a stream of nonsense. 'Who the bloody hell are you? And why are you sending me those sick texts? Is this some type of morbid game to you? And why now? Oh, and I do care. More than you can ever imagine! Are you wearing coloured contacts? Do you get some weird pleasure from trying to fuck with my head?' I only stopped shouting when I ran out of breath.

'I...I...I'm Rachel.' She was holding the wall for support. 'I'm Eleanor's...um...I'm her sister.' She started crying as my world shrank and a buzzing started in my ears. I desperately tried to make sense of this new load of crap. She was a lying bitch. Ellie didn't have a sister. This woman standing in my hallway was twisted and evil, and she wasn't getting out of here until I had my answers.

I slammed the door hard, gripped her elbow and practically dragged her into the kitchen.

CHAPTER 4

I surreptitiously sniffed the milk before adding a dash to Rachel's mug, relieved I drank my coffee black – full caffeine kick without the listeria risk. Bringing her inside had seemed like a good idea, but now that she was snivelling into a crumpled tissue at my kitchen table, I wasn't sure what to do next. All I knew was that I was intrigued to hear her bullshit story.

I'd grabbed a semi-clean shirt hanging off the bannister as I steered her, blubbering and inconsolable, into the kitchen. My mother would have been proud that I'd offered her a cup of tea before launching another tirade of questions at her. Boiling the kettle and fussing with mugs had given me much-needed time to marshal my untidy thoughts, and now I was ready to begin the interrogation.

Rachel remained unresponsive to my growing impatience and I slammed her mug down loudly in front of her. She flinched and looked up at me. A quiver ran up my spine as I saw the obvious similarities between her and Ellie. She looked down at her tea as if unsure how it got there. We were getting nowhere. I knew she'd sent the text messages, and it was only the colour of her eyes that kept me from throwing her out. If it turned out she was wearing coloured contact lenses I was going to lose my shit.

Ellie had been born with a rare condition called congenital

heterochromia, which she believed she'd inherited from her biological father. In layman's terms, Ellie had two different coloured irises. Her left eye was light blue and her right a warm chocolate brown. Some colour variations were subtle and hardly noticeable, others, like Ellie's, were quite pronounced. I loved her eyes and thought it gave her beauty a fascinating twist. The snivelling woman at my kitchen table appeared to have the same affliction. As I studied her eyes more closely, I realised that the blue was a shade or two darker, and the brown was more honey than chocolate.

'Rebecca?' I tried a little louder. Eventually, she lifted her head and looked at me, her expression slightly glazed. Apparently she was still in shock.

'It's Rachel. Rachel Bates. Are you sure she's dead? How did she die? When?'

This wasn't going the way I'd planned. It was my questions I wanted answers to – I didn't have the patience for hers. I snapped.

'You have precisely ten seconds to tell me why you're here, then I'm throwing you out. And if you send one more text I'm going to the police.'

A little taken aback by my outburst, she took a quivering breath before hitting right back at me.

'Listen, arsehole. I don't know what texts you keep jabbering on about, but Eleanor contacted me and invited me to come up. She emailed me about four months ago, and sent copies of documents proving she was my sister. I work for an international law firm but I've been out in our Singapore office and only arrived back in the UK yesterday. I came up here to finally meet her...' her voice trailed off and she blew her nose and mopped her eyes. She was either Oscar-worthy or genuinely upset. I wasn't sure which.

'What the...? What proof for God's sake?' I asked, incredulity temporarily dampening my anger.

'She sent me a copy of her birth certificate. We have the same father. Thomas Hudson.'

I laughed, gripping the kitchen counter for support, light-headed from lack of sleep and relief. She totally had the wrong house and the wrong person. 'You've got your facts so wrong it's ridiculous. My wife's name is... um... was Ellie, and her maiden name was Grainger. Her parents died when she was a little girl,' I said, shuddering at the irony. They too were killed in a horrific car accident.

Rachel sighed, and with a dramatic flourish pulled some papers from her handbag. She rifled through them and placed one on the kitchen table. 'This is a copy of her birth certificate. See? It says her name here clearly. Eleanor Elizabeth Hudson. Parents: Thomas and Elizabeth Hudson. She was born on June 4th in Cambridge.' She sat back sipping her tea triumphantly.

I wasn't going to be outdone. Ellie kept all our 'important stuff' in a drawer in the kitchen, and I opened it with unnecessary dramatics. I pulled out a folder of plastic wallets, each holding some significant document chronicling all the critical milestones in Ellie's life. I hadn't quite brought myself to add her death certificate to it yet, but the rest was there, all neatly filed away. Her GCSE and A-Level results, her nursing degree from the University of Southampton, our marriage certificate and, near the front, her birth certificate. Each one displayed her real name; Ellie Grainger. Not even Eleanor. She was always just Ellie.

I placed her birth certificate next to Rachel's bogus one. Our heads came together as we leaned over comparing them. Her parents were listed as Norman and Shirley Grainger, and she was born in Lewisham. Only the date of birth was the same.

'There you go. Completely different person. The only thing they have in common is their birthday.' Ellie always maintained I took smug to a whole new level.

'But…but that's not possible,' Rachel stammered, holding my version of Ellie's birth certificate up to the light as if it might be a forgery. I grabbed it out of her hands.

'Well now we have that cleared up I think you need to tell me exactly what you're playing at, right… now…'

My tone started off threatening and might have had the desired effect until we both saw something in the folder that made my words go dry in my throat.

In the same plastic wallet, hidden behind the one I'd just pulled out was another document. Another birth certificate. This one was identical to Rachel's and looked to be just as genuine, only the name read Eleanor Elizabeth Hudson.

What the fuck?

'There! You see? Why are you lying to me?' Rachel demanded, glaring at me victoriously.

'Me? Lying? Listen you silly cow. You arrive here unannounced, three months too late, with a load of crap about a long lost sister and a forged birth certificate—'

Rachel slammed the file down on the kitchen table with a thud, wobbling her tea mug. The sudden noise effectively staunched my tirade mid-flow. She visibly shook herself and took a breath before starting in a voice that resonated calm and reason.

'I think we got off on the wrong foot here. I understand it must be a shock to you, but how dare you speak to me like that? You're incredibly offensive. I appreciate you say you've recently lost your wife, but that doesn't change the fact that she was also my sister. Maybe if we can both calm down and discuss this like adults we can get to the bottom of this misunderstanding.'

I slumped down on the hard kitchen chair unsure what to believe. She had a point. It wasn't like me to be so rude, even if I wasn't exactly having the best year. Maybe I owed her at least the courtesy of hearing her out before I tossed her back on the street.

My phone lay on the table next to last night's almost-empty bottle of Jack that I hadn't bothered to hide or excuse, and it was vibrating with a text message. A cold dread filled my gut. I opened it up, knowing what it would say.

I know who murdered Ellie.

Day 95 didn't seem to be shaping up any better than the 94 days that came before it.

CHAPTER 5

I flipped the phone on its face, but not before Rachel had managed to read the message. Bollocks. I needed to compartmentalise my problems. First I would hear this woman's outrageous tale of long lost sisters, then I would deal with my prolific texting buddy – although so far I hadn't come up with a plan for him.

Because the messages were coming from an anonymous number, there was no way I could reply. I'd spent the previous evening trying everything I could think of as I sank deeper into the whiskey bottle. I eventually resorted to drunk-calling a tech-savvy friend of mine from my uni days who had agreed with me that the message was completely untraceable without government-grade spyware or something.

I'd even thought about contacting the police for about two and a half seconds, but after being shot down by my liaison officer for even suggesting that Ellie's accident could be suspicious, I decided to give it a miss.

'Right then, Rachel Bates, let's start with you.' There was no way I was going to apologise, even if my behaviour had been out of order. She shouldn't have woken me up so bloody early.

'I'm not hiding anything and I can prove it,' she said with confidence. 'But first could I have another cup of tea, please? Black this time. I think your milk is off.'

Picky cow. I poured the rest of the milk down the sink and made her a fresh cup as she dug around in her pile of papers, marshalling her lies.

When I sat down with my second coffee she was keen to get started. The way she tucked her hair behind her ear reminded me so much of Ellie, but I had to push those annoying thoughts out of my head. I categorically knew that Ellie had no family. She was an only child, orphaned at a young age and brought up for the most part in foster care.

'My mother's name was Catherine – Catherine Bates – and she was a single mum. There was no father listed on my birth certificate and I shared my mum's surname. Growing up, I didn't even know my dad's name.'

She pushed what was clearly her own birth certificate across the table, which I rather immaturely chose to ignore. There were too many of the bloody things flying around the kitchen today for my liking.

'Mum has suffered from mental illness for a long time. She was diagnosed as bipolar when I was a child. She coped well, for the most part, as long as she took her medication and didn't get too stressed.' She seemed to hesitate awkwardly as she divulged her family's secrets, her eyes darting around the kitchen, never quite meeting mine.

'When I was younger, she always dismissed any questions about my dad, fobbing me off with tales of drunken university parties. It sounded like there were multiple candidates for the role of "father of the year".' The pain under her words was evident in her pseudo-flippant tone. 'But I don't think my mother was like that, not even when she was young. Before she became ill, she was a junior lecturer at Cambridge with a very bright future. Then she fell pregnant with me. She was always very serious and ambitious – not really the partying type.'

She took a sip of her tea and shot me a look as if she were daring me to interrupt her and suggest that before becoming a single parent her mum might have lived by a less studious code. I didn't give her the pleasure.

'Anyway, in the last ten years or so she's gotten a lot worse, to the point where she can no longer live independently. And now,' she sighed, 'as an added bonus, she's developed early-onset dementia. She has to live in sheltered accommodation and has a dedicated mental health nurse.'

I waited patiently as she organised her thoughts. Not interrupting people's stories was part of my job description and it gave me time to study her body language – another occupational hazard. She came across genuinely concerned as she shared the details about her mother and the tough hand she'd been dealt in life.

'There are some stolen moments of clarity. She even worked with her nurse to make a video for me. It was like seeing my mother before I lost her to the demons inside her head. She was rational and articulate. It's still pretty hard for me to watch of course. It's like I've lost that part of her, but she managed to find her way back – at least temporarily – to give me this information.' She took a fluttering breath, making me worry that she was about to start crying again. She seemed to steel herself, pulling her shoulders back and continuing, 'This is a transcript of her video.'

She produced three or four folded pages stapled together, and smoothed them out on the table. They looked well-read and Rachel seemed a little reluctant to hand them over. I imagined that losing a parent to mental illness must be every bit as hard as them dying. I wondered how I would cope with a message from Ellie beyond the grave. I broke down every time I read her last text message, so I suspected I'd be a quivering wreck if I ever had to sit through a video made in her last days.

'It's long and a little rambling, so I'll give you the abridged version,' she said, sipping her tea, needing a little respite perhaps. 'As I said, my mother lectured at Cambridge in modern history and was quite brilliant. She had a successful career ahead of her. Then she met my father.' She paused, lost in her memories. I wasn't sure she was even aware I was there anymore.

'His name was Thomas Hudson and he was finishing his Masters in economics. They fell in love, but there were complications. She was a lecturer and he was still a student and...' again she hesitated, her eyes heavy with the sadness of what could have been, '...and he was engaged to be married. But Thomas was a bit of a player, and around this time his fiancé also fell pregnant. My mother was devastated. Thomas promised to break off the engagement and marry her instead, only his father went ballistic, threatening to disinherit him. Seemingly his fiancé was from a wealthy family too and Thomas was all but forced into marrying her.' She threw her fingers up in irritated little air quotes. 'He never even knew my mother was also expecting. Mum was too embarrassed to stay at Cambridge so she took a leave of absence to cover her maternity period and transferred to a smaller, less prestigious university near her parents' house in London. She carried on working until she became too ill to cope. Thirty-odd years ago being a single parent was still a shameful thing, I guess.'

'So this Thomas Hudson – your father – never knew about the other baby? Er... I mean you. He didn't support your mother? Not even financially?' Despite my better judgement, I felt myself being drawn into her tragic story, even though I had hundreds of counter-arguments swarming in my head.

'No,' Rachel sighed, draining her cup. 'As far as I know she never saw him again. She knew he'd joined his father's firm after graduating from Cambridge. He and his new young wife were quite the socialites. My mother followed their lives in the papers for a while. His wife also had a daughter – Eleanor.' She looked at me, trying to gauge my reaction. I purposely gave her nothing, which took quite some control on my part.

'Then, when I was about six or seven, Thomas and his family

were all killed in a car crash. That's why Mum never bothered telling me about him. I'm not sure why she decided to tell me at all in the end, and it's impossible to ask her now. She's no longer lucid. She tried hard to be a good parent, juggling motherhood and her career and her growing mental issues for as long as she could. I felt very loved and my grandparents were always there for me, so finding my father was never a huge priority. It was only when I heard from Eleanor that I decided to pursue it. I thought I'd lost my sister a long time ago. I couldn't quite believe it when she contacted me. She said she would explain everything when I came to see her... but now it's too late of course...'

Her voice trailed off as she returned to the reality of my kitchen. She looked emotionally drained, but I was still unconvinced. So far, besides some pieces of paper, it was just a vaguely feasible yarn and told me nothing that couldn't have been found on a Google search. And then there was the obvious complication. Ellie. My Ellie didn't die in the crash as a child.

I shoved my chair back suddenly and Rachel jumped. She was very edgy, but I needed to move – the caffeine was making me jittery. I tossed the dregs of my coffee down the sink. I had a million and one questions for the illegitimate love child of a man who, as far as I was concerned, had nothing to do with my dead wife.

I turned around to find Rachel chewing her nails nervously. She had something else to say. More lies, no doubt. A thumping headache was building behind my eyes from last night's over-indulgence and I didn't know if I could cope with any more of her bullshit.

'Listen, it's a fascinating story but quite honestly I still think you have the wrong person. Ellie was never Eleanor. Her surname was never Hudson. And the most obvious flaw – she didn't die as a child with her imaginary parents.' I couldn't and didn't want to start trying to explain the erroneous birth certificate. I really just wanted this woman out of my kitchen.

I also needed to hydrate. I picked up a glass from the draining board and filled it from the tap.

'Finn, please, you need to listen. I have—'

A low hum filled my ears as I threw the water glass down and watched a hundred shards of glass spew across the stone floor. I'd had enough of her ridiculous nonsense. All the pain and misery of the last few months washed over me, destroying my last frayed threads of self-control.

'Get the fuck out of my house. You're talking absolute bullshit. I don't know what you want or why you're doing this to me, but I've bloody well had enough.' I reached for my phone on the table and began hitting nines. 'Get out. Now. Or I'm phoning the police and then you can show them all your fancy bits of fucking paper.'

Rachel stood up, tears welling in her eyes.

'How dare you speak to me like that, you cold-hearted bastard,' she spluttered. 'I came to finally meet my sister and you... you—'

'999. What service do you require?' The voice on my phone interrupted her tirade.

Bloody hell, I'd actually got through to the emergency services. I started apologising to the woman on the phone.

'I'm so sorry. I dialled the number by mistake. I don't need anything. I'm sorry to have wasted your time.' I finished the call before she could have a go at me, and at that moment I heard the front door bang.

Rachel had left and I turned to follow her – I wasn't done yelling. A piece of glass sank painfully into the sole of my left foot. I yelped and fell onto the nearest chair. Could this morning get any worse?

I yanked the shard out of my foot and stared for a second at the bright crimson blood that pooled on my skin. Then I jumped up and flew out of the kitchen and after Rachel.

Out on the road I saw a white car pulling away quickly. I idiotically sped off after it, my bare feet slapping the dewy tarmac.

For a moment it seemed I was going to catch up, miraculously, but then the car picked up speed and pulled ahead before taking a sharp right into Duggar Avenue. I kept chasing it around the corner like a demented dog, desperate to catch its number plate at least, but it was conveniently smeared with mud and I couldn't make out much more than W-----Y. And maybe a 5 or a 3 in the middle somewhere? Completely useless.

Out of breath and with my left foot beginning to sting I slowed to a stop, defeated. I bent over, my hands on my knees, breathing hard. I hadn't been out running much since Ellie's death and was feeling it.

From Duggar Avenue there were a couple of options leading out of the village. Even if I ran back and grabbed my car, Rachel would be long gone. 'Alright then, fuck off!' I yelled after the car, disturbing the otherwise peaceful street. Feeling suddenly completely ridiculous, I limped back home.

Michelle from next door was heading out of her house, shepherding her twin boys to the car for the morning school run. Her husband was something important in the city. She looked at me, barefoot and in my shorts, and asked: 'Morning Finn, you been for a run?' Concern oozed from every word.

'Hi, Michelle. Did you see the woman who just left mine? She looked a bit like Ellie.' My words sounded ludicrous spoken out loud. Maybe I was having a breakdown. Maybe this was all some vivid alcohol-induced dream, and I was desperate for some corroboration that Rachel was real.

Michelle smiled, a sympathetic look flashing across her face. 'No sorry, only just came out. Eliot couldn't find his school shoes. He'd lose his head if it wasn't screwed on! Hey, I'm cooking chilli tonight and I always make too much. I'll drop some round.' Thankfully, she got in her car and didn't hear my caustic reply. My mother would not have been proud.

As Michelle's car drove away, I trudged through my front door. I carefully sidestepped the scattered glass fragments on the floor and picked up Rachel's mug, quickly slamming it down again.

The bitch had stolen Ellie's folder of documents.

CHAPTER 6

If you're going to die or pretend to die, you can't come back as yourself. You have to reinvent yourself, reinvent your life and your reason for living. You have to create a new identity and a new name. And you have to give up everything that was part of the old you.

And that's what they did. They sacrificed everything. Their way of life, their friends, their family and even their children. They reinvented themselves, detached from anything connecting them to their former life – they were reborn.

Thomas and Elizabeth Hudson, socialites and heirs to their families' respective fortunes, became Tom and Liz Harper. Everything changed.

Tom Harper sat on the bench holding yesterday's newspaper while his neighbour's dog sniffed around the newly budding daffodils before lifting his leg. Early morning joggers and fellow dog walkers passed him by, some even nodding in recognition. Tom spent many hours on this bench, watching the Murray house across the road. Even now that Eleanor was gone, he still continued his vigil.

He watched as the woman ran out of Finn's front door and sped away in her shiny white BMW. Annoyingly, he wasn't able to get a good look at her face. Seconds later he saw Finn dash out of the house after her, barefoot and wearing only cotton shorts. He chased the car halfway up the road.

To his surprise, the woman had already been sitting at the kitchen table when he arrived at the park. Had she spent the night? Had there been a lover's tiff? One minute they were having a pleasant chat over an early morning cup of tea, and next thing she was running out of the house with Finn chasing her in his pyjamas.

Could this stranger be Finn's lover? So soon after his wife's tragic death? Surely not. Even Finn wouldn't be that cold-hearted and uncaring, would he?

Peering over the top of his newspaper, Tom saw Finn limp back up the road and chat briefly to his neighbour before going back inside and slamming the front door.

Tom rose painfully on his arthritic knees and stretched out his back. He called the dog who was busy fretting over a young poodle.

He could never understand what Eleanor had seen in that young man, but he guessed that was the burden of all fathers. No one marrying your only daughter was ever going to be good enough.

Not that he was her real father – not anymore. He and Elizabeth had given up their right as parents when they arranged for her to go into care, but they'd never quite been able to let go entirely, so he'd kept a watch over their beloved daughter from a distance.

Until she died in that horrific car accident.

Seeing Finn with company so early in the morning could only mean the woman had spent the night. The bastard had found himself a replacement for Eleanor in less than three months, even down to the same hair colour. Although they seemed to be having a rough time of it if this morning's little drama was anything to go by.

Tom wasn't sure he would tell Liz. She'd be crushed. She'd always had a soft spot for the young doctor. She claimed he was very good looking and had kind eyes.

Tom slipped the dog's lead on. He didn't particularly like dogs but it gave him an excuse to come to the park. Besides, his elderly neighbour was very appreciative.

As Tom walked to the car, Finn's infidelity continued to gnaw at him. The man had the gall to be with another woman with Eleanor barely cold in her grave.

And then the irony sank in. It was his own inability to remain faithful that had led to the ruin of all their lives. How dare he be angry at Finn?

Tom checked his watch, a present from his own father – all he had kept of his former life. He had to get back to Liz. It would be time for her meds and her breakfast, and they would be in for a hell of a day if she didn't have her tablets on time.

CHAPTER 7

Finn

I flung my stethoscope into my desk drawer with an enormous sense of relief. I'd survived my second shift back at work, and for over twelve hours I'd managed to ignore the emptiness I was feeling inside. I'd done my job well, and I'd laughed and joked with my colleagues. This was my new normal.

After chasing Rachel's fleeing car up the road I'd spent the rest of the previous day wallowing in a blur of self-pity and confusion. The more I replayed her bullshit story of uncles, infidelity and unwanted pregnancies in my head, the more ridiculous it all sounded. I had loved Ellie completely, and I'd known everything about her. We hadn't kept secrets from each other, and there were no hidden cupboards filled with skeletons and unknown members of a strange extended family.

By lunchtime I'd convinced myself that it was nothing more than a huge misunderstanding, and that Rachel would revisit her facts and realise her mistake. Thankfully, my malicious texter had given up his sick little game and left me in peace.

Hopefully I could now get back to my pathetic attempt at reconstructing a life without Ellie.

Late that afternoon I went for a long, therapeutic run through the woods surrounding the village, and I came home sweaty and exhausted to find that Michelle from next door had been true to her word. There was a delicious-looking tub of chilli on my doorstep, complete with salad and homemade garlic bread. I ate it alone while watching some crap on TV. Another new normal.

In the early hours of the morning I'd woken with a start, breathing hard, my heart hammering in my chest. I had gone a whole day without visiting Ellie's tree. It was the first day I'd missed since her accident. Torturous pangs of guilt kept me from getting back to sleep, and I'd surprised the night staff by arriving early at A&E, ready and willing to start work.

Having started my shift early, I had an excuse to leave early. The department was quiet and I was shattered. At the gift shop near the front of the hospital I bought some fresh yellow roses. Going now would give me longer with Ellie, and I could make up for yesterday's inexcusable lapse.

I didn't notice the weather until I stepped outside. A fresh westerly wind was swirling the heavy dark clouds around the sky, and it was raining heavily. I'd lost whatever daylight I'd hoped to enjoy, and was going to get soaked sitting at the tree. I almost decided to head home instead but knew I couldn't let Ellie down, again.

The car park was empty and quiet. Dark shadows edged around the pools of the security lights as fat raindrops hammered noisily on the asphalt. By the time I'd run to my car, my shirt and jumper were already sodden and sticking uncomfortably to my skin. The roses were also looking a little worse for wear.

My phone buzzed in my pocket as I got my car keys out. I opened the text without thinking and blew out a breath. The vindictive bastard hadn't given up after all.

I know who murdered your wife.

Something hard crashed down on the back of my neck. Unimaginable pain radiated up and down my spine. My vision swam as I staggered into the side of my car, my phone and keys dropping from my numb fingers. The car kept me from collapsing to the ground but also kept my head perfectly positioned to receive another strike. It connected agonisingly hard below my ear and the earth tilted away. Bile forced its way into my mouth as I toppled helplessly to the tarmac. Darkness pulled at my brain but I fought to stay conscious. I had to get to Ellie's tree.

Confusion and sheer anger drove me up awkwardly onto one knee and I shook my head trying to clear my vision. My attacker must have thought I was fighting back. I saw a heavy black boot flying towards me and there was nothing I could do to avoid it. This time, there was no coming back, and I pitched forward into a small puddle. The last image I had was Ellie's flowers lying halfway under my car next to my phone.

Piercing shards of light bubbled through the blackness and waves of agony-induced nausea washed through my consciousness. My brain was short-circuiting, unable to connect the impulses. Far away voices, low and hard were yelling and groaning. I was swimming up through a barrel of thick black molasses, the top always just out of reach.

Icy water splashed over me, running into my mouth and nose. An embryonic instinct made me cough and splutter to clear my airway. Fuzzy images sharpened; a dark, menacing figure loomed over me. Conscious thought floated, detached beyond my grasp. Vomit rose from my stomach and sensation turned instantly to panic.

Someone shoved me hard between my shoulders, rolling me onto my side as vomit spewed from my mouth and soaked my shirt, leaving an acidic stink in my nose.

My name echoed from a great distance as I fought to catch my breath through the smell. The voice got nearer, dragging me up from a void. I opened my eyes and shut them again twice as fast, willing the blackness to return. My neck was on fire; multi-coloured starbursts exploded inside my head. Something slapped my face, and I began to recognise the stinging sensation from earlier. The slaps got more vicious until my eyes flew open and bile rose again, foul in my mouth.

Memories drifted into focus. The rain. The car park. A black boot. Ellie's flowers in a puddle under my car. And pain. Lots of pain.

I was lying uncomfortably on a cold, damp surface of rough concrete. My arms pulled awkwardly behind my back by plastic strips that cut into the flesh of my wrists. I sensed someone nearby. A man crouched down, but his outline swam in and out of focus. I could barely raise my vision past his shiny shoes. He must have noticed, because he grabbed my face and tilted it up towards him. I yelled as the vertebra in my neck threatened to snap.

'Murray. Open your eyes.' His voice was low and compelling and resonated around the room. Inexplicably, I tried to comply.

'Where...' I tried to ask.

'Be quiet and listen.'

I lifted my eyes to get a good look at my attacker, and shuddered with terror. He had no face. A few more brain cells rebooted before I realised he was wearing a black ski mask which showed only his eyes. Dread swirled in my gut, threatening another wave of vomit. I swallowed hard. Nothing made sense. He knew my name?

'What y'want?' I mumbled. God, talking was no easier than thinking. My throat felt like sandpaper and my tongue was sticking to the roof of my mouth. My words slurred and sounded pathetic. He slapped me harder. My cheek stung and my eyes watered. He was wearing thick leather gloves.

'Just tell me where she is and I'll get you medical help,' he hissed.

My head swam. 'Who are you? Where am I?'

Cold anger flashed in his steel-grey eyes and fear flooded my veins. I shivered.

'Eleanor! Your wife! Tell me where she is and no one needs to get hurt.'

My brain connected some fuzzy dots. 'So you sent the texts? You bastard!' I squeezed the words past the razor blades in my throat.

'Texts? What the fuck are you on about?' He slapped me again before grabbing my face, forcing my head up to look at him. 'Where… is… Eleanor?' he repeated slowly and deliberately.

'Ellie's dead arsehole. And her name was never Eleanor.'

CHAPTER 8

The man in the ski mask hit me a couple more times and the stitching on his glove caught my lip. My skin ripped and my teeth rattled. I tasted blood.

'Tell me where Eleanor is hiding and you get to live.'

'Are you fucking kidding me? Were you not listening? She's dead! Stone cold dead!' I yelled up at him, my blood-tinged spit speckling the exposed skin around his eyes. Anger suppressed the pure fear churning inside of me.

He drew in a slow breath and deliberately wiped the blood off his face. His eyes were solid grey slate, hard, cold and terrifyingly empty. He was pissed.

'Where… is… Eleanor?' he repeated as if I were severely educationally challenged. I returned the compliment, exaggerating every syllable.

'In a fucking urn on my mantelpiece, you sick fuck.' At least my words were coming out coherently.

'Bullshit, Murray. She's alive and you know where she's hiding. Her parents fooled me once, Eleanor won't fool me again. If you tell me now, things will go better for you, and maybe even for her.' A touch of crazy was creeping into his tone and a shudder of dread swept up my spine. I had no clue what he was talking about or what her long-dead parents had to do with anything. I needed to keep him rational and diffuse the situation.

'Ellie is dead. Dead and cremated. Twice. Once when she hit the goddamn tree and then again at her funeral. If I had her hidden away somewhere I'd be right there with her, you idiot.' I had aimed for a conciliatory tone, but ended up failing hopelessly. I flinched as his eyes hardened.

He gripped the front of my jumper and yanked me into a sitting position, bouncing my still aching head off the damp wall behind me. An eerie silence filled the space and I could hear the rain outside running in the gutters. He clearly wasn't happy with my answers and seemed to be replaying my words, taking counsel with the demonic voices inside his head.

I focused on calming my ragged breathing and making sense of my fucked-up situation. My head throbbed in time with my racing pulse as I turned to look around. There wasn't much to see. The lighting was poor, but it looked like we were in a basement. The walls and floors were rough brickwork covered with mould and years of neglected grime. A sickening aroma of cat piss and decay exuded the entire space.

Debris covered the floor, and along the wall I could see black rubbish bags lined up. It was hard to see into the shadowy corner, but I thought I could make out a sleeping bag and some neat piles of clothes. I pulled at my wrists but there was no give in the plastic. I tried rubbing them against the brickwork behind me but I only managed to catch my swollen wrists instead. Warm blood dribbled down my fingers.

Through the half-open door in the far corner and I could see some stairs – stairs that I supposed led up to escape and safety. For a split second I imagined jumping up and sprinting out of the dank basement. My quads twitched with possibility. I looked at my masked abductor and didn't move a muscle – there was no way I was going to get past him.

The man was well over six foot with impressive biceps that filled his tight black shirt. He had an intimidating air of authority, and I was sitting on the floor in my own sick with my hands secured behind me. I felt as weak and pathetic as a two year old.

I spotted some ink on his wrist where his sleeve had ridden up slightly, but I couldn't identify the tattoo as anything more than a collection of intricate lines. Suddenly he was back in front of me, yanking me to my feet and snarling like a wild animal. I forgot all about escaping and tattoos.

'Last chance, Murray. Where is she?'

I shook my head trying to find words that he would understand – and believe. He drove his fist hard into my midriff, forcing my diaphragm up and successfully emptying my lungs in a painful whoosh that left me breathless and limp. I couldn't seem to draw in any oxygen and my lungs screamed in agony. I'd only had a few fistfights in my life and only as a schoolchild, none of which I'd actually won. I lacked any frame of reference. I was entirely at the mercy of this raving lunatic who could kill me in the blink of an eye, right here in this foul room. Visions of my decaying body being found in this horrible basement weeks from now only fuelled my fear. I didn't think it could get any worse.

That's when I saw the glint of something in his hand and felt my insides turn to liquid. A new terror overran every cell of my body.

CHAPTER 9

He was holding a knife.

A fucking huge knife. It was all shiny and silver with a matt-black handle and a serrated edge that looked capable of taking my head off. He gripped it comfortably, like an old friend.

Sweat rolled down my back soaking my shirt, and I trembled uncontrollably. I'd seen my fair share of stabbing victims in A&E and knew the level of pain and damage a weapon like this could cause – especially in experienced hands. I wanted to vomit, blackout and run all at once, but instead I just stood there, my back against the wall and my muscles like jelly.

A few days ago I'd almost been ready to overdose and end it all, but now that I thought I was going to die I desperately wanted to live. I wanted to smell roses and see the sky through the branches of Ellie's tree. I wanted to do a million different things. What I didn't want was to bleed out in this filthy room.

It took a moment before I realised he was telling me something, his tone frighteningly calm and conversational. I tried hard to listen but all my focus was on the knife. I kept picturing it tearing through my flesh, severing blood vessels, ripping apart organs and...

'...in Iraq I worked alongside the American special forces interrogation teams. Total psychopaths, but they knew more ways of causing pain than you'll ever imagine, Murray. And sometimes just the fear of what is to come can be enough. Well let's hope that's the case for you, Doc. You won't be much of a doctor with your fingers missing now will you? So let's start again. Where... is... Eleanor?'

'You have to listen to me. You have it all wrong. You have the wrong person. My wife's name was Ellie, just Ellie, never Eleanor. Ellie Grainger. This is all a huge mistake. Please just let me go and we can forget all about this...this misunderstanding. I swear I don't know where your Eleanor is or anything about her.' Panic had me rambling at a hundred miles per hour and I could hear the beseeching tone in my voice. I was beyond caring and scared shitless. I badly needed him to see sense and let me go.

He made an odd sound deep in his throat, halfway between a laugh and smirk. The knife came up to my throat and its jagged edge pressed down.

'Don't fuck with me, Murray. Ellie Grainger? That was nothing more than a stupid alias dreamt up by her father. Her name is Eleanor Hudson. My beautiful Eleanor with the captivating eyes and the ugly scar. There is only one Eleanor.'

As he spoke, I felt a sharp bite. The knife slid through my skin into the soft tissue of my neck. My carotid artery pulsed mere millimetres away. He was describing my Ellie. But none of what he was talking about made any sense, and I had no idea what he wanted me to say back to him.

The knife was slowly sinking deeper. I felt blood running down my neck. One more push and I would...

'What the fuck's going on here, mate?' a rough voice slurred. The masked man turned his head and the sharp edge of the blade moved away from my throat. I pulled in a quick desperate breath, relieved at the interruption.

He let go of my jumper and turned to face two scruffy men

standing just inside the open doorway. Neither of us had heard them come down the stairs. They were dressed in identical large dirty overcoats and each carried an assortment of bags. They gawked incredulously at my masked tormentor, gripping his knife streaked with blood. They were slow to decipher the situation. I didn't want them to leave me to this madman but I couldn't let him hurt them too.

'GET OUT!' I yelled. 'Run and get help, please! MOVE!'

His elbow slammed into my nose and fireworks exploded in my brain. My legs crumpled even before the pain took hold, and I collapsed, retching on the floor as blood gushed freely down my face.

My attacker reached the two homeless men with alarming speed, grabbing a broken brick en-route. There was an audible crack of bone and the nearest man dropped to the floor wailing, holding his head, his bags flying in all directions. His friend looked on confused, still too slow to react. The masked man swung the brick again, hard, into the second intruder's face. His destroyed nose erupted in a torrent of bright red blood and his hands flew to his face.

Both men were now moaning loudly and writhing in agony on the dirty floor, and although they were no longer a threat, I knew he would move in to finish them off. More voices floated down from above. The attacker hesitated, torn between his obvious desperation to torture me and the temptation of getting away before more people turned up. Decision made, he strode back towards me.

If he was going to kill me, I wanted to be on my feet, at least. With adrenaline and fear driving me, I somehow managed to raise myself onto one knee. I wobbled and swayed, but couldn't get any further.

I could barely focus through the blood and tears filling my vision. He came closer and pulled me to my feet. I flinched, convinced he was going to bury the knife deep between my ribs, but instead he shoved something in my face. A photo swam into focus and stopped my heart beating altogether.

As calmly as if we were chatting about last night's football he said, 'Don't tell the police anything, Dr Murray. Just say you were mugged or I'll pay *them* a visit, you have my word on that.' He stuffed the photo down my jumper. 'And have better answers for me next time we talk.'

He spun me around and cut the plastic ties off my wrists while he whispered threats in my ear, his breath warm and moist.

I turned slowly as I felt him move away. He walked to the door, stepping over the two homeless men on the way.

'Rest assured, I will find Eleanor. And the baby. Nothing will stop me. Not you and not her pathetic excuse for a father.'

And then he was gone, through the doorway and up the stairs. I heard sounds of a scuffle up above, but I was beyond caring. The fucker was gone. I slumped down on the ground, totally spent. I couldn't stop my fingers from shaking as I took the photo out from underneath my jumper and stared at it.

CHAPTER 10

Before. 1995.

Shirley Grainger patted her perfectly-lacquered hair and smiled at her reflection, pleased with the result. It was so important to look her best. After all, today was the day she became a mother. A shiver of excitement skipped down her spine – she would make such an excellent job of it.

'Oh Norman, do stop messing about with your tie, they'll be here soon. And put your jacket on. We have to look perfect.'

Norman's mumbled answer was lost in an excessive whoosh of hair spray. Not a hair would dare be out of place. The doorbell rang out a melodious tune and Shirley strode down the stairs, her heart fluttering in her ample chest, to greet her children.

Of course, it was Norman's fault they were being forced to foster. He was infertile or impotent, she could never remember which, and of course, it was far too late for her now. She'd complained to her knitting group at church about it and they had suggested adopting. Shirley felt that fostering was a better way to go before making anything too permanent. She'd heard that some of these children could be a handful. Better to have a trial run first, so to speak.

Carole Butterfield, the agency social worker, stood on the doorstep holding the hands of two young children. A pigeon pair. Although of course they weren't biological siblings and looked nothing alike. Ellie and Harry. Shirley wished she could rename them. Arthur and Mary-Jane would have suited her better. Perhaps if she did decide to adopt them…

'Welcome, welcome! Come in Carole. Hello Ellie, hello Harry. I'm going to be your new mother!' she gushed, too busy spreading pink lipstick on small unwilling cheeks to notice the social worker rolling her eyes. Foster parents for older children were hard to come by, so Shirley Grainger had to be tolerated. Harry squirmed out of Shirley's grasp – he wasn't one for kisses. Ellie was more amenable, more polite. A better class of child altogether, thought Shirley.

Shirley knew a little of the children's unfortunate backgrounds. Harry's mother had died of a drug overdose in a dilapidated council estate flat over two years ago. He was small for an eight year old and a few inches shorter than Ellie who was almost a year younger than him. He had a mass of unruly dark red curls and a mischievous look in his eye. Harry had already been in two foster homes but Shirley was confident she could sort him out. The boy just needed boundaries and he would flourish in her lovely home.

The girl was a different kettle of fish. Her extremely wealthy parents had recently died in a car accident. Although she didn't have all the details it seemed all the money was gone, tied up with the lawyers in trust funds and the like. The poor little girl had been left with nothing. There would be no more ponies and private schools. Ellie would have to go to the local state school now with Harry. Shirley was going to join the PTA; she fancied the role of chairwoman.

'Come through to the kitchen. I have Ribena and biscuits as a special treat and then I can show you to your rooms!'

'Do you have a dog, Miss Shirl?' Harry asked, wiping his snotty nose on his sleeve as he pushed past her into the pristine kitchen.

'You should call me Mother now. And oh no Harry, dogs are messy creatures, they drop so much hair. Ah, here's Norman, your father. Come say hello to the children Norman.'

Norman smiled kindly and sort of waved, the uncertainty in his expression evident to the children. This clearly wasn't his idea.

'Now then Harry, you sit here and Ellie over there. Norman put the kettle on. I'm sure Carole here could do with a cup of tea?'

'My name is Eleanor,' the little girl corrected politely, her voice clear and her diction perfect. She would make a lovely daughter, Shirley thought. Harry, on the other hand, would need tutoring. His manners left a lot to be desired.

'No, no dear, it says Ellie on your birth certificate,' Shirley quickly corrected. She still thought Mary-Jane would better suit the serious little girl.

Shirley was delighted when the social worker declined the cup of tea and left, promising to be in touch. She was excited to be alone with her new children. She couldn't wait to show them to their rooms. She had told everyone that she was going to be fostering not one, but two orphans. They all thought she was a saint to take on such a huge responsibility, but she'd explained it was just her Christian duty to give these poor homeless waifs a good home.

As Norman showed the social worker to the door, Shirley took a good long look at her new family. Harry was all skin and bones with a ridiculous amount of freckles on his small nose. Ellie was really quite beautiful with her unusually coloured eyes. Shirley had been assured that they would not affect her vision. Of course, the sizable pinkish scar covering her cheek and chin detracted from her prettiness. Again, she'd been assured it would fade in time. Her shiny long blond hair hung down her back. It was lovely but totally impractical. Shirley would take a pair of scissors to it tonight. That would make it so much easier to manage.

Shirley noticed how the children held hands, ignoring her homemade oat and fennel biscuits. She would need to put a stop to that, after all, they were brother and sister now and there would be no inappropriate behaviour under her roof. No doubt it was the council estate upbringing that Harry had endured that led to such nonsense. Well, her own mother had never spared the rod on Shirley or her brothers and she may need to follow that example.

'Finish up, children, then we'll go see your bedrooms and get you changed into some smart clothes before Mrs Fisher comes to visit. She's the chairwoman of the WI, you know. We'll all have to be on our best behaviour for her now, won't we?'

CHAPTER 11

Finn

The cab dropped me at home after midnight, exhausted, sore, confused and still shit-scared. I kept imagining the balaclava-clad maniac in every noise and shadow. I put all the lights on downstairs.

Someone must have called the emergency services as the masked man ran off. The basement was in an abandoned building on the edge of the hospital ground frequented only by a community of homeless people.

While he was busy threatening to cut off my fingers, several itinerants had wandered into avoid the continuing storm. I still had no idea how he'd gotten me there from the car park. The police had promised to check the CCTV footage.

I'd never felt so terrified or defenceless in my life, and if the homeless crew hadn't arrived when they did... I couldn't finish the thought; a shudder swept down my spine. I reached for the unopened bottle of JD that I'd found in the cupboard and sloshed an over-generous measure into the nearest glass, spilling it on the table as my hand shook. What the hell. I needed a drink even if it messed with the painkillers.

The paramedics were the first to arrive and took my two homeless rescuers and me to my own A&E department. One had a broken nose, the other a fractured skull. They were woozy on details but earned themselves a clean bed and some dodgy hospital food for a few days.

The police listened to my story, one I'd modified while I was waiting for my x-ray. I understood their scepticism. A masked mugger who dragged his victim from a car park to a basement, sliced his neck, bashed his nose, but left his wallet – it didn't ring true.

When pushed, I hinted it might have been something to do with my wife's accident. I said it more to gauge their reaction than anything else. I wished I hadn't bothered. Having little else to go on, they made a half-hearted attempt to check the details of Ellie's crash, again confirming that there was no suggestion of foul play. 'It was an accident' and 'she was very dead' were the words the young constable so elegantly used before his older colleague glared at him for his insensitivity. I was way too tired to take offence.

Luckily, Toby, a good friend of mine, was the doctor on duty. He checked me over and asked if I wanted to stay overnight. I politely declined, shamelessly threatening to tell his girlfriend about what really happened on the boy's trip to Ireland last summer if he made me an in-patient. I just wanted to go home to my own bed.

But now that I was here, I couldn't be arsed to go upstairs. My whole body hurt, everywhere, and my cut lip stung as the whiskey eased passed it. My nose was swollen and bruised, but miraculously, not broken, although it hurt like hell especially when I stupidly tried to breathe through it. Thankfully, my headache had subsided into the background thanks to the potent painkillers Toby had prescribed me, but I could still taste the vomit and smell my fear.

I'd given the police the best description I could of the attacker; tall, strong, well-built and bat shit crazy.

They were confident the 'mugging' was a one-off, and that my assailant had been scared off and wouldn't bother me again. They suggested I avoid poorly-lit car parks and pissing off my patients, and promised to do all they could to find him. They didn't sound very hopeful.

They took the view that most of the inaccuracies in my story were down to the fact that I'd been hit over the head several times.

Of course, I hadn't mentioned the questions my attacker was asking about Ellie. I was still trying to process them myself. I also didn't bring up the text messages claiming Ellie had been murdered. I wasn't keen on landing in the psych ward. And I most definitely didn't show them the photograph the bastard had shoved down the front of my jumper before running off.

The maniac in the balaclava thought Ellie wasn't dead, but in hiding. And my texting buddy believed she had died, but that it hadn't been an accident. They were both delusional.

All I wanted was to be left alone, to grieve for my wife and unborn child and start the overwhelmingly difficult job of putting my life back together.

I smoothed out the photo on the table and took a large swallow from the glass. Acidic fear rose again in the pit of my stomach. It was a recent shot of my parents walking in a park with their loopy chocolate labrador, Kim. It was either taken close up or with a very effective telephoto lens. You could see the wrinkles around my mother's eyes and count the buttons on my father's cardigan. They were both smiling as Kim scampered ahead of them, chasing her orange ball.

My hands trembled as I turned the photo over to see their home address scribbled on the back. I felt the masked man's breath again in my ear as his whispered words circulated around my head, leaving icy threads of dread. In a few short sentences, he'd described what he had planned for my parents if I were to deviate from my mugging story. I was left with no doubt that he was sociopathically evil and totally capable of what he threatened.

While I'd been at the hospital waiting for a head CT, my boss had popped her head into my cubicle. As Head of the Emergency Department, she didn't usually pull the night shift, but she was helping out as the team was short-staffed. She took one look at my battered and bruising nose and gave me a few extra days off. I would have hugged her if I'd been capable of moving off the gurney. Somehow I knew she would be the one covering my shifts. I was going to be in her debt forever.

I also rang my parents from the hospital, downplaying my injuries and keeping to the story of a random mugging. My father told me to go and work at a hospital in a nicer area.

I quizzed him as much as I could about anything odd at home; strangers hanging around the house or when they were out walking the dog. He told me the Kent countryside was safe from gangs of hooligans and to worry about myself and not them. I didn't know how to warn him without sounding paranoid, and I knew the police weren't going to mount a guard on my parents 24/7 even if I managed to convince them of the validity of the threat. It was better to say nothing.

I downed the rest of the whiskey. It swirled uncomfortably in my empty stomach as I finally headed for the stairs. I'd left my car in the hospital car park before catching a taxi home, having got one of the security guards to salvage my phone from underneath it. It was a compromise Toby had insisted on. I was in no shape to drive. I'd thrown away Ellie's bunch of roses – they were ruined. Day two of not visiting her tree.

I switched off my drowned phone and flung it on a shelf in the airing cupboard to dry out, hoping it would be working in the morning. I headed for bed, not really caring.

CHAPTER 12

The sound of knocking woke me up. Mid-morning sunshine streamed through the open lounge curtains promising a glorious spring day. I felt like crap. The noise was insistent and very annoying, bouncing around the inside of my fragile skull. I groaned as I rolled off the couch. I hurt like fuck. Everywhere. My head, nose, abdomen and even my wrists where I'd torn the skin on the rough bricks.

Despite Toby's kick-arse painkillers and last night's whiskey, I'd had a restless night. I'd woken at every noise and panicked as my imagination ran wild in the darkness of the bedroom. I came downstairs at about four in the morning and dozed on the couch in the living room. I brought Ellie's purple jumper with me. It still smelled like her.

I stumbled through to the hall and opened the door expecting to find the postman or a concerned neighbour.

'Let me in, Finn. We have to talk.'

Rachel was once again on my doorstep. I felt like shit but she looked worse. Her eyes were red and swollen and her blond hair was a piled mess on her head. There was fresh, angry bruising around her throat.

She pushed past me into my kitchen.

I found myself following her, unsure what else to do. She sat down with an audible sigh and accepted my offer of tea. This was becoming an uncomfortable habit.

'I'm sorry, I was so...so scared. I didn't know where else to go. My God, what happened to your face?' she asked staring up at me, genuine concern clouding her expression. She'd only just noticed the state I was in. I gently touched my nose. The swelling was still quite pronounced. I wasn't sure how or when we'd moved from being perfect strangers to co-dependent victims.

'You first,' I insisted, but from no sense of gallantry. My head was aching and I doubted I could articulate yesterday's events meaningfully having only had one coffee. 'Those bruises on your neck look painful. What happened? Have you iced them?' I would get back to the missing birth certificate in a moment.

Rachel tucked some wayward strands of hair behind her ear. The simple gesture was so reminiscent of Ellie that my heart ached inside my chest. There was a quiver in her voice as she began talking.

'He came to my flat,' she said, 'late last night. Forced his way in. I was so scared. The things he said – the threats. He was so different...' Her voice trailed off.

I was more than a little confused. 'Sorry, who visited you?'

'Robert.' Her tone suggested I should have known all along. 'Eleanor's uncle. *Our* uncle. I didn't even know he knew where I lived.'

Maybe it was the combination of lack of sleep, pain medication and concussion, but I had no fucking idea who she was talking about.

'Uncle? Seriously? I thought you had no contact with your father's family. You told me that you didn't know anything about anyone until Ellie contacted you.' Something about her story didn't sit right.

Rachel's eyes dropped to her half-empty cup. 'Well, yes. Sort of. She did invite me here but...but it was Robert who contacted her to begin with.' She coloured with embarrassment.

'Just tell me what happened last night,' I snapped. I'd had the night from hell and yet this woman was back in my kitchen suggesting that Ellie had been keeping secrets from me in the days and weeks before her death. Her unnerving similarity to Ellie was the only reason she was still sitting at my table.

She took her time sipping her tea, avoiding any direct eye contact. Her words when she spoke had a rehearsed feel to them as if she'd practised in the car on the way over.

'After I watched my mum's video, I decided to find out about my father's family. I knew he was dead, but I wondered if he had siblings or cousins or something, and if maybe they were looking for me. There could have been a whole family out there I didn't even know about.' She lost herself in thought for a few moments and I started thinking about food. I hadn't eaten since yesterday lunch, and surely Rachel's latest crisis didn't have anything to do with me?

'So late last year,' she continued, 'I contacted one of those DNA sites and sent in a sample.' Seeing the look on my face, she quickly added: 'It wasn't a dodgy one. It was a reputable company and I'd seen it advertised on TV. I sent the sample in, not expecting to hear anything, and certainly not so soon. But he did. Find me, I mean. And very quickly.'

'And by *he*, I'm guessing you mean this Robert guy, right?'

'Yes. Robert Hudson. Our father's brother and therefore our uncle. He knew all about my mother. About her being my father's lover and falling pregnant, and that my father got married and never saw her again. It was... well, sort of exciting finding some lost family. I'm an only child of an only child. My grandparents are both dead and now I'm slowly losing my mother. Suddenly I had an uncle – a blood relative who was interested in me and my life. He took me out to dinner at fancy restaurants. He had lots of money, and he even bought me presents and...and things...' There was clearly something she wasn't saying.

'And then in November he told me about Eleanor. How he'd found my father's *other* daughter – alive. He didn't know how or why she hadn't died with her parents, but he'd found her somehow. He said that he'd spoken to her and that she was desperate to meet me. She emailed me right away. I was away working in Singapore at the time, but as soon as I got back I came up here to see her. I was so excited. I'd always wanted a sister. And suddenly I had one. I guess that's why I was so shocked when you told me about her accident.' Tears welled in her still-puffy eyes.

'I'm sorry Rachel, I'm still confused. Why didn't this Uncle Robert come and visit Ellie himself?' I didn't want to believe that my Ellie belonged to this chaotic-sounding family. But what really churned my gut was that this man had contacted her, perhaps in error, and she hadn't told me about it.

'He couldn't get away from work. He has something to do with the military, a consultant or something, and he's often out of the country. But he told me Eleanor wanted to meet me and that he gave her my email address. So as soon as I landed, I came here to meet her and found you instead.' I ignored her barb. My mind was beginning to whir. Rachel carried on speaking, but something had changed. I recognised an echo of fear in her voice.

'Anyway, I phoned him after seeing you and told him that Eleanor had died in an accident. He'd seemed genuinely fond of her and I thought he would be upset. Instead, he went ballistic. He swore and yelled at me on the phone. Said you were lying. That you knew exactly where she was hiding. He was ranting, not making any sense. I put the phone down and decided to forget it all. Forget about finding family. I didn't need the stress. Not with my mother getting worse and everything.' She snagged a breath, and again lost herself in the cup of tea.

'And then...' she swallowed, 'and then late last night...' The quiver in her voice almost broke my heart. I reached over and gently took her hand. Our bodies trembled with remembered fear.

CHAPTER 13

'It's okay. You're safe now. You don't even have to tell me if you don't want to.' I didn't like where this conversation was going and I was quite happy for it to end. I needed to take one of Toby's painkillers. My nose was killing me.

'But I have to tell you. Don't you understand? Robert told me to,' she said, her voice rising in panic.

'Now I'm really not following,' I deflected, again. 'What has this got to do with me?'

'It's got everything to do with you, Finn. Robert knows you're lying about Eleanor.' Her tone was as emphatic as her suggestion was outrageous.

'What the fuck?' I couldn't cope with this. I pushed away from the table, absolutely furious. How dare she come into my home, wake me up, and then accuse me of lying about my wife dying?

'I'm sorry, Finn. I really am,' she quickly interrupted. 'Can you calm down for a minute and listen to me? I've had a horrific night and I have to tell you what he said. Please sit back down.'

I didn't want to, but the pleading tone in her voice won me over. Seething, I sank back down on my chair and let Rachel carry on.

'I'd just gone to bed when Robert banged on the door. I

shouldn't have opened it. I could tell he was furious, but I was worried he'd disturb my neighbours. I thought I could calm him down. Anyway, he pushed inside and just lost it. He was yelling and threatening me, saying you were lying and that I hadn't told him the truth – that I was working with you to hide her.'

'Wait, what does he look like? This Uncle Robert?' Deep down I already knew the answer, and cold fear was churning my insides.

'Um, well he has grey hair, short like a soldier. And his nose—'

'No, not his face,' I interrupted. 'His build.'

'Oh, right.' She seemed confused by my questions but tried her best to answer. 'Well, he's tall. Taller than you even. And he's well-built like he works out. And he has a large tattoo. What do they call it?' she asked, gesturing to her arm. 'A sleeve right? All the way up from his wrist. Mainly angel wings and geometric shapes.'

I couldn't breathe. The same psycho who had held a knife to my throat had also threatened Rachel. I think part of me had known the truth when I saw the awful bruising around her neck. It had to be the same man. I only vaguely remembered the attacker mentioning Ellie's parents, I'd clearly been more focused on keeping my fingers attached to my body. I didn't want to believe it was Ellie's uncle.

'He had a knife,' she said. Her words reverberated around the kitchen. I didn't want to hear any more, but she carried on regardless. My fingers found the steri strips on my neck and I shivered, despite the warmth of the kitchen as the April sun shone through the window. I failed to dissipate last night's fear.

'It was a huge, horrible knife. And he kept telling me what he would do with it. To me. To my mum...' Her tenuous hold on her emotions snapped and she began sobbing. Her hand was still in mine, resting on the table. I understood her pain. I'd seen the bastard's knife and heard his threats. I squeezed her hand as reassuringly as I could. I didn't have the words to comfort her.

'He described awful things he would do if I didn't give you a message. In person.'

'What message?' I asked quietly. I knew what the sick bastard wanted. The police were wrong – he hadn't been scared off. He simply went to terrorise his next victim.

'He was crazy, rambling on about how you lied. Demanding to know where Eleanor is. He's adamant she's alive and that you know where she is. He told me to find her or...or he would come back and... do things...'

She snatched her hand back as if burnt, dropping her head and covering her face. An uncomfortable silence ballooned in my kitchen as I tried to get a grip on the fear growing inside me. How was I going to convince this deluded knife-wielding imbecile that he had it wrong? That my Ellie was dead?

Rachel seemed to go from upset and vulnerable to flat out furious in a millisecond. 'What's going on Finn? Where is my sister? What haven't you told me? Was that whole story about the accident just bullshit?' she spat, glaring at me as if I were suddenly the villain.

I wasn't even going to start revisiting those fucking stupid questions. So I asked one of my own instead. 'How did your neck get hurt?'

Rachel pushed back her chair and began pacing. Her facial expression flickered between anger and fear.

'He pulled my hair and pinned me up against the wall. He was far too strong. He made me promise I would come here and get the truth from you, and I agreed. I would have agreed to anything. I was so terrified.' She was shaking so much that she had to grip the counter to keep her balance. 'That didn't stop him putting his hands around my neck. I thought he was going to kill me. He just kept squeezing. I couldn't breathe. I couldn't fight. I... there was nothing I could do about it. I tried. I really tried. He just squeezed harder and then...then I must have passed out.'

'He compressed your carotid arteries,' my medical brain automatically announced. 'Did you go to the hospital or the police?'

'Are you out of your mind?' Her unmatched irises bored into me in horror. 'He said not to. And anyway... he left a photo. It's of my mum in the garden at her care home. Her address is even written on the back. He knows where she lives. We're not telling anyone – ever. Do you understand me?' Her hands were on her hips as she loomed over me. 'You don't understand how threatening he is. I came as soon as I thought you would be awake.' She was lucky I was here. If I hadn't been attacked I would have been at work.

'Okay, okay. I'm with you on the no police. I really do understand.' Fuck did I understand. The photo of my parents flashed through my mind.

She slumped down in her chair, exhausted. 'Please, Finn. Just tell me where the hell Eleanor is. I can't let that man hurt my mum. Please.'

'Rachel, I swear on my life, Ellie is dead. She is not missing or in hiding because she isn't alive. Even if I wish with all my heart that she was. That's the honest truth.' I poured every ounce of sincerity into the words. I needed her to believe me, then maybe I could convince this Robert Hudson too. It didn't matter who they think Ellie may have been because she was gone now, and that was a fact we all had to accept.

I collapsed in my chair as fatigue washed over me. I was totally spent. For the last three months I had been running on grief. I didn't have any reserves left to cope with Rachel and Robert and their utter bullshit.

'Robert is convinced you're lying, Finn. What are we going to do?'

I had no bloody idea.

CHAPTER 14

T om Harper parked his car and sat for a while. He was a little early for his appointment.

His mind wandered as it was prone to do more these days as he grew older, and it was always the old days he reminisced about. The days when his name was Thomas Hudson and his future shone with an all invasive light. When he was heir to a fortune, a successful businessman in his own right. A husband, a father. He was happy.

His life had been mapped out since birth. The right schools, the right university, the right friends and even the right wife, one who aligned his family with one of equal importance and influence. Then followed the perfect home, the perfect children; both blond and beautiful. His brother proved to be the only fly in the otherwise perfect ointment.

How his reality had changed. A downward spiral had taken hold of his life and his sins were finally catching up with him.

Gone was the big house in London and the country estate near Oxford, the yacht on the Med and the ski chalet in Verbier. Their lavish, opulent lifestyle; their friends and their social standing. All abandoned. All sacrificed. But to what end?

They had new names and new identities. Empty and soulless and hidden from the world. And in the end, it had all been for nothing – Eleanor still died.

Now he and Liz lived their small lives in their two-bedroomed bungalow in a nondescript part of Essex, with its garden the size of a postage stamp and a scruffy old cat.

Tom worked as an accountant for a small software firm in Chelmsford. They had a few savings, but nothing that would attract attention. There was a time when they had everything; the golden couple, featured on the society pages of every London tabloid. The toast of the town. Now they had nothing and lived in quiet obscurity.

Tom roused himself from his morbid recollections as he entered his lawyer's offices. He trusted the lawyer with his life. After all, Lawson had been there from the beginning and was instrumental in facilitating his and Elizabeth's deaths and rebirths.

'Mr Lawson will be with you shortly,' the secretary said as she led him through to the conference room, her chubby thighs rubbing together under her polyester skirt with a fraying hem. The conference room wasn't as grand as it sounded. Julien Lawson received all his clients in here. His office was small and cramped, but at least this room had pleasant views out over the park.

Tom stood at the window, waiting. The April sky was cloudless and blue, with the first hints of summer on the pleasant breeze. Bikes and picnic blankets had been recovered from storage, and everyone was making the most of the sunshine.

Watching the children chasing around the park transported him back once again, to when he had watched Eleanor and Benjamin running across the lawns in Oxfordshire – a million years ago. Eleanor was tall and leggy even at five, and she moved with a grace and beauty that melted his heart. Benjamin, just two, was podgy, his chunky legs below his nappy pumping hard to keep up with his sister.

The image of his lost children dissipated the instant the door opened and Lawson entered. He was short and as overweight as his secretary. He seemed to be stuffed into his ill-fitting pin-striped suit, his wobbling neck sticking out like a tortoise. He was sweating and looked flushed, and not for the first time, Tom found himself worrying about the man's blood pressure. Lawson sat heavily, his bulk overwhelming the chair. He opened a thick file.

'Good to see you again, Tom. What was so urgent that you needed an appointment on a Saturday?' Lawson's voice was roughened by his thirty-a-day habit, but his eyes were bright and intelligent. A small-town lawyer whose bread and butter had been dull divorces and the odd contested will. He was still a shrewd man.

'It's about the money. Eleanor's trust fund money. What happens to it… now? Now that she's gone?' Tom stumbled over his words, his grief still a fresh wound. He'd been so devastated after Eleanor's accident that he hadn't thought to check before. But now, getting access to the fortune that he had so cleverly concealed for his daughter's future appealed. He would use that money to permanently put an end to the problem that was his brother, once and for all. And then, finally, he and Elizabeth could find the peace that had eluded them all these years in hiding.

The hidden funds were difficult to ignore.

Lawson looked at Tom for a moment. He was surprised his client hadn't asked about the money earlier. Clients always wanted the money. Well, he was going to be sorely disappointed.

Lawson paged slowly through the comprehensive trust document he had drawn up for Eleanor Elizabeth Hudson when she was just a little girl, and her parents were planning their disappearance. He had provided for every contingency. Even the ironic twist that Eleanor would die before she was eligible to inherit the substantial funds.

Following the words with his finger, he paraphrased the provisions of the trust for Tom, 'In the event of Eleanor's premature death, the monies revert to her next of kin.'

He heard Tom's considerable sigh of relief. Hiding his smile, he looked up and explained further, 'As there are no other siblings and your daughter was married at the time of her death, her next of kin is her husband, Mr Finlay Murray.'

Tom's face dropped. 'It's all his? It all goes to the doctor?'

Lawson continued, 'After all Tom, you said you wanted nothing to do with the money – that it was hers to do with however she wanted. Now it belongs to the husband, as we agreed all those years ago.'

'He gets everything?' Tom repeated softly, almost to himself. A vision of the woman sipping early-morning tea at Eleanor's kitchen table filled his vision, and his mild mistrust blossomed to instant suspicion.

'Of course, if Finn were to pass away before the trust matures, there may be the possibility to revoke the trust and return all the funds to you as the original donor,' Lawson added.

Tom ignored the lawyer's words, changing the subject. A plan was forming at the back of his brain. 'Did he know?' Tom asked. 'Did Murray know about the money? And that he would be next in line to inherit if something happened to Eleanor?'

Lawson hesitated, unsure what Tom was insinuating.

'No. Not as far as I know. I've never even met the man, but if Eleanor chose to tell him, well... I did warn her not to tell anyone, like we agreed. But...' Lawson paused, searching for words Tom would understand. 'She was very, um, confused when she found out about the trust fund. Confused and extremely upset to be honest. It was a huge shock. The sheer amount of money was staggering to a girl who had grown up in foster care, but I still doubt she told her husband.'

'And you didn't tell her that Elizabeth and I were still alive?' Tom knew the answer. After all, Julien Lawson had broken many laws himself helping Tom orchestrate their bogus deaths. Still, Tom needed to hear him confirm it.

'Of course not, Tom. I've kept my side of our arrangement. That's what you paid me for.' Lawson's contempt at being doubted was obvious, but Tom was oblivious.

He took a deep breath as he fought the growing anxieties that were eating at him. Out of necessity, he had few friends, and the lawyer was the only person who he could share his fears with. 'Julien, I think… I think that maybe… that maybe someone murdered Eleanor. Made it look like an accident. Perhaps for the money.' Tom blurted out his rambling thoughts, a little surprised that he could articulate them.

Lawson sighed, and asked, 'And you think the husband did it?'

'Yes. No. Maybe. I don't know. Maybe it was Finn. Or maybe…' he inhaled, 'or maybe it was Robert.'

A chill settled over the room. Both men knew Robert was more than capable of killing Eleanor. After all, he had already tried once in her lifetime, so why not again now?

Lawson broke the silence, 'But Robert believes she died in the crash. Your crash I mean. He wouldn't even know to look for her. Would he? Honestly, Tom, I think you're jumping to conclusions. Eleanor's death was a tragic accident, nothing more.'

Tom wished he hadn't said anything. It was nothing but the grieving ramblings of a devastated father – a father needing someone to blame. He returned to the practicalities of the situation. 'When will the money be released?'

'There can be no change in the timeline. The trust matures on Eleanor's birthday at the beginning of June, which means I need to contact Murray soon. There will be a lot for him to sort out prior to that date. You do realise that don't you, Tom? The money is his now. And he needs to know about it. I can't just pitch up on his doorstep in June with a cheque.'

'But what if—' Tom wasn't finished, but Lawson had heard

enough.

'Tom, my old friend, I know it's been incredibly difficult for you, but you need to let it go. There is absolutely no evidence that there was any foul play. Not from the police or the coroner. I have to abide by the stipulations set out in the trust documents, and quite honestly, I thought the husband looked genuinely devastated at the funeral. I doubt he would have the backbone to kill someone.'

'Looks can be deceiving,' Tom mumbled, thinking again about Finn's lady visitor and the row they'd had. Had they been fighting over the money? Had his mistress pushed Finn to kill Eleanor, and was now afraid she wouldn't get her share of the funds? There were too many variables to think about. Truthfully, Tom would rather focus on Finn as the culprit than addressing his real fear – that Robert, his own brother, had murdered his beloved daughter.

Lawson closed the folder with a soft thud, signalling that their meeting had ended.

He watched dispassionately as Tom headed back to his car. A forlorn, grey man.

CHAPTER 15

Finn

I know who killed your wife.

I know who killed your wife.

I know who killed your wife.

I stopped counting the messages; there were at least a dozen of them. They flashed on the screen one after the other as soon as I switched my now dried out phone back on.

Rachel looked utterly worn out and it felt a little mean expecting her to drive back to London. When I suggested she stay for lunch and then have an afternoon nap in our spare room, she jumped at the chance.

I left her in charge of the boiling water and popped down the road to the small Co-op. I got some tea bags, fresh milk, pasta and some paracetamol, regretting throwing all mine out the other day.

I cobbled together some pesto pasta which neither of us wanted, but which we ate in a strained silence. There wasn't much to say. She wanted answers and assurances and I was fresh out of both.

Happy to escape the kitchen, and me probably, she took her cup of tea upstairs with her. I showed her to the room that was going to have been our nursery. I hadn't gone in there much lately.

Before heading back downstairs, I retrieved my phone from the airing cupboard. As soon as I switched it on the bloody thing started pinging non-stop with messages.

I was tempted to drown it in water again and keep the madness at bay. My persistent texter wasn't showing any signs of tiring from his sick game.

I made a strong black coffee and slumped down on the couch, relieved to be having a break from Rachel. My hands were shaking, and it was annoying the hell out of me. I blamed it on my pounding head and aching nose. I felt like the freight train that ran over me yesterday had backed up and hit me a dozen more times during the night.

The texts were messing with my head. They were the same and all from the anonymous sender. What was the sick fuck expecting me to do? How did he not realise I couldn't reply – even if I wanted to?

It was bad enough that this delusional 'Uncle Robert' with the big knife believed Ellie was alive – but to have 'anonymous-is-us' suggesting that an unknown third party had deliberately killed my wife was beyond comprehensible.

All I wanted was to hold on to the memory of Ellie as she was. My gorgeous, gentle Ellie. But the last few days were making that frustratingly difficult. I was even beginning to imagine a different Ellie to the one I'd known and loved; one with a hidden family of knife-wielding maniacs. Could Robert have caused Ellie's accident in some way that even the authorities couldn't discern? I would have laughed if anyone had even suggested such crap a week ago.

My imagination was in freefall, chasing idiotic questions around my over-tired brain. Why would anyone want Ellie dead?

My headache had gotten worse. Perhaps I needed to take some more time off work. A sabbatical of sorts. I could go and stay with my parents. Let all this nonsense blow over. Ellie was dead, and surely both Robert and the texter would have to face that reality soon enough – just as I was so desperately trying to do. Visions of the photo Robert had stuffed down my shirt shifted my perspective. I couldn't allow that lunatic any excuse to go near my parents. I'm sure Rachel felt the same desperate need to protect her mum.

The sudden sound of the post landing on the mat sent hot coffee sloshing over my hand. I hadn't realised I was so jumpy.

Feeling closer to 103 than 30, I bent and picked up the pile of envelopes off the hall mat. There were a couple of bills, some junk mail advertising the karaoke night at the village pub and a small brown padded envelope. As I turned it over my heart sank.

Mrs Ellie Murray

22 Brambly Hill

Littleton

Berkshire

I didn't think I would ever get used to seeing post addressed to Ellie. Usually it was a Next catalogue or an appointment reminder from the dentist. I didn't recognise the untidy handwriting, and I only hoped it wasn't any more deluded family members wanting to poke through Ellie's ashes.

Sitting back on the couch, I took another swallow of my coffee and stared at the envelope. Seeing Ellie's name in such a normal context was a horribly painful reminder that she was gone. I missed her so much, but she was never coming back. I had to live with that reality. I couldn't shake the overwhelming feeling of emptiness that her loss had left in my life. I took a moment before I opened the envelope, waiting for the ache in my chest to decrease to an almost-manageable level.

It took three tries to rip the package open as my trembling fingers struggled with the flap. I tipped the contents onto my lap: a handwritten letter, some photographs and a silver bracelet.

I would recognise that bracelet anywhere.

For our first wedding anniversary, I bought Ellie a silver bracelet with a very distinctive filigree pattern. A one-of-a-kind original. She loved it and always wore it when she wasn't working.

I didn't touch the bracelet or turn the photos over. I just sat there, numb. Ellie's bracelet should be upstairs in the small wooden jewellery box on her chest of drawers, not falling out of envelopes. Once again, I was heading down the rabbit hole.

Eventually, I gathered up the courage to open the letter. 'Letter' was an exaggeration. It was half a page of writing on a page torn clumsily from a spiral notebook. The untidy handwriting matched the envelope.

I know who killed your wife. You ignored my texts.

Don't you want to know?

The first sentence was achingly familiar. My stomach flipped over as bile edged up my oesophagus like liquid fire. This unknown person had reverted to the Royal Mail to get my attention. The rest of the words literally took my breath away, and a heavy pain gripped my chest as I read on.

Ellie's NOT dead – they killed someone else instead. Ellie is alive! Her accident was a scam. I want £5,000. CASH. Here's her bangle and some photos. For proof. Don't tell ANYONE. Meet me at McDonald's in Leicester Square at 1.30 pm on Sunday. Don't be late. Bring the money and I'll tell you how to find her.

If you don't want to find her, I'll let HIM have her.

I stumbled to the sink and only just managed to keep the vomit off the floor. My stomach emptied completely as I spewed over the dull stainless steel, vaguely relieved I'd washed the dishes after lunch. The smell alone had me retching a couple more times. I was sweating and couldn't get my breath. I was going to have a complete meltdown if I didn't get it together.

Dead. Alive. Murdered. My world was imploding. Nothing made sense anymore.

I took some slow, deep breaths as bile sloshed in my stomach and it took a few minutes before I could make it to the kitchen chair. I was still clutching the envelope and its macabre contents. I sat staring at them on the table for the longest time.

Perhaps I'd been a horrible person in a previous life. This had to be some twisted form of retribution for my past sins. Who hated me enough to do this?

Reluctantly, I picked up the bracelet, feeling its weight in my hand. Perhaps someone had found an identical bracelet. There was an inscription engraved on the inside of Ellie's where no one could see; a message just for her. My fingers gently caressed the inside of the metal circle, my eyes refusing to look.

I felt only smooth polished silver and then, like a blind man fumbling his Braille, my fingers found the intricate little indentations that I'd had made for her. I knew what the words would say.

You are my perfect imperfection. Forever and for always.

Shit. They must have stolen it from Ellie's still untouched jewellery box upstairs, but I didn't have the courage to head up and check. And anyway, the photos were still lying face down on the table, waiting for me. What if it was of Ellie – Ellie alive? Ellie alive with another man, holding hands and kissing? I couldn't get my head around what I should think, how I should feel. All those years of studying human anatomy and I never realised a heart could be ripped apart – twice.

I'd never thought of Ellie with another man, but what other reason could she possibly have for faking her death than to be with another man?

There were two photographs, both taken from a distance; the images were blurred and had been poorly reproduced, making any identification difficult. They showed a young woman wearing jeans and a sweatshirt walking along in front of a parade of shops. She was carrying some grocery bags and eating an apple.

The hair was the right colour and roughly the right length. In both images, the apple obscured her face. I couldn't see if there was a scar, and the definition was way too poor to see her eye colour. She was the right build – except the woman in the photograph was at least six months pregnant. Her belly eased over her jeans, pushing up her shirt a little. I ran my thumb over the baby bump as tears spilt stupidly down my face. She could have been anyone. Anyone except Ellie – Ellie was dead.

Tomorrow was Sunday. I needed to get my hands on some cash. I knew it was a lie. I knew Ellie was dead. But I had to meet with this person and find out why they were doing this to me.

I had to make them stop.

They were destroying Ellie's memory as fast as the flames had destroyed her body.

CHAPTER 16

Arriving home from his meeting with the lawyer, Tom found his wife sitting quietly on the couch, her legs tucked neatly underneath her. She sat too quietly, not even acknowledging his presence as he entered the small sitting room. She simply gazed at the bare wall above the mantelpiece with eyes glazed and her face slack and devoid of expression. A thread of drool edged down from the corner of her pale mouth.

Tom was a little surprised to see that Liz was dressed and her hair brushed. He'd left her in her dressing gown at the kitchen table eating cereal. She'd even washed the bowl and spoon. Her colourful knitting sat discarded on top of her ever-present scrapbook.

Tom could only guess at the kaleidoscope of thoughts that revolved behind his wife's unfocused eyes as she drifted through life lost in a sea of memories.

The house was simply furnished. There were no cluttering knick-knacks and no family photographs. To the outside world, they were the dull, childless couple who kept themselves to themselves. They had few friends and next to no social life. Liz stayed home either knitting tiny hats and cardigans for the premature babies at the local maternity unit or paging through her scrapbook.

She hadn't always been like this. Once she had been a beautiful and intelligent young woman, brimming with vitality and potential, already making her mark on London society as his wife. But that was all before.

Of course, while Eleanor was alive, Liz had a purpose. A mission in life. A reason to carry on. She could still regard herself as a mother, even if only in abstention.

Over the years they had watched their daughter. First into care and then to the awful foster home. Through school and on to university, and then working at the hospital. They knew when she was ill, or scared, or unhappy, and they panicked the time she fell off her bicycle aged ten. They knew her friends and that she loved playing netball. They watched anxiously as she grew up and discovered boys, learnt to drive, became a young adult.

And then she met Finn Murray. Straight away, they knew he was special. He followed her around campus like a smitten fool and it was soon apparent that she was just as captivated. Their engagement followed shortly afterwards. They had travelled down to Kent for the wedding, slipping into the back of the packed chapel and watching as Eleanor walked down the aisle on the arm of her soon-to-be father-in-law. They had left quietly before the end of the service.

All the important landmarks of a parent's journey through life with their daughter – but only as spectators. It was all carefully documented in Liz's precious scrapbook.

Now Eleanor was gone, and Elizabeth was left with nothing but pain – a living entity destroying her tender hold on reality.

'Hello, Lizzie,' Tom kept his voice purposely calm, not wanting to shock her out of her reverie. 'I'm back!'

'Tom?' she took a moment to recognise him, her expression so sad and vulnerable. He'd thought they could escape and make a new life; different but still happy. After all, they still had each other. But he was wrong – they had nothing. Now they had lost Eleanor too, and would lose all the money to Murray in a couple of months as well.

'He phoned back.' Elizabeth held out a piece of paper. 'He left his number. His name was Andrew, I think.' Her words were slow, but at least she was in the present. And she'd answered the phone and taken a message – a rare occurrence in itself.

'Oh right, of course. Andrew's one of the young men I work with,' he explained, although by that time she had already lost interest in the conversation. 'I'll give him a ring back. It's probably just about work. Shall I pop the kettle on Lizzie and we can have a nice cup of tea before your medicine?' She nodded distractedly, finding a loose thread on her skirt.

Tom went into the kitchen before he dialled.

'Hey Tom,' said Andrew when he picked up the call, 'thanks for getting back to me. I found him. Your mystery man. Just like I said I would.'

'You found Robert?' Tom's voice broke as fear closed his throat. He swayed on the spot and held the wall. 'Are you sure?'

'Yes, it's him alright. As I said, no one can hide in this electronic age. Everyone leaves a footprint. You just need to know where to look.'

'You found him.' Tom repeated in disbelief.

'Yeah, so it looks like Robert Hudson is no longer with the army. I can't find out exactly what happened. No one is saying much but it was pretty major and all very hush-hush. Now he's back in the UK. He recently bought a property in London which, to be honest, made him even easier to find.'

Tom's hand squeezed the phone, his knuckles white as dread and desperation enveloped every cell in his body. He remembered the shock of seeing Robert at Eleanor's funeral... and Robert had seen them.

Liz had been hysterical with fear, and by the time Tom had extracted her from the pew, Robert was gone. Tom had almost convinced himself that would be an end to it all. The child was now dead after all. Robert finally had his wish. Except, of course, Robert now knew they were alive and was back in London. There could be only one outcome... Robert would never be done.

'...electricity and Council tax bills since September have been registered for a flat in Stratford in his name.' Andrew was still talking. 'It's one of the blocks that they built for the Olympics.'

'Yes, thank you. You've done a brilliant job, thank you so much. Could you text me the address over?' Tom replied automatically. His brain was struggling to process it all. So Robert had been back since September. He hadn't just come over for Eleanor's funeral; he had been there all along. His mind raced as new and frightening possibilities escalated.

'And...' Andrew hesitated, '...I've got that other info you asked for about the dark web. You said it was for a friend. Do they still want it? Shall I send that as well?'

Tom's mouth was dry and he was now slumped on the floor, unsure how he'd gotten there.

'Yes please, Andrew. That would be great,' Tom managed to answer. 'My friend will be very grateful.'

CHAPTER 17

'You got something fun planned for that cash?' The bank teller gave me a sugar-coated corporate smile as she passed the notes over. I almost blurted out 'actually no, it's a payoff to a blackmailer who has proof my dead wife is still alive,' just to wipe the stupid grin off her face. Instead I just smiled, mumbling, 'Yeah, something like that.'
The cost of Ellie's funeral had left our savings dangerously depleted, and I had to call in a few favours to raise the cash. I only got £3,770 as it was, but what the hell. It would have to do. The thin pile of shiny red £50 notes didn't look like much.

I'd left a quick note for Rachel saying I'd just popped out. I planned to bring back some groceries to cover my absence, but I doubted she would be waking up any time soon. Of course, I thought about doing the sensible thing by ignoring the letter and its demand for money – that lasted for all of three seconds. It was non-debatable. I had to know.

I rationalised my need to follow up on the ridiculous letter by telling myself that by meeting this bastard, I could get to the bottom of whatever outrageous scam he was running. Perhaps his livelihood was preying on vulnerable widows and I could stop him doing this to someone else. Then I could get back to rebuilding my life, albeit devoid of my Ellie.

But was there the smallest glimmer of hope egging me on?

I so wanted to believe it was her in the photograph; happy, healthy, heavily pregnant – and not dead. But where did that leave me? And why would she put me through the agony of thinking she had died in that crash? Was she with someone else now? It wasn't like we had some rockstar Hollywood prenup that meant our divorce would be financially ruinous. And the million-dollar question: if Ellie was alive, shopping and eating apples, then who the fuck died in that car?

The more confusing the questions, the more determined I was to find the answers. But there was one particular question that was gnawing at my insides like a starving parasite. If Ellie had gone to all that trouble to fake her death and get away from me, then was the baby she was carrying mine? I couldn't go there without crumbling.

I tucked the fresh notes into the same brown envelope the letter had arrived in. The couple of friends I'd texted to help me make up the shortfall with stories of broken boilers and emergency car repairs had quickly pinged me the money along with messages of undisguised sympathy. I wanted to scream at them, but I needed their help, and if I'd told them the real reason for asking for it they would have had me straight-jacketed and down the crazy farm in seconds. I knew it was a scam deep down, but I was still prepared to hand over the money – just in case.

Walking into my kitchen I found Rachel sitting at the table, severely pissed off. Bugger, I'd forgotten to pick up some shopping to cover my absence.

'Where the hell have you been?'

'Hi Rachel, so nice to see you too,' I spat back. 'Do you feel better after your nap?'

Tears began falling from her red-rimmed eyes and she wiped them away with the back of her hand. She'd clearly worked herself up into quite a state. 'You've been to see her, haven't you? You made me go to sleep so you could slip out of the house and go see her. Robert said if I didn't find her he'd come back a-a-and hurt me—'

'Whoa, hang on. Went to see who?' I interrupted.

Rachel sprang to her feet, her tone challenging me to lie as her eyes locked onto mine. 'Who? Oh don't act stupid, Finn. You know exactly who I mean. Eleanor, of course. You went to see Eleanor. You know where she is.' It wasn't a question.

I slumped down in a chair. I was tired and hungry and emotionally drained, and I couldn't stop my words from spewing out at her. 'Ah bloody hell Rachel, Ellie is dead. Don't you get that? I don't care what some juiced up idiot with a big knife claiming to be her long lost uncle thinks. I saw her burnt-out wreck of a car – what was left of it at any rate. I sat in a coroner's court and heard the judge say how she'd died by misadventure, for fuck's sake. I organised her funeral service and the cremation of her already-charred body. I don't know why people like you think she's alive and get a kick out of sending me photos and shit. My wife is dead!' I was almost yelling, desperate for her to understand.

'Photos? What photos?'

Crap, I hadn't planned on mentioning that. I was struggling to think straight. I could blame it on the recent concussion, but quite honestly, I was done. Rachel seemed to know exactly how to push all my buttons. I took a deep breath and began counting to ten very slowly.

Rachel only let me get to three before she rounded the table to stand in front of me, invading my space. Her hands on her hips reminding me of my mother when she was in her 'take no nonsense' mood.

'What photos?' she repeated, fury bubbling in every syllable.

I shoved my chair back a little to give myself some space from her and held my hands up in supplication. One of us needed to diffuse this situation before it spiralled out of control. It may as well be me.

'Sit down and I'll put the kettle on. When you're calm I'll tell you about it. Not before.' My voice was rock solid. There would be no negotiation on this.

It must have taken some effort, but Rachel slowly regained a little control and sat back at the table. This Uncle Robert had obviously scared her shitless, even more than I'd realised. But that didn't automatically make her my best friend. We simply shared a common enemy. I decided there was nothing to lose by telling her about the blackmail letter.

I made tea with the last of the milk and brought her up to date. I told her how the envelope arrived addressed to Ellie, and about the letter and photos. I kept the bracelet to myself. That part was just too personal to share. She listened quietly. It was impossible to read her expression.

Soon enough she unleashed her opinion. 'You're seriously going to go through with this? You're actually going to go into London and meet this… this psycho and hand over thousands of pounds because of a blurred photo? Are you absolutely out of your idiotically stupid mind?' Her words were filled with derision, and even I was beginning to have massive doubts. But how could I not go? And then she asked the question that I had been carefully ignoring.

'What if it's him? What if it's Robert? What if he's waiting and he has his knife? Or even a gun? We don't know what he's capable of, Finn. All this could be his way of luring you to him. Then what are you going to do?'

I had no fucking clue, but I scrambled for a defence anyway. 'Firstly, I really don't think it's him. And anyway, it's a busy area of London so there'll be lots of people about, and this time I won't be slugged from behind.' I paused. 'And I'll have you there as back up, right?'

She looked at me for a long moment, and behind those mismatched irises, I could almost see her processing her thoughts and deciding. All I wanted at that moment was to defrost a neighbour's meal from the freezer, sink a few beers and try and get some sleep. Tomorrow would handle itself.

I decided to hurry things along. 'Look, forget it. You don't need to come with me. This isn't your problem. You can just walk away. But I have to know who is sending me the texts and now the photos, and I need to know why...' I hesitated. I was going to say 'I need to know how he got hold of Ellie's bracelet which should be upstairs in her untouched jewellery box', but I didn't have the energy to finish my thought. I needed to know why anyone could even suggest Ellie was alive. She wouldn't leave me. We loved each other. We were having a baby together. The dark alternatives were just too awful to contemplate.

I almost missed Rachel's words when she spoke, her voice barely above a whisper, 'I can't walk away. He threatened my mum and I'm so scared that if I don't at least try to find out what's going on, then he'll come back and—'

'So you'll come with me then?' The thought of meeting the hooded man again filled me with trepidation. I didn't for a moment believe it was him – the letter was too subtle for a knife-wielding lunatic, but selfishly, I liked the idea of having Rachel as backup, even if I had to reluctantly, and somewhat pathetically, admit it to myself.

God, I missed Ellie so much. She would have had my back. But then again she wouldn't have let me waste the last of our savings on such an obvious fool's errand. She was always so sensible and careful where money was concerned. I shook my head to direct my mind away from the diversion it had taken. If Ellie were alive, I wouldn't be looking for her anyway. She'd be here with me.

'I guess so. We should stick together, right?' I could hear the hesitancy in her voice. She was no keener than I was. 'Can I see the photos and the letter?'

I'd forgotten that she hadn't seen the contents of the envelope, and if we were going to be partners it was only fair. Full disclosure and all that. I got the items out of Ellie's important stuff drawer and handed them over. Still not ready to share everything, I slipped the bracelet into my pocket when my back was towards her. I was surprised at how reluctant I was to even show her the photos. It felt disloyal in some way, although I didn't know why.

She read the letter, absorbing its short message before studying the photos.

'Oh my God!' she exclaimed, grabbing the back of the kitchen chair for support. 'She's pregnant? My sister's pregnant?' The expression on her face was, for the briefest few seconds, a mixture of shock and horror. It was such a strange reaction I almost thought I'd imagined it. I guess I'd never thought to tell her Ellie was pregnant when she died, and I watched, mesmerised, as she traced the protruding belly of the woman in the photo, tears welling in her eyes once again.

'No,' I said, 'she's not pregnant. She's dead.' I wasn't even sure if I'd said the words aloud or if they were just on repeat inside my head.

CHAPTER 18

'**I**'ll drive.'

God, Rachel was annoyingly bossy. She must have inherited that from her mother's side of the family. To be honest, I was more than happy to go in Rachel's nice new car. I'd hardly slept the night before and had a thumping headache threatening again behind my gritty eyes.

Rachel, on the other hand, was bright and breezy this morning with an air of excitement I certainly wasn't sharing. The bruises on her neck were darkening angrily. She smelt citrusy with a touch of lavender, and was wearing yet another pair of new-looking designer jeans. I recognised the expensive brand as one Ellie used to lust over in the adverts. I'd promised to buy her some when I became a registrar – maybe.

The sky remained dull and overcast, packed with threatening clouds, but it was warm and hordes of daffodils seemed to have appeared overnight – or maybe I just hadn't noticed them before. Ellie loved springtime, and she loved flowers, especially yellow ones. When this ridiculous crusade was over, I would plant some daffodil bulbs under her tree and if the council wanted to arrest me for it, well tough shit. Ellie would love some sunshine-yellow daffs at her shrine.

Rachel took the quickest way out of the village, and it wasn't until we were on the motorway that she spoke.

'Finn, was that Eleanor in the photo?'

She'd stayed over last night and we'd shared a bottle of wine, both enjoying a lie-in this morning. It felt both weird and calmly reassuring having someone else in the house after all these months of ghastly solitude. We'd both avoided discussing our trip to London, or anything to do with Ellie over a surprisingly delicious lasagne provided by Miss Rice at number 8. We'd both needed the break, but now she was ready to push me for answers.

'It's a terrible photo; it's out of focus and I can't see her scar or her eyes, so it's impossible to tell. It could be anyone. Well, anyone with her basic colouring and build who happens to be pregnant. It could even be you with some pregnancy padding or something. And besides, as I keep saying I know Ellie's dead. There's no real question about that. It can't be Ellie in the photograph.'

'A scar? What was the scar from?' Her focus shifted from the road and she didn't notice the car braking in front of us.

'Shit. Rachel stop!' I yelled, smashing my right foot uselessly into the floor. She braked with loads of room and looked shocked at my outburst.

'Sorry. I...I'm just a little nervous in traffic. You know, after Ellie's accident,' I mumbled apologetically.

'Oh gosh of course. I didn't even think. Sorry, Finn. Are you ok?'

'Yeah, yeah I'm fine. Just keep your eyes on the road.'

'I will, I promise.' She stared dutifully ahead and dropped her speed. 'But please tell me more about Eleanor's scar. I want to know everything about my sister.' I kept forgetting how little Rachel knew about her half-sister.

'She couldn't actually remember how she got it. It was before her parents died and she went into foster care. She had a large keloid scar across her chin and up her cheek. It looked like a peculiar burn to me. She could've had plastic surgery to improve the look, and she did hate it. But at the same time, it was her only connection with her birth parents and her past in some weird way.' I paused to draw breath. It felt so wrong discussing how Ellie felt with a virtual stranger. I didn't share the ironic twist of fate that two car accidents twenty years apart had annihilated an entire family.

She was visibly shaken and covered it by quickly asking another question, but I could see the scar had affected her for some reason. 'I didn't know that, we only emailed and never exchanged photos or anything. So what about her eyes?'

'She had heterochromia. Like you. One blue eye, one brown.'

Rachel gasped softly as I explained, her grip tightening on the steering wheel. Another thing I'd omitted to tell her. Their mismatched irises were a genetically inherited condition, which could theoretically indicate they shared a common parent. I was slowly coming around to accepting there was a good chance they were sisters, although I still couldn't believe Ellie had contacted her without even mentioning it to me. We shared everything. Or least I thought we had.

'Oh, really?' She took a moment to process this, no doubt evaluating its significance. 'What was she like, honestly?' she asked in a kinder tone, almost as if this was the real information she needed. 'I mean, I know you were married and all, and you loved her, but what was she really like? As a person?'

All I wanted was to get to London, find and pulverise the sicko sending the texts and go back home to grieve my dead wife in peace. I certainly didn't want to answer Rachel's loaded questions.

'She was amazing. The love of my life. Kind, generous, clever and funny. Everyone loved her.' The clichés tripped off my tongue effortlessly like a message on a Clinton's greetings card. But they weren't Ellie. How did you describe someone in just a few sentences without sounding like a dodgy dating website profile? I'd loved Ellie with all my heart, but she wasn't perfect any more than I was.

In the last few weeks before her accident we had fought more than ever. She was pregnant, tired, worried about having the baby and, it seemed, extremely hormonal. The day before she died I'd come home from work shattered, having had the shift from hell in A&E, desperate for a rest before I headed back to cover a colleague's night shift, and I'd forgotten to pick up the damn milk. It didn't go well.

Ellie yelled and I yelled back and soon it wasn't about the milk at all. We'd only been married for three years, had a mortgage draining our finances, jobs that kept us apart and utterly exhausted and now we had a baby on the way. There were a lot of issues. It soon escalated into a horrible fight.

Ellie often talked about emigrating. Medical personnel were in demand across the globe and we'd discussed, at least in theory, moving to Australia or Canada. She wanted to get away; make a fresh start. I was reluctant to leave my parents and my sisters. With the baby on the way, I'd thought that the whole 'let's move overseas' lark had been put to bed. Boy was I wrong.

Ellie seemed more obsessed than ever, berating me for being a mummy's boy, spineless and inconsiderate. I foolishly argued back that with the baby coming it would be ludicrous to consider moving countries right now. I may not have articulated my objections quite that diplomatically.

Uncharacteristically, Ellie was like a dog with a bone, providing counter-arguments to everything I said. Suddenly, she was obsessed with 'getting away' and 'starting again'. After a lot of shouting back and forth, she grew almost hysterical, and it took me ages to realise that there was a lot more that was worrying her.

Eventually, she calmed down and admitted she was panicking

about becoming a mother. Having spent most of her childhood in care, I guess she was worried she wouldn't know how to be a good mum. Immigrating was simply her way out of facing the fact that we were going to be parents in a few months.

As she broke down sobbing, I held her in my arms whispering how much I loved her and what an amazing mum she was going to make, that we didn't need to run away; we just needed to work together to make this parenting thing work. I told her everything she wanted to hear until she stopped crying. Although I knew there was more to her outburst that she wasn't saying, I was too tired to argue anymore and simply accepted her acquiescence.

No matter how badly Ellie and I argued, we always made up – often sealing it with some awesome make-up sex. But I only had a few hours before I needed to head back to work and the London derby had just started on TV. Idiotically, I offered Ellie a cup of tea which brought us back to the lack of milk. We had a good laugh this time, and Ellie suggested I go watch the football while she went out to buy some. She said she had a few errands to run and not to worry if she wasn't home before I needed to leave for work.

If I'd known I'd never see her again, I would have held her in my arms every last second and told her how much I loved her, always. I never told anyone about the argument, not my parents, nor the police investigating the accident. I barely admitted to myself the awful way we had spent our last few hours together. And my biggest regret? The commentator was reviewing the upcoming match as I switched on the TV, and I didn't even say 'I love you' back as she dashed out of the door to the shops. There was no way I was going to tell Rachel that now. This would be my cross to bear for the rest of my life.

'She was perfect,' was all I could manage as my voice cracked. I turned my head and stared out the window. I was done sharing.

CHAPTER 19

The rest of the journey passed in uncomfortable silence as I stared out at the countryside flashing past beside the M25. Rachel knew her way, leaving the motorway and negotiating London traffic like a pro. She found some astronomically expensive parking near Leicester Square without batting an eyelid at the cost. I should have been a lawyer.

We headed towards Swiss Court and the McDonald's on the corner, and I recognised the queasy feeling in the pit of my stomach as panic. Every possible scenario I ran through my head ended horribly. Even the ridiculous one where Ellie was alive but wanted to be with someone else, and had left me, taking my/our/his baby with her. I gave myself a mental kick. I had to get a grip and concentrate. We had no idea who we were meeting and the only weapon I possessed was a pocket full of cash. Grappling with a thousand what-ifs was not helpful.

The restaurant was on the corner. It was heaving with a cosmopolitan Sunday lunch crowd as tourists and locals alike queued rowdily for Big Macs and shakes. My cholesterol began to rise from the smell alone.

I had no idea how we were going to find the person who had sent the letter. I kept looking for a large, tall man with a mask and a huge knife – but that was just me being paranoid. He wouldn't have the knife out in the open.

'I don't even know who we're looking for,' I grumbled, peering through the glass doors and feeling like a pervert as I scanned all the kids with their Happy Meals.

Rachel nodded her head in agreement, peering over the queuing customers. 'Maybe he'll find us. Plus, if it is Robert, I'll recognise him.' The anxiety was apparent in her voice as she scanned the jostling crowds. I began to feel bad for bringing her with me; she was obviously still terrified after her encounter with Robert.

'You're jumping to conclusions,' I said in the most reassuring tone I could muster. 'We don't know it's Robert who's been texting, or that he's even the man who abducted me.' That was meant to calm her down but all it did was confirm the fact that there could be a third party involved and that I had no fucking clue what was going on.

Rachel smiled weakly at my attempt to comfort her, and we both refocused our attention on searching the throng of people.

I spotted several threatening-looking individuals in the crowd. A tall, intimidating man who was staring at us intensely turned out to be blind, walking with a cane and the cutest guide dog. Another man was checking out the crowd in the same way that we were, but soon found his girlfriend and left with her happily, hand and in hand. My paranoia was escalating. If we didn't find him soon, I was going to lose it altogether.

My phone vibrated in my pocket and I jumped. I held my breath as I tapped open the message.

Did you bring the money. Whos the woman

One-track-mind and lousy grammar. My texter was back. This time, the message came from a regular mobile number and not the anonymous one like before, so at least I could reply. My nervous fingers stabbed at letters, keeping it short.

Yes. A friend. We meet you together. I didn't have time to explain the whole 'she may be Ellie's sister' thing.

It took me a moment and then the realisation dawned. We were being watched. The hairs on the back of my neck tingled.

It seemed an age before the reply came back, and my hands were so sweaty I almost dropped the bloody phone.

Sit at the bus stop.

Face the road.

Dont turn round.

Rachel and I both read the words on the screen at the same time and turned our heads in unison to look for the bus stop. It was only a few metres away and, mercifully, it was empty. There were two rows of seats separated with blue tubular metal backrests. One side faced inwards onto the pavement and the other towards the traffic.

We both hurried over to the bus stop and sat down obediently. Sweat trickled down my back and my head swivelled left and right as I searched the crowds. I still had no idea who I was looking for. I felt for the envelope of cash in my jacket pocket. Did I just hand it over? Would there be proof? What if Ellie was...? I stopped myself. Ellie had died in a tragic car accident in late December; I was only there to get this man to stop harassing me, nothing more. I couldn't start imagining Ellie behind every corner. Not again. And I fucking needed to stay focused in case it was Robert.

'You got the money?' said a voice directly behind my left ear. I'd been expecting to hear a man and nearly ignored the girl's soft words. She sounded young and anxious.

'I said don't turn round,' she hissed as I involuntarily began turning my head. I could feel Rachel stiffen next to me. If I didn't handle this carefully, the girl would bolt.

'Okay, okay. I'm not moving. And yes I have the money, but you have to tell me about Ellie. First you said she was murdered and now you claim she's alive. So which is it?' I tried to keep the desperation out of my voice, but now that I was here, I wanted answers.

'We can't talk here 'cause someone might see us. The Queen's Theatre is around the corner. The stage door's unlocked and it's almost empty. We talk there.'

'No fucking way!' I snapped. 'You tell me what you know now, or the deal is...' I felt the girl stand quickly, and by the time I'd turned, she'd already melted into the throng of pedestrians.

'You bloody idiot!' Rachel yelled at me as she scanned the crowds. I climbed up on the plastic bus shelter seats, desperate to spot her. My temper had just lost us the girl.

'Give me your phone.' Rachel's tone brooked no arguments, so I handed it over. Of course! We had the girl's number! Rachel walked off to get away from the traffic and began dialling. I stood there feeling like a total dick with my heart beating furiously in my chest, pleading with the patron saint of mobile phones that the girl wasn't too spooked to pick up.

I ran our hopelessly short conversation through my head. What on earth did she mean by someone seeing us? I hadn't liked the idea of going somewhere quiet to talk – I was way too nervous as it was. Was she working with Robert to lure us closer so he could use his knife on us in private? My brain reeled with different scenarios. I desperately needed to find the girl, stay calm, give her the money and then find out the truth. Not knowing was ripping my heart apart.

I watched Rachel talking into the phone. At least the girl had answered the call, but even at this distance I could see that Rachel was arguing the case for a second meeting with all her worth. Her left hand was gesticulating wildly; her face tensed in concentration. It didn't look like it was going well. In fact, it looked like I'd just lost my one opportunity to find the answers I craved so desperately.

CHAPTER 20

L iz Harper rocked quietly at the dining room table. Her thousand-yard stare was fixed firmly on the past; nearly catatonic. She struggled terribly with change. Even though Tom had sold their next disappearance as a holiday, Liz had still reacted badly.

The cab was due in a little over an hour, but he would have to wait until Liz was fully functioning before they could leave.

Knowing Robert was back in England had changed everything. They were no longer safe. Liz was no longer safe. For twenty-three years they had remained hidden, but now his brother would find them.

Seeing him at Eleanor's funeral was such a shock. They should have run then, but Tom hoped and prayed his brother would have forgotten his old hatreds and slithered back under the rock where he had been hiding – especially now Eleanor was dead. His brother could only be back for one of three reasons. One: he'd found Eleanor and murdered her in what had appeared to be an accident. Two: he'd heard of Eleanor's death and had come to claim the money in the trust fund. Or three – Tom shivered in the warmth of the lounge – he was back to finish the job on Liz and himself. Or it could be a combination of all of the above.

Either way, he and Liz were in greater danger now than they had been twenty-three years ago. At least they had been young back then and Lizzie had been mentally stable and able to help with planning their disappearance. Now it was all down to him. So Tom had come up with a new plan, this time without consulting Liz. But if his plan worked then not only would they be rid of Robert, but they would have the trust money as well, and then he could get the help Liz needed. Maybe this time their new life would be better. But first, they had to disappear again.

Liz fed off his tension. She had been difficult all morning, refusing to get dressed or eat her breakfast. She wouldn't even take her medication. Tom didn't have the time or the patience to spend coaxing her into complying. He was too busy packing.

Tom looked around the lounge, trying to decide what they needed to take with them. He wouldn't miss this place much, he decided. It had been a house, but never a home. He began collecting some essentials for their trip. Lizzie's knitting. Her scrapbook.

The scrapbook was open on the table next to his wife. Tom glanced at the article on the open page which had been cut from the local newspaper and lovingly pasted in. Clearly this had happened when Liz was having a more lucid moment. The headline read:

Local footballers spread Christmas cheer to hospital patients.

It showed a photograph from the Christmas before Eleanor's accident. She was dressed in scrubs, caught in the background amongst her colleagues as the footballers distributed festive goodies to A&E patients.

Tom's heart squeezed in his chest as the realisation dawned. This was how Robert had found her. Ellie had always been so careful, but she'd obviously been caught off guard with this photo. The scar on her cheek was plain to see. Had it just been extreme bad luck that Robert had seen the same photo? Or perhaps he had some advanced software programmed to look for just such an anomaly. Tom had heard of such things from the young whizz-kids at work. Everything was possible these days, it seemed.

The way Eleanor was trying to avoid being captured on camera made Tom realise something about his daughter. She had remembered all that he had told her and had spent her life trying to obey him. She had been so careful on social media, and on the odd occasion that she had been tagged in another person's photos, she had always ensured that her head was turned and her scar concealed.

With a heavy feeling in his chest, Tom recalled the last time he had ever spoken to Eleanor.

Twenty-three years ago, outside the social services office in Southend, he had explained to his daughter how her life was going to change irrevocably. It had been just him and Eleanor sitting in the car – Elizabeth was unable to face this last goodbye. He'd explained to Eleanor that her name would now be Ellie, and that she must never ever tell anyone about what had happened, or about the man who had hurt her. If she did, he would come back and hurt her more. She must forget her old life and her family and reinvent herself – a word the distraught six year old hadn't understood. He told her never to let her scar be photographed, or the bad man would see it and find her. He and her mother had to go away; to hide from the bad man. They wouldn't be coming back.

The scar on her cheek was still red and raised and angry, and her tears stung it as they flowed over her skin. But his Eleanor was so brave. She knew she was saying goodbye to her father forever, but somehow she understood it was for the best, and the only way to keep everyone safe.

Carole Butterfield – the social worker who had come to collect Eleanor from the car – had been paid an exorbitant amount for her part in the deception. Eleanor would enter care as Ellie Smith, recently orphaned. The woman already had a suitable foster home lined up, and hopefully Eleanor's name would then change again as the foster mother was keen to adopt. All of this would make the paper trail even harder for Robert to follow. When the social worker read about his and Elizabeth's deaths in the newspaper, she would inform Eleanor that her parents had both died in the accident. It would give the child closure – he hoped.

So much effort, and all it had given Eleanor was twenty-three extra years before Robert had found her. The more he thought about it, the more convinced Tom became that Robert had been instrumental in Eleanor's accident.

He reluctantly finished off the packing, gratefully noticing signs that Elizabeth was slowly returning to the present. Perhaps they would be ready for the cab after all.

CHAPTER 21

Finn

T he stage door was located down the side of the theatre on a quiet lane and was, as promised, unlocked. It opened onto a dimly lit corridor with tired-looking wallpaper and dog-eared show posters.

Rachel stepped inside with no hesitation. I followed her more cautiously. She must have been a first-rate negotiating lawyer; she'd successfully managed to coax the girl into agreeing that we could come to the theatre and meet with her. Seemingly she worked there part-time as a cleaner and knew it would almost be empty at this time of day.

Rachel would have left me and come alone if she could. She only needed me there for the cash that was burning a hole in my pocket. I needed to know the truth, and so, it seemed, did Rachel.

'Come on Finn,' she urged. 'She's waiting backstage.' Rachel must have sensed my apprehension – images of body part amputations were flashing through my mind. I wasn't keen to walk down the gloomy corridor not knowing who or what was waiting for us.

Rachel clearly had no such misgivings and she strode off purposefully, leaving me no option but to man up and follow her.

For the first time in my life, and as ridiculous as it seemed, I wished I owned a weapon of some kind. A baseball bat? A submachine gun? Something lethal at any rate.

A door opened on the left, halfway down the passageway. A girl stood glaring at us. She was dressed in skinny black jeans and was waif-thin, with an extensive collection of ingeniously placed piercings. She had the whole emo thing perfected. The girl also looked scared, which started me sweating.

'In here.' She disappeared back into the room, and like lambs to the slaughter, Rachel and I followed.

The room was small and artificially bright, and it was lined with mirrors. It looked like a cramped dressing room, with two chairs and a small couch. Thankfully, there were no knife-wielding psychopaths, so I breathed a little easier.

'You got the money?' She sounded really desperate, and I got an inkling she had an expensive habit that needed feeding. I bet I'd find track marks if I pushed up the long sleeves of her black hoodie. I'd treated enough addicts in the Emergency Department. I knew the signs. No wonder she was so skittish. I made sure my voice was soft and calm, not wanting to spook her again and knowing Rachel would have my balls if I did.

'Yes, I have the money, and it's all yours I promise, just as soon as you tell us everything. And I do mean everything.'

Rachel seemed unconvinced I could keep my composure and interrupted, 'Let's all sit down and talk'. She sat on the sofa, jerking her head at me indicating I should join her. It was a tight fit, but no doubt sitting my six-foot-four frame down would look less intimidating. 'My name is Rachel, and this is Finn as you know. What's your name?'

The girl hesitated, eying us up and shuffling from one foot the other. Eventually, she answered, 'You can call me Cassie. And I want the money. All of it.'

'Relax, Cassie. I've got the money. It's right here.' I patted my jacket pocket feeling like a character from a second rate gangster movie.

'Cassie, please come sit down,' Rachel persuaded. 'We're here to give you the cash, but we need to talk first. That's the deal.' At last, the anxious girl grabbed a chair and sat, glancing at the closed door every few seconds. Her anxiety was real. She was evidently afraid of something or someone.

'What do you know about Ellie's accident?' I asked impatiently.

'Finlay, calm down,' Rachel warned, giving me an annoyed sideways glare. Using my full name as if she really knew me set my teeth on edge. 'Why don't we let Cassie tell us her story and then we can give her the money. Just like we promised.'

Telling me to calm down wasn't particularly helpful, but I let it pass and gave Cassie my very best 'I'm not here to fuck you over' smile that I generally reserved for toddlers with beads up their noses in A&E. Thankfully, she was completely focused on Rachel and was ignoring me.

'You promise I get the money?'

Rachel nodded emphatically, motioning for me to show Cassie the envelope. I wasn't sure who put her in charge but she and the girl seemed to have a connection, so I dutifully took out the envelope and showed them both the red fifties inside. I bloody well wasn't going to just hand it over.

'You won't like it,' Cassie started, and a vice squeezed my chest. Suddenly I didn't want to hear what she had to say. I wanted to run for the hills and be anywhere but here. She carried on, 'I lied before about her being alive. I'm sorry. I just had to make you come. But he killed her. Murdered her. Making her crash her car into a tree.'

My head spun as I tried to make sense of her words. Calm was no longer an option. I was instantly up on my feet yelling.

'What the fuck are you playing at? You sent photos! You said she was alive! Now you say she's dead again? Is this some kind of sick game to you? And why would anyone kill Ellie?' My microscopic vestige of hope dissipated like a wisp of smoke and my heart tore apart. It felt like I was losing Ellie all over again.

'Shut up and sit down Finn.' Softening her tone, Rachel addressed the frightened girl who now had a very stricken look on her face, 'Cassie, it's all right. Finn's just upset. We're just trying to understand what's going on here. Who died in the car? Who was the girl in the photos you sent? Do you know where Eleanor is? You said she was alive.'

Rachel sounded as confused as I felt, and her litany of questions weren't doing anything to calm Cassie down. The girl stood, bouncing from one foot to the other, her eyes large and scared. I perched on the edge of the sofa trying to get a grip on my emotions, but also ready to grab her if she tried to run.

'Please, Cassie. I have to know. What happened to Ellie?' My voice cracked with desperation.

With her eyes on her boots, she shook her head before slumping back onto the chair. Pointedly ignoring me, she faced Rachel, drawing a breath before she started.

'The photos were just a friend. She had the same colour hair and we made her look pregnant. I'm sorry. It's just I wasn't hearing from you, and I really needed the money.' She paused, her gaze now fixed on the envelope of cash. I picked it up and shoved it back in my pocket without saying a word. I hadn't realised how much I'd dared to believe Ellie might be alive. I was such an idiot.

Seeing the money disappear clearly gave Cassie the encouragement she needed to get on with her story. 'You ignored my texts. I had to get your attention. You didn't get back to me when I told you she'd been murdered, so I sent the photo.'

I was halfway to my feet again but Rachel stopped me with

a hand on my arm. 'Finn wasn't able to reply, Cassie,' she explained calmly. 'You used an anonymous number. There was no way for him to get hold of you. He wasn't ignoring you.'

Cassie tucked her lank black hair behind her metallic studded ear. Realisation was beginning to dawn on her and her fingers trembled as her addiction gnawed.

'Oh. I wasn't sure how it worked. I didn't want you to be able to trace me or anything. So I just thought you didn't care. That's why I sent the photos. I thought maybe you'd give me the money if you believed she was still alive.' She suddenly sounded about twelve, and I had to lean in to hear her soft words. I almost felt sorry for her. Almost.

'There are things we still don't understand,' said Rachel. 'When and where did you meet Ellie? And who killed her?' Rachel wasn't the only one struggling to make sense of what the girl was actually saying. My brain was doing backflips trying to process it all.

'Was it a big guy? Tall?' I interjected. 'Cold grey eyes, tattoo on his right arm?'

She looked at me and shrugged. 'Don't know who you mean. It was my boyfriend who killed her. Well, ex-boyfriend now I guess. His name's Harry. Harry Grainger.'

CHAPTER 22

I carried three overpriced lattes and a plate of pastries back to the table where Rachel and Cassie were sitting half-hidden at the back of the coffee shop.

I hadn't even known that Sunday matinees were a thing until we heard members of the cast arriving in the theatre. Cassie began to panic and Rachel had diplomatically suggested getting coffee, so we decamped to the nearest Starbucks. I wasn't worried about Cassie running off – I still had the cash. She would follow me to the ends of the earth for it.

I hoped the pastries would give her enough of a sugar boost to keep her focused as she fought the demons of her addiction. She looked even paler, and her nervous twitches were growing more pronounced. The girl needed rehab, not a couple of thousand pounds she could squander on further destroying her life.

'Right Cassie. Start at the beginning and tell us everything you know.' Even Rachel was getting impatient and I didn't blame her. All we had so far was Harry the ex-boyfriend.

Cassie blew over her latte, ignoring the food. After a moment she tilted her head a little but kept her eyes on the table. Her voice was soft and edgy, as if she was trying to make herself sound tough while falling apart inside. I couldn't decide if it was fear or the addiction alone that was fuelling her anxiety.

'Back in December, Harry and me were doing fine. And then

your Ellie pitched up out of nowhere and ruined everything.' I gulped my coffee, scorching my tongue. Listening to Cassie talk so disparagingly about my wife was hard to stomach.

'He said they were old friends from being in foster care together and he owed her. Harry made me stay in the bedroom. Told me to watch a movie with headphones on while they talked. Ellie wanted him to do her this big huge secret favour.'

Ellie seldom spoke about her time in foster care – I knew it had been challenging to say the least – but I knew for sure she'd never mentioned a Harry Grainger. I added his name to the growing list of things that I didn't know about my wife's past.

Cassie paused and sipped her drink, lifting her eyes to mine briefly to see if I was following. I did my trick with the envelope again, placing it on my side of the table with the notes peeking out. The implication was clear. I wanted the whole story before she got the cash. Cassie eyed it hungrily.

'Only I didn't. Use the headphones, I mean. I listened at the door because... well because I thought Ellie was there to steal Harry away from me. She was clever and pretty, even with the scar. And they seemed to have this really close connection. I didn't trust her one bit.'

Another long pause. This was like pulling teeth. Mentioning Ellie's scar was either exceptionally manipulative or an honest observation. I was reserving judgement.

'Keep going!' I ignored Rachel as she kicked me under the table. I couldn't help myself. She was just as keen to find out the girl's story, but it was my money and I was getting tired of waiting. 'What did they talk about?'

'I couldn't hear it all, but I heard Ellie say she had to die and she wanted Harry to kill her. Or help her die at any rate. But he had to make it look like an accident so you could still get all the money.'

'What fucking money?' A shiver swept down my spine.

'Shut up Finn. Just let her talk,' Rachel hissed.

'They made a plan to crash her car and make sure it burned so she'd definitely be dead and the police would think it was an accident and then you would be safe.'

She was rambling and I needed her focused. She knew so many details about Ellie and it scared me that there could be some truth in her story. Trying a more gentle approach, I probed, 'Safe? Safe from who? From what? Cassie, please focus. This is very important.'

Her fingers twisted and picked at her bitten nails. Without looking up, she replied, 'I only heard bits, but I think she said her uncle was trying to hurt her again. Harry seemed to know all about him too. He did something to her when she was a kid and now he was back and would hurt you and the baby. So she had to die. She had a place picked out and everything. On a quiet road with a big tree.'

We'd agreed not to tell anyone about the baby until after Christmas and I was about to ask how she knew about it when her next sentence took my breath away.

'She said she loved you too much to let him hurt you.'

Bloody hell. My insides liquefied and my eyes stung with unshed tears. There were aspects of Ellie's life that were a mystery to me, but she'd loved me. It took an effort to clear the lump from my throat and get my words out. I needed to change the subject.

'How did you get her bracelet?' my voice came out choked. My thoughts and emotions were like a confusing stew churning in my gut. Rachel shot me a look. I'd forgotten she hadn't known about the bracelet. I gave her a *Reader's Digest* version of the story, ignoring her indignation at not being told before. 'It was in the package with the letter and photos. It was Ellie's. Sorry I meant to say.'

Cassie was staring at the money and hugging herself as if she were cold. She was struggling to stay on track, but there was still so much I didn't know.

'Cassie? The bracelet. How did you get hold of it? Did you steal it?'

'No fucking way. I don't steal!' Cassie exploded. 'Not like your precious Ellie.'

'What the hell does that mean?'

'Ellie stole something from the hospital. I'm not sure what because I couldn't hear everything but she and Harry were talking about taking something from the hospital where they worked.'

'Harry worked at the hospital?' My heart was somersaulting in my chest. Her ex-foster brother/boyfriend/lover or whatever he was worked at our hospital and I didn't even know about him? I shuddered as I thought about what else my wife had failed to mention in our five years together.

'Yeah, Harry said they'd worked together for years and saw each other at work all the time. When I got pissed, he said they were just like brother and sister. But I wasn't so sure. Hang on, didn't you know him? He knew all about you.'

Her comment, innocent as it was, had me squirming in my seat. No I didn't fucking know a damn thing about this man who had played such a massive role in Ellie's past. There was just too much information. I would need to replay and process everything Cassie had said later, but right now I just couldn't deal with the Harry/Ellie equation, so I repeated my original question instead.

'Where did you get her bracelet, Cassie?'

'She gave it to me. Ellie said to keep it in case I needed to use it. She said you'd give me cash for it. But she made me promise not to use it before April, no matter what.'

The empty ache of complete bewilderment settled through my core, a feeling I was getting horribly used to. Nothing made sense.

'Ellie said what? And why April?' I needed clarification.

Cassie looked up at me, defiance in her bloodshot eyes. 'You heard me. She gave it to me to keep and said you'd give me good money for it. Almost as if she knew Harry was going to leave me. I didn't steal it. And I have no fucking idea why it couldn't be before April. These last few months have been difficult, but I promised, so I waited.'

'Harry left you?' Rachel's calm voice interjected. I'd almost forgotten she was there. 'But you know where he is, right? We need to speak to him.' She was totally focused on this Harry Grainger.

'I don't know where the bastard is or why he ran off, and I don't care,' Cassie answered aggressively. You could tell she cared a great deal by the way her shoulders had slumped. 'After he murdered her he never came home and it was all her fault. Harry loved me and now he's gone. Disappeared. And I need money for rent and food a...and stuff.'

'How did you know how to get hold of Finn?' Rachel asked.

'Ellie gave me an address and phone number one of the times she visited Harry. She said to make sure you couldn't trace the text, so I used this weird site to make it anonymous. A friend said you wouldn't know who was texting you.'

One of the times she visited Harry? For fucks sake, what was Ellie playing at? Why didn't she come to me? Why had she gone to Harry for help when she believed her life was in danger? I thought she knew I would always be there for her. I would have found a better solution than suicide. But clearly she trusted Harry, not me.

'I want my money now. You promised,' Cassie said, her bottom lip quivering. She was close to tears.

'How many lives had Ellie's unfounded paranoia screwed with?' I wondered silently as I reluctantly handed over the envelope.

CHAPTER 23

'Umm, this is delicious. So who made this Finlay?' Rachel asked.

'Seriously, just Finn. Only my mother calls me Finlay. And tonight's tasty homemade chicken pie has kindly been provided by Helen at number 34. She has been most prolific in her delivery of meals and offers of 'being there' whenever I need her.'

I'd had too much wine and was prattling on a bit. The chicken pie certainly had been delicious, and it was complemented perfectly by the frozen sweetcorn I'd microwaved so artfully. Rachel and I sat at the kitchen table having finished off our gourmet meal, both still trying to process our trip to London.

'Well, it was excellent, so thank you to your kindly neighbour.' Rachel's words were ever so slightly slurred, so maybe the wine was affecting her too. We were on our second bottle of red.

The elephant in the room grew bigger. I topped up both our glasses and blurted out, 'So was it money well spent?'

Rachel eyed me over her wine glass for a time before answering. Her eyes were so annoyingly reminiscent of Ellie's that it brought a lump to my throat every time I looked at her. Her tone when she answered was calculated and cold, and that was where all similarity ended.

'It was a hell of a lot of money for that young girl and we both know full well what she's going to spend it on.' Less wine and I may have reacted to her reproachful tone. I was getting tired of her judging me, but I was just mellow enough to let it pass. Plus I couldn't exactly argue with her assessment.

'Actually, I didn't give her all the money. I took out a chunk of it when I was up at the counter getting the coffees. I'm not a complete moron. Cassie was too keen to get away to bother counting it, but she only got a little over a grand.'

Not paying her was maybe a dick move. After all, she'd held up her side of the bargain – but I didn't want to be responsible for her overdose.

'Still too much for a girl with a serious drug addiction,' she shot back, her eyebrows arched accusingly. She clearly wasn't going to let it go.

'Hey, I tried offering to help her get a place in rehab, but you heard her, she wouldn't even admit she had a problem. You can't force someone into getting help if they don't want it.'

Rachel's disapproval was obvious, but Cassie had refused all my offers of help, taken the money and practically sprinted out of the coffee shop. She did accept Rachel's business card and promised to think about it, but that was the best I could get from her.

'So how well did Eleanor know this Harry?' she asked. 'And why did she ask Cassie to contact you? And why not until now?'

'Let's just get something straight,' I repeated for what felt like the hundredth time. 'My wife's name was Ellie. Never Eleanor. I don't give a damn what some fictional birth certificate says that my ten-year-old niece could have knocked up with Windows 7.' Rachel's expression stiffened but I carried on regardless. 'But no, she never specifically mentioned a *Harry* from her childhood, but she never said much about those days anyway. She didn't have a warm and fuzzy childhood and preferred not to talk about it. And I have no idea why Ellie – if it was even her – would give anyone her bracelet. It was really special, and she loved it. And I certainly have no bloody idea why she supposedly gave my number to some random smackhead and told her to contact me in April.'

'If it was her?' she said incredulously. 'What on earth do you mean by that, Finn? Do you seriously think Cassie just made all that stuff up? She knew about Eleanor's scar and the baby.'

I took a mouthful of wine, giving myself time to marshal my jumbled thoughts. I tried to keep my tone calm. After all, it wasn't Rachel I was pissed at.

'Firstly, all that could have been found on a Google search or Facebook,' I lied. No one, not even my parents, had known Ellie was pregnant. She hadn't even been to the doctor yet. We were only just coming to terms with the news ourselves. 'And secondly,' I continued, my frustration building, 'besides the bracelet, for which I'm sure there's a logical explanation, all I have is Cassie's word that Ellie was even at her house. And if she was, then my pregnant, happy, well-adjusted, beautiful wife purposely set out to kill herself. And I can't accept that, not for a minute. Not ever.'

'Finn, can I speak, candidly?'

I just glared at her. I really didn't want to be having this conversation at all. I wanted to forget everything Cassie had said and inferred. Rachel carried on regardless.

'I know you loved Ellie very much, and yet there's an awful lot you don't seem to know about her. This Harry guy for one. The fact that she contacted me. Her real name.' She ticked the points off on her fingers. 'I think you may have to face the fact that the woman you loved and thought you knew kept things from you. Maybe things that led her to believe that suicide was the only way out.'

A jagged-edged dagger sank deep into my heart, twisting as it went. These were the precise assumptions I'd been conscientiously avoiding. Hearing them spoken out loud in such a clinical way was devastating. The thought that Ellie had basically been lying to me for our entire time together was something I just wasn't ready or able to face. I stood up quickly, nearly knocking my glass over, and began to noisily clear the dishes. I didn't trust myself to speak.

As I stacked the plates in the sink, my brain running through every devastating permutation, my eyes grew hot and heavy with tears. This time I didn't bother to fight them. I held the edge of the sink and shuddered with grief. Why couldn't I just have been left with my perfect and untainted image of Ellie?

Rachel came up behind me and put her hands on my arm, awkwardly turning me around to face her. Our bodies were barely centimetres apart. I could smell the claret on her warm breath and feel her body pressed against mine, soft and inviting. The last few months had been lonely, lacking in human comfort, and it felt good to connect with another human being to share my misery. I wept onto her shoulder like a five year old, but it felt so wrong.

Pulling myself together, I gripped her arms and gently moved her away. I knew she only meant to comfort me, but still, it felt like a betrayal of Ellie. I took a breath and was surprised at how almost normal I sounded.

'Ellie was my whole world, my...my everything. I know it sounds cheesy but we had something special. But if she did this, if she kept this stuff from me and conspired with someone to end her life... well then I have to believe she had an incredibly good reason.' I sighed. 'But did she have a whole secret past she didn't tell me about? I don't believe it. Not for a minute. We shared everything. Everything.' Even to me, my words sounded hollow and contradictory. The proof of Ellie's dishonesty was getting harder to refute.

Rachel eased out of my grip and began fussing with the dirty dishes, not meeting my eyes.

'But she didn't tell you everything. Did she?' Her tone was gentle and conciliatory, and it hurt all the more for it. 'Not about the money, and nothing about the man she was so afraid of or why she felt she needed to protect you—' I tried to cut in, but she held up her hand to stop me interrupting her. 'I know we can't put much faith in everything Cassie says, but she did have the bracelet and—'

'There is no money!' I interrupted, my voice loud with anger. Anger felt safer than the sheer misery that was tearing me apart. 'I had to borrow from my parents to pay for her fucking casket. She didn't even have a will, let alone a life insurance policy or a hidden bank account. *That* I would have known about. We counted every damn penny. There is no fortune hidden in her knicker drawer. Cassie is a strung-out junkie who found a bracelet, went on Google and embroidered a story.'

Rachel was trying hard to get a word in edgeways, but I was on a roll. 'For all I know, Cassie may have come to A&E at some point and Ellie treated her. Or they met at the gym or something and Cassie took her bracelet then.' I knew I was grasping at straws. I slumped down in the chair glancing up at Rachel. 'And I'd know if someone was trying to hurt my wife, wouldn't I?'

Rachels expression softened, acknowledging my despair. Her look of undisguised pity was too much for me to cope with, so I stood up, rattling the table.

'I'm going to bed,' I announced, effectively putting an end to any further discussion about the fuck-up my life was warping into. 'The spare bed's made up and there's a clean towel in the airing cupboard. Or just go *home*. Whatever.' I stormed out of the kitchen and took the stairs two at a time, desperate to get away from the reality check Rachel wanted to have me face.

CHAPTER 24

I poured coffee into the Garfield mug Ellie had given me last Easter. It was only half five, but I'd been up for over an hour already. I knew Rachel had stayed. I'd heard her in the bathroom late last night and the kitchen this morning was spotless – even the wine bottles had made it into the recycling.

I looked at the pile of gaily wrapped presents sitting in the centre of the kitchen table and groaned. They would be this morning's Ellie related challenge, and I wasn't sure that coffee alone would be enough to get me through this.

When I couldn't sleep last night, I'd started searching for Ellie's bracelet. I was desperate to disprove Cassie's version of events, but I couldn't find it anywhere. Instead, from the back of Ellie's cupboard, I unearthed three presents all neatly wrapped in Christmas paper. They were all addressed to me – from Ellie.

Ellie's funeral had been the week before Christmas – we'd had to wait for a break between nativity plays and Christmas parties for a slot at the village church. It was seemingly an inconvenient time for a funeral. I didn't have much festive spirit after the ordeal of cremating my wife.

Christmas day was an awful mess at my parent's house. My sisters and their families tiptoed around me while I lay on the sofa, drinking to fill the black void that compressed my heart.

I refused to even acknowledge it was Christmas day.

I never for a moment thought Ellie would have bought and wrapped presents for me. We were both more last-minute Christmas Eve shoppers. But here they sat on my kitchen table, completely out of place in April. I sipped my coffee, trying to decide if I should bin them or open them.

'Morning.' Rachel stood in the doorway eyeing me nervously, trying to gauge my mood this morning. Her hair was pulled back in a short ponytail which emphasised her cheekbones, and she was wearing yesterday's clothes. Her bruises were now somewhere on the yellowy-purple spectrum.

'Hi, want some coffee?' I wasn't going to apologise, but I could try and be polite.

'Thanks, but I'd prefer tea if you have fresh milk.' She moved into the room and flicked the kettle on. She was far too familiar with my kitchen appliances.

Rachel sat down opposite me at the table, the small pile of presents between us. The silence grew as she looked at me, clearly expecting an explanation I wasn't keen to provide.

At last, curiosity got the better of her and she asked, 'And these are?'

'Christmas presents,' I replied. I just wasn't in a sharing kind of mood. Rachel reached over and read one of the cute reindeer gift tags aloud.

#22

Dearest Finn

Merry Christmas

Love you always

Ellie

The other two were identical except for the numbers – they were marked *#12* and *#38*.

Having read the other two gift tags, Rachel looked up and

asked, 'Where are the others?' She sounded annoyed, as if she thought I was holding back on her. 'There are loads of missing numbers. Did Eleanor always number your presents? Why didn't you open these at Christmas?' She certainly had her cross-examining lawyer head on this morning.

I sipped my coffee, pausing as long as I dared just to piss her off. I was in a foul mood – too much wine and too little sleep. Finding Ellie's gifts from beyond the grave hadn't improved matters. Eventually I gave in, answering her questions robotically in the order she asked them.

'These were all I found. We've never numbered our presents, who even does that? It's weird. And I only found them this morning when I was searching for her damn bracelet.' Guiltily, I admitted, 'I haven't exactly got round to going through her things, yet.'

'You really aren't a morning person, are you?' she said. I decided to treat that as purely rhetorical.

I had to open these bloody presents and quickly before I lost my nerve forever. Like pulling off a band-aid, rip and be done with it. I started with number twelve, hoping Ellie had a bloody good reason for numbering the damn things.

I ripped at the blue snowman paper and revealed a small volume of poetry. It was entitled *Jammer* by someone called F.D. Osterveld, and its leather binding looked old and worn.

Rachel picked up the book and thumbed through the pages. 'It's not in English, right? Why? What language is it? Can you read it?'

Ellie had loved languages. She spoke passable French and had studied Italian for fun at night school while doing her nursing degree. I was useless, with even English proving difficult at times.

I sighed, wishing now I'd opened these alone without the running commentary and stream of questions. That seemed to be the way Rachel conducted most of her conversations. Honestly, I'd been too nervous and had been waiting for her to come downstairs and provide moral support, but I was seriously questioning the logic of that decision now.

'I'm fairly certain it's in Afrikaans. My mother grew up in South Africa, so she learnt it at school. She taught me the odd phrase and how to count to ten. It was my party piece for a time – a bit pathetic really.' I paused, and then continued loudly, 'And no, I have no idea why Ellie would give me a book of poetry in a language I can barely recognise more than two words in.' The last sentence reverberated around the small kitchen.

'I'm sorry Finn, I realise this is difficult for you, I really do,' she said with the right amount of empathy and understanding. 'I remember what it was like going through my grandmother's things after she died. I'm just so confused about all of this. Would it be better if I left?' She made to stand up.

'No, please don't go,' I said quickly. I realised how much I actually needed her there, or at least how much I didn't want to be alone. 'I'm just being a dick. I'm sorry. You're right, it's tough going through her stuff. It's so…so final.' I forced a breath past the growing lump in my throat. 'To be honest Rachel, I'm not even sure who I was married to anymore. We never did this sort of thing. We needed loads of stuff for the house and didn't do individual gifts. Last year our joint Christmas present was the mirror in the hallway and the matching Fitbits we bought together in the Boxing Day sales. None of this makes sense.' I let my head drop into my hands and felt a familiar heaviness begin to build behind my eyes. Shit, I'd promised myself I wasn't going to cry again today.

Rachel leaned across and put her hand on my arm. 'It never goes away, but it does get easier, eventually. And finding out about Ellie, well, it may help give you the closure you need. Try another present and see if that helps.'

She was right, of course, I had to know. It felt like a virus was burrowing away in my brain, demanding answers.

The gift labelled #22 was wrapped in festive silver paper with falling snowdrops. I ripped it open and an extra-large-sized t-shirt fell out. It was in hideous avocado green, and there was no way Ellie would have ever chosen it for me. It was also at least two sizes too big.

Rachel shook it out and held it up. It looked even worse. On the front was a badly reproduced photograph of a giraffe, slightly out of focus and blotchy. She read the inscription on the back.

'Colchester Zoo. A fun day out for all the family.' Looking at me around the enormous t-shirt, she asked, 'Colchester? That's Essex, right? Have you ever been there?'

'No, and neither has Ellie.' I added quickly, 'At least not with me.' Maybe in her alternative life about which I know nothing, I thought to myself. Before she could ask any more questions, I opened the last present.

A DVD of *Hunt for Red October* and a *Wham!* CD entitled *Fantastic* were neatly stacked inside.

'That's a good movie, if a little dated, and an even more dated taste in music!' Rachel declared. 'Favourites of yours?'

'Actually yes. One of my favourite movies up there with *Shawshank Redemption*. And my mum was a big *Wham!* fan. She played them every Sunday when I was growing up. My sisters and I used to dance around the kitchen with her while dad carved the roast. Those memories stay with you.'

'So besides the foreign poetry – fairly sensible presents,' she decided as she scanned the song list on the back of the CD. The relief was evident in her voice. I wondered if she wished she'd never bothered coming to meet her half-sister. She was wrong though. There was something not right about this bizarre pile of belated Yuletide gifts.

'Not really, no. I already have copies of both of them and Ellie knew that. She bought me a DVD of the movie not long after we met as I only had it on video, so it makes no sense that she'd buy me another copy of either.'

Rachel hefted the CD and the book of Afrikaans poetry, one in each hand, deep in thought. 'There has to be a reason,' she mumbled, almost to herself. She'd clearly entered full-on puzzle-solving mode. For me, I just wanted to find out who my wife had been.

'So, do you fancy a day out at the zoo?' she asked enthusiastically. 'There has to be a reason to go see the giraffes.' It sounded more like a decree than a suggestion, and I was about to offer a weak argument against a wasted trip when a knocking at the front door interrupted me.

A cold shiver swirled through my gut, recognising the sound of urgency and bad news. I saw a uniformed police officer through the kitchen window which confirmed my fears. He was standing next to a man in a suit. A light drizzle had started while I'd been opening the presents and neither man looked happy. It had to be bad news if the police were standing on my doorstep – again.

Oh, God no. My parents.

I was gripped by sheer panic. My heart hammered uncontrollably as I thought back to Robert's threats and the photograph showing them innocently walking the dog. With everything else going, on I'd pushed the abduction to the back of mind.

CHAPTER 25

Before. 1993.

Eleanor Hudson gripped the buggy's handle tightly. She looked into the blue eyes of the baby lying quietly inside, willing him not to cry. Thankfully, he was in a happy mood for now, gurgling and swinging his limbs in the direction of the cow and moon mobile hanging from the buggy's brown-checked hood.

Eleanor didn't like it when Baby Benjie cried. It was such a pathetic sound, so sad. He got so much attention when he was upset, of course – not that Eleanor minded. She wasn't jealous. She loved her little brother. There wasn't much not to love. He didn't interfere in her world from inside his cot yet, and Mummy and Daddy still loved her and played with her, reading her lots of stories. So her life had hardly changed since Benjamin came out of Mummy's tummy.

But right now it was very important that he didn't cry. They had come into town because Mummy said Eleanor needed new shoes. Only now Mummy had left her at the door of the shoe shop, telling her to hold the handle of the pram, keep Baby Benjie happy and not to move for two minutes. Then she went to the edge of the pavement to speak to the man in the grey car. Eleanor was sure it had been much longer than two minutes, and she was getting worried.

If Baby Benjie cried, Mummy might think she wasn't doing a good job as a big sister, and then she might buy her boring blue shoes when Eleanor had her heart set on shiny red ones with bows like the ones Annabel from nursery had. So she pulled funny faces, stuck out her tongue and blew raspberries on Benjie's tummy like Daddy did. Her brother rewarded her with grins and giggles.

Mummy was taking so long talking to the man. Eleanor didn't like him. Last time he came to visit, he and Daddy shouted horribly at each other and it made Mummy cry.

Eleanor was so focussed on Baby Benjie that she jumped when Mummy called her name. She reluctantly let go of the buggy and stepped shyly to Mummy's side, her fingers winding the hem of her pretty floral skirt.

'Eleanor, you remember your Uncle Robert? Come and say hello.' Mummy sounded upset again. Eleanor looked at the big man with sunglasses. She raised her hand in a vague wave, not really knowing what to say. If she were a grown-up, she would tell him off for shouting at her Daddy and upsetting her Mummy. Mummy carried on speaking. 'Look, Robert. Look at her eyes. There, you see? She is Thomas's daughter no matter what you think!'

Something in the tone of Mummy's voice made Eleanor reach out and grasp her hand. Mummy liked to show everyone her eyes saying they looked so pretty and that they made Eleanor look so special. Eleanor tried to see past the dark glasses to see the man. He sounded angry when he spoke.

'That's complete bullshit, Elizabeth, and you know it. The eyes don't mean anything. You know what happened that day. She's mine and I will get her. And you. Thomas doesn't deserve either of you.'

The man had said a naughty word. Mummy squeezed Eleanor's hand so tightly it hurt and when she spoke, Eleanor could hear the fear in her words. 'Don't be ridiculous, Robert. Thomas is Eleanor's father. That's indisputable. And what we… what you did was… wrong. Vile. And anyway, we have another baby now. We're a family.' Mummy indicated to the buggy and a soft whimper sounded right on cue. Benjamin had realised he was all alone. 'Please, Robert. I'm begging you. Leave me alone and leave my children alone.'

Eleanor pulled away from her mother and skipped back to the buggy. She leant over, gently put Benjamin's dummy into his little mouth and started to rock the pram the way she'd see her parents doing. She didn't like the man in the car at all. Grown-ups were so confusing. She didn't understand the things Mummy was saying. Daddy would never allow anyone to hurt her or Mummy. And Eleanor would never let anyone hurt her baby brother.

Mummy was still talking to the nasty man, their voices low and mean, and Eleanor didn't want to hear what they were saying. She would tell Daddy about the man and he would sort him out just like he did some of the silly people he told her about at his office.

Then Eleanor heard a smack, more shouting, and then the car raced off.

When Mummy turned she was crying. Her eyes were already red, and tears fell quickly down her cheeks. When Eleanor saw the spreading red handprint on Mummy's cheek, she put both her hands up to her face and felt her own blemish-free skin.

The nasty man had hit Mummy. Eleanor couldn't believe what had just happened. No one had ever hit her Mummy. Eleanor couldn't imagine what it would feel like to hurt your face.

At least not yet she didn't.

CHAPTER 26

Finn

T he two police officers sat awkwardly in the small lounge. The uniformed constable, I think his name was Dobson, had spiky blond hair that glistened with gel. He didn't say much but kept his head down, scribbling away in his notebook.

Detective Renshaw worked in the homicide division. He was the older of the two, with serious brown eyes that seemed to penetrate your soul. It was obvious who was in charge. So far he hadn't said much either, except to introduce himself and confirm that he wasn't here about my parents.

'Why did you think your parents could have been hurt, Dr Murray?' he asked.

I'd flung the door open, desperate to know what had happened to my mum and dad.

'Well, they're getting older, my dad's driving isn't what it was...' I mumbled, at a loss for what could possibly excuse my paranoia. 'So why are you here?'

The last time a police officer had sat in my lounge, he'd told me Ellie was dead. The déjà vu situation had my head spinning and my shirt damp on my back.

Rachel came in carrying a tray of teas. She'd even found a packet of chocolate chip cookies and a plate to put them on.

Detective Renshaw ignored the biscuits and looking straight at me asked, 'So do either of you know Cassandra Sykes?'

Relief washed over me. This wasn't about anyone I knew or loved.

'I don't recognise the name myself,' Rachel was quick to answer, 'but Finn and I have really only just met. We don't have mutual friends. Are you sure this concerns both of us?'

Renshaw's expression was unreadable. 'A young woman was found dead in her flat this morning. She had *your* business card in her pocket, Miss Bates, and yours was the last number she dialled from her mobile phone, Dr Murray,' he said, glaring at each of us in turn. 'When we couldn't find you at the hospital, or you, Miss Bates, at your flat in London, we came here. And that's when we found both of you. Together.'

The detective's words were edged with disapproval. I was about to justify the fact that Rachel was here in my house when I suddenly connected the dots.

'Cassandra? You don't mean Cassie, do you? Skinny, dyed black hair, lots of piercings? I heard Rachel gasp to my left, and the spiky-haired constable wrote furiously.

'Yes. That sounds like our victim,' the detective confirmed, and then he let the silence do his job for him. It worked – I fell in, feet first.

'We only met her yesterday,' I explained. 'She had some... um... information for us. We tried to talk her into going to rehab, so we gave her Rachel's business card in case she changed her mind and wanted our help. We tried to tell her not to spend the money, at least not all at once. I guess she couldn't help herself.'

I could sense Rachel willing me to stop talking, the lawyer in her not wanting me to incriminate either of us in Cassie's death.

'You gave her money? How much? And for what, exactly?' I didn't like Renshaw's tone, but now that I'd started I didn't know how not to stop.

'About £1,000. And we're trying to find her boyfriend, Harry. He was a friend of my late wife and we wanted to talk to him, but Cassie didn't know where he was. I thought... I thought she would be okay. I know it was a lot of money but...' I stopped talking as guilt clouded my thoughts. I'd given a vulnerable and desperate young woman a shed load of cash and then just left her. I should have made her accept some treatment, held back the money until she did – I should have done something. Anything. She was dead and it was my fault.

The detective weighed up my answer for a second. His next question took me by surprise.

'How do you think Miss Sykes died, Dr Murray?'

I looked at Rachel but she just shrugged. Surely it was obvious.

'I gave her a lot of money, Detective, and she was a drug user. I presume with all that cash, I mean, I'm guessing she over-dosed...' I stumbled, less sure than before.

Renshaw stood up, walked over to the window and looked out at my back garden. Looking past him, I saw Ellie's scraggly rose bushes by the side of the garden shed. She would have pruned them back by now, ready for the spring. The detective took his time before speaking.

'Dr Murray,' he said at last, turning to look at me, with his penetrating gaze evaluating my reaction. His next words made my stomach flip over. 'Cassandra didn't OD – she was found hanging, naked, from the ceiling fan in her bedroom.'

'Oh my God,' Rachel gasped next to me on the couch.

'She hung herself? Shit.' I gulped. 'How awful. I mean, the poor kid. I didn't realise she was depressed or that narcotics would...' as I spoke my guilt intensified – the girl I'd abandoned had committed suicide.

Renshaw ignored me and said, 'We found the cash you gave her in an envelope next to her bed. Miss Sykes didn't kill herself. Well, not unless she first beat herself black and blue and inflicted several deep knife wounds over her breasts and genitals before disposing of the knife, and all while her hands were tied behind her back and a plastic bag secured tightly over her head.' He took a breath, his eyes switching between Rachel and me, gauging our responses. 'Cassandra Sykes suffocated to death, slowly and painfully. Of course, we're waiting for the official autopsy to confirm the cause of death but we both know what death by asphyxiation looks like, don't we doctor?'

If his words were intended to shock, they had the desired effect. Rachel's head hung in her hands and I could hear her sobbing quietly. We'd obviously both come to the same conclusion. The masked man, aka Robert, had found Cassie – the use of a knife removed any potential doubt. I'd underestimated him, and poor frightened Cassie had paid the price. I'd led him right to her.

An icy shiver drifted down my spine. He must have been following us. How else would he have known we were meeting?

We spent the next two hours telling Detective Renshaw and his note-taking constable almost everything. The texts from Cassie, meeting her in London, about Robert attacking Rachel and possibly being the same guy who abducted me. I even told him about the photo of my parents. He asked a few questions but mostly he let me prattle on. Rachel added in that she was Ellie's step-sister, although she had never met her.

For some reason, we both played down Harry's possible involvement in Ellie's accident. For my part, I wasn't anywhere near ready to acknowledge the ridiculous possibility that Ellie had actually set out to deliberately kill herself that cold December morning.

'And did Miss Sykes tell you where her boyfriend and your wife's friend – this Harry Grainger – actually is?' Renshaw asked.

'No, she said he'd disappeared back in December, and that she had no idea where he was. I believed her. She really wanted the money but actually had very little useful information.'

'And Harry Grainger has the same surname as your wife's maiden name, correct? Were they related?' His tone was light and conversational like he was asking me about the weather, but I could sense he was gauging my reaction.

'Yes. I mean, no. I mean it's the same name but they're not… they can't be related. At least I don't think so. As far I know, she was an only child. Well until Rachel… frankly, Detective, I honestly don't know anymore.' I let out a breath and fought to stay calm as a wild cyclone of questions whirled around my brain.

'Ellie told me she had no family, that her parents were killed in a car accident when she was just a little girl and that she went into care. Cassie said Harry met her in foster care, but Ellie never mentioned him to me,' I added, feeling pissed off once again at how little I knew about my wife. 'Why would they have the same surname?' I asked to nobody in particular. I felt desperate for answers.

'Eleanor's surname was also Hudson,' Rachel added, confusing the police officers even more. 'She had two birth certificates; I have them both at my flat. I took them from Finn by accident.' She glanced at me apologetically. '*Our* father's name was Thomas Hudson. At least that's what my mother told me.'

'And you definitely believe her to be your step-sister, Miss Bates?'

'Um, well yes, absolutely. Everything fits.' I could hear doubt creeping into her words. She'd been extremely nervous talking to the police and seemed to be questioning her facts now. 'Eleanor emailed late last year asking me to meet, but we never had a chance to find out—'

'I'm pretty sure they are half-sisters or whatever,' I inter-rupted, admitting it to myself as much as to the detective. 'They both have a rare genetic condition. It's called het-erochromia – different coloured irises. It suggests that they share DNA from a common parent.' I sounded like my genet-ics professor at uni. Renshaw studied Rachel's eye colour care-fully but didn't make a comment.

That seemed to bring our interrogation to a close. Renshaw gave us his card in case we remembered anything and then he and his sidekick left.

I couldn't get the image of Cassie hanging dead and mutilated out of my head, and acid churned in my stomach. Rachel was half a step away from having a massive meltdown herself.

'It was Robert, right?' she blurted out the moment the door had closed. 'He tortured and killed her. He believes Eleanor's alive and that Harry knows where she is.' Her whole body shuddered as she said, 'I let him hurt that girl.'

'It wasn't your fault, or mine.' I forced credibility into my reply. 'He's a sick psycho, Rachel, and I don't think we could have saved Cassie.' It was a lie. I was convinced I had a part to play in her death. 'I mean, perhaps we could have listened bet-ter. I guess she said she was scared of someone. She said there was another man—'

'I never believed he would actually murder someone,' said Ra-chel, her words so soft I wasn't sure I'd heard correctly. 'He's searching for my sister... for Eleanor. He'll come back... he'll come back and d-d-do the same things to me. He won't stop until he finds her.' She looked at me defiantly, and said, 'That means we have to find her first, Finn.'

And just like that we were back to the 'Ellie must be alive' crap. It was too much.

'For fuck's *sake*, Rachel. ELLIE'S DEAD.' I yelled brutally. 'How is that so bloody difficult for you to understand?'

Rachel turned, her cheeks wet with tears, and slapped me – really hard.

'You cold, uncaring bastard. That could have been me hanging from the ceiling.' She grabbed her bag and keys and stormed outside to her car.

I didn't know if I should follow her or let her go. I didn't seem to know much of anything anymore. The only thing I knew for certain was that I should have gotten to know my wife better.

CHAPTER 27

A warm sun, dazzling with the promise of summer, was chasing away leftover wispy clouds as I drove into work the next morning. A profound sense of relief seeped into my subconscious as I pulled into the hospital car park. At least the organised chaos of the Emergency Department was something I could understand, and to some degree, control. The total shitshow that was my personal life could be neatly parked for the duration of my twelve-hour shift.

After Rachel stormed off, I'd bitten the bullet and started sorting Ellie's things, praying there were no more surprises to be found hiding in amongst her shoe boxes.

I boxed some stuff up for charity as my mum suggested and put the boxes in the small room that should have been our nursery. I kept a few items that reminded me of my Ellie; some pieces of jewellery and a wooden elephant that we bought on our honeymoon, and then I threw them in a box too.

Predictably, it wasn't long before I gave up and sat on the floor sobbing like a two year old. It was as if I didn't know who Ellie was or who she'd been, and it seemed stupid to feel so sentimentally connected to things that belonged to a virtual stranger – a stranger who'd consumed my life and shared my bed.

I knew the boxes would sit there for weeks or even months, but I'd made a start. Unfortunately, I didn't feel any tremendous cathartic relief like I thought I would. Just immense sadness coupled with so much anger that my jaw ached. If I hadn't been working today, I would have drunk myself into numb oblivion.

I hadn't heard from Rachel, and maybe that was for the best. It was time to let this whole thing go, so I could remember Ellie as she was instead of searching for some crazy truth that would destroy the memory of the woman I loved.

Work was long and busy with mercifully little time to think. My face was healing and hardly anyone questioned me about it or asked how I was coping. It was business as usual.

At about three in the afternoon, I grabbed half an hour and a chicken sandwich in my office. Stupidly, I googled the name *Harry Grainger* and got 986,000 hits. How did I seriously think I could find him on Google? I narrowed the search down by adding London and only got 553,000. 'So much easier', I thought sarcastically. I should have been using this time to catch up with my paperwork, but instead, I found myself typing in *Ellie Grainger*, which returned over 300,000 possibilities. That's when I gave up and got on with writing my medical notes. There was no way that I'd ever find Harry bloody Grainger.

The thought of some mystery man from Ellie's past helping her die was like a hot poker twisting in my belly. So much for letting it go. Why had she gone to *him* for help? I was right there! And why the hell had he gone along with it? I would never have let her do it. There just had to have been another way.

I closed my eyes and sighed as I realised that's precisely why she would have turned to Harry. He was willing to help her die – something I would never have done.

On the way home, I stopped at Ellie's tree. I'd forgotten to pick up fresh flowers, and the yellow roses from my last visit were brown and wilted. As darkness fell, I sat with my back up against the rough bark begging the universe to explain why

Ellie had left me with so many questions and no ability to find the answers.

A blue estate car came zipping along the winding country road towards me. The man inside was driving stupidly fast and with his lights off. Arsehole. Didn't he realise how dangerous this corner was? Perhaps I should devote my energy into setting up a petition on Facebook or something, getting the council to make this stretch of road safer for other drivers so no one else had to die unnecessarily.

The driver realised in time how tight the turn was and brought his speed down. His headlights were still off. Perhaps he'd blown a fuse.

The car slowed even more as it took the final bend before the tree. Something flew out of the driver's window and landed less than a metre from my feet. By the time I reacted, the car had accelerated off around the next bend in the road.

A crumpled brown paper bag lay in the dirt. Did the bastard see Ellie's makeshift shrine and decide it would be hilarious to decorate it with his fast-food litter?

Pissed off, I got to my feet. There was a bin across the road in the layby next to my car. As I bent down to pick up the paper bag, I froze. Written on the bag, in bold black ink, was my name. The man in the car hadn't taken any chances; he'd written it on both sides. I couldn't have missed it if I'd tried.

My hand shook as I walked over to the bin and held the package over it – the urge to throw it away and pretend none of this was happening was overwhelming. I could sell the house, move back in with my parents, retrain as a GP and move to New Zealand. I could forget Rachel and the man with the knife and dead Cassie. I could even forget my Ellie. Forget, move on and make a new life. Nothing good could come of opening this parcel.

I flicked on the interior light in my car and sat holding the still tightly closed paper bag. How could I forget Ellie? She was my wife, my best friend, the love of my life. I thought what Ellie would do if it were me who had crashed into a tree, revealing a hornet's nest of unanswered riddles. She would never stop searching for the truth.

My phone rang and my paranoid brain immediately assumed it must be the littering driver, eager to push me a little further over the edge. Instead, the caller ID insisted it was Rachel. I'd been dreading our first conversation and I seriously didn't expect it to go well. I really hoped she wasn't going to yell – I wasn't in the mood.

'Hi,' I answered.

'Finn, hi, it's Rachel,' she began unnecessarily. 'We need to talk, something has... um... come up. I'm just leaving work now and can be at your place in just over an hour. I'll pick up a Chinese on the way. Are you home?' She sounded distracted and I could hear voices in the background.

'What came up?' I pictured her with a similar paper parcel.

'I can't talk now I'm just getting into the lift. I'm about to lose you. Are you okay if I come round? I have something I need to sh—' The call dropped and I sat holding the dead phone to my ear, desperate to hear what was so urgent she was driving all the way out to me. I sent a quick text.

I'll be home. Bring pork dumplings.

Then I added another message.

And milk if you want tea.

I tore open the paper parcel. My gut was clenched so tight I could barely breathe. My normally dexterous fingers struggled to pick off the sellotape and it took ages, but at last it fell open.

There wasn't much inside, but my eyes filled with a familiar warmth as I took out each item. First was Ellie's yellow sunflower-shaped fob watch – the one she would have been wearing when she set off to work and died against the tree. Next was the logbook from her car. Last time I saw it, it was in the glove compartment of her battered Citroën and should have been incinerated in the accident. The very last item was a small plastic box with a green lid. Tears dripped off my cheeks. Inside was Ellie's wedding ring. A simple gold band engraved on the inside with the date of our wedding.

Ellie didn't wear her engagement ring to work because it had a protruding setting with a small diamond, but her wedding ring never came off. Even as her fingers started to swell a little with the pregnancy, she still kept it on.

When I asked the police if they could get it back for me after the crash, they said the intense heat from the fire had fused the metal around the bone and asked if I wanted them to cut her finger away. I declined – it was only a ring, but now it lay in the palm of my hand. I slipped it onto my little finger.

All three of these items should have been destroyed with the car. How the hell had they got here? More questions buzzed around my brain like lasers on speed, and my head started pounding. I wiped away my tears that were no longer bringing me any comfort and let the anger wash over me instead. Someone was fucking with my head.

Throwing everything back in the bag, I noticed a photograph I'd missed. At first glance, all I could see was the green of some trees. Would this be what I had been dreading all along? A photo of Ellie with this Harry guy in a loving embrace? Walking hand in hand along a sun-drenched Jamaican beach? My imagination ran on overdrive.

Instead, when my eyes eventually focussed, all I saw was a giraffe glaring at me out of one eye as it nibbled leaves off a tall tree. What the fuck? I flipped it over and all of a sudden lost my ability to breathe. Glued on the back was a scan photograph of a foetus in utero.

I did a rotation in obstetrics during my training, and looking at the skeletal development of the baby in the photo, I guessed it must have been about seven or eight months old. Roughly the age Ellie's baby would be now. Our baby.

There was no name or date on the scan. It could be anybody's. People posted baby scans on Facebook and Twitter with annoying regularity as April Fools pranks or to frighten their partner or parents. What the hell was the blue car man hoping to achieve besides causing me unbelievable pain and leading me to seriously question my sanity? And what was this obsession with giraffes?

The questions circulated like water around a plug hole, leaving me numb. I started the car and drove home. I was starving – I hoped Rachel had remembered the dumplings. I would need to line my stomach. I could hear the alcohol calling.

CHAPTER 28

'There's a bit of pad thai left,' Rachel said, wiping her mouth on the paper napkin with one hand and passing me the container with the other.

She had brought Thai instead, and although I hadn't gotten my favourite pork dumplings, it was delicious, and the carbs were coping well with the lager I was pouring in after it. She was dressed very corporate and intimidating; her hair was dragged back in a bun and there was a slightly masculine cut to her new-looking trouser suit. She would have scared the shit out of me in the boardroom – but at least she'd brought milk.

I went for a run when I got home to try and clear my head and I'd got back to find Rachel sitting on my doorstep with the bag of food. I'd jumped in the shower while she re-heated the takeaway, and on coming downstairs, I'd found the table laid and the food ready to be served. She certainly knew her way around my kitchen. She'd refused to talk about whatever had made her rush up here until after we'd eaten. In retaliation, I'd told her about the bag being thrown from the window, but not about what was in it. We ate quickly and in near silence.

'No thanks, I'm stuffed.' I could always finish it off for breakfast. 'Thanks again for bringing it over.'

'No problem,' she said. 'Finn, I... er... firstly I need to apologise for the other day, and for hitting you. That's honestly so unlike me. But hearing about Cassie dying so horribly... she must have been so frightened and all alone... I guess you're used to death. I'm certain it was Robert wh...who tortured her...' She closed her eyes and I could imagine the gruesome image of Cassie's last few hours lodged in her head. 'I'm so scared. I know he's coming after me next. If I don't find out what happened to Eleanor, he'll kill me too...' She dabbed at her eyes with a scrunched up tissue, as her shoulders heaved with fear and misery.

I didn't trust myself to answer right away, so I got two more beers out of the fridge instead. Cassie had suffered horrendously, and I couldn't ignore my part in her death.

Rachel was back on her favourite bandwagon. She needed to find out the truth about Ellie because Robert had threatened her if she didn't. What I was struggling with was why this psychopath, Robert, believed Rachel was the most likely person to get to the bottom of Ellie's death. Rachel didn't know Ellie from a bar of soap.

'There's nothing to apologise for,' I sighed. 'It was a shock and you reacted. I was a total arse, and to some extent, I think you're right, Cassie died because she knew about Ellie and this Harry character. Or at least because of whatever that knife-brandishing nutjob Robert imagined she knew about them.' I took a breath and ran a hand through my hair. I needed to decide how far I was going to trust Rachel. Something was nagging at the back of my mind, but I was so adrift in this nightmare that the thought of having Rachel by my side to help sort the bullshit was outweighing the doubts.

'I have to find out what happened to Ellie.' The statement fell unplanned from my mouth. I felt I should defend my decision for my own sake as much as hers. 'For peace of mind, or closure or whatever. I know you didn't know her, but Ellie wasn't a quitter. She'd been through so much as a child but had come out a fighter. I can't believe she would kill herself – unless she had absolutely no other option. I need to find Harry and ask him what he knows about Ellie and the accident...' I added quietly, '...before anyone else finds him.' Rachel's fear was contagious. The thought of Robert hurting anyone else didn't sit well with me.

Relief seemed to flow through Rachel's body, and her shoulders relaxed. 'I agree, we have to get to the bottom of this,' she said. 'We have to find them – I erm... I mean Harry.' She avoided making any eye contact, perhaps hoping I hadn't noticed her faux par. Bloody hell, did she really still believe Ellie was alive? She carried on, 'I got this at work this morning, Finn.'

She handed me a plain white envelope with her name and a company address typed neatly on the front. Inside was a voucher for two tickets for Colchester Zoo, dated for this coming Saturday. There was also a map of the grounds and highlighted in bright yellow marker pen was the giraffe enclosure. Subtle.

'I guess we're off to the zoo then?' I asked, keeping any hint of sarcasm from my voice. She'd shown me hers, so I showed her my bag of bits and boiled the kettle while she looked it all over.

'So I understand the things from the car and the ring. Perhaps she handed them over before the crash, knowing it was going to happen? I guess that goes with Cassie's story of a planned suicide,' she said thoughtfully. 'But the baby photo? That suggests she's alive, right? If you've aged it properly. Did she have a scan before she died?'

'No, it was still too early.' This wasn't a conversation I was comfortable having. I thumped Rachel's mug of tea down in front of her and collapsed into the chair. I would never get used to discussing Ellie like the protagonist in an episode of CSI.

Rachel got the point. 'Oh God Finn, I am sorry. I can't imagine how hard this must be for you, but we have to consider every possibility if we're going to find out what actually happened.'

She had her logical lawyer head on again and it drove me over the edge.

I jumped up. 'Do you seriously think that if Ellie is alive, carrying my baby, that she's fucking hiding from me? With Harry? Some guy she may know from her childhood?' I snarled, partly furious, but mostly petrified of the answer. If Ellie had felt so compelled to take her own life to escape Robert, why had she gone to Harry for help? Why hadn't she come to me? The question gnawed at my heart. Why hadn't she trusted *me* enough to help her?

'I honestly don't know. You have to calm down. We have to think rationally – look at all the options.' She was annoyingly calm now that I'd agreed to carry on looking into Ellie's death. In contrast, I was teetering on the brink of a full-scale breakdown.

She continued, 'Maybe she had to hide from Robert for some reason, like Cassie said. She couldn't tell you and... maybe now she *wants* you to find her. Or at least find out what happened to her. Maybe she made a plan, with Harry, to leave you clues to follow, like telling Cassie to send you the bracelet.' I couldn't fault her logical approach. She added the bleeding obvious as an afterthought, 'Perhaps it was Harry driving that blue car?'

And then something caught my eye. In small writing on the bottom of the scan photo were three numbers; numbers that I immediately recognised. *38-22-12*. I'd been so distracted seeing the fetal scan that I hadn't noticed them before.

I ran and fetched the pile of incongruous Christmas presents from the sideboard and dumped them down on the kitchen table. Everything was spinning out of control. I was caught in a horrible loop of mind-bending paradoxes pushing me down a path I feared to follow. But what choice did I have? I owed it to Ellie to find the truth. The deep desire that raged inside me to beat Harry into a bloody pulp when I found him was definitely a contributing factor.

Rachel looked at me a little nervously before realising the numbers on the scan photo were the same as the ones on the presents.

'Oh, I get it. These presents really are clues. Let's see what we have here.' She began rummaging enthusiastically amongst the odd collection of items. '*Hunt for Red October*,' she said, emphasizing the first word to make sure I was keeping up. 'A story about a search for a submarine that's hiding right? So is this suggesting they want you to search for her?' Rachel was waffling away, holding up each exhibit like it was a piece of damning evidence in court. Again, I got stuck on the 'they'. Ellie was dead, for God's sake.

'Yeah… I mean, not exactly the storyline, but what about the *Wham!* CD and the book of Afrikaans poetry? Where do they fit in?' I asked.

'Not sure about the CD, because there are only eight tracks on it so it can't relate to Ellie's numbers. But…' she continued thoughtfully, 'the numbers could be page numbers in the poetry book. Although we'd need to translate the Afrikaans, but then Eleanor knew you'd be able to ask your mum, right?' Rachel already had her phone out and was busy on Google while she talked. She certainly had that in common with Ellie – they could both multi-task very efficiently. 'Or we could use Google Translate to follow the clues? It's not particularly accurate, but it may give us an idea.'

I made a note not to offer Rachel any more alcohol. She was in full flow and clearly warming to her theme. She had, however, piqued my interest, and if this is what Ellie had planned, then I had no choice but to try and follow up on it as best I could. I paged through the book before finding the index page.

'No page numbers, oddly, but the poems themselves are numbered so we could try those,' I suggested. 'Twelve first, right?' My hands trembled ever so slightly as I paged through the book to poem number twelve, not knowing what to expect.

What if this was just some cruel and incredibly elaborate Dear John letter? Then I found the poem and an invisible hand squeezed my heart to near-breaking point. The title of poem number twelve was highlighted in pink. I hadn't even noticed any highlighting when I'd flipped through the book before.

'Oh, fuck...'

'Finn, if this is too hard—'

'No, I'm fine,' I lied, pulling myself together through sheer willpower. I showed her the poem's highlighted title and her fingers started typing into the Google Translate app.

'It says, *Ek het jou baie lief.* Don't bother, Rachel, I know what it means. My mum always said it to me. It means, "I love you very much".' I swallowed the lump in my throat that was threatening to cut off my oxygen supply and moved onto the next one. That poem was also highlighted, but this time I didn't recognise the one-word title. 'Number twenty-two is *Jammer.*'

Rachel looked up from her phone, confused. 'Okay, so that translates as "pity" – although in which context, I'm not sure. Let's do the last one, number thirty-eight, see if that helps.'

'*Kom soek saam,*' I pronounced carefully. My mother was a night owl – the after-effects of years of night duty on the maternity wards. I knew she'd still be up. I dialled her mobile so as not to disturb my dad.

Rachel read the translation out loud while it rang, 'It means "come search together".'

My mum answered on the first ring, 'Finley, darling, what's wrong?' Shit, it was past eleven, no wonder she was ready for bad news. They'd taken Ellie's death as hard as I did.

'Hey mum, so sorry to disturb you, everything's fine. I'm at a pub quiz with some friends and there's a foreign language round.' I was talking such bullshit, and I hoped she wouldn't question me too closely. 'There's an Afrikaans word. Can you tell me what it translates as quickly? It's the word *Jammer*.' I spelt it out, not trusting my pronunciation.

'Oh that's easy. It means "sorry", as in apologising. Is that all you need?' she added a little too hopefully, making me feel even worse for lying.

'Yes, that's it. Thanks so much, Mum, sorry I worried you. I have to go, they're starting the next round.'

'No problem Finn darling. I'm so pleased you're getting out and about with your friends. Well done. Perhaps we can FaceTime at the weekend?'

I could hear the love and affection in her voice. It made me want to start telling her the truth, but then I remembered the photo of her and Dad walking the dog. I couldn't put them in danger. I made some vague promises to visit soon and ended the call.

Rachel had heard the translation and put it all together. 'I love you. Sorry. Come looking together.' She sipped her cold tea as we both mulled over the so-called 'message' in the three poem titles.

'It seems like we're meant to be on this journey together, Finn,' Rachel decided, and then added with a smile, 'I guess we may as well start by going to see the giraffes at the zoo! Are you free for a road trip to Essex on Saturday?' She waved the tickets she'd received in the post.

I couldn't shake the feeling of dread that sat heavy in the pit of my stomach. Ellie didn't even like giraffes. At least I didn't think she did.

CHAPTER 29

The roads were slow with Easter weekend traffic, and we didn't arrive at Colchester Zoo until mid-morning on Saturday. As we got nearer to the Essex coast, the smell of impending rain became stronger, and it peppered the air as the clouds darkened around us.

The car park was packed with buses parked nose-to-tail alongside neat rows of cars disgorging families carrying picnic baskets, all headed for the growing queue at the entrance. Standing in line, I began to feel a little self-conscious since we hadn't brought either a picnic or a child.

The zoo was impressive, stretching over twenty-four hectares according to the brochure Rachel had picked up at the entrance. It was home to over 260 different species of animals, and the proverbial needle in the haystack came to mind.

Rachel had been strangely quiet on the drive up, spending most of the time texting on her phone. I hadn't been particularly chatty myself. The realisation that I was potentially about to meet a man who had been an integral part of Ellie's life, who may also have been involved in her death, filled me with emotions I was struggling to process.

Having checked the map, Rachel set off in the direction of the giraffes. I followed slowly, watching the families around us, imagining having a day here with Ellie, pushing a pram around a zoo, having a family picnic. A crushing glimpse into what life might have been like.

'Finn. Finn, come on, it's this way,' Rachel whined at my tardiness. The more her phone had pinged on the drive over, the grumpier she'd become. But then I guess I knew nothing of her life – we weren't friends, just strangers thrown together by a bizarre set of circumstances.

I picked up my pace.

Welcome to the African Plains!

The sign pointed the way and listed the animals that were on display. Giraffes were fourth on the list.

'Excuse me?' I accosted a uniformed zookeeper. 'Is Harry working today?'

'Harry?' the man asked. He looked slightly older than most of the other zookeepers we'd seen, and he carried an official-looking clipboard. 'Oh, Harry. Um, yes, I think so. Let me check,' he offered helpfully and disappeared through a door marked *Private Staff Only*.

'This is probably just a huge waste of time. We don't even know if he'll talk to us,' I told Rachel as we waited. A nervous wave of panic washed over me. What was Harry going to tell me? Was it anything I actually wanted to hear? The overwhelming odour of zoo poo rose from the animal enclosures and I felt light-headed. Rachel just shrugged her shoulders and looked away.

'Hi, I'm Harry. You asked to see me?' asked a woman in her mid-twenties with long blond dreadlocks and a bucket of carrots. We both just gawked at her, so she added, 'Can I help you?'

'But you're a woman,' I replied stupidly. 'I mean... er... I'm looking for a man.' This wasn't going well. 'Do you know anyone called Cassie? Or Ellie?'

'Or Eleanor?' Rachel chimed in.

'I don't really understand. I'm Harriet Lowe, Head of Education for the *African Plains*.' She made it sound terribly important. 'Was there something specific you wanted to ask me?' She gestured to the bucket of carrots to indicate she had better things to do with her time than play twenty questions with us.

'Um... yeah, is there anyone else named Harry who works here? Harry Grainger? Specifically with the giraffes?'

'I don't know anyone called Harry. Unless he's one of the interns. You could ask at the main reception.'

I thanked her as she hurried off with her bucket. We had stupidly presumed Harry worked at the zoo, even though Cassie had told us that he worked at the hospital with Ellie and I. I couldn't place a Harry Grainger amongst any of the staff there, and believe me, I'd tried. The idea that Ellie had a best friend and confidant right under my nose without me even knowing was still a festering wound.

'Finn, are you listening?' Rachel's irritated tone pierced my thoughts. But there was more than frustration in her voice – she sounded a little scared.

'Sorry, yes. I guess Harry doesn't work here after all. Now what?' I was out of ideas.

'We should spend some time around the giraffes.' It wasn't a suggestion.

'Seriously?' This was all turning into a colossal waste of time as far as I was concerned. Rachel sensed my lack of enthusiasm.

'We've come all this way, we may as well have a look around,' she said, softening her delivery slightly. 'Perhaps the plan all along was for Harry to find us here.'

Did she think Ellie's long lost lover was hiding behind a clump of pampas grass? This was ridiculous – I should be at home sorting out my life, not chasing around stinking zoos searching for a man who now seemed unwilling to come forward. I would give it an hour and then I was leaving, with or without Rachel.

The giraffes lived in a large, circular pen with a raised viewing platform at one end. We went up the stairs, joining the excited children and frazzled-looking parents strolling around the exhibits and educational displays.

To actually see the giraffes, you had to carry on through some automatic glass doors and out onto an outdoor deck and look down. It reminded me of a gladiator pit in Ancient Rome, but the giraffes seemed quite happy with the setup and strolled around majestically, nibbling the leaves from high up in the trees. Just your average day on the rolling plains of Essex.

Across the other side of the faux-African habitat, a suspended wooden walkway meandered between the dense trees that rose high above the animals. An excellent place for a sniper to hide, my overreaching paranoia suggested. In reality, kids were running up and down it howling like Tarzan.

Why the fuck would Harry Grainger want to meet here? I felt like I was missing something. I walked back inside, leaving Rachel to watch the giraffes, and I began to read the blurbs on the various exhibits. I learnt that giraffes are pregnant for about fourteen months and live in groups called 'towers' led by an adult male – fascinating stuff, yet completely useless.

'Daddy, Daddy, watch me! I'm like Spiderman!'

A boy of about seven had scrambled up onto the back of the bench seating that ran around the room and was attempting to scale a wall made of neatly inscribed brass plaques as if it were a climbing wall. The plates were arranged in rows and sat slightly proud of the brick, affording the kid tiny toe holds. Each plaque was engraved with the details of companies, families or individuals who had explicitly donated towards the upkeep and continued happiness of the zoo's giraffe contingent.

It was not an ideal climbing wall, but young Spiderman was undeterred. My A&E head saw him tumbling down, hitting his head, breaking an arm and losing his teeth. I even began to check for suitable ambulance access. Ellie always said I could look at any happy scene and imagine a medical disaster scenario worthy of an episode of Casualty.

Thankfully, Spiderman's father – a large and formidable man with a completely shaven head and half an ear missing – stepped up and grabbed the child under one arm and marched off, placating him with offers of ice cream.

'Finn quickly, we have to go.' Rachel was suddenly at my side, pulling my arm, her eyes shining with fear. 'He's here, I saw him. He's coming up the path. Come on.'

'Who's here? Harry? You found him? But—'

'No, you idiot, not Harry.' She paused only long enough to make me understand. 'It's Robert. He's coming this way. Come on we have to move. NOW.'

'Robert?' I parroted, my voice shrill. Robert? Oh fuck. Here? Dread swirled in my stomach with flashbacks to that hideous basement and a knife at my throat. But there was something else; something I'd just seen, and my brain couldn't let it go. When I was watching the young Spiderman wannabe with the death wish, something had caught my eye amongst the plaques. With Rachel hauling at my arm, I looked back and saw it straight away. Maybe this wasn't a wasted trip after all.

CHAPTER 30

I followed Rachel as she ran out of the giraffe house. Panic filled my cells and drove my legs. She slowed fractionally opposite the flamingos and I caught up just enough to grab her arm.

'Are you sure it was him? Here? Now?' I asked stupidly, panting. People began to stare.

Rachel's mismatched irises looked at me incredulously. 'Yes I'm fucking sure it's him,' she spat. 'I'm not waiting for him to catch me. There's no Harry here, Finn. *Robert* must have set this up.' And then she was off again, sprinting across the pathway and narrowly avoiding being hit by a coloured Dotto train which was filled with squealing children.

Confusion buzzed in my head. Why was Robert here? Why lure us hundreds of miles to a zoo in Essex? He knew where we both lived. And anyway, I'd seen something.

'Hang on Rachel, there's something I need to check—' I stopped talking. She was already out of earshot around a corner. I hesitated, torn between verifying what I'd seen and chasing after Rachel. A vivid replay filled my head. I saw a basement and a masked man with an icy stare, presumably Robert, with a huge knife shouting evil threats. That helped me to make up my mind. I ran after Rachel.

I had the car keys, so I knew she wasn't going anywhere without me. Picking up my pace, I tried to catch up.

'Rachel, Rachel. Wait, for God's sake! That's not the way to the car park!'

She ignored me and kept up the half jog instead, glancing over her shoulder from time to time with dread etched on her face. Perhaps the howler monkeys smelt her fear, or maybe they were just acting up – either way, they began shrieking loudly as we passed under their high fenced enclosure. The noise of their agitated screams was enough to goad anyone's anxiety.

Rachel veered left, heading even further from the exit.

'Rachel you're going the wrong bloody way!'

She left the path and ran between two buildings, one of which was the butterfly house. The buildings formed a narrow alley which must have made her feel safer than the open path because at last she slowed enough for me to catch up. I grabbed her arm and yanked her to a stop.

'Let go of me!' Her breathing was ragged and her eyes were wide with fear; the blue one almost translucent. At least she was standing still at last. 'I don't care if you don't believe me but I saw him. We have to get away.'

'And we will. But first you have to calm down. We're heading in the wrong direction. I'm sure the car park's the other—'

A sledgehammer drove into my left kidney and blinding pain arched across my lower back. I yelped and sagged to one knee, consumed with pain. I heard Rachel scream but it was short-lived and quickly muffled. I knew she was in trouble, and adrenaline drove me to my feet. I only managed to stay standing long enough to be on the receiving end of a boot in my stomach.

I dropped again and rolled into the side of the building, desperately trying to hang onto my breakfast. I could hear myself groaning in agony, but my brain was in overload. The pain was too much to process. I just lay on the dusty ground, shock, agony and pure terror fighting for priority in my head.

It felt like forever before I managed to move, dragging myself slowly and painfully to my knees. The world spun gently and I swallowed a mouthful of vomit.

A tall, muscular man with a neatly trimmed and greying buzz cut was standing behind Rachel holding a terrifyingly familiar knife to her throat. His other hand was clamped down tightly over her mouth. He sneered down at me kneeling pathetically in the dirt.

'No heroic moves, Murray.' His voice kept me frozen on the ground as images of the basement scene flashed through my head. I would never forget that voice. 'Stay exactly where you are. It's time we all had a little chat.'

To emphasise his order, he eased the point of the knife into the soft tissue of Rachel's neck, millimetres away from her throbbing carotid artery. Her body stiffened, and a small moan escaped from under his hand. Her frightened eyes bore into mine as she tried desperately to stay still, willing me to save her. A bright crimson dribble of blood oozed out over the dull blade, and for a few seconds we were completely motionless in our strange tableau of fear.

'Where is she? You came here to meet her, so don't fucking lie to me. Where is Eleanor?' His eyes swung back and forth between us, and I wasn't sure who he was asking. I didn't for a moment imagine that he would hesitate to sink that blade deeper into Rachel's neck, just for the sheer hell of it.

With exaggerated slowness, I drew myself up onto my feet, keeping my arms out and my palms up – the perfect picture of defeat.

'Leave her alone. We can talk. You don't need the knife and you don't need to hurt her.'

'Take another step and I'll slit her fucking throat. Tell me where you're meeting Eleanor. Now.' Slight hysteria coated his words. He was bat shit crazy and he was holding a knife to Rachel's neck. I had no idea what to do. I had no experience with this level of irrational violence.

'Listen – Robert, is it?' I aimed for a conciliatory tone. I took a breath and felt the pull of aching soreness growing in my core from the bastard's fist and boot. Adrenaline and fear were keeping the pain dampened down, for now. 'Please, we want to help you, honestly, but Ellie is dead – she died in that accident. No one wishes it wasn't true more than me, but she's dead. Very dead. Rachel and I are just here for a day out, to see the animals, enjoy the sunshine. We never came to meet anyone, least of all Ellie.'

'Bullshit!' he yelled. 'You're lying Murray. You came to meet Eleanor. I know you did.'

I'd found something at the giraffe house, but there was no way I was sharing it with this sadistic bastard right now. Not unless I really had to. I couldn't even bring myself to look at Rachel – I knew how frightened she must be feeling, but I needed to keep my head clear.

'You're wrong. We're not meeting anyone. We just came for a day out,' I lied again, speaking slowly, searching his cold grey eyes for a modicum of sanity. 'Ellie is not here, Ellie is dead,' I repeated again, and made the mistake of taking a small step towards him.

Immediately, the knife sank a little deeper into Rachel's skin and more blood leaked down her neck. I froze. Rachel whimpered softly, making my heart rate rise. My hands flew up, emphasising how little threat I was. Rachel was trying to say something behind Robert's hand until at last he removed it, allowing her to speak.

'Please, Robert. He's telling the truth. There's no one here. I looked. Please don't hurt me.' Her voice was full of fear, but surprisingly strong. She obviously had little faith in my negotiating ability when it came to talking this manic out of killing her. Still, Robert didn't look convinced. Desperate to distract him before he slipped the knife any deeper, I said the first thing I could think of.

'Robert, why do you think Ellie's still alive?'

It clearly wasn't a question he was expecting. Confusion crossed Robert's face and the knife moved away from Rachel's neck by a fraction. I had his attention now and pressed home my minuscule advantage.

'Why do you keep saying she's alive? You must know she can't be. No one could have survived that crash or the fire.' My voice stumbled a little as the image of the burnt-out wreck that had been Ellie's car flashed before my eyes. It was etched in my brain and would haunt me forever.

Robert clearly wasn't someone who enjoyed being challenged, but my verbal attack was much more effective than anything I could have achieved on a physical level. His eyes clouded with what could have been doubt, or maybe just annoyance – it was hard to tell.

'*They* survived,' he said, '*they* lied. So why wouldn't she? They're alive, so why wouldn't she be?' I had no fucking clue what he was on about and I really didn't care. While he was talking, he wasn't stabbing and kicking either of us, so I kept the conversation going.

'I don't understand, Robert. Who's still alive? I don't know what you mean.' My voice was astonishingly calm and bore no reflection of the terror building inside me. I tried to keep using his name, eager to establish a connection. I wasn't sure if I'd learnt that on an NHS 'conflict resolution' training course or something, but I was taking a hell of a chance. The knife was still being held in the general area of Rachel's exposed throat – one flick of his wrist and her blood would be gushing out and there would be precious little I could do to save her.

'Her parents, you imbecile, you know exactly who I mean! Thomas and that saintly bitch Elizabeth. They faked their *ac-*

cident and so did—'

'The public aren't allowed back here. Not ever. Didn't you read the signs?' Robert's diatribe was interrupted by a young man pushing a steaming wheelbarrow of manure. He was standing at the entrance of the alley wearing a green uniform with his hair in a man bun. He didn't look happy to find three zoo visitors playing silly buggers in an out-of-bounds area. He seriously needed to go away and take his load of shit away with him before Robert turned the knife on him.

'Of course, so sorry. We're leaving right now.' I grabbed Rachel's arm and tugged her towards me, unsure where the knife was but desperate to believe even Robert wouldn't stab her with a witness standing there.

Clearly Robert had other ideas. He shoved Rachel into me, hard, and we fell awkwardly into the side of the building. I felt a white-hot slash on my arm and Robert's warm breath brushing my ear.

'This isn't over, Murray. You better pray I don't find her first. I'll squeeze that bloody baby out of her and kick its head in.'

By the time I'd helped Rachel to her feet, he was gone. He'd pushed past the youngster, upending the wheelbarrow in the process. The load of manure had landed on the ground across the mouth of the alley, coating the zookeeper's work boots. He jumped back in horror, slipped and landed on his arse. Even if I had wanted to chase after Robert, there was no way I could untangle Rachel and get past the kid in time. Robert was long gone.

CHAPTER 31

I concentrated on following the satnav out of Colchester heading for the A12, while desperately trying to make sense of what had just happened.

We had left the young keeper cursing and complaining loudly over his scattered load and legged it to the car park, this time following the map. We moved quickly, but not too fast to attract attention. I wanted to get out without having to answer any questions from nosey zoo officials.

We didn't see Robert anywhere, even though I imagined him in every tall, threatening man we passed.

Neither of us had said a word as we turned onto the motorway, but with every mile I could feel Rachel growing more agitated next to me.

'Finn, we need to go to the police.' She had a wad of tissues she had found in her bag pressed to her neck.

'No fucking way.'

'He threatened us, for Christ's sake, he threatened me. He had a knife to my throat. He's out of control.' The adrenaline and fear had burnt out, leaving her ghostly pale and trembling. She was also totally wrong. The police could and would do nothing.

'What are we going to tell them? That some maniac wanted to know where we were meeting my dead wife? And why were we there in the first place, Rachel? Because I found some old Christmas presents and you got a couple of free tickets in the post? Many more of those conversations and they're going to send the men in white coats after me.'

'He could have *killed* me, Finn.' Her voice cracked.

'I know, I know,' I said, trying to reign in my frustration and soften my tone, 'but going to the police is a waste of time. We have to find out what happened to Ellie.' Then I added, 'We have to follow her next clue.' Shit, I hadn't meant to say that last bit out loud. It all seemed like pure madness to me, and I was seriously doubting what I thought I'd seen.

'What the hell are you talking about, is Robert's insanity contagious or something? Finn, you said so yourself, there was nothing and no one there.' Her face darkened. 'Oh my God. Oh shit. Your arm, Finn, you're bleeding! You need to go to hospital!'

I looked down and was surprised to see blood soaking through my grey jumper, then I remembered how Robert had slashed my arm just above my left elbow as he made his escape from the alley.

'I don't need a hospital, I'm a doctor, remember. I just need to stop the bleeding. It's not too deep.' I hoped it wasn't anyway.

I pulled into a layby a few miles up the road. There was a concrete picnic table and a blue rubbish bin with wasps buzzing around some discarded coke cans. Hardly a sterile environment, but it would have to do. My arm had started quivering during the last few miles and gripping the wheel had only made the wound bleed faster. The shock I had felt was wearing off, and the pain was increasing exponentially.

I awkwardly opened the boot to get the medical kit I kept in there and yelped in pain when I used my hand. Rachel climbed out of the car and came over to help me. Being left-handed, I felt particularly useless.

'Take off your sweatshirt.'

I really didn't want to. It was going to hurt. A lot. But clearly Rachel had recovered enough from her ordeal to have her bossy head on again, so there was no point in arguing.

I was right – it hurt like fuck. I was pretty sure I was going to fall over if I didn't sit down. I slumped into the back seat of the car to get away from the traffic that was whizzing past us at over seventy miles an hour. Thankfully, they were going too fast to pay us any attention.

There was a lot more blood than I thought there would be, and Rachel started talking about hospitals and police stations again. I was having none of it.

'I just need to clean it up and dress it. Now, do you want to help me or stand there arguing while I slowly bleed to death?'

She glowered at me but stopped talking and opened the medical kit. It was well stocked and she was surprisingly easy to direct. Packets of saline and antiseptic wipes cleared the worst of the blood off, and Robert's blade, sharp as it was, had narrowly missed any major blood vessels as it sliced a neat eight cm-long gash in my upper arm. Rachel held the wound closed as I crisscrossed some steri-strips to pull the edges together, then I covered the whole mess with gauze and wrapped it tightly in a wide crepe bandage. It would hold until I got home.

'I can sort it out properly when I'm home,' I insisted as Rachel repacked the first aid kit and threw the bloody wipes and gauze into the bin, 'and then we need to make a plan to go to Southampton. That's where the next clue is, or whatever.'

She walked back to the car with her eyes glued to her phone. She had a strange expression on her face, like she was trying to make a decision.

'We've missed lunch!' she suddenly announced. I'd been expecting her to have some profound insight into our awful predicament. 'Your arm's stopped bleeding for now. How about we go find somewhere to eat and then you can tell me why the hell we need to visit Southampton, for God's sake. I'll drive.'

I just wanted to go home, but we'd missed breakfast and my stomach growled at the thought of food. Some fluids certainly wouldn't go amiss. 'You're not insured on my car,' I remembered.

The look she gave me would have shrivelled the most battle-hardened warrior.

'You've been stabbed by a madman and you're worried about car insurance?' she scoffed and headed for the driver's door.

Rachel drove us to a pub a few miles down the road. The place was a well-known chain and was Saturday lunchtime level busy. It seemed to be packed with all the families that weren't picnicking at the zoo. The predicted rain started to fall softly as we arrived, and we were lucky to get a small, noisy table near the kitchen door.

Rachel ordered drinks and food up at the bar while I surreptitiously lifted my t-shirt, examining my stomach. There was a spreading redness where Robert had kicked me, but he'd mostly missed my ribs – by accident or not I wasn't sure. I had taken some painkillers back at the layby and hoped they were strong enough to numb everything that was starting to ache.

Rachel brought a pint of lager and a coke to the table. I grabbed the lager, needing the alcohol. She was keen to drive anyway.

'So come on now, what hidden message did you find?' she asked, her sceptical tone suggesting that she'd had her quota of fool's errands for one day.

I sighed, wishing not for the first time today that I'd kept my mouth shut. I'd planned to send Rachel home and follow up on this on my own, but it had just slipped out, and now I knew Rachel wouldn't be able to let it go.

'I saw something in the giraffe house,' I started slowly, trying to find the words to explain without sounding completely delusional. 'I tried to tell you.' I hesitated, less sure now, reality blurring as I grasped at straws, desperate to believe the impossible. I'd convinced myself that what I'd seen was another message from Ellie. I just wasn't sure how believable it would sound to anyone else. 'Don't get me wrong, I know she's dead, but I think she left me another message before she died. Did you see the wall of plaques acknowledging all the donations for the giraffes?'

'Yes, of course, you couldn't miss them. I read through the lot. Harry's name wasn't up there and neither were any other names I recognised.'

'I know, me too, and this one was so obscure I nearly missed it. It said *Francis, Edith and Aloysius, Southampton.*'

Rachel looked at me as if our traumatic encounter and my subsequent blood loss had resulted in my complete mental breakdown. 'I beg your pardon, but how is that even relevant?'

I paused a minute before answering, reluctant once more to share intimate details of my life with Ellie.

One Sunday morning, a few weeks after Ellie had found out she was pregnant, we were lying in bed. We'd just made love, and I remember thinking that I had to be the happiest man in the world at the moment. I had a beautiful wife who I adored and who loved me, and now we had a baby on the way.

We lay there cuddling, Ellie's head on my chest, and we started meddling around with names for the baby. Ellie came up with this ridiculous notion that we should all change our names. It went hand in hand with her crazy plan to emigrate. I pretended to play along and the names got even sillier. Eventually we landed up as Francis and Edith and a baby called Aloysius. I left our bed to make tea before she started suggesting a new surname as well.

I gave Rachel the PG version, and predictably she didn't look convinced, her frown above those mismatched irises so reminiscent of Ellie that I had to fight to stay focused.

'Just hear me out, okay? Those names, no one else would have known them. We told no one, but they became, well, sort of nicknames for a week or two. I even sent her some flowers addressed to 'Edith' as an extravagant joke. It was just some harmless fun.' I stopped trying to explain, realising how stupid it was sounding. I wanted to add 'you had to be there'. It was the shared language of a couple in a loving relationship, sharing personal moments that outsiders wouldn't understand.

I was saved from Rachel's cynical reply by the waiter who came over and set out a selection of condiments and cutlery. He assured us that our food would be along shortly.

'So you were going to call the baby Aloysius?'

'Hah! Of course not.' I laughed, despite how crap I was feeling. 'Not in real life. We didn't even know the sex. And you're missing the point here Rachel, what's important is that no one else would recognise that particular combination of names. Only me and Ellie.'

Rachel played with her straw, thinking through what I'd said. For once, her tone carried a hint of sympathy when she remarked, 'But she could have told this Harry friend of hers.'

Fuck that hurt. My shoulders slumped and I felt a pull on the steri-strips holding my wound closed. I hadn't even considered the Harry option.

'She wouldn't have told anyone,' I answered, pushing away the creeping doubt. I'd been so sure a second ago. 'It was... it was just something between us. She wouldn't tell *him* that kind of thing, surely?' I hated the despair evident in my voice.

'Finn, I don't think you know what Ellie may or may not have told Harry. I know you loved her, but I don't think you knew her very well. And you certainly didn't know what her relationship with Harry was.' She read the devastation of her words on my face, then added more kindly, 'Perhaps it was even done before she died, like the Christmas presents. She could have set it up as a surprise, maybe another Christmas gift? There were missing numbers—'

She stopped as I shook my head vehemently. 'No. There was a date. March, *this* year. Three months *after* the accident. And it said Southampton.'

'Why Southampton?'

'That's where we met at university. No one else would know all of that. She must have organised the plaque before her accident—'

'Or she told someone else,' she insisted quietly, not looking up from the table.

Our food arrived, only now I felt too sick to eat it, but I made the most of the time to gather my very jumbled thoughts. I jumped in as soon as the perky waiter was out of earshot.

'Just for a moment, imagine that Robert is right.' I held up my hand as she prepared to argue. I needed to make her listen. 'Bear with me. For the sake of argument, imagine Ellie is alive,' I felt a deep tug of desperation in the pit of my stomach, but I carried on regardless, 'and that everything – the presents, the message in the poems, the zoo tickets, the plaque for the giraffes – are all clues. Clues that she wants me... us... to follow, to find her. What if this childhood friend, Harry, helped her fake her death somehow. But now she needs *me* to step up and find her. What if...' God I was grasping.

'So now you think Robert's right? And she *is* alive?'

'No. Yes.' Could I sound more indecisive? 'No, of course not, not really. She can't be alive. I know that. But the plaque...' I was struggling to get my meaning across. 'There are just so many what-ifs. I mean maybe she knew this Robert was after her and she needed to disappear. What I do know is what that bastard said to me when he cut my arm open, about me needing to find her first.' And what he planned to do to my baby. Although how he even knew she was pregnant was something I was trying hard not to think about. No one had known, not even my mother.

I took a long gulp of my beer, needing some time to process this weird version of the facts that my brain was busy creating. 'Imagine for a second that Ellie's actually out there, alone, scared and pregnant, and I don't even try to find her. And he finds her. We can both attest to how screwed up he is, and you saw the hate in his eyes when he spoke about her, right? I can't let him get to her.'

Logical thought prevailed as I relived the events surrounding Ellie's death. I needed to stop believing this crap. I added, 'And anyway, I need to know what happened to Ellie – why she killed herself and left clues and went to Harry – now more than ever.' I shuddered as I realised it was the first time I had admitted that Ellie might well have committed suicide, and now I was willing to chase her ghost rather than face that heart-wrenching fact. Yet, a second ago I'd been imagining her alive! I couldn't even keep up with myself.

Exhaustion washed over me as I finished my little monologue. I picked at my fries, unable to look at Rachel, aware of how pathetic and desperate and totally certifiable I must be sounding. Did I honestly believe I was going to find Ellie hiding out somewhere, waiting for me to come and rescue her? I just knew I could never live with myself if I turned my back and gave up on her. I understood Rachel's arguments about the plaque – they were logical – but for me, it offered a minuscule, one in a trillion-billion chance of Ellie being alive.

I was expecting another tirade of objections and arguments, but all she said was: 'So what do we do now? To find the next clue, I mean. What's in Southampton?'

'You still want to help?' I couldn't keep the surprise from my voice, convinced that after all the crap we had just been through she would be heading for the hills. I wouldn't have minded, to be honest. I would have been happier to do this on my own. I'd begun to have serious doubts about Rachel's motivation for sticking with me.

'She was my half-sister,' she offered by way of an explanation, before adding what was perhaps the more honest answer: 'and anyway, I still have Robert threatening my mum if I don't at least try to find out what happened. What choice do I have? He's as deranged as you are.'

The last bit was a final kick in the teeth. Something in the tone of her words hit a nerve, and I felt my anger surge out of control. Rachel's only concern was getting Robert off her back. She cared nothing about Ellie. She didn't even know her. I sprang up out of my chair, knocking it over backwards.

'*If* Ellie is alive and *if* I find her, if you think for one fucking moment I'm going to let you hand her over to that... that fucking MANIAC then you're out of your fucking mind...'

Slowly, I began to notice everyone looking at me, and that the barman had come round from behind the bar. I stormed out, leaving Rachel to deal with my mess and the bill.

The rain was now hammering down and I stood in the car park shivering uncontrollably. I'd left my car keys on the table, and I sure as hell wasn't going back to get them. Icy water was finding its way down the back of my jumper and the steri-strips on my wound must have popped open. I could feel fluid seeping down my arm, but I just couldn't be arsed to look.

I was shocked at the intensity of my feelings. I knew I was utterly delusional about Ellie, but no matter how hard I tried, I couldn't shake the what-ifs that swirled through my head, distorting my logical thinking. I damn well knew that Ellie would never give up on me. Ever.

Rachel came out, her expression a confusing mixture of anger and embarrassment. I braced myself for the verbal onslaught. I just hoped she'd brought my keys.

'Oh, Finn. It's okay. I know what you're going through and I feel your pain.' It sounded slightly contrived, but it was preferable to her yelling at me. And then she hugged me.

I felt myself relax into her unexpected embrace. I didn't need or want her approval, or even for her to agree with me, but it was comforting to know that at least she wasn't going to try and stop me.

'You're soaking wet and bleeding again. Come on, let's get in the car and go home.'

CHAPTER 32

The police were waiting when Rachel pulled into my driveway. Two police cars were parked out front; one still had its lights flashing.

I'd slept most of the way home from the pub, cradling my aching arm, selfishly leaving the driving up to Rachel. I was almost too sluggish to panic. Almost. I felt my mouth go dry and nausea build in my stomach. Had they come to tell me something terrible had happened to my parents, or even one of my sisters? Between the holiday traffic and stopping for lunch, it had taken us hours to get home. Would Robert have had enough time to get down to my parents in Kent?

Rachel seemed less concerned. 'Calm down Finn. Let's just find out what they're doing here before jumping to any conclusions.' Her hand gripped my arm as I moved to get out of the car. 'Maybe we shouldn't say anything to the police yet, I mean about the zoo and your wound and... erm... everything.'

Everything covered a lot of ground. I headed for my front door, careful to hold my left arm as naturally as possible. I'd changed out of the wet, blood-soaked jumper into an old baggy sweatshirt I'd found in my boot as we left the pub, which thankfully covered the bulky bandaging on my arm.

'Ah Dr Murray, come in. I'm afraid we have some bad news.' The spiky-haired Constable from the other night met me at my door.

My world tilted and my head spun with awful possibilities. I shoved past him and slumped onto a kitchen chair, unsure my legs would hold me.

I heard Rachel ask, 'What's happened, Constable?'

'Have you two been out for the day? Together?' His tone was infuriatingly judgemental. My fist subconsciously clenched and a shriek of pain shot through my arm. I bit my tongue and felt a fresh drizzle of blood slide out beneath the bandages.

I fought to calm down and keep my voice friendly. I failed miserably.

'Yes, we were out together, not that it's any of your goddamn business. Just tell me what the fuck happened. And what exactly are you doing in my house? My door was locked when I left. Why is it such a mess in here?' Only now I started looking around. Cupboards hung open and stuff was scattered everywhere.

'Now there is no need to get aggressive, Mr Murray.' I noticed he'd dropped the Doctor title. 'We were called by your neighbour, er... a Mrs Winchester from number 34.' He flicked through his ever-present notebook, checking his facts. 'She thought she saw someone acting suspiciously near your house, and when she noticed your car wasn't in the driveway, she very sensibly dialled 999. When we arrived, the front door was open and the lock broken. I'm afraid you've had a break-in, Mr Murray.'

Relief flooded through me. A break-in was nothing compared to the gruesome images circulating my brain. Now the chaos in the kitchen started to make sense. The place had been ransacked. I realised Spike was still talking, couldn't they have sent someone else?

'...perpetrator was no longer in the house when we arrived. We think he or she may have escaped over the back fence. We need you to take a look around and see if anything is missing. We don't think they had time to take much. You're lucky to have such good neighbours.'

Yeah, I felt really lucky. I almost showed him my stab wound so he could see just how my luck was holding out. Instead, I pulled myself wearily to my feet and began to check the house as instructed.

It was surreal looking for something that was missing amongst the mess. Upstairs was worse; the bed was stripped, clothes had been pulled from drawers and all the neatly stacked boxes in the spare room of Ellie's things I'd packed had been torn apart, the contents strewn over the floor. Her jewellery was still there as far as I could tell, lying in small clumps on the carpet, and so were our laptops, my iPad and games console. Even the cash I'd held back from our meeting with Cassie was where I'd left it on Ellie's dressing table.

'Gosh, you really are a lucky man, Mr Murray,' Spike declared again. 'They even missed the money! I think you owe your neighbour a big thank you – seems she saved you the trouble of an insurance claim. You'll have to get that lock taken care of though.' God, he was annoyingly chipper.

'Interfering busybody,' I muttered, barely under my breath, leaving the subject of my abuse open to interpretation.

It took the police another half hour to finally leave. Rachel chattered amiably with young Constable Spike while his colleagues dusted for prints around the house. I was sure he was dying to ask Rachel how she'd enjoyed our day out together.

It was a relief to have my house back and I took two painkillers to celebrate. My arm, back and stomach were all throbbing in unison.

'You were extremely rude to the police, Finn. They were only trying to help,' Rachel announced acerbically as soon as Spike and his friends were out the door. 'They saved your house from getting seriously trashed by whoever broke in here. You could at least have been civil.'

My arm was bleeding again and hurt like hell. Perhaps it was the blood loss or the exhaustion, or just the fact that my house was a disaster area and horrifically symbolic of the chaos in my life, but I'd lost all patience. I couldn't understand how she hadn't connected the dots, instead buying into Spike's theory that it was kids who got spooked before they could nick anything.

'Oh for fuck's sake Rachel, grow up. This wasn't your run-of-the-mill-burglary by some bored adolescent. Think about it. This place was thoroughly searched but everything of any value was ignored.' I softened my antagonistic tone when I saw the distraught expression on her face. She still didn't get it. 'Rachel, this wasn't a petty thief. This was Robert. Robert was here. In my house. Going through my stuff. And through Ellie's. Presumably looking for clues as to where I've hidden my wife.'

'Going through your stuff? But you told the police nothing was missing.'

I dipped my head in the direction of the countertop. 'The Christmas presents from Ellie. They're gone. And besides, you were the one who told me to say nothing to the police.'

Ignoring the jibe, she quickly asked, 'What, all of them? Are you sure? There's quite a mess.'

'Yes, I'm sure. They're nowhere. The book of poetry, the DVD, even the ugly green t-shirt. They're all gone.'

'Oh God.' She paled. 'Robert was here? Oh, my God.' She stood up and began pacing the kitchen as if at any minute he might jump out of the washing machine. 'But how? I mean, he was at the zoo with us—'

'But we stopped for lunch,' I chimed in, keeping any hint of accusation out of my voice. It had been her idea to stop off, but she had no idea what Robert was planning. 'The bastard must have beaten us home. I just don't know how he knew about the presents.'

'The thought of him being in your house...' She paused for a moment, processing the thought. 'He probably read the gift tags saying "from Ellie" and guessed they were important.'

'Nope,' I countered, 'the tags weren't with the presents. I'd... well... I'd put them away.' I'd put them in a pathetic shoebox at the back of my cupboard with a few other mementoes of Ellie I couldn't part with. They were still there – I'd checked when I was upstairs.

'Oh,' was all she could manage before tears began spilling down her cheeks.

From instinctive chivalry, I stood and slipped my arms around her protectively. It was awkward at first, but slowly she relaxed into me. 'I know I don't like it either. But he's gone now. And we can't let him intimidate us.'

I thumbed her tears away and she visibly pulled herself together, drawing away from me. 'I know, I just feel so vulnerable, especially on my own. Would you mind if I stayed here again tonight?'

'Sure, of course.' What else could I say? I couldn't send her back home, frightened and alone. 'I'm going to sort my arm out and then tackle the mess.' Only the worst of it, I thought. The idea of repacking Ellie's boxes was too much to deal with right now.

'Thanks, Finn.' She looked relieved that I'd let her stay. 'I can start sorting out down here if you want and find us some dinner, or do you need help with cleaning your arm first?'

I declined her help, keeping my tone polite and friendly. I was happy to go upstairs and have some time on my own. I was starting to feel slightly claustrophobic around Rachel. Or was it just the fact that she was reminding me more and more of Ellie?

CHAPTER 33

Ellie woke me up. Her hand on my shoulder was feather-light but I stirred at its touch. I smelt her grapefruit flavoured shampoo even before my eyes opened. I knew it was her.

Her dress was pale pink and her shoulders were sun-kissed brown with summer freckles. Her long hair was caught in a high ponytail and it flicked when she moved her head, just the way I remembered it. I couldn't believe she was back. Questions flooded my brain and I opened my mouth to speak. Ellie placed her finger gently on my lips before leaning down to kiss me.

The kiss was all-consuming, driven by passion and love, and it overwhelmed us like molten lava. Her lips were soft and warm and tasted of summer berries. Her tongue probed gently against my lips before slipping inside, and I sensed the safe familiarity of the woman I loved. Ellie was alive and real and back where she belonged, here in our room, and she was kissing me as if nothing had happened.

I pulled away. 'Ellie, what happened? Where've you been? What's been going on? Why—'

She held up her hands and smiled. That glorious, radiant smile that I fell in love with the first time I saw her. She reached over and switched on my bedside lamp.

'I know I have so much to explain, and I will Finn, I promise. I'll tell you everything. But first, just hold me. I've missed you so much.'

In the soft glow from the bedside lamp, I saw her beautiful mismatched irises and the shiny whiteness of her scar. She was my Ellie. Nothing she could tell me could ever change how much I loved her.

I reached up to cup her face and slowly brought her mouth back to mine. I felt her weight as she moved on the bed, straddling me. This time *I* kissed her. Long and hard, my tongue exploring her mouth desperately. I felt the kiss permeate through every cell of my body. I'd missed her so much; her touch, her laugh, her friendship, the level of intimacy you only achieve with a long term partner. I'd missed my wife.

She groaned and I felt both our bodies responding. It felt so safe and so familiar. So right. I wanted answers, but more than anything, I wanted Ellie. Every inch of her. I came up for air.

'God, I love you so much, Ellie. I've missed you so much. You broke my heart when you went away.' I couldn't say 'when you died' because she wasn't dead. She was very much alive.

'I know, I'm so sorry. But you have to believe I never stopped loving you.'

And that was enough for me, at least for now. Reaching up, I slipped off her shoulder straps. Her nipples strained at the thin cotton of her dress as I eased it down off her shoulders, needing to see all of her.

I touched her nervously like an inexperienced teenager, still caught between disbelief and desire. Ellie smiled as my hands savoured her familiar contours, and as I felt her soft, warm skin, my brain slowly accepted that she was real, alive and with me in our bed. Her eyes held mine with heart-shrivelling intensity, and in that moment I knew everything was going to be alright.

Her dress bunched around her waist with only the duvet between our nakedness. My erection pushed against her, and for the first time in months, I felt truly happy – complete. My Ellie was back.

Her mouth found mine, her breasts heavy on my chest... but then I froze.

Her belly was flat.

'El, the baby? What happened?' And in that heart-stopping instant, I knew it was a dream. Ellie was dead.

I woke up in our cold dark bedroom with an embarrassing mess on the sheet. I was very much alone.

It wasn't the first time I'd dreamt of Ellie since the accident, but never like this. Never so real, and never in such a sexual way. I felt utterly bereft, and I was covered in sweat with a quickly dying hard-on. I closed my eyes and I could still see her, smell her, taste her. But she wasn't real.

I staggered into the shower and turned the water to freezing – I needed to punish myself. I'd just tried to make love to my dead wife. What kind of a sick bastard was I? Somehow I managed to keep the dressing on my arm mostly dry.

An hour before my alarm was due to go off, I left the house to drive to work. No one would mind me starting early on a Sunday morning – Saturday nights were always frantic. Rachel had stayed over. She was fast becoming a permanent fixture in my house.

We'd spent the remainder of Saturday afternoon tidying up the house before sharing a defrosted beef casserole and watching some meaningless TV program. I was in bed by nine. I'd cleaned up the knife wound but would get one of my colleagues to take a closer look today if there was time, maybe even filch some antibiotics. First though, I would need to come up with a plausible reason for having such a deep gash in my arm.

I still felt sore everywhere, but I couldn't not go to work. They had been incredibly understanding, but having another day off would just be taking the piss. I'd cope if I used my arm carefully and didn't need to pull any dislocated shoulders. I sent up a small prayer that all sport enthusiasts would stay in one piece today during their Sunday fixtures.

I was scheduled to work most of the week and Rachel had her own work commitments, so we decided that our road trip to Southampton would wait until next weekend. That was fine by me. It gave me a few days to come up with a plan. I had no idea where to start looking. Sure, Ellie and I had spent our first few years as a couple there and had shared some favourite haunts, but nothing stood out as a starting point. I was worried that we would drive around reliving my student days with nothing to show for our endeavours.

I couldn't shake my dream of Ellie as I drove to the hospital. It had felt so real. Was it an omen? A warning to stop this futile search for answers that could only lead to enduring the agony of losing her all over again? I knew it was a dream, brought on, no doubt, by wishful thinking and desperate longing, but somehow it also felt like a message.

Unfortunately, I was no closer to interpreting it when I pulled into the car park. For now, I needed to focus on work and keeping my shit together. Messages from my late wife – whether they be on zoo plaques or in vivid wet dreams – would have to wait until I was off duty.

CHAPTER 34

Adam Benning hadn't been a particularly good soldier. In fact, he hadn't been particularly good at anything his whole life. His choices on leaving school were severely limited due to apathy and a lack of decent grades. The army recruitment officer who had addressed his Year Eleven group had promised that an army career would enable him to reach his full potential whilst also offering the chance to travel the world and have incredible adventures. He also mentioned how girls fell for men in uniform, and that had Adam hooked.

The reality, however, was entirely different. Basic training was brutal and unrelenting, and Adam rediscovered he had little respect for authority and zero aptitude for following rules. There was also a noticeable lack of fawning girls. The only ones he met were hardened soldiers who outranked him and wouldn't give him the time of day.

Life somewhat improved after basics, but not much. He still didn't enjoy the day-to-day routine and discipline, but at least the demanding physical requirements had eased off some. Then the bloody army decided he ought to go overseas and put all that they had taught him into action by fighting the Taliban.

He lasted less than two weeks. Active service highlighted his inadequacies as both a soldier and an adult. He spent his days hiding from his superior officers and praying to be sent home with some minor injury, and after only a few weeks he got his wish – sort of.

Having been ordered to re-clean his rifle, he lashed out in frustration and caught his corporal on the jaw with a lucky right hook. Adam was shipped back to the Military Corrective Training Centre in Colchester to serve a three-month sentence for assaulting a superior officer.

The army was not unduly saddened when Adam Benning elected not to return to active duty after his spell in military prison and to leave the army instead. Back on Civvy Street, Adam had high hopes of joining one of the many close pro-tection firms providing bodyguards and mercenary soldiers in hot spots around the world. He had heard that there was ser-ious money to be made for minimal effort, and without the discipline he had found so tedious in the regular army.

After several rejections, it slowly dawned on the twenty year old that his record of insubordination and assault, coupled with his lack of actual combat experience, meant that there were no lucrative job offers flooding in.

Adam blamed his miserable situation on the army rather than any shortcomings of his own.

He sat bemoaning his unfair treatment in his cramped council bedsit in South London, playing video games and searching for new porn sites in less conventional areas of the internet. That was when Adam stumbled across a strange chat room where an old loser named Tom was looking for someone to carry out some less-than-legal work for him. Intrigued by the idea of making some fast, easy money, Adam made contact.

The work that was required turned out to be the murder of two men who Tom claimed were 'bad people'.

Adam wavered. This was serious shit, but the money was too good to turn down. And after all, the army had trained him to kill; he was merely using his skill set in a less orthodox way.

The money removed any moral objections he may have had to taking a life, and he didn't let the insignificant detail of having never faced an enemy in anything other than a training scenario stand between him and the big pay-out this Tom was offering.

He had no real idea *how* he would kill these men. Although he thought of himself as being tremendously streetwise, he lacked useful connections to obtain an illegal firearm. Perhaps he could use a knife. The biggest problem would be not getting caught – he didn't fancy any more jail time. He would have to be careful about fingerprints, DNA and all that other stuff they showed on telly.

Tom, using what he claimed was an untraceable email account, had sent him details of the two victims. Adam felt excited at his new employment opportunities. He would look into running an advert on the deep web – Tom could give him an endorsement when he had completed his mission.

The first target was a young doctor. He would be easy. Adam decided that he would carry out some recon work on the doctor like he'd been taught in the army, and so he arrived at A&E complaining about a sore throat. He signed in at reception using his own name, thinking afterwards that it may have been a good idea to use an alias, but by then he was already on the computer. Still, he doubted there would ever be any follow up into past patients once he had dealt with the unsuspecting doctor.

He cleverly manoeuvred his visit so that he was eventually seen by Doctor Murray himself. He was pissed off that it took nearly three hours for his turn, but spent the time assessing his victim as he worked. The doc seemed a little slow and distracted, and his left arm, which he moved stiffly, appeared to be slightly weakened.

He wasn't much of a doctor either, taking mere minutes to examine Adam's sore throat before suggesting he go home, rinse with mouthwash and see his GP if his symptoms persisted. Adam thought the bloke seemed decent enough, nice and polite, and he wondered what Tom had against the man – but it wasn't his place to question the source of the money.

The only problem was that a busy Emergency Department wasn't in the least bit conducive to carrying out a murder. Not if he didn't want to get caught at any rate. The doctor was never alone, at least not in the public areas, and Adam couldn't work out how to get through the security doors without a pass card. And then there was the problem of all the cameras and security guards.

After a wasted morning, Adam decided the doctor would have to wait. Except for that left arm, Murray looked quite capable of fighting, so maybe it would be better to work up to him.

He would start with the other man on the list instead. He was older, lived alone, and Adam doubted he would offer much in the way of resistance. His name was Robert Hudson and Adam had his home address.

CHAPTER 35

Adam regained consciousness, utterly bewildered and in tremendous pain. Unable to move and struggling to breathe through his smashed nose, he tried to open his eyes. They were wet and sticky and gummed shut from the blood oozing from a deep gash above his left eye.

His hands were tightly secured behind his back, and the strips of hard plastic binding his ankles together were cutting into his flesh. His clothes were gone and he was only wearing his white underpants. Adam was scared shitless, lying almost naked and utterly vulnerable on the floor of an empty room.

It had all happened so quickly – Adam barely had time to register the attack, let alone defend himself. He had reached Hudson's door at the top of the stairs with absolute confidence that his victim was completely unaware of his presence. He hadn't noticed the hidden cameras that had been tracking his movements since the moment he entered the small apartment building from the street.

Adam's plan was simple; he would knock on the door, overpower the old man and stab him with the kitchen knife he'd brought from home. Then, he would simply leave before he could leave enough forensic evidence for the police to find. It would be a walk in the park and a very profitable walk at that.

Just as Adam raised his fist to knock, the knife still out of sight in his coat pocket, the door was yanked open and something heavy hit him in his unprotected face, breaking his nose. While he was still recoiling from the initial attack, another blow caught him on his temple. His unconscious body slumped to the ground like a marionette with the strings cut.

Now he was awake, bound and bloody with an aching head. He could feel the broken bits of bone in his nose grate on each other every time he took a breath. He tried to make sense of his environment. There were heavy curtains pulled across the window, stopping any daylight from entering. A bare bulb hung down from the ceiling, barely illuminating the corners of the small room.

Adam grunted in pain as he pulled himself into a half-sitting position. He had to wait for his vision to clear as his head was spinning. Unfortunately, his circumstances looked no better sitting up. The walls of his makeshift cell were covered in small foam peaks that he'd once seen used inside a recording studio. For the first time, he wished he had paid closer attention when the army lectured him on escape techniques.

He was still trying to process his fucked-up situation when the door opened and a tall man walked in, filling the small room with his bulk and attitude. He was suntanned, with close-cropped greying hair, and he wore a sleeveless t-shirt which showcased both his impressive biceps and collection of elaborate tattoos. He matched the photo Tom had provided, but the picture did nothing to highlight the malicious gleam in the man's cold grey eyes. Adam's bladder grew weak with fear. This man was here to hurt him.

'So nice to see you're awake.' His tone was light, conversational almost, but it was all the more frightening because of it.

In one hand the man held Adam's wallet which he had stupidly brought with him, and in the other was a brown gym bag.

'You can't keep me 'ere. I need a fucking doctor. Broke my nose you 'ave.' It came out as *dose* and his voice sounded whiny and pathetic.

'Yes of course, but first we're going to have a little chat. Then we'll sort out getting you some medical attention.'

Relief washed over Adam. This guy would help him, he just wanted answers. He watched as the man put down the bag and began unpacking it slowly, one item at a time. A bulbous club hammer, some bolt cutters, several screwdrivers with sharpened tips and the biggest knife Adam had ever seen. Most of the tools were old and rust coloured, but the implication was clear. He was not here to complete some DIY project.

Adam was not a particularly brave man, but he wasn't completely stupid. He had no loyalty to his client – he was nothing more than a name and a promise of easy money on some dodgy website.

'Y-y-you don't… you don't need those,' he stammered. 'I'll tell you whatever you wanna know, but it ain't much.'

'Oh, you will tell me everything,' Hudson replied in his booming voice, 'your kind always does. To be honest, it takes all the pleasure, all the challenge out of it. Nevertheless, I don't like the idea of you just thinking you can come here and break into my home, so I think we should have some fun first, don't you? I'd hate for you to have had a wasted journey.'

Terror radiated through Adam like an electrical current. What sort of a sick bastard was this? So unlike that nice doctor at the hospital. Tom might have been right to want this one dead.

'Please mate, er, Mr Hudson, there's no need to hurt me. I was only doing this for the money. I was never really gonna go through with it…' Adam rambled, desperately.

'So you know my name? Interesting.' The tall man began arranging his macabre set of tools on the floor in front of Adam. 'So why did you come here with a knife and threaten me, Mr Benning?'

Adam desperately wanted to tell the man everything, but he

also wanted to get out of this fucked up torture room. He would need to play it very carefully. 'Please mate... look, I need a doctor. I will tell you but—'

Hudson moved so quickly Adam hadn't even managed to close his eyes before the heavy bolt cutters connected with his left cheek. The bone cracked, the snap audible like a piece of fine bone china hitting the floor. Seconds passed before his high piercing scream filled the room. Blood gushed from the open wound, pooling in Adam's mouth. The scream culminated in a gurgle.

'You need to spit out the blood,' Hudson explained calmly as if he were instructing a child on dental hygiene. Adam tried his best, but his entire face was buzzing in agony. He shook uncontrollably as tears fell and mixed with the snot and blood streaming down his ruined face. Hudson took a step back, watching the man wail and writhe in pain. If there was any empathy for his fellow human's suffering, it did not show on his face or in his dead, expressionless eyes.

Hudson waited for Adam to quieten down before gingerly lowering himself onto his haunches. He casually opened Adam's wallet and began to study its contents. Adam fearfully watched his every move, unsure when the next blow would come.

'Adam Jeremiah Benning. 12B Fairfield Gardens, Woolwich.' Hudson read off Adam's driving licence in a bored tone. 'And what else do you have in here, Mr Benning? Twenty-five... ah no, thirty pounds, a Tesco's Club Card and some rather old condoms. Nothing that says who you work for?'

Adam wasn't sure what the question was exactly, but he desperately wanted to answer it. Fighting pain and waves of nausea, he tried his best. 'I-I-I don't work for—'

The club hammer was in Hudson's hand before the words had left Adam's mouth. The heavy instrument shaped like a miniature sledgehammer swung down in a graceful arc and connected with Adam's right knee cap. There was nothing human about the sound Adam made as he lay on the bare floor. There were no words to explain the intensity of the agony that filled his entire being.

Hudson ignored his screams, waiting patiently.

'This hammer might look pretty small, Mr Benning, but it weighs 1135g, and when wielded by an expert like me, it's actually pretty powerful,' said Hudson. There was nothing small about the destruction of Adam's knee. 'You see, your patella – the triangular-shaped bone in your knee – never stood a chance. It disintegrated on impact. It looks like small shards of bone have spun away, cutting and shredding your tissue and muscle. You see how it's already started to swell and discolour? Well that's the internal bleeding for you.'

Adam quietened and slowly returned to the room, only to find Hudson waiting for a reply, casually swinging the hammer.

'The human body is nothing if not resourceful, Mr Benning. Your brain has realised that your body can't cope with this degree of onslaught, so it has begun to shut down your pain receptors, minimising the effect... if not the damage.' Hudson smiled. 'As long as you keep that leg immobile, your brain will do everything in its power to ignore the pain.'

While Hudson began to whistle tunelessly, Adam did his best to pull himself together. He steadfastly refused to look at his destroyed knee.

'H-h-he just gave me your address,' he stuttered, panting hard. 'Never told me his name, just sent a photo in an email. I don't work for nobody. I'm unemployed. Look... mate, I'm sorry I came, but I needed the money...' Benning wanted to stop talking. He wanted to lie down and slip into the darkness, away from the pain, but Hudson raised his eyebrows and the hammer, both ever so slightly.

Adam garbled on, desperate to make his tormentor understand. 'It was just some old geezer on the internet. He'll pay me £100,000. Cash. For you and the other guy.' He squinted up through his rapidly swelling left eye, still cowering in fear and pain.

'You're making no sense. Start at the beginning,' Hudson demanded. 'What other guy? And who was going to pay you to kill me?' He frowned scornfully down at the man lying bleeding and broken on his floor. 'Just give me the facts. *Go on.*' He raised the hammer, knowing he wouldn't need to take out the other knee but relishing the thought. 'GO!'

Adam swallowed more blood than saliva, and bile burned the back of his throat. He mustn't throw up now. If he did, his body would convulse and his leg... He began babbling, trying hard to be concise. He was still hoping that if he told this madman everything, he would let him go, or maybe even take him to a hospital.

'His... his name was Tom. That's all I know. I s-s-swear. He asked if anyone would carry out a hit. For cash. It was on a chat room in that bit of the web where you can find anything but everything is anonymous. Said I'd do it, didn't I. Just wanted the money. I was never really gonna hurt nobody.' He glanced up to see if the man would punish him for this lie before quickly continuing, 'He emailed me the info and two photos – yours and the doctor's. I decided to start with you.' His words grew quieter, hope beginning to fade. What had he been thinking? He hadn't even killed anyone when he was a bloody soldier. What on earth made him think he could do it now? And certainly not against this maniac who wielded all these tools like he was some pro with seemingly no remorse.

Hudson was quiet for a beat while Adam racked his brain for more to add but came up empty.

'Did this *Tom* have a surname?'

'No, no, only Tom. I didn't ask no more.'

'So you were happily going to kill two men, men you'd never met, because someone named *Tom* promised you some money? Not only does that make you an idiot, Mr Benning, but also not a very nice person, don't you agree?'

'I needed the dough,' Adam whined. 'I have debt. It's hard getting a job as an ex-soldier. I fought for my country ya know, and then just got dumped, with nuffin'. I was desperate.'

'A most unlikely soldier,' Hudson commented with disdain, slowly getting to his feet, wincing slightly as his back straightened. The hammer hung casually down the side of his right leg. 'What was the name of the doctor, the other man you were going to murder?'

'Murray. Dr Finlay Murray. I went to see 'im at the hospital where he works, but there were too many guards and cameras and shit...' Adam's voice was growing weaker, and Hudson leant in to hear better.

'So you thought you'd start with me? An older man, an easier target?' his mirthless laugh echoed off the padded walls.

Adam nodded his throbbing head, not trusting himself to speak, realising how little he was helping his cause. Moving his head brought fresh agony to his wounds and more blood leaked down his face. He had told the man everything. He had been helpful. Surely his ordeal was nearly over?

'Is there anything else you wish to tell me, Mr Benning?'

'No there's nuffin' else, I fucking swear. Please, you have to let me go. I need a hospital. You'll never see me again. I won't tell no one, I'll just—'

'Oh don't be ridiculous, Mr Benning, we're only just getting started. But you are absolutely right, of course, you won't ever tell anyone. That's a given. Oh, and in case you're wondering, this room is completely soundproof. No one will hear you, so feel free to make as much noise as you need.'

Hudson was already reaching into his brown gym bag as Adam pissed himself, the smell rank with fear. His pleas and tears were ignored as Hudson went to work, grinning to himself as he realised he had the perfect place to dump the body. If his brother was desperate enough to hire this Neanderthal, it could only mean he was getting close to finding Eleanor, but Robert had the perfect way to slow down the opposition.

CHAPTER 36

Finn

Work kept me almost sane that week. I was desperate to go to Southampton, although I was still clueless about where to start. I needed to find answers so that I could finally put Ellie and her convoluted past to rest. A stubborn flicker of pathetic longing refused to die, bringing nothing but more pain with it. I had to end this. I needed closure of some kind.

The thought of Ellie needing someone else, turning to them for help over me, was almost as crushing as the idea of her driving her car into that tree on purpose.

I was almost too afraid to sleep at night in case her ghost revisited me, yet I was desperate for her touch at the same time. Thankfully, she hadn't found her way into my dreams again that week.

Rachel had finally gone back to London. I'd magnanimously offered her unlimited use of my spare room, even though it would have meant her commuting into London for work each day. I argued that we could watch each other's backs. It sounded like the right thing to say, but to be honest, I doubted it would stop Robert from getting to either one of us. He seemed to be a most resourceful psychopath.

Despite all this, I was more than a little relieved when she turned me down. I wasn't in the best of moods to play host. She did make me promise that I wouldn't do anything without her though, as if she still believed I knew where Ellie was hiding, alive, and that we would disappear together into the night. If only.

Instead, we implemented a protocol where we would talk twice a day to ensure the other was still alive. Ineffectual, but it made her happier, and it gave her an excuse, I thought, to check up on me regularly. God, I was growing more paranoid by the day.

She was coming over on Friday night after work and we planned to travel down to Southampton first thing Saturday morning. We were still in high-level negotiations as to who would be driving.

I finished an early shift on Thursday and I was just reaching for a beer when the doorbell rang. I had recently spoken to Rachel and had just finished cleaning and redressing my knife wound, which I had explained at work rather clumsily as a cut from a screwdriver. I said I'd been hanging a picture of Ellie at the time and lost concentration. The mere mention of my recently dead wife had stopped even my most sceptical colleague from asking any follow-up questions. I didn't even feel ashamed. I allowed a newbie doctor to practice his stitching skills. The result was messy, but it would keep the wound closed and infection-free. Dressed and cleaned it hardly even hurt. Hardly.

'Mr Murray, Finlay James Murray?'

It wasn't Robert, thank God. My shoulders relaxed.

'Yes?'

'My name is Richard Lawson. I'm a solicitor. Here's my card, may I come in?'

He shoved his business card into my hand even as he stepped

into the hallway. He was a little on the chubby side and took up a lot of room. I stupidly took a step back, allowing him in.

We headed into the kitchen. Lawson made noises about the lovely view of the back garden. The lawn badly needed mowing, so I knew he was talking crap. I put the kettle on, forcing a smile.

'So why exactly are you here?' I had worked a busy shift and could almost taste the beer I'd planned on downing. I didn't have the energy for small talk.

'Of course, down to business. I'm here about your late wife. We need to discuss some financial details.'

I looked at him blankly. An uneasy feeling was creeping up on me. Not more outstanding expenses from the funeral? I thought I'd paid for everything. If he was working for a bailiff I was screwed. I barely had enough to cover the mortgage and the bills this month. Working part-time had severely decreased my pay – pay I usually topped up with overtime and unsocial hours.

'What's still unpaid? I thought all the funeral costs were accounted for?' I asked, my stomach beginning to churn. Was it some debt Ellie had failed to mention to me?

'You misunderstand me, Dr Murray. I'm not here to collect money. Quite the contrary. I'm here to discuss your wife's trust fund. It matures in June on her thirtieth birthday.'

God, I'd completely forgotten Ellie would have been turning 30 this year. Before the accident, I'd been thinking of organising a surprise party or a special holiday. But our funds were limited. Then she fell pregnant and our plans changed completely, and then she died of course.

'What trust fund? And anyway, she's dead.' I was certainly getting better at sharing this fact. If she were here, Rachel would no doubt complain I was being rude again.

'Yes, I am very sorry for your loss.' He put no effort into

sounding sympathetic. 'You see, Eleanor's father established the trust fund and she was to inherit it when she turned thirty. In the event of her death before that date, the monies pass to her next of kin. And, as long as you have proof of being legally married and that there are no other close family members, then that would be you. Did she mention this to you at all before her death? I spoke with her back in early November of last year to begin sorting the transfer of funds.'

No, of course she didn't. Ellie didn't bloody tell me about it. Politeness was no longer an option.

'What the fuck are you saying? Ellie knew about this? You spoke to her? When? Where? And what father? She was an orphan and in foster care almost all her life.' I almost added *at least I think so*. I hated having to question everything I ever knew about my wife.

Lawson seemed unmoved as my anger ratcheted up a notch. His tone was slightly bored as if this task was really beneath him, and he should be at home sipping expensive brandy from a crystal glass instead.

'I wrote to Eleanor in early September to remind her the fund was pending, and that we needed to begin planning for the transfer of the various investments. She came to see me at my offices in Chelmsford.'

He lost me at Chelmsford. When the hell had my wife travelled to Essex without even mentioning it to me? Hang on, wasn't Chelmsford on the way to the zoo in Colchester?

'She knew about this trust fund? From when exactly?' The words tasted bitter on my tongue. 'You said you were reminding her...' I couldn't finish my sentence. I couldn't put into words yet another incidence of being the clueless, idiot husband. Dear God Ellie, I loved you with all my heart but you kept so much from me.

'Oh, Eleanor has known for some time.' He sounded so smug, and there was that name again.

'You do know her name was Ellie, not Eleanor?' It was a pathetic argument, growing weaker each time I used it. But it was all I had.

'No, her name was most definitely Eleanor. Eleanor Elizabeth Hudson.'

Oh shit, not this again.

'Her name was Ellie fucking GRAINGER!' My voice was so loud now that Mrs Winchester at number 34 could have joined in our conversation. I was past caring what the neighbours thought. 'You have the wrong woman. You *all* have the wrong woman. Get the fuck out of my house.'

Lawson ignored my outburst almost as if he had been expecting it. He opened his briefcase with the flourish of a practised magician and withdrew a buff-coloured folder.

'The photo on the fridge,' he said, pointing over my right shoulder, 'that's Eleanor. *That* is the woman who visited me in my offices. Eleanor Hudson. Or at least she was until she married you and changed her surname.'

I turned and stared at the photo as if seeing it for the first time. It was a lovely picture of Ellie. She looked so happy and carefree. Her smile was radiant and beautiful. You could clearly see her scar and even the magical colours of her eyes.

'You don't bloody understand, do you?' I sighed, slumping back on my chair. 'The woman I married was called Ellie Grainger, an orphan with no trust fund, no lawyers and no other names.'

'No Dr Murray, you are very much mistaken.' He began removing documents from the folder, a déjà vu moment from when Rachel had brandished her own pile of papers on my kitchen table. That seemed like a lifetime ago.

'Bullshit. I know Ellie… I *knew* my wife, and I don't have to listen to this crap.' My response lacked all conviction. The knife in my heart twisted with every word this annoying, pompous asshole uttered.

'If you don't mind me saying, you don't seem to know much about anything, Dr Murray, and there are lots of reasons why you should listen to what I have to tell you. 5.3 million reasons to be exact.'

'What the hell are you talking about?'

'Oh, didn't I mention it before?' His supercilious smile made my fist ache to pound his chubby face, but the bastard just kept on talking, spinning my universe 180 degrees once more. 'Your wife's trust fund, which now reverts to you as her next of kin, is worth 5.3 million pounds, give or take a hundred thousand or so.' Lawson positively beamed at my shock. The bastard was enjoying every minute of this. 5.3 million? How the fuck did Ellie forget to mention 5.3 million pounds to me?

'Of course, there was also a brother.'

I was ahead of him there. 'You mean Harry?' I said knowingly, desperate to show that I wasn't completely clueless.

Lawson sighed. 'No not Harry. I suppose you mean Harry Grainger, the boy from her foster home? No, I'm talking about her biological brother. Benjamin Thomas Hudson. If he came forward he may contest the terms of the trust fund, but I think that's highly unlikely.'

'Brother?' It came out as a strangled whisper. This was even more shocking than the thought of Ellie having over five million pounds tucked away somewhere. We often spoke about my sisters and she would berate me if I didn't keep in touch with them regularly, saying how much she would have loved a sibling and making me feel like a shitty brother. Now this arsehole was sitting in my kitchen saying Ellie had a brother all along.

I fought the building tears by getting angry. I no longer knew what emotional response was expected of me. Was I mourning someone I didn't even know?

'Well guess what, you pompous arsehole.' God, what was I, twelve? 'Did you know that Ellie also has a half-sister called Rachel? So the family tree is growing!' I announced this fact triumphantly, and it was worth it to see the total look of shock on his fat face. Continuing with my immature outburst, I yelled, 'Now get the fuck out of my house!'

Lawson was desperate to question me further. Rachel's existence was obviously news to him, but the look on my face must have dissuaded him from pushing it. He eventually stood, gathering his papers and walked towards the hallway.

'We will need to talk about this further, Mr Murray. There is a lot of red tape to sort through before the beginning of June. I will leave you the file. Read it. It may help explain something of Eleanor's past, and it details her extensive portfolio of investments.' He paused at the door before adding, 'I'll be in touch. Soon.'

The front door slammed. I sat at our kitchen table with tears I could no longer contain streaming down my face. God Ellie, if you weren't dead already...

Who was I kidding? I still loved her so much it hurt. Even if our life together was a complete lie and she'd been nothing but a fraud and a charlatan. She was my fraud, my charlatan. She was my Ellie.

CHAPTER 37

The alarm shrilled in my ear and I obediently dragged myself out of bed to go for a run. It didn't go well. I now had 5.3 million more questions buzzing around my head, and I couldn't find any rhythm. My usual thirty-minute route took me well over forty, and I was breathing hard by the time I got home, sounding like an eighty-year-old emphysema patient.

My slower pace meant I was now running late, and with a sense of remorse bordering on shame, I realised I was already establishing a morning routine that didn't involve Ellie. I'd even lost count of the days since her accident.

I was in a sombre mood by the time I eventually headed downstairs to leave the house that Friday morning, and would have given anything for an excuse to head back upstairs and under my duvet. I almost ignored the fact that our shed door was swinging gently in the fresh spring breeze.

Our shed was small and needed re-roofing. It housed the lawnmower, some empty plant pots, Ellie's easel from her abandoned artist stage and not much else. It was always padlocked, but now the padlock was missing and the door stood ajar. I was short on time but I walked over to close it anyway.

The average adult male has about four grams of iron in their blood, and when this combines with the natural oils on the skin, it creates a very recognisable metallic smell. As I neared the shed, I immediately got a strong whiff of blood, faeces and death. As an A&E doctor, I would recognise that smell anywhere.

I nudged the door open with my foot and peered tentatively inside. I immediately wished I hadn't. I should have left the bloody shed door and gone to work.

There was a body lying in my shed.

I didn't need a medical degree to know that it was very, very dead. I didn't recognise the person, and to be honest, although I was used to dead bodies, this wasn't one I wanted to study too closely. Death had not come easily and not without tremendous pain. Put plainly, the man in my shed had been tortured and died horribly. He was dressed in nothing more than white boxers, and his almost-naked body was a mass of cuts, scrapes and arrested bruising.

Both his knees were swollen grotesquely and his fingers and toes were bloodied and deformed, more resembling mincemeat than human digits. I'd seen a movie with Mel Gibson once where someone took a hammer to his toes. Perhaps the person who did this had seen the same movie. The man's boxers were soaked in dried blood, and I had absolutely no desire to see what trauma had caused that amount of bleeding.

Even these horrific injuries could have left the man in my shed hanging to life by a thread, but what sealed his fate was the clear plastic bag over his head. My mystery man had suffocated. His eyes were wide and staring, and his blue tongue protruded, grossly swollen from between his death-grey lips.

I'd watched my fair share of NCIS episodes on TV, and knew all about contaminating the crime scene. If I believed for a second that the corpse had even a flutter of a pulse, I would have gone in and tried to help him. Instead, I stood at the door and dialled 999.

The operator asked a lot of questions when I explained I had found a body in my shed: Was he conscious? Was he breathing?

Was he talking? I explained that I was a doctor and eventually they agreed to send the police. I said there was no need for the ambulance to hurry.

Next, I phoned work and spent over five minutes convincing my colleagues that they should believe my reason for not coming in this morning. One of the young nurses I spoke to even asked to see a photo of the body as proof.

Shamefully, my first, almost joyous hope was that maybe it was Robert lying brutalised on my shed floor. Standing at the door, I studied what I could see of the face. I couldn't be sure. His nose was smashed and his cheekbone had suffered a depressed fracture, giving his face an odd flattened appearance. The bloodied plastic bag wasn't helping either. Even his mother would have struggled to identify his ruined features. I leaned in a little further but couldn't see a tattoo on his wrist, and the body appeared shorter and stouter.

I heard the wail of sirens coming through the village and went out onto the road to wave them down.

If it wasn't Robert's body in my shed, then I had a horrible feeling I knew who had tortured and killed the poor sod. And I could make an educated guess as to who the victim was too. Harry Grainger was laying practically naked and battered to death on my shed floor. Robert must have found him and questioned him like he had Cassie. But why the fuck leave him in *my* garden? A warning of what he was capable of – as if I needed reminding.

I'd been running so late this morning that I'd forgotten my daily call to Rachel. I quickly dialled her number and caught her on her way into work. After completely freaking out she announced she was heading straight over. I tried to explain that it wasn't a great idea, and that I would no doubt be tied up with the police for most of the day. In response, she mumbled something about being a lawyer and me not being able to keep my mouth shut.

By the time Rachel arrived well over an hour later and had fought her way through the cordon of police and crime scene technicians wearing white plastic overalls and stupid blue booties, I was on my fourth recounting of this morning's events.

When she rushed in, I was sitting on Ellie's side of the couch holding a cold cup of tea, feeling a little queasy. I wished she hadn't come. Detective Renshaw sat opposite me in the armchair with Spike perched uncomfortably on one of the kitchen chairs he'd dragged through. The inseparable crime-fighting duo had arrived less than ten minutes ago, having been alerted, no doubt, by the responding police officers that yet another incident had occurred involving me.

We were just getting to the open shed door part of the story, and I decided to keep going so Rachel could hear all the grue-some details without me having to repeat them again later. Renshaw nodded, encouraging me to continue, perhaps ac-knowledging that if Rachel had made it this far into the house, he wasn't going to be able to get rid of her either.

She paled and gripped the door frame as I catalogued the injur-ies to the corpse I'd seen from the doorway, and described how I knew there was no hope that the man was still alive.

Renshaw glared at Spike who eventually got the message. He stood and guided a trembling Rachel to his chair. He stood hovering, notebook in hand, perhaps hoping I'd suddenly de-cide to confess to the murder.

'It's him. Isn't it? He did this,' she blurted out, looking right at me, undisguised fear in every word. And she accused me of not being able to keep my mouth shut?

'It's *who* exactly Miss Bates?' Renshaw pounced. I was getting confused about who knew what. Had we told the detective about Robert? I gave up and zoned out. Now that the adren-aline was gone, I was feeling completely drained, and I kept seeing the horrific state of the body flashing before my eyes.

Nothing would ever remove that grisly sight from my memory.

Rachel brought Detective Renshaw up to date on our various run-ins with Robert, including our latest incident last week at the zoo. It didn't sound in the least bit credible to me, and I'd been there. She gave a vague description: a big tall man with short grey hair, cold eyes and an extensive tattoo. His main crime to date, besides his habit of waving a knife around carelessly, was to ask stupid questions about the location of my dead wife who he unequivocally believed was still alive.

A kind woman constable replaced my cold tea with a fresh cup which I sipped gratefully, unable to stop myself imagining the dead man's last few hours spent at the hands of his tormentor.

'Dr Murray? Dr Murray? Er... Finn?'

'What?'

'Are you with us, Dr Murray? Now, you claim this man – this Robert Hudson – is hounding you, wanting to know about your wife. So why do you think he believes your wife is still alive?' Renshaw's tone was laced with scepticism.

'Fuck knows.' I shrugged, too tired to care anymore. 'Maybe it's because of the money.'

'What money?' Rachel and Renshaw asked in unison.

I sighed, knowing I was about to open a new and bottomless can of worms. 'The 5.3 million pounds I'm going to inherit about six weeks from now.'

CHAPTER 38

It was early evening before we had the house to ourselves. There were still people milling about in the garden and my shed was lit up like Blackpool Tower on a bank holiday. Renshaw suggested I might prefer decamping to a hotel for a few days, but I was determined not to be kicked out of my own house. Rachel didn't offer her place, which considering how often she'd enjoyed the hospitality of my spare bedroom, seemed a little selfish.

The body had been wheeled out an hour ago and Renshaw left along with it. The forensic team had been through the house with a fine-tooth comb and a UV light looking for blood and other evidence that would presumably indicate I'd murdered the poor bastard. They even showed me close-ups of his poor unfortunate face hoping I could identify their John Doe and perhaps save them some leg work. They seemed as confused as I was as to why he'd been dumped, already dead, in my garden shed, but when the time of death was confirmed as the previous day while I was at work, even Renshaw couldn't come up with a reason to arrest me – as much as he would have loved to dearly.

'5.3 million?' Rachel spat the words at me. I wasn't sure if it was a question or a statement. She was pissed I hadn't told her before.

'Yep. 5.3 million pounds,' I echoed.

I considered the money. My parents hadn't been wealthy but were certainly comfortable. Dad was a GP and Mum worked as a midwife part-time when I was young, but she mostly concentrated on her charity work as I got older. I never wanted for anything and my parents were even paying back my student loans to help out now that I was paying the mortgage on the house without Ellie's salary. I had no frame of reference to even visualise what point three of a million looked like, and couldn't begin to imagine the spending power of the other five. Could I buy a big house with a swimming pool and a tennis court? And a sports car? Maybe a Porsche. In bright red. It was like one of those silly games you play imagining what you would do if you won the lottery.

'There is, however, a fly in this very lucrative-sounding ointment. Ellie may have a brother. His name is Benjamin. And I guess half the money is his too. But I have no idea who or where he is.'

Rachel's expression was a mixture of confusion and incredulity. We'd opened a bottle of wine, a reward for enduring Renshaw's questioning for the better part of the day, and we were now sitting in the lounge after dinner.

'A brother? Are you kidding me? Now there's a bloody brother? Where's he, for God's sake?' Rachel reacted as if I'd announced I had the plague. She instinctively reached for her phone, perhaps to check with Google or something, but slipped it back into her bag when she realised I was watching her.

'I have no idea. The lawyer said something about him maybe contesting the terms of the trust fund if he's alive, which he doubts anyway,' I answered, vaguely. Honestly, with everything else going on, the existence and/or whereabouts of a brother wasn't top of my 'Ellie's anomaly list'. I didn't understand why Rachel was so spooked by the news.

'As her half-sister, am I entitled to a share?' She neatly steered the conversation in a different direction.

'I honestly hadn't thought of that. I'll have to ask my newly acquired Essex lawyer friend. So perhaps a three-way split?' Maybe no tennis court and only a mid-range Porsche then. My pot of unspeakable wealth I hadn't known existed was dwindling fast. And who knew, maybe there were still more siblings out there, perhaps even a husband or two hiding in the wings? I wasn't naïve enough not to appreciate that an inheritance, especially one of this size, could bring out all types of opportunist would-be family members. And Rachel could even be one of those. Not to mention murderous *Uncle Robert*.

'That's a serious amount of money, Finn. Did you honestly know nothing about it? And I don't mean to be insensitive, but now that you have it do you still want to go chasing down to Southampton? You have no idea what other misery you'll uncover down there.'

'I don't give a flying fuck about the money,' I countered, surprising myself at how honest a statement that was. 'What I *want* is Ellie back, happy, healthy, and pregnant with my baby. Like it was before. And without the rising sibling count... no offence. But since all that's no longer possible, then what I really want is the 'truth'.' I threw up finger quotes to emphasise my point. Although I wasn't sure I would even recognise the truth and how it pertained to Ellie if it sat up and bit me on the arse. 'The honest to God truth. About Ellie, her past, Harry, her brother, you, her psychotic and misguided uncle, her hidden fortune. The whole ugly truth about the woman I loved so much she consumed my *soul*.' My declaration tripped effortlessly off my wine-lubricated tongue.

Rachel didn't comment on my outburst, and her expression was passive and controlled once more. I continued rambling, caught again in a vortex of pain and regret.

'You know Ellie and I talked about taking out life insurance, in case the worst happened to one of us, but there was no way we could afford the repayments. It went on to our, 'to do next year' list, along with swimming with whale sharks and skiing in Japan. She had so many opportunities to tell me the truth. About everything. The money, her birth parents, her brother... *you*. Why didn't she? Why did she keep lying to me? And for all those years!'

I looked at Rachel over my glass of red wine to find that she was blurring slightly. I didn't expect answers from her – they were rhetorical questions. After all, she had less idea of who Ellie was than I did.

A growing virus was consuming my insides, insistent to know why everything I thought I knew about my wife was a total lie. 'I'm going to Southampton tomorrow, with or without you. I'm driving and I'm leaving at eight.'

I was done negotiating and emphasised my point by deliberately slamming my now empty wine glass on the coffee table.

'Finn, all I'm saying is Renshaw warned us not to interfere. This is now an official murder investigation. They're looking for Robert. And after what he did to that poor man in your shed... well, perhaps we should leave it to the professionals?'

'I'm not interfering. And I'm certainly not looking for Robert. He's an unstable sociopath and I have every faith the police will catch up with him soon. But considering that body was in my garden shed, staying at home is hardly the safer option. I'm going to Southampton in the morning, end of. You can come if you want. It's up to you.'

Her reluctance for our joint field trip had caught me off guard. I thought she would have relished the idea of being seen to be doing her best to get to the bottom of Ellie's death, if only as a way of placating Robert. She took a long moment to make up her mind, and she finally looked at me in that supercilious way of hers, like *I* was the one needing a psychiatric evaluation.

'Of course I'll come with you. As I said, we're in this together.

But I think you should let me drive. You're still so... so emotional.' She looked up at me and must have seen the resolve written in bold on my face, because she quickly added, 'Okay, okay I guess you can drive.'

CHAPTER 39

Saturday's azure-blue sky was for the most part hidden behind threatening grey clouds, but it felt warmer than it had done in weeks, as if spring was trying its best to get a foothold on the dying winter.

Rachel had stayed over again. Her overnight bag was in the car, so she hadn't even needed to borrow my spare toothbrush.

Detective Renshaw had phoned as I was brushing my teeth before bed the night before to let me know they had identified the body. I'd been so convinced it was Harry Grainger that it came as a bit of a shock when he said it wasn't.

Renshaw explained that the poor sod's name was Adam Jeramiah Benning, an ex-soldier who had served a short time in a military prison and fallen on hard times. I spent twenty minutes convincing the Detective that I didn't know him before the penny dropped. Then I reluctantly confessed that I'd treated a man in A&E a couple of days ago with the same name. He'd come in with some minor complaint I couldn't even recall, and the only reason I remembered him at all was because of his middle name. The song *Jeremiah was a Bullfrog* jumped into my head the moment I read his name on the chart, and it stayed there, annoyingly, on repeat until the end of my shift.

Renshaw didn't sound thrilled that I was on some level acquainted with the victim, and said they would check the hospital records. The man seemed to automatically distrust anything I told him. He also seemed annoyed that I hadn't mentioned it before, but there was no way I would have connected the horrific death mask in the plastic bag with a patient I examined for less than ten minutes.

I begrudgingly agreed it would be in my best interest if we met first thing on Monday morning to discuss the developments in the case. Renshaw had been seriously blindsided when I told him about the money, and I hadn't even told him about the brother yet.

The roads were busy. The Easter holidays were in full swing and it took us longer than expected to reach the outskirts of Southampton. Not that I was in any hurry. I was still hoping for a bolt of inspiration to at least provide a starting point for this ridiculous odyssey.

Rachel was growing increasingly distant. I wasn't sure which was pissing her off more: finding out about Ellie's trust fund or finding out about Ellie's brother. Either way, she was in a foul mood. I'd even asked a few times before we left if she really wanted to come with me, but she assured me she was up for the hare-brained road trip cum treasure hunt we were embarking on. I took her at her word, but I was far from convinced. I didn't blame her. My enthusiasm was waning fast too.

After a few sleepless nights of introspective tossing and turning, I was less sure of what I'd seen and certainly questioning its relevance. Secret messages from beyond the grave on a wall at an Essex zoo... seriously? Yet I desperately needed closure or at least the beginnings of it. I needed time and space to heal, not just from the loss of my wife but almost more importantly, the loss of the person I thought I knew. And this journey was, I felt, the first step towards that goal. I needed to prove to myself that there was nothing to find – no obscure messages and no more clues to chase. My best-case scenario would be to find nothing.

We drove in near silence which at times was more than a little awkward. Rachel spent most of the time messaging on her phone, absorbed in what must have been her normal life.

'So, now what?' she demanded as we entered the outskirts of the city. 'Where do you suggest we start?' As if I had the fucking answers.

During the drive down, between graphic flashbacks to the body in my shed and questioning my sanity, I'd compiled a list of places in and around the university where Ellie and I had shared moments, but I had no way of guessing which one, if any, may be significant. I couldn't shake the nagging feeling that I was missing something, some other clue amongst the stolen presents.

'I've got a few ideas, maybe I'll see something like I did in the giraffe house.' The most pathetic plan of action I'd ever heard, and Rachel jumped on it.

'*Seriously*? That's your master plan? Drive around until you *notice* something.' Her caustic tone set my teeth on edge.

'I told you not to come,' I hissed.

'Yeah, well I'm here now, so let's get on with it. Take me on a tour of your misspent youth, Dr Murray.' The growing gulf between us widened to canyon proportions as I swallowed a host of scathing retorts. There was no point in making the situation worse.

She sent yet another text as I pulled into one of the university car parks.

Our first stop was the library. Or least that's what I'd planned. 'This is where I first met Ellie, amongst the medical periodicals. We were both looking up information on juvenile arthritis. She shared the articles she'd found with me, and the rest, as they say, is history.' I narrated, as we walked towards the entrance, reliving our courtship. I hoped to sound flippant as a torrent of mixed emotions threatened to overwhelm me. This wasn't going to be as easy as I'd thought. Being back here was bringing all sorts of memories to the fore – things I hadn't thought about in years. Whoever orchestrated this macabre fishing expedition for me had a cruel and twisted sense of fun.

It wasn't long before we hit our first obstacle. I was no longer a student there, and I had no way of getting through the electronic barriers without a working ID card. We stood in the foyer looking lost.

'So this was an important place for both of you?' Rachel looked around dubiously, probably wondering how we were going to find a message in a library we couldn't even access. Unless there was a giant banner hanging from the ceiling announcing 'Ellie's message' in fluorescent paint, we were hopelessly searching for the proverbial needle.

'It was where we first met, but we came here loads of times during the years, both together and individually. But it was never that *special* to us, there was a nice view from the window upstairs where we'd meet when I was running late. I mean, it's just a library. I thought it was as good a place as any to start, that's all. I didn't realise we wouldn't even be able to get in.'

The silence between us stretched uncomfortably. We were both doing our best to be civil. For something to do, I woke up one of the computers in the foyer area and tried logging on with my very outdated student details. If my old email was active, perhaps there was a message there. The system didn't even recognise my username.

'Oh well, lots more places to try,' I announced with mock cheerfulness. I looked away quickly. I didn't fancy seeing Rachel's pissed off expression. I wondered how much an Uber back to London would cost for her before remembering that her car was back at my house.

For the next two and a half hours, I subjected Rachel to a tour of our favourite campus haunts. The coffee shop where we would meet between lectures, the campus nightclub where

Grad Ball took place, Ellie's first-year halls, our lecture theatres and labs, bus stops, a great pub where we'd shared our first real kiss, the gym, the pool, the woods behind the science block where we'd shared more than just a kiss.

After all of that, we retrieved the car and toured the student houses I had shared with friends during my five years at university, and the rugby pitch where Ellie watched me play a few times.

Around midday, we stopped for lunch at a local restaurant Ellie and I had frequented occasionally as students, and ate in mutually frustrated silence. It started raining softly on the drive over, and there was a briskness in the air as if winter was determined to hang on a little longer.

I sipped my soft drink and watched the lunch crowd – normal people enjoying their normal Saturday. No one here was searching for messages from their dead spouse while ducking psychotic murderers who left mutilated bodies in sheds. When had my *normal* life taken such a skewed turn?

I gave in to the recollections and let the past pour over me. We had shared so many good times, so much happiness. I was drawn to Ellie from the first time I saw her in the library, and soon we were inseparable. She'd been one of the most honest and open people I'd ever met – or so I thought. What an idiot I'd been. Now her lies and deceit threatened to shatter my heart, and I'd thought losing her in the accident was the worst pain I'd ever feel in my lifetime.

'So where to next?' Rachel broke my reverie. 'I mean, it's been fun and all, reliving your youth, but I'm not sure what we're achieving. I thought you'd have it all figured out. You seemed so sure you'd find something.'

I ignored the dig and shared yet another memory. 'You know Ellie and I had one of our biggest fights of all time in this pub. We'd only been going out a few months and came here for dinner after one of my rugby matches.' I didn't care if Rachel was paying attention. I couldn't fight the memories engulfing me.

'So what did you fight about?' she asked, more from a sense of duty than interest.

'Her scar, of all things. I asked her how she got it. She got very defensive, saying she was too young to remember and no one else was alive who could tell her. Actually, I offered to search her medical records and that's when she really lost it. Big time.'

'Her scar?'

'Yeah, well sort of. Ellie didn't mind her scar, she wasn't at all self-conscious about it, but she was adamant that I didn't look into her records. She even threatened to break up with me. I thought at the time that maybe she didn't want to relive it. Her childhood was miserable by all accounts so I understood why she maybe just wanted to put it all behind her.'

'You think she was hiding the truth? That she *did* know what happened to her face?'

'Ah hell, I have no idea,' I said, shrugging as I thought back. 'The weird thing is, a year or so later I did look at her records, just out of interest. I never told her because I knew she'd be furious. I guess I also kept secrets.' I swallowed hard, remembering I had kept that from her. But Ellie's secrets were huge in comparison. 'Not that it mattered, there was nothing to find. No mention of how or when or where she acquired the scar anyway. As far as I can remember, it just listed the usual run of the mill children's illnesses and a fall off a bike. There was no mention of the scar at all, which was odd. I couldn't understand why she'd got so furious at me that day.'

Rachel sipped her tonic water and picked at her scampi and chips, mulling over a suitable reply. I beat her to it.

'We hardly ever argued, you know. Not about important things anyway. Ellie was always so easy, so accommodating. Sometimes I used to think she only agreed to marry me so I'd stop pestering her...' I stopped as realisation dawned. There was one place I had inexplicably forgotten, and it was even signposted on the bloody CD in the Christmas presents.

I got up and went to pay the bill, abandoning Rachel at the table in front of our half-eaten meals.

We were in the wrong part of the city.

CHAPTER 40

Before – 1987

Elizabeth's future was bright. Her exams were finally over, her dissertation was complete and her Cambridge days were coming to an end. Her new life was just beginning, and this weekend was all about making Thomas Hudson part of that future.

They were off to the Norfolk Broads for the weekend and she was sure he would propose. And if he needed a little prompting, she was ready for that too. She'd secretly been off the pill for the last three months. She would become Mrs Thomas Hudson one way or another.

Halfway through her packing, the doorbell rang. Thomas was annoyingly early. Elizabeth checked her hair in the mirror and squeezed some colour into her pale cheeks.

Only it wasn't Thomas. Instead, his younger brother Robert stood on her doorstep, his short hair dishevelled and a wild, haunted look in his grey eyes. Robert gave her the creeps.

'Um, hi. Thomas isn't here.'

'I know. I came to see you. I have to speak to you. Can I come in?' He pushed past her into the small front room with the saggy couch.

'Robert, this really isn't a good time. Thomas is coming over soon and we're leaving for Norfolk.' She wasn't interested in whatever deluded nonsense he would try and unload on her this time. Nothing was going to ruin her special weekend.

'Elizabeth, you have to listen to me. Thomas isn't the man you think he is. He's no good for you.' Robert's aggressive tone sent a shiver down her spine.

Not his again, Elizabeth thought. Robert was always bad-mouthing his older brother. Their sibling relationship thrived on open animosity. 'Please, Robert, just go. I need to finish packing. We can talk about this next week.' Maybe once she and Thomas were engaged, he would finally let it go.

Robert shuffled from one foot to another, clearly agitated, and Elizabeth knew she wouldn't get rid of him until he had unloaded his latest anti-Thomas paranoia. Of course, she'd heard the rumours – Thomas had a reputation as a ladies' man. But all that was in the past. Now they were a couple. He'd settled down with his wild oats days well behind him.

'Elizabeth, I have to tell you something. It'll be painful but you have to listen to me,' he insisted.

Robert was on extended leave from the army; something to do with a misconduct enquiry or something. He was wasting her time and she wanted him to go. She needed to redo her makeup before Thomas arrived.

'Honestly, Robert, I'm not interested in anything you have to say. I'd like you to leave now, please.' Her tone was determined.

'I followed him today. I saw him. He was with *her*.' Robert was rambling and she didn't like what he was insinuating. 'He doesn't love you and he doesn't deserve you. He's with her right now. I saw them kissing on the doorstep.'

'Oh just stop it, Robert, please. Thomas loves me. We're going away and he's going to ask me to...'

His eyes flamed with anger and her words stuck in her throat. Why had she let him in?

'Love you?' he sneered. 'He doesn't love you. You're not listening. He's at her house. Right now. Another woman's house. Don't you get it? You're just the convenient heiress, a good business merger my father approves of and probably ordered.'

'Now you're talking rubbish. Why would you even say things like that? Of course, he loves me...' Elizabeth fought to put enough conviction in her voice. Thomas couldn't be with another woman, not today, could he? 'I want you to go,' she repeated.

'He will never love you, can't you see that? Not like I do. I'd never cheat on you. I would worship the ground—'

'Stop it, Robert. Stop this nonsense,' she interrupted. 'I love Thomas. Not you. I could never love *you*.'

Robert ignored her outburst. 'She's a lecturer, you know, at your precious university. Older, but still pretty. Not as beautiful as you though. Lives about ten minutes away, on Barley Road, very convenient for my dear brother.'

There was an edge to his voice and the first glimmers of panic stirred in Elizabeth's chest. Robert was taunting her, his words were poison-tipped barbs. They raked her heart with their truth.

Elizabeth took a deep breath to steady herself. She reminded herself that Thomas was an excellent catch, regardless. He was the heir to his father's estate and not just because he was the older brother. Everyone knew that Robert wasn't a 'true' Hudson; their late mother having had a scandalous affair, the result of which was the tall, irrational, strange man currently filling her lounge.

'That's enough. I've heard enough. Thomas is at the library, working. He told me. He wouldn't do this to me. I'd know.' The confidence drained from her words as she continued, 'I'm not interested in his past. Our future together is all that matters. Now for the last time, Robert, I'm asking you to *leave*.' Elizabeth kept her voice steady. Robert seemed more obsessive today than usual.

'His past? Are you kidding me? You're an idiot, Lizzie. This is happening right now. He is fucking her right this very minute. And you need to face—'

'Get out. GET OUT!' Elizabeth shrieked, no longer able to contain her fury or fractured emotions. 'Thomas would never cheat on me.' Involuntary tears slid over her cheeks. 'You're nothing but a jealous bastard, Robert. You've always been jealous of Thomas and now that we're going to be married you ca—'

He hit her.

Elizabeth had never been struck as an adult. Her hand flew to her face in disbelief.

'He does not love you.' Robert's words reverberated off the walls. He gripped her shoulders, seemingly intent on making her understand his brother's infidelity and the depth of his love towards her. The look on his face frightened her, Robert was enjoying this. He was enjoying her pain and her humiliation.

Elizabeth felt weak with shock as Robert towered over her, his breath warm on her face and his hands preventing her escape, bruising her arms. Anxiety gurgled in her stomach.

'Robert, please, let go of me,' she protested quietly.

'Why won't you listen? Why can't you see the truth? He's just using you. I love you. Only I can love you.'

Everything was escalating alarmingly quick. Elizabeth managed to wrestle her right arm free and struck him across the face with surprising strength that was fuelled by her mounting fear.

He barely flinched, but his expression changed. His grey eyes burnt with a cold, emotionless fire.

Thomas had hinted to her about his brother's sociopathic tendencies, how Robert had been haunted since their mother's suicide and father's intolerable disinterest. He'd explained how this had left Robert with uncontrollable anger that surfaced from time to time, but Elizabeth had always dismissed the stories.

She was beginning to realise that Thomas hadn't been exaggerating. And now, Robert was jealous. Jealous of Thomas and their relationship. Jealous that they had found happiness together. He knew now he would always be the second-best brother.

And she also realised, in that terrifying moment, that Robert was here to take what he believed – in his deluded state – was his.

He lurched forward and grabbed a handful of Elizabeth's hair, twirling it around in his strong fingers. He dragged her, flailing and screaming, into the bedroom. He was oblivious to her shrieks of pain and dread.

Robert hurled her onto the neatly made bed and loomed over her cowering body. He reached down and tore at her silk blouse, sending delicate pearl buttons scattering across the floor. He'd snagged her lacy bra in the process, ripping it apart. Elizabeth screamed and covered her naked breasts with her arms. Her body trembling in terror beneath his gaze.

He hit her again.

This time it wasn't a slap, but a fierce punch that split her lip and left her head reeling.

'Robert no. Please. No.' She pleaded and squirmed beneath his immovable body, but Robert had become unreachable. His eyes were icy cold and glazed with cruel purpose.

He ruched up her tartan skirt above her waist, momentarily mesmerised by the sight of her slender feminine hips. As he gripped her lace panties, Robert felt the quiver of her repulsion shudder through her at his touch. Her reaction just spurred him on, building on the hatred that seethed, unchecked, inside him. He ripped the flimsy material from her body, balling it up and shoving it deep into her mouth as she whined and sobbed.

'Shut up you stupid bitch or I'll shove it right down your fucking throat. You think you're too good for me, don't you? I'll show you who's the better brother. I'll show you what a real man feels like.' He reached to undo his belt. 'Thomas won't be here for hours, sweetie, he's with his whore. We have the whole afternoon to *play*.' His words drained her of any fight she may have had left. He was strong, powerful and vicious beyond her understanding.

Elizabeth lay shivering under his weight, her spirit broken. She knew she would never be the same woman again.

CHAPTER 41

Finn

Mo's Café was down a side street near the cruise boat terminal, and it buzzed with a lively lunchtime crowd. The windows were hazy with condensation as the heat generated inside met with the cooling spring air outside. I all but pushed Rachel through the door.

The steamy café was loud with clashing plates and competing voices, and it was filled with the smells of burgers and strong coffee. I spotted an empty table and steered Rachel towards it. Truckers and family groups rubbed shoulders as trays of food fought their way out of the kitchen.

Mo's had always been popular in Southampton, but it was in no way a student hangout. When Ellie and I had first started dating, she used to work here as often as her hospital shifts and lecture schedule allowed. Ellie had an NHS bursary to pay for her nursing course and accommodation, but with no family to support her, she needed a job on the side for any other spending money. She'd lost touch with the Graingers and wouldn't have wanted to take their money even if they had offered.

'More food? You're joking, right?' Rachel's tone was understandably annoyed. I'd refused to answer any questions she had on the way over regarding our double-quick exit from the restaurant, too consumed with the whirlwind of thoughts competing for attention in my brain. Why the hell hadn't I thought of this place before? Would there be another clue here? And if so, what would it lead me to? And to whom? Thankfully, she'd been too engrossed in her phone to push me on it.

I motioned for Rachel to sit and handed her a menu encouragingly. I owed her an explanation, but I wasn't sure where to start.

'Ellie used to work here,' I began, opening my menu to give me something to do. I was surprised to see how little it had changed – all-day breakfasts, chips with everything and a surprisingly wide selection of homemade cakes still made up the bulk of choices.

'When? During Uni?' Rachel sat down reluctantly, taking a little more interest in her surroundings.

'Yeah, to supplement her income. She enjoyed working here and this place was always special. Oh and the bloody CD even told me to come here,' I added ruefully.

'What? The *Wham!* music? You're joking, right?' I ignored her scornful tone, hopeful that I was finally on to something. Her frustration with our total lack of progress had been growing steadily.

'It's a long story—' A waiter appeared at our table with a friendly, if slightly harassed smile and notepad in hand, ready to take our order. Rachel ordered her obligatory pot of tea, and I settled for a coffee and a slice of carrot cake I had no intention of eating.

Now that I was here, I was no closer to understanding

what it was that I was looking for than before. I had a growing feeling of dread that I was going to find nothing except more painful memories – memories I was nowhere near ready to face.

'Start talking Finn. What are we doing here? As quaint as it is…' Rachel looked around with apparent disdain. She was losing patience with me fast, and this place obviously didn't measure up to her trendy London wine bars.

'Right, well… so, as I said, we met in the library and spent most of our time together on campus as students.' I was stalling, nervously questioning the logic of coming here. It had sounded so perfect inside my head, but would saying it out loud make it nonsensical?

I took a deep, uncertain breath. 'Even when Ellie gave up working here, we always came back. It's cheap and the carrot cake is seriously good. It was definitely one of our 'special places'.' I threw up the air quotes just as our waiter unpacked his tray. He gave me an odd look as he thumped down my coffee, his dark ginger curls sticking damply to his forehead.

Rachel began fussing with her tea and asked, 'So this was a significant venue? More so than the numerous others we visited today? And how exactly did the CD tell you this?'

Her stark cynicism hit me hard. A sense of hopeless isolation in a crowded restaurant threatened to overwhelm me. Instead, I forged ahead, compelled by pride to justify our being here.

'This is where I asked Ellie to marry me. It's where I proposed. It's where she said yes. Where she promised to be my wife and to love me forever.' My voice choked embarrassingly and the familiar sting of tears prickled behind my eyes.

'Oh God, Finn, I'm so sorry. None of this can be easy. But why didn't we come here earlier? Of course this place is important.' Her compassion sounded almost genuine.

'I don't know,' I answered honestly. It's what I'd been asking myself on the drive over from the restaurant. Now we were here it was so blatantly obvious. Had I been subconsciously avoiding it, knowing how gut-wrenchingly difficult it would be?

Rachel's sympathetic understanding didn't last too long. 'So how was the CD relevant? How exactly are they connected?' she questioned me in her typical lawyer-ish manner.

'I told you my mum loved *Wham!*, and Ellie was subjected to listening to it whenever she came to stay with my folks, which happened a lot. She soon spent Christmasses and Easters with us, and summer holidays if she wasn't working. She didn't have anywhere else to go and my parents loved having her. There was a track on that CD called... um... *Young Guns* I think. And it talks about marriage... and not in a good way, but Ellie loved the song and her and my mum would dance around the kitchen singing...' I stopped and gulped my scalding-hot coffee. This was too fucking hard.

Rachel took my hand and gripped it firmly until I eventually looked up. My pseudo-Ellie stared back at me, willing me to continue.

'It was sort of our song, and it's about getting married and giving up your friends and stuff. So when I wanted to propose, I spoke to Mo and he...'

'What? *Mo* is real?' she interrupted, lost, annoyingly, in

irrelevant details.

'Yes he's real, and he was super-fond of Ellie when she worked here, so he was happy to help,' I sputtered, giving her the *Reader's Digest* version, afraid that if I was interrupted again, I'd lose my nerve completely. 'I asked Mo to help me set it all up. The place was almost empty and he played the *Wham!* song when I went down on one knee. Cheesy as hell, but Ellie loved it.'

I stopped, unable to say more.

'So you proposed here, in this café?' She waved her arms around, her look of disdain highlighting how different Ellie and Rachel were. Ellie thought it was the most romantic thing ever. At least that's what she told me. 'So the song was special, but now what? Is there anything here? Would this Mo character know anything?'

'I doubt it, as far as I know, they lost touch years ago. I was so sure there would be something obvious to find here.'

Rachel clearly wasn't at all convinced, but did a good job of looking around the café. There wasn't much to see. The limited wall space was painted an industrial grey and for the most part, it was devoid of any artwork or decorations. It wasn't that sort of place. And for Rachel, this was just one too many stops on the Finn and Ellie memory trail. Her phone pinged yet again and she quickly read the message. Our friendship had nosedived way past the level where I could ask who was constantly messaging her. Although she was sitting right opposite me, I felt terribly disconnected. This was my problem, and if Rachel had better things to do...

Wiping the dampness from my eyes and mentally pulling myself together, I went up to the counter. Maybe Mo would have a message for me after all. Could it be that easy?

Our waiter was standing at the cash register and seemed to be watching me. He looked a little familiar and I wondered if I knew him from somewhere, maybe back in my uni days. I couldn't place him.

'Hi, is Mo here? Could I have a quick word?' I asked him as he handed me my bill. 'I'm an old friend.' A *slight* exaggeration.

'Ah, sorry mate. Mo sold up and moved away years ago. The new owners decided to keep the name. Hah, you know how important a name is, right?'

'Yeah right,' I answered distractedly. 'Oh and did anyone perhaps leave anything here for me? I don't know what, like a letter or a message? My name's Finn Murray.'

He looked back at the table where I'd left Rachel sitting before answering. 'No mate, there's nothing here – and I would know. Is there anything else I can help you with?'

Feeling a little foolish and unsure what else to ask, I shook my head and handed over a twenty for the coffee, not looking at the printed bill. The waiter shook the ginger curls from his face as he gathered my change and handed it back with the bill which he had folded neatly.

'Listen mate, you'll want to check the bill once you're outside.'

I was too preoccupied for his words to register – something had caught my eye. I'd left my phone on the table and now Rachel was fiddling with it. She must have sensed that I'd spotted her because she quickly placed it back on my side of the table.

I pocketed the change and the bill, unsure of what I'd just

seen. Rachel stood and headed to the toilets at the back of the café. I mouthed 'nothing here' and tipped my head to indicate I'd wait outside. As I walked out, I scanned the interior one last time but came up depressingly empty.

With no Mo and no messages in the café, I was entirely out of options. Mo's had been my last ditch gamble and I'd been so sure – but there was nothing. Just another dead end and I had no idea where to look next. It was time to go home.

I stood outside in the soft rain, breathing in the fresh, clean air and fighting growing waves of disappointment and misery. Was I so desperate to believe that there would be something here because I couldn't accept a life without Ellie? I flashed back to the handful of pills I'd nearly used to end it all. Surely that would have been the easier way.

Then the waiter's words echoed back through my head. I took out the bill, unfolded it and found some words scribbled at the bottom.

Meet me at the prawn bin. At 6. Lose the girl.

Come ALONE.

Don't get followed.

H

CHAPTER 42

Rachel joined me on the pavement just as I stuffed the note back inside my pocket. Her phone was still in her hand and she looked a little agitated.

'Finn, listen this has been fun, but I don't honestly think we're getting anywhere. A friend from London just messaged me and needs my help. Would you mind if I trained home and picked up my car tomorrow sometime? I really need to get back there and help them out.' Her eyes stayed glued to the pavement as she spoke. I'd heard some bullshit stories in my life and this ranked up there with the worst.

'Yeah, of course, no worries. Hope your friend's okay. Shall I drop you at the station? I think I might as well call it a day anyway, there's nothing here but old memories. Think I'll head down and visit my parents. They've been nagging me for weeks.' I could lie my arse off too and at least mine sounded more genuine than her 'friend-in-need' crap.

'Er, yeah that would be great, if you don't mind. So you're giving up on Southampton and heading off to Kent? Will you go straight down—' She paused as a car whizzed past, noisily interrupting her. 'Or have you got more places to check first? I feel bad bailing, but my friend—'

'Honestly, it's fine. There's nowhere else I can think of to try, and if I leave now I'll beat the traffic. Thanks so much for coming with me, Rachel, I really do appreciate it. I'm just sorry it wasn't more productive. At least my mum will be thrilled to see me.' My need to deceive her took me by surprise. Was it just the note or her weird change in behaviour that was feeding my paranoia?

We didn't talk much on the short drive to the station. I thanked her again for giving up her day off and she waffled on about her needy friend and even read out the text she'd sent telling him/her (she hadn't been gender-specific) that she was on her way. Before she got out of the car, she leaned over and kissed my cheek and I felt her warm hand on my chest. Completely out of character. And then she was gone.

I sat for a moment, gathering my thoughts. She wasn't the most demonstrative person I'd ever met.

Next thing I knew, I'd jumped out of the car and was sprinting after her. Rachel had left her scarf on the front seat. The next train to London left in five minutes from platform two – she should have been waiting for it, but then I spotted her across the tracks. She was climbing into the passenger door of a silver utility van. There was writing on the side, but I couldn't make it out from this distance. It looked like a handyman's vehicle of some sort.

The angle of the van meant I couldn't get a clear look at the driver, but I could see that they were sat talking as the London bound train pulled into the station. I turned to leave, totally confused. Who did she know in Southampton? I knew why I was misleading her but I couldn't work out why she had lied to me. I didn't believe for one minute that meeting this van man was anything to do with her needy friend story. I jogged back to my car, her scarf still in tow. I'd give it back to her tomorrow. Besides, right now I had other things to do.

With a couple of hours to kill before I was due to meet with the mysterious 'H', I used my phone to google directions to the nearest café with good WIFI. Over a particularly strong latte, I did a little untraceable research, disappointed I hadn't thought to do it earlier.

At half-past five, I parked the car in the multi-storey car park and headed into West Quay shopping centre. It looked a little tired now even though it still contained a movie complex and a few floors of shops and restaurants.

On the first floor, there was a small restaurant where Ellie and I had celebrated my birthday one year. It was nothing special, but it turned out to be quite a memorable evening for all the wrong reasons. I'd had the prawn linguine, and as we left the restaurant, I began to feel extremely ill; sweating, nauseous, light-headed. Ellie quickly led me towards the nearest public toilets, but I knew I wouldn't make it. In desperation, I found a rubbish bin and proceeded to empty the contents of my stomach into that. It was not a pretty sight. Barely-digested prawns and wine-soaked spaghetti filled the grubby plastic receptacle.

It wasn't a big deal, probably just a bad prawn, and I felt better almost immediately, but to the two of us the bin became known as my 'prawn bin', and we used it occasionally as a landmark when meeting up. It was nothing more than one of those stupid jokes you share as a couple. I certainly couldn't remember ever telling anyone about it. Obviously Ellie had.

It certainly seemed that 'H' knew all about my infamous prawn vomit. But who the fuck was 'H'? Was he going to turn out to be the infamous Harry Grainger? God, I hoped so. Then I could finally get some answers out of the bastard who seemed to have played an integral part in both Ellie's former life and her death. Then I planned to break his goddamn interfering neck. I just hoped his answers were going to be things I could cope with hearing.

The seafood restaurant was gone, replaced with a trendy tapas bar, so maybe I wasn't the only one who they had tried to poison with their dodgy shellfish. I carried on going and was pleasantly surprised to find my bin exactly where I'd remembered it – near the entrance to a corridor with a sign for the public toilets above its entrance.

The shops were still open and people were drifting into restaurants for early pre-movie dinners. I leant against the wall near the bin and started watching the people as they rushed past, laden down with shopping bags.

'Are you alone? Where's the woman? Were you followed?' The waiter's nervous voice sounded in my ear. He'd managed to sneak up on me and was standing on my left. He wasn't looking at me. I felt terribly foolish as I tried to emulate every bad spy movie I'd ever watched, barely fighting the urge to answer out of the corner of my mouth.

'She went back to London. And I know shit about being followed, but I don't think I was. So now what? Who are you? How do you know about this bin? I need some answers—'

'Not here. Go into the toilets, find a stall but leave the door unlocked and I'll come find you.'

'You've got to be kidding me. In the men's toilets?' I could see the headlines now: *Doctor and waiter caught in a compromising situation in a public convenience.* 'Can't we just go to the tapas bar and chat? I could do with a dr—'

'The men's toilets,' he interrupted. '*Now.* If I'm not there in ten minutes, then run and don't stop. I need to make sure you weren't followed.'

'Run? Run where? And who would be following me?' I asked, but he'd walked off and was standing with his back to me at the railings, watching the escalators. I hesitated, trying to weigh up my options. Waiting in a toilet stall for this melodramatic waiter wasn't my preferred course of action, but if I wanted to hear what he had to say there seemed no other choice. I genuinely believed he could have the answers I craved so desperately.

I turned and headed for the toilets, wondering when I should start timing the ten minutes. I really wasn't cut out for this cloak and dagger bullshit.

CHAPTER 43

The toilet stall was claustrophobic. I stood looking at the door, feeling like a total idiot. The toilets were old and less than pristine. There were only two stalls and both were occupied when I'd rushed in. I took my time at the urinals until one became available.

I tried to listen for sounds on the other side of the door but the bathroom now seemed empty. I had stupidly lost all sense of time, and the whole 'wait ten minutes' thing had gone out the window. I stood uncomfortably inside the stall with sweat leaking down my back, breathing in ammonia-laced stale air and wondering for the hundredth time what alternative universe I'd been catapulted into. And where the hell was Harry? If that's who he was.

Again I thought about just heading home, but the man had known who I was and about my prawn bin and only Ellie could have told him about that. He was someone who knew Ellie – someone who, worryingly, seemed to know more about her than I did.

I heard a noise outside moments before the door crashed open. I stepped back, hitting the back of my knees on the toilet bowl and nearly losing my balance.

'Come on, we need to go.' The red-haired waiter seemed

to be beside himself, pale, flustered and breathing heavily.

'Go where? What's happening for fuck's sake?'

'What's happening is you were fucking followed mate. Now enough with the questions, we need to move.'

He grabbed my elbow and pulled me out of the stall. The bathroom was empty. My waiter seemed to be suffering from an extreme case of paranoia.

Instead of rushing out of the door and back to the shopping centre, the man pulled an oddly-shaped key from his pocket and opened a small, barely-noticeable door that sat flush with the wall.

'*Move!* Come on, get inside and start running. I'm right behind you,' he instructed, half pushing me through the narrow opening and locking the door behind us.

'How did you do that? And the key?'

'I wasn't always a waiter, mate. Now for fuck's sake, get a move on – Robert's coming.'

Robert's name had the desired effect and I legged it into a dimly lit service corridor. The man's footsteps thudded behind me, pushing me to pick up my pace. There wasn't enough space to run side by side and it was impossible to ask questions, so I just put my head down and ran. The maintenance corridor was grimy and was full of paint tins, ladders and other assorted junk. It was like running an obstacle course.

It widened a little around a corner and he took full advantage of the space, pushing in front of me. He mumbled that he needed to lead the way. Once he was past, he took off at a full sprint and I had to work to keep up.

The passageway began to reveal options left and right;

a sort of maze that must have encompassed the entire mall. I tried to keep track of our route, but I soon became hopelessly confused. *He*, on the other hand, was very sure of where we were heading and didn't hesitate at a single junction.

After a series of turns that left my head spinning, he stopped and I ploughed into the back of him. Ahead lay a dead end and another door. He used his key again, opened the door and stepped through it. I followed, and as I looked around, I was vaguely aware of him re-locking the door. We were out of the passageway and seemed to be in a dark corner of the car park.

Maybe it was time for me to find my car, drive home and see a therapist instead of chasing ghosts with an unknown waiter.

'Come on.' The man took hold of my elbow again, but this time I'd had enough.

'No fucking way.' I planted my feet, determined, questions pouring out unchecked. 'Not until I know who you are. How do you know Robert is here? And what the fuck does he want? What's any of this got to do with Ellie? How did you even know her?' Even saying the last question out loud felt like a punch in the gut. I didn't think I would cope if I learnt they'd been secret lovers for all these years.

'It's not what you think. We should go somewhere safe and talk.' He looked me in the eye and sighed. 'But you have to know, I've always loved Ellie.'

Before conscious thought could intervene, I hit him in the mouth with all my pent up frustration. He went down hard on the rough concrete floor.

I shook my hand, my bruised knuckles stinging. There

was blood oozing from where I'd split his lip. Slowly, he stood up and held out his hand, introducing himself as we were meeting at a cocktail party. I fought the desire to knock him straight back down on his arse. I needed to give him a chance to explain, but he'd only get about three seconds.

'Let's start again, shall we mate? My name's Harry. Harry Grainger. I'm Ellie's foster brother. And *you*, of course, are Finn.' His words lisped a little, his lip already swelling. My head began to spin. Harry was real and he was standing in front of me. I had to know: 'Did you help Ellie drive into the tree? Did you kill her?'

'Don't get mad, okay? And don't hit me again. But yes, I was there,' he answered quietly, his expression impossible to read in the dim light. Time stopped and I forgot to breathe. Logical thought regressed to an instant primal need to inflict pain on another human being. The man in front of me had just admitted to murdering my wife. I stepped forward, my left arm cocked, my fists tight... that's when I saw movement over his shoulder.

I recognised Robert immediately and froze in shock. He was standing less than a metre behind Harry and was holding a gun. Although pistol-shaped, it looked odd and vaguely familiar, with a yellow bulbous end to the barrel. It wasn't a gun, it was a taser. The police had run a workshop for A&E staff about tasers and their effects last May.

I wanted to call out and warn Harry, but like slow-motion footage, I watched as two barbs catapulted from the yellow barrel, trailing coils of wire behind them. They connected somewhere on Harry's back and he gave a high-pitched yelp.

The effect was instantaneous as the high voltage surged through his body. He trembled violently before losing all his motor ability. I watched in horror as his limbs failed and he began to slump towards the hard ground. Instinct and stupidity made me lunge forward to cushion his fall, and my outstretched arms that were ready to pulverise his face milliseconds before, now reached out and took his weight, holding him semi-upright.

He continued to convulse violently in my arms and it took all my strength not to drop him. The unspent electricity flowed through him and into me, leaving an odd taste at the back of my throat. The doctor in me wanted to lay Harry down gently and assess his injuries, but my pragmatic side wanting to throw his body into Robert's smug face, who was still depressing the trigger of the taser, and run like fuck.

'Stop it you arsehole, he's unconscious. That's enough. You'll kill him.' I was surprised my voice worked at all. It was getting harder to hold Harry and I could feel the overload of current beginning to weaken my own muscles. But I couldn't just let him fall, and that also meant I couldn't move. We stood frozen in time like a macabre sculpture.

Robert lifted his finger off the trigger. Harry sagged completely and I struggled to support his dead weight. The barbs were still stuck through his shirt and embedded in his flesh.

'Carry him to the van or I taser him again. This time I won't stop until he's dead. The choice is yours.' Robert's voice cut through my fear and I watched his finger hover near the trigger guard. Harry wasn't moving in my arms, and except for some residual muscle spasms, he was completely out of it. His breathing was worryingly shallow. His heart wouldn't cope with another surge of electricity. I again considered throwing his body towards Robert and running, but my arms were shaking with fatigue and felt pathetically weak. Robert seemed to read my thoughts.

'Don't even think about it, Murray,' he warned, taking a small step backwards, careful not to dislodge the barbs in Harry's back. 'Carry him to the van. It's just around the corner.'

'He needs medical attention,' I pleaded desperately. I couldn't abandon him even if he had killed Ellie. I'd taken an oath.

'In the van and then you can help him, or I give him another jolt and he dies right here. I only need *you* alive, Murray. Now move.'

CHAPTER 44

Tom's plan to have Finn and Robert killed and to claim back the trust fund had backfired. It was only a matter of time. He felt a fear so intrinsic and so familiar that it invaded his core. His entire being flooding with panic. His brother had found them.

Tom had used the dark web – something he knew little about but believed to be secure – to recruit an assassin. He had chosen poorly and the man had failed. Worse than that, Robert had caught him.

Tom had opened his email account expecting to hear of his recruit's successful mission, only to find a horrific video waiting for him instead. It depicted the poor man being brutally tortured – Robert's unsubtle way of letting his older brother know he was coming for him. So Tom had run again. Another quiet Airbnb further up the coast, another change of name, another excuse as to why they preferred to pay cash.

But he knew his precautions couldn't prevent the inevitable, and besides, Thomas was too old and too tired to keep running. He could no longer keep Elizabeth safe. She would never be safe.

Tom needed a new plan. Robert would come, if not today, then soon, and he would hurt Elizabeth. His brother was nothing if not predictable when he was angry, and he would be very, very angry to discover how Thomas had thwarted him so ingeniously all those years ago.

After Robert's attack on the children, Thomas began to painstakingly plan their escape. He'd evaluated several options including emigrating, but he knew that Robert would never give up searching for them all the while he believed they were out there somewhere. So, he devised a strategy where Robert would no longer feel the need to hunt them down at all.

First, Benjamin was sent to one of Elizabeth's distant cousins in Canada, but the family were only able to take one child on the understanding that there would never be any further contact. The ruse worked perfectly, even though it had broken their hearts. Even the lawyer didn't know Benjamin had survived. Next, Tom arranged for Eleanor to be taken into care, the second-worst day of his life, and today would be the third – the last.

He couldn't take it anymore. He was bone-weary of constantly looking over his shoulder. He had spent his life trying to protect his wife and children, and he had failed miserably.

Eleanor had stayed nearer home, easier to watch over and to follow from afar, but all that had achieved was to put a target on her back for Robert to aim at. That and the trust fund he'd set up in her name. He had honestly believed that by the time Eleanor turned thirty, the risk she faced from Robert would be negligible. That mistake had cost his beautiful daughter her life. Tom was no longer in any doubt that Robert had killed her, causing that horrendous car crash in an ironic copy of how Tom himself had orchestrated their pseudo-deaths. So cruelly typical.

Now, Tom was conceding defeat. But while Robert had won, Tom would not give his brother the pleasure of causing them any more physical or emotional pain. He still had a duty to protect Liz. His mind was made up. There would be no more running.

His only regret was that he couldn't stop Robert from getting his hands on Eleanor's trust fund. If Robert and Finn weren't working together, then Robert would have killed the man and taken the money for himself somehow. Of this, Tom was absolutely convinced.

He had thought about warning Finn, but couldn't think how without giving himself away. With so much money being dangled before him, Tom doubted that Finn would even listen to his story of long-dead parents and a murderous, vindictive uncle. And if Finn had anything to do with Eleanor's death, then he deserved everything that was coming for him.

Back at the new Airbnb, Tom found Elizabeth quiet and subdued, but at least she was showered and dressed. She was confused about all the moving around, but was trying hard to stay positive.

As the lazy spring sun began to dip into the ocean off the Essex coast, Thomas led his wife out onto the shale-hard beach. It was almost deserted with only a few dog walkers as their companions. He would wait for them to leave.

A stiff evening breeze was picking up as he and Elizabeth sat huddled together, looking out to sea. Elizabeth leant back into him, for once calm and almost serene. Perhaps she knew it was all coming to an end, all the fear and constant worry. More likely it was just the effect of the sleeping pills he had slipped into her afternoon medications, making her more compliant.

He hadn't discussed his latest decision with her. He would never have been able to find the words. It was better this way. She would be the victim of his choices once more, but then it would all be over. Thomas had taken her youth, her happiness, her children, and now he would take her life – or what was left of it now that they had lost Eleanor.

Feeling Elizabeth's body against his, Tom felt an old stirring and considered taking her behind the huts on the now empty-beach to make love to her one last time. But that would only be for his gratification – she would just lie there, disappearing into her lost world, unresponsive. To his shame, he had used her like that before, on occasion, where his physical need outstripped his self-control.

Instead, he wrapped his arm around her protectively, his hand soft on her thigh. With his other hand, he adjusted the uncomfortably heavy diving weight belt that was fastened around his waist.

The sun was dropping fast now; a radiant orange ball, dripping like a flare, falling into the darkening sea.

He gently urged Liz to her feet. He had researched this stretch of the coast. There was a strong riptide that ran full strength around dusk, and it would more than suit his purpose.

If their bodies ever washed ashore they would be miles from here. Elizabeth wore heavy shoes and a thick wool cardigan, and she was a weak swimmer – still, he took no chances. She wouldn't cope alone without him. Robert would find her and inflict his sadistic rage on her. They were forever joined by their sad existence. He slipped the cord from her dressing gown around their wrists, fastening it tightly, then he took her hand. She barely noticed the cord's gentle bite as he led her down to the water's edge.

Tom struggled to walk with the weights, and took a breather as the waves began to lap lightly around their feet.

'We're getting wet,' Liz observed groggily, with no alarm in her voice. Once again, Tom wondered if he should have discussed his decision, but he didn't think he could have made her understand their complete lack of options. No, this was the best course of action; there was no other way to keep her safe.

He tested the knot of the dressing gown cord. The weights would take him under and keep him there, and Elizabeth would have no choice but to follow.

Thomas and Elizabeth began walking into the sea as the sun slipped below the horizon, its light and warmth disappearing from the world.

CHAPTER 45

Finn

T he sun shone uncomfortably warm and bright, the harsh glare forcing my eyes tightly shut. I'd given up reading the novel I'd bought at the airport and lay listening to the waves gently swishing, lullaby-like in the background. Ellie was in the sea, calling me to join her, but I was too comfy lying on the sand and couldn't be arsed to move. She wouldn't give up, calling my name and even coming out of the water to nudge me in the chest.

I forced open a reluctant eye. The sea and sun melted away as confusion and dread flooded into its place.

There was no beach and no Ellie.

I was lying awkwardly on a hard metal surface. It was stiflingly hot and the sound of the ocean was, in reality, the sound of a car engine. I was in the back of a moving vehicle and I wasn't alone. Harry was lying next to me in the confined space. It was him nudging me and calling my name.

'Finn! FINN! Wake up for fuck's sake!' His urgency fuelled my panic. I tried to sit up but it just wasn't happening. My hands were pulled behind my back and I felt hard plastic strips bite into my wrists. Bits of memory came back to me – Harry tasered into unconsciousness, falling, Robert standing behind him, me dragging Harry's dead weight around the corner, the open double doors of a waiting silver van.

'We have to get out of here, Finn. You *need* to wake up.'

I shook my head to clear away the fog – a serious mistake. A concrete brick bounced around the inside of my skull. I didn't remember the impact that caused this pain. My throat was dry and my shoulders were cramping – oh how I wanted to drift back to my fictional beach.

'Where are we? How do we get out?' Stupid questions. Harry's hands were also fastened behind his back. We were fucked. The van was closed in; there were no windows in the sides or doors and our compartment was shut off from the cab. We were handcuffed in a small metal box, whizzing along some road with Robert driving, presumably. I knew this wasn't going to end well, which had my stomach churning with dread. The only light seeping in was from around the doors, and it came and went as car headlights shone through. We were trapped with no way out.

Harry, however, had other ideas. 'Next time we stop, we have to move. Start getting some feeling into your legs. You'll need to be ready to run. We can't let him get us out of the city.' His voice was barely audible above the swoosh of tires on tarmac.

'Run where? How?' He ignored me as he busied himself with his bound hands.

'What are you doing?' I hissed. I started flexing my leg muscles just in case Harry had a real workable plan.

'I've got a small blade in the waistband of my trousers.

I'll be free in a minute and then I'll cut you loose.'

'A blade in your... what kind of waiter are you?'

'Roll over.'

I felt the sharp blade nick my skin in his haste, but then my hands were free. We both sat rubbing our wrists and collecting our thoughts. My head was throbbing in time with my racing pulse, but adrenalin was keeping the pain manageable. I could see the sheen of fresh blood on Harry's hands. Cutting through the plastic cuffs behind his back must have been trickier than it looked.

The gears grated and the van shuddered as it slowed. Harry moved towards the back doors and I followed him less confidently; my legs felt wobbly and the thought of running made my mouth go dry.

The van rolled to a stop. Above the idle engine, I could hear music on the radio and the sound of other traffic. It was now or never. Harry quietly turned the handle to open the door. Considering he'd been electrocuted to within inches of his life, he was coping remarkably well.

'Ready?' he whispered, not looking back at me. I nodded, but by then he'd already flung the door open and jumped down. I followed, landing hard on the tarmac and almost stumbling into the car queuing behind us. The driver stared open-mouthed as the two of us flew out of the back of the van and ran off. I looked over my shoulder and saw that the van we'd escaped from was silver.

Honking horns and shouting heralded our escape. We were at a large junction with a petrol station opposite us and we were surrounded by a motley collection of houses and shops. I set off after Harry's fast departing form.

Harry weaved between the cars on the petrol station forecourt before heading past the carwash and out the back. We sprinted down a street. Fast. I could easily match his speed for now, but Harry looked like a runner – a 'marathons are super fun' sort of runner. His sinewy legs were eating up the ground. He started taking lefts and rights; the blocks were short and we changed direction several times as we headed out of a housing estate and carried on through an industrial park. His pace wasn't slowing and he didn't look like he was ready to stop anytime soon.

We both kept checking back for the van and Robert, but no one seemed to be following us – yet. Trees and fields of spring wheat slowly took the place of suburbia, and we left the roads, jumped (or in my case fell over) a stile, and headed across a newly ploughed field to a small cluster of trees.

It was much darker away from the city lights and being in amongst the trees made me feel safer. Besides, I was fed up with running. I caught up with Harry and jerked him to a stop. I wasn't going to carry on following the man regardless. I wanted answers and a plan, and more than anything I wanted my normality back. That involved an existence that didn't include being shackled in a van and having to run for my life.

'What the—'

'I'm not going any further… Harry… not until you tell me… what's going on.' I was breathing so hard that my words were coming out in spurts, like bullets from a gun. 'Explain what you said… about Ellie. Why did you kill my wife?'

'Not here. We need to keep going.'

'NO!' I shrieked desperately, holding onto his arm as he turned to go. He may have been able to out-run me, but I was a head taller and a lot heavier. I took some deep breaths to gain control of my ragged breathing. 'I'm not going any further. You either killed her or helped her die and at the very least I deserve to know why. If you don't start talking, then I'll take you back and hand you over to Robert myself.'

Harry paused and we glared at each other in the pale moonlight that was managing to shine through gaps in the gathering clouds. Soon he relaxed and the fight went out of him.

He tugged his arm away, stepped over to a tree stump and slumped down on it, his black brogues incongruous on the leaf-covered mud. Once I felt sure he wouldn't run off again, I leant up against the nearest tree, desperate to see the expression on his face when he told me how he'd helped Ellie die. Then I was going to kill him. His little hidden blade wouldn't save him this time.

Leaning against this tree reminded me of Ellie's – her makeshift shrine and the closeness that I felt to her there. This tree, in some arbitrary wood in the middle of God knows where, offered me nothing.

'I was with her when her car hit the tree...' he hesitated and then lifted his head, looking me straight in the eye.

'Finn, Ellie's not dead.'

My entire universe flipped 180 degrees.

CHAPTER 46

Before. November last year.

R obert slid the knife from its sheath and held it flat against his thigh, savouring its weight. It was by far his favourite and had served him well through the years. Statue-still, he waited for his prey.

He watched as the woman struggled through the heavy fire door that led from the shopping centre into the quiet, almost-empty underground car park. She was burdened with bags of shopping and appeared distracted, unaware of his presence behind the thick concrete pillar to her left.

Robert rehearsed the plan in his head – get the bitch in the car, question her, kill her, take her purse to mislead the police and walk away. Job done.

Doubt unexpectedly bloomed in his brain. Would a quick death redress the humiliation and shame his brother's sickeningly cunning duplicity has caused him? For years he had believed they were all dead, but Eleanor was still very much alive and was the very embodiment of their transgressions against him.

He watched as she crossed the car park, juggling her purchases and trying to find her keys. A roll of Christmas wrapping paper escaped her clutches, rolling under her car. He heard her swear softly before setting down her bags to scramble after it. Silently he moved behind her.

Robert flashed the knife quickly and she caught the metallic glint in her peripheral vision before it settled sharply under her chin.

'Not a sound, my dear.' His voice was low and charged with animalistic anticipation. 'You scream, you die. Right here in this car park. Nod that you understand.' Eleanor nodded briefly. He could feel the fear in her accelerated breathing and the rigidity of her body pulled tightly against his.

'Stand up, unlock the car, and open the back door. Then move all the way across.'

She hesitated for a moment, so he eased the knife deliciously through her paper-thin skin, enjoying her sudden gasp of pain. She obeyed his order reluctantly, rising slowly from the ground. With weak arms, she struggled with the door, perhaps sensing that she'd have less chance of escape from inside the car. Losing patience, Robert wrenched it open for her, and with the knife at her throat, Eleanor clambered across the back seat. He allowed himself a small grin. This was the part he was really looking forward to.

'Please... who are you? What do you want?' Her words were laced with panic as she dragged herself across the seats and curled up in the corner, as far away from him as she could get. 'If you want money, just take my purse...'

She looked up at his face.

'Robert,' she breathed with an absurd mixture of reverence and pure terror. He was the man of her nightmares.

'Hello, Eleanor, my dear. Gosh, don't you look well – for someone who's meant to be dead.' He got into the back of the car beside her, wincing slightly, and shut the door behind him.

'Get away from me you sick bastard!' she shrieked. Robert saw unadulterated hatred chase the worst of the fear from her mismatched eyes.

'Hush now, you have some questions to answer, that's all.' The lie tripped off his tongue as he studied her like an insect before dissection. 'Obviously you didn't die with your parents, so where have you been all these years?' Reaching across, he traced the edges of her scar, feeling her shiver with repulsion at his touch. 'If I hadn't spotted your unique scar in that photo with the footballers in the paper, well I would never have known you survived, and well... I guess this lovely family reunion wouldn't be happening.'

Robert eased the knife down Eleanor's vulnerable neck and between her breasts, relishing her discomfort. He paused begrudgingly, searching his feelings as that good-for-nothing army psychiatrist had taught him. He found nothing. He genuinely believed this woman was his daughter, but she'd been corrupted by his brother and his worthless whore. The knife didn't falter. His heart was too twisted with hatred, too empty of love and empathy.

A little pressure through his wrist would plunge the blade between her ribs and up into the chest cavity. She would bleed out quickly enough and he could be gone, but her pain would only be short-lived. He hesitated, needing more. He needed to see her anguish and fear as he'd done when she was a child. She'd rejected him then after all. The spoiled little princess would never have accepted *him* as her father.

He looked at her mismatched irises, identical to his brother's. Robert slid the knife back to her exposed throat. His expression was passive, uncaring, but his cloud grey eyes never left her face. He still had questions and they needed to be answered.

'What happened to your little brother? Is he still alive as well? And your parents? Are they even dead? You better not lie to me.'

Eleanor seemed confused by the question. 'What do you mean? They're dead. They're all dead. Ben, Mum, Dad. *Everyone*, and it's all your fucking fault.' Her voice was strong with a ferocious courage Robert couldn't help but admire. He'd had enough experience of enhanced interrogation to recognise fear-driven honesty.

'So tell me, how did *you* survive the accident?' Robert demanded, his voice filled with pent up rage.

'How the hell should I know? I was only a little girl. I went to an orphanage and they gave me a new name—'

'What and you didn't think to ask for your dear old Uncle Robert? You preferred to be alone?' he mocked.

Although she was clearly petrified, she managed to hold eye contact with him. Her words, dripping with loathing, hurt him more than any injury he'd ever had.

'I hated you. We *all* hated you,' she spat. 'What you did to me...' Her hand instinctively rose to her cheek. 'What you did to my family lead to that car crash. They had no other choice. You made them take their own lives. *You* made them abandon me in an orphanage. *You* ruined my family – and for what? Because your mother didn't love you and your father despised you? No wonder you were such an unwanted bastard.' She paused, took a breath and hissed, 'I didn't want you anywhere near me.' Despite the knife at her throat, her words rang with defiance and her honesty made Robert flinch. This stubborn bitch was nothing like the weak little daddy's girl he hurt all those years ago – he couldn't decide which Eleanor he hated more.

'So you grew up a poor, discarded orphan.' His smile was as cold as his words. He could easily imagine how lonely and desperate her childhood must have been – so similar to his. Perhaps they had more in common than she realised.

Eleanor nodded and glanced out of the window. He sensed she was looking for an escape. He merely nudged the knife deeper – deep enough to draw blood. Eleanor grimaced. Once more, he had her undivided attention.

'Surely you understand I can't let you live?' he announced quietly, and watched as a little of her resolve dissipated. 'But I'll let you choose, a slash to the throat or a strike to the heart?' Robert enjoyed describing impending death to his victims – it was the ultimate trick for achieving fear and focus.

'So which will it be?' he asked casually as if he were taking her coffee order.

Tears filled Eleanor's mismatched eyes as anger, hatred, fear and other emotions he could barely read played out on her face. She wasn't worth any more of his time. It was her words between her sobs that ultimately stayed his hand.

'No, no, no... please don't do this... *please*... I'm pregnant... please don't hurt my baby.'

A baby?

Robert's mind flashed back to Elizabeth – her body writhing beneath him as he took what should have been his all along. He watched from afar as her belly swelled with *his* child all those years ago, and now Eleanor was carrying his grandchild. The knife meandered to her stomach as he imagined the cells forming beneath the gentle swell.

He'd never experienced the luxury of having a family of his own, of being the father that his was not. Thomas had stolen even that from him. Elizabeth was the only woman he had ever loved. Every woman since had failed to live up to her and failed to meet his expectations. Women found him cold and distant, and relationships often ended violently. Ever since he was a boy, he had longed to feel loved, but his family had only ever despised him and treated him as an outcast. Even his mother had shunned him, ignoring his very existence. It was always Thomas who had everyone's attention. The golden boy. The heir.

He looked at Eleanor. His daughter may mean nothing to him – he had lost her a long time ago – but a baby, a grandchild, *his* grandchild. His legacy. A child he could mould as his own, one who would love him and sooth the demons of hatred that coiled around his heart. The knife wavered.

Was this what he had been chasing his entire life? Was this his chance to experience unconditional love?

'How far?'

She looked confused.

'How far is the pregnancy?'

'Just a few weeks – I'm due the beginning of May,' she murmured, her eyes wide. 'Its heart is beating and I think I can feel it moving already. It's just an innocent baby. Please I'm begging you, it's done nothing wrong. Please don't hurt my child.' She was pleading, desperate to save her life and garner his sympathy. Her arms were folded protectively over her belly as if she were already cradling the infant. 'And I'll have the money soon. I can pay you.'

The point of the knife hovered a millimetre from her belly button.

'What money?' he demanded. He knew instinctively that she was talking about the missing millions that disappeared after Thomas and Elizabeth's accident.

'My inheritance from my parents. My trust fund matures in June. There's over five million pounds and you can have it. All of it. It's yours – if you don't hurt me or my baby. And only if you go away. Forever.'

In that moment, hope flickered across Eleanor's face. Robert looked away in disgust. Hope is for fools and the weak... but what was she talking about? A buzzing filled his ears as he recalculated his brother's litany of sins.

Not only had Thomas escaped his clutches by dying with his slut of a wife, but he'd hidden Eleanor, making him believe that she too was dead. Then to add insult to injury, Thomas then dared to leave the girl the family money – money that had been rightfully his.

All his life, Thomas had everything, everything Robert had ever wanted – everything he deserved. That only left him wanting revenge – revenge that Robert carried in his heart like a living, breathing thing. But now it really was time for him to have retribution for his brother's sins. It was his turn to take *everything* back.

And perhaps there was a way – a way to have it all; his vengeance, a family, the money... *his* money.

He calmed his breathing and reset his temper. Now would not be a good time to lose control.

'To be clear,' he sneered, 'if I come back in June, you'll just hand over five million pounds? Just like that?' The pull of a fortune and a life with a child of his own – a future he'd only ever dreamt of – conflicted with his deep, ingrained need to inflict pain.

With money, he could take the child anywhere. Europe maybe, or South America. He would hire a nanny, of course, and the child would love him as they lived their privileged life together. After all, wasn't it his duty to provide a loving home for this child, like the very one he had been denied? The child was his blood. It was *his*.

It was time that he took his ultimate revenge on them all. Thomas, Elizabeth, his parents and even Eleanor.

'Yes,' Eleanor cut through his reverie, 'I swear on my baby's life. You can have it all. I never wanted it anyway. It didn't do my parents any good, did it? I didn't want their money – I just wanted them.' Robert watched as memories of her cold, lonely childhood in care crossed her face. He felt no empathy.

The deal was sealed amidst more tears. It's a small risk to take, Robert thought. He had found her once from a random photo in a newspaper – he would find her again, even if she ran. He knew her new name, where she worked, where she lived. This pathetic, snivelling woman wouldn't outsmart him as his brother had.

He was merely postponing her death until after she gave birth and handed over the money. In the meantime, he would relish the anticipation of taking everything, if not from his brother then from Elizabeth's bitch daughter. The ultimate revenge. He would – at last – have everything he so richly deserved.

He was gone.

Ellie trembled uncontrollably, sitting for what felt like hours in the back seat of her car, unable to move. Revulsion, fear and pregnancy hormones roiled in her stomach, and when she opened the door at last, it was to vomit on the oily floor of the car park.

Her tears flowed unchecked as she climbed unsteadily behind the wheel, sobs catching in her chest. She had saved her child's life by brokering a deal with the devil himself.

She brushed her cheek and her scar throbbed with remembered agony. She knew that Robert would never settle for the money, no matter how much she had to give him. He would always want more – he always wanted more. Soon the baby growing inside her would be born and vulnerable to her uncle's particular brand of hate and depravity.

Robert would come back and take the money, and he would kill her, her child and Finn. Her thoughts flew in terrified confusion.

But Ellie was a survivor, made so by her parent's abandonment. She was the poor little rich girl left to the mercies of foster care.

She needed a plan and she needed help, but there were

only two people she could turn to.

Finn, her husband and the love of her life. But then she would have to explain all her lies and deceit, and she doubted he would be able to comprehend the scale of evil Robert was capable of. He would only want to go to the police and do the right thing, and that would get him killed trying to protect her. She remembered with a shudder that Finn didn't even know about the money.

And then there was Harry. There had always been Harry. She scrolled down to his number hidden in her contacts under the name 'Janet' in case Finn ever accidentally checked her phone. She had lived a lifetime of caution, even where Finn was concerned.

Harry would know what to do. He knew the lies she lived with and understood how truly psychotic Robert was. He would help her. A vague plan was beginning to form in her head.

Her hand rested on the near-indiscernible bulge of her belly, and the life it harboured inside – a life she was now solely responsible for. Ellie's tears started to flow again in earnest.

She wanted so desperately to have this baby with Finn by her side, but she was caught between her need for him to be there and her desperate desire to keep him safe from Robert.

Her mind whirled in desperation.

There was someone else who could help her. Another family member of sorts. She would gather her thoughts and send an email tonight. She would need all the help she could get.

Ellie thumbed the dial button, but only managed to reach Harry's voicemail. She had forgotten he was only half-way through his porter's shift at the hospital.

'Harry. It's me. Robert found me. Meet me during your break outside the morgue. I need you.'

CHAPTER 47

E llie Murray woke bathed in sweat, trembling with fear. Her dream was back. No, it wasn't a dream – it was her fully-fledged, terrifying nightmare. Slowly, the hideous images of Robert, blood dripping from his knife and Finn's lifeless body merged with disjointed childhood memories of unbearable agony receded, and her breathing slowed.

As a girl, her nightmares had gotten so bad that Mrs Grainger took her to a councillor of sorts who said it was nothing more than the overactive imagination of a wilful child. Her foster mother had punished her when her unnecessary screams had woken the household. Only Ellie knew the dream represented an actual event, details of which were tightly locked away in her subconscious. Her only proof was the scar on her cheek.

The nightmare never left her, but with Harry's help, she learnt to weather its storm. Most nights, Harry managed to get into her bedroom before her screams were heard by their foster parents. He would hold her hand and his voice would slowly soothe the fear that raged inside her, then he'd stay with her until she finally managed to fall back to sleep. Harry was her rock.

Ellie's vague memories of her birth parents were tied up in knots of pain and abandonment – everything she found so hard to forget. There were so many holes in her early memories; a shadowy man who plagued her sleep, a missing baby brother, her parent's fatal car crash and knowing her name could no longer be Eleanor.

Going to university provided a welcome escape from the Graingers, although it presented a far more daunting prospect: how would she cope living with strangers and without Harry in the room next door? People would find out how pathetic and weird she was.

She had needed Harry to stay close. While she attended university, he worked in a café near the docks and as a janitor at the shopping mall.

Ellie had to learn how to live in uni halls. She took sleeping pills, tried hypnosis and practised meditation – anything to keep the night terrors at bay. Relationships proved tricky, but she wasn't really looking for a boy-friend. No one would love the peculiar, scarred girl after all, but at times she still yearned for physical intimacy.

The occasional one night stand suited her perfectly. She always left before falling asleep, so the guy wouldn't wake up next to her screaming her head off. Besides, she didn't exactly have time for much else while she worked two jobs and balanced shifts at the hospital and lectures. She certainly didn't have time for a man in her life.

That was all true until she met Finn Murray. Kind, sweet, completely adorable – Finn turned her world up-side down and melted her stone-cold heart. He followed her around campus like a love-struck puppy. He brought her flowers and McDonald's breakfasts after long night shifts. He wrote her terribly cheesy poems and he even made her nachos while he helped her with her anatomy and physiology assignments.

Finn loved her scar and her funny coloured eyes, but she still made sure she never spent the night. Then, on one fabulous summer day spent picnicking down on Bournemouth beach, they went back to his student house. They'd drunk a little too much wine in the warm sun and after making love, Ellie fell asleep in his arms. She didn't wake up screaming and terrified. There was no nightmare, not that night nor the next nor any night she slept alongside Finn. Finn Murray became her safe place. His embrace kept her demons at bay.

And to top it off, he loved her. He actually loved her. And she loved him back for it.

But she couldn't be with Finn now.

Ellie flicked the bedside light on and pulled herself awkwardly to her feet. Her stomach felt huge. The baby was growing well – it was head down and engaged. It wouldn't be long now. A shiver of fear passed through her. Having a newborn to protect was going to make her even more vulnerable.

Finn had been thrilled when she told him she was pregnant. She was much less happy about it at first, unsure even how to be a mum, but his positivity and sheer excitement won her over. Not for a moment did she imagine it would end like this. Having the baby in hiding and without Finn was an unimaginable idea. She missed him so much. Her heart burned with longing.

She knew Robert would be watching Finn's every move after her 'death', and that he would only be convinced that she was really dead if he saw Finn's genuine heartbreak and grief at her loss. She had put Finn through a terrible ordeal to keep him and the baby safe, but what other choice was there?

Now, with the birth barely weeks away, she needed Finn just as she knew she would. And with Harry's continued help, she had set a trail for him to follow – although that hadn't been until after everyone had seen the measure of his grief. She had given Cassie strict instructions not to send him the bracelet until April, and then Harry had used Ellie's backdoor key to leave the presents where Finn would find them. Finn would work it out. He would follow the clues to Harry and then Harry would bring him here, to her mother's house. At least that was the plan.

But of course, Robert didn't give up. Ellie had idiotically underestimated her Uncle's vicious cruelty and dogged perseverance.

She waddled to the toilet. The baby was enjoying its nocturnal bouncing session on her bladder. On returning to her cold bed, she tried to sleep, but her imagination ran wild with panic. For Harry, for Finn, for her unborn child.

Cassie's horrendous and unnecessary death had shocked Ellie to the core. Then Finn was mugged, although she knew few details about that, and now a mutilated body had been left in their shed. It was all down to Robert – of that she had no doubt. He was coming for her, and she knew she couldn't stop it. Not now. Not with the baby coming. But she desperately wanted to see Finn one last time. She needed to apologize and explain, and then say goodbye properly.

She would make Finn take the baby away to safety and give Robert his blood money, sacrificing herself to his vengeance if it would save her husband and their precious child. Finn's mother would help him raise their baby, she was sure. She just had to get him here before Robert tracked her down. She could already feel him baying for her blood out there in the dark somewhere – her nemesis about to claim his prize.

God, where was Harry? She needed news. She needed Finn.

Checking her new phone for the umpteenth time, hot tears dribbled over her scar. Harry had promised he would text when he was on his way with Finn.

There were no new messages.

CHAPTER 48

Finn

A soft rain started to fall, dripping down coldly between the branches. Unnerving nocturnal noises filled the undergrowth and a chill was growing in the air. Harry was only wearing his thin monogrammed Mo's Café work shirt and must have been feeling the cold now that we had stopped running. I hugged my arms around my body, grateful for my jumper as my sweat cooled down. My quads were already starting to stiffen.

'What the fuck do you mean "Ellie's alive"?' I barked, rage tainting my words, my fists bunched. I'd never wanted to hurt anyone so much before in my life. The urge to do actual bodily harm to this man threatened to overwhelm me. 'Start talking Harry or by God I'll pulverise your—'

'Alright, Finn, give me a moment.' He interrupted my verbal tirade, his hands high in supplication. 'Let me catch my breath, mate. It's a long story, starting when we were kids.' He took a breath but seeing the look on my face, he carried on quickly. 'We met in a children's home and were together for years at the Grainger's. Eleanor and I were very close.'

'Her name is *Ellie*. Not fucking Eleanor,' I growled, miserable at hearing of their intimacy. A man I'd never heard of until a few days ago was claiming to have played an integral part in my wife's past.

'It was Eleanor first, actually, that's what she told me. Eleanor Hudson. It only changed to Ellie when she came to live at the children's home, and then, when we were adopted, she officially became Ellie Grainger. It was safer that way.'

It was like being drip-fed information. 'Okay whatever. Just keep talking.'

'Finn, mate, I'm freezing to death out here. Let's find some shelter and I'll tell you everything, I promise. There's a barn in the field over there.'

'Everything? You better not be messing—'

'Yes, everything. Believe it or not, we're on the same side mate.'

I followed him reluctantly out of the trees, keeping close and alert in case he took off. The rain was coming down harder and the night was turning an inky black. I jumped at every shadow.

We clambered over a fence into a field with an open-sided barn piled high with hay. We moved towards the back and went behind the neatly-rolled bales where it was drier and a lot warmer. I actually felt safe and fought a ridiculous urge to lay down and sleep.

This time, Harry didn't need threatening. He started talking almost as soon as we got comfortable on some stray hay bales. He was still shivering and it was hard to tell if it was the cold or the residual effects of the electrical storm his body had suffered. I had no sympathy. I only wanted answers.

'Right, where were we?' he said, rubbing his hands together. 'Oh yes, me and *Ellie* growing up together. We always stayed close. When she went to uni in Southampton I got a job at the West Quay mall as a janitor. When she married you, I got a job in the same hospital. She liked me nearby, you know, in case she needed me.'

No, I didn't fucking know. He'd looked familiar at the café but I certainly couldn't place him from work. 'Where in the hospital?' I snapped.

'I was a porter, in the morgue mostly. I tried to avoid making runs to A&E if you were on duty. Ellie didn't want us meeting, even by accident.' His supercilious grin had my blood thrumming in my ears and I had to fight the urge to smash it from his face.

Suddenly I didn't want to hear anymore. Ellie had purposely kept this man hidden from me, right under my nose. The pain in my heart was unbearable. Bloody Harry just kept talking, his words blurring, shredding my life into meaningless little pieces. Ellie had lied to me about absolutely everything.

'...then back in November she was attacked by her uncle, Robert, and we had to do something. He threatened her with a knife when she was out shopping. He cut her neck, the sodding bastard.' The concern in his eyes was genuine and overwhelming, and I knew in that moment that he loved Ellie at least as much as I did, if nothing else.

'She never even told me,' I protested weakly, my voice cracking with regret. I was devastated that I'd been so blind to her awful predicament.

'She was petrified, Finn. I've never seen her more scared

in her life. But more than anything she was scared for you and the baby and what Robert would do to you both. We came up with a plan together. She needed a way out. So we staged the crash and faked her death. She knew I would do anything for her.'

I stood up and started pacing furiously. What was he implying? That I wouldn't do anything for her? God, I was going hit him again, the obnoxious prick. His meaning gradually found a way past my anger, and I realised what he was saying.

'You mean... you mean Ellie is... Ellie really is alive?' I couldn't quite believe what I was asking. My mouth formed the words but my brain was still playing catch-up. 'But the body... Ellie burnt in the car.' Part of me was unwilling to be lulled into this false reality he was feeding me. I'd been down this road before. It felt like I was continuously having to relive her death over and over.

'Like I said, we had it planned. Working in the morgue, I um... I borrowed a body – a Jane Doe, a homeless woman. Ellie changed the name on the death certificate and all the paperwork, her DNA, dental records the whole nine yards. It was a slow night shift and I paid one of the security guys to switch off the cameras. Told him I was showing my girlfriend the morgue. I parked my car at the vehicle entrance and I rolled the body out on a trolly. Easy as. It was going to be cremated anyway because no one had claimed it. No one would notice it was missing for a few months at least, and by then I'd be long gone. There would be no connection to Ellie anyway.'

'And Cassie?' I threw at him. I needed time to digest what he was saying and figure out if it was bullshit. I almost regretted what I'd said. His head slumped and when he looked up, I could see tears welling in his eyes.

The pale moon had snuck between the dripping clouds. The rain was easing off now but the wind continued to whip up the valley. The crack in Harry's voice was utterly authentic.

'Ah, shit. That was terrible. No one deserves to die like that. We didn't think for a moment Robert would target Cassie. She was a good person, damaged, but she had a kind soul. I just couldn't bring her with me. She had, um… issues, and my priority was helping Ellie.'

I had no option now but to ask the one question I most feared the answer to. 'So tell me, were you fucking my wife? Was it while we were married or before? Or are you still doing it now?' The shock on his face was obvious, and I realised I was holding my breath, waiting for the reply.

'Fuck no mate! How can you even ask me that?' Harry looked horrified. 'I told you we grew up together since we were about seven. She's like my sister! She *is* my sister. And anyway she's in love with you, dickhead. Always has been.'

Relief flooded my entire body as the realisation that Ellie hadn't cheated on me sunk in. She loved me. And she was alive. Her lack of trust, the lies and dishonesty I could work through.

'Where is she?' My voice sounded strange, as a cacophony of thoughts crowded my brain. Where was she now? When would I see her, talk to her, hold her?

Reality came crashing down, overwhelming me. I dropped to my knees. *Ellie was alive.* Tears filled my eyes and fell down my face. Tears of joy, of misery for not being with her, tears of pure, beautiful hope. A hundred emotions clashed in my head.

When I was following the string of ridiculous clues with Rachel, I never dared to believe I'd actually see Ellie again. I'd been looking for closure and perhaps a welcome distraction from the emptiness and longing that was consuming me. Chasing around the country meant I didn't have to face the fact that my reason for living had been incinerated against a tree.

'I don't know.' Harry's gaze shifted to his filthy shoes and his voice was so soft I nearly asked him to repeat himself. When he carried on talking, his words were almost lost in the wind. 'She has a new phone, a burner, we keep in contact, mate, but I don't know exactly where she—'

I shot to my feet and yanked him up, my hands bunched in his shirt collar. 'What the fuck do you mean, you don't know? Where is my wife? And a burner phone? Seriously? What the hell are you playing at?'

His hands failed uselessly at my grip which was tightening around his neck, anger fuelling my strength. He had no chance.

'I swear I don't know where she is. She said it was safer for me that way—'

'Okay then, so phone her. Right fucking now. Let me hear her voice.' I was yelling at him, saliva hitting his face. I threw him to the ground struggling not to kick him as he lay vulnerable at my feet. I wasn't a violent man, even rugby tackles left me feeling sorry for my opponent. I didn't recognise myself as I stood over his cowering form in the barn.

'A burner is just a pay-as-you-go phone, to keep it untraceable mate,' Harry explained, looking up at me from the floor. Fearfully, he added, 'I haven't got my phone or I would call her. I guess Robert took that and my wallet.'

I forced a breath past my clenched up throat and stupidly felt my pockets. My phone, wallet and car keys were no longer in my jeans. I sat down heavily on a pile of hay. I was cold, sore, wet and tired and stuck in the middle of nowhere with no phone, money or car keys with an idiot who knew far more about my wife than I did. Ellie was out there somewhere all alone and I had no idea where or how to contact her.

Things couldn't get any worse.

CHAPTER 49

'And then, of course, there's the money.'

I held out my hand to help him up which he accepted with understandable trepidation. We sat opposite each other on the hay bales.

I'd be damned if I was going to apologise for attacking him – again. The mention of the money, however, wasn't doing anything to help me hang on to my tenuous sense of self-control.

'What money? You mean the trust fund I also didn't know a bloody thing about?' I hadn't meant it to come out like that but sensed I was about to hear more unknown facts about Ellie, facts that Harry bloody Grainger seemed to have chapter and verse on.

'Ellie's birth parents were absolutely minted mate, like, *extremely wealthy*. Before they planned their joint suicide and Ellie's first fake death...' he grinned at the irony and I almost crossed the ground between us, '...they set up a trust fund in her name.' None of this was even remotely amusing. I wanted to make him refer to my wife as *Mrs Murray* or something else equally juvenile because that was easier than struggling with the excruciating but undeniable fact that Ellie had chosen to confide in him and not me. My thoughts were all over the place as he kept talking.

'I have no idea how they fooled Robert into believing she died in the crash, and she was too young to remember any details. As far as anyone knew, she was an orphan with no family. The money wouldn't be released until she turned thirty, of course.'

'So Ellie knew about the money when she was growing up? This trust fund of hers, I mean.'

'Oh sure. Well, not as a kid of course but a lawyer contacted her when she turned eighteen, some man named Lawson, I think. Slimy bastard, but her father trusted him it seemed. The lawyer explained it all to us.'

'*Us?*' I flew up off the bale and had him by the throat again. Ellie and I met and started dating during her first year at Southampton. By her second year, we were already officially living together and seriously discussing marriage. All that time she kept this all from me? It was clear which man she trusted the most.

'Let me go, you fucking twat. You want the whole story, don't you? And I already told you we were close. I was the only one who knew the truth about her past.' He panted, his face turning red.

Another question forced its way through my anger: 'Do you know how she got her scar?'

He could barely get enough breath to answer, so I let him go but didn't move away. I hoped I could intimidate him into telling me the truth. Ellie's scar had always been a touchy subject.

'No. She didn't remember much about it. It happened even before her parents died. She just knew it had everything to do with her insane Uncle Robert.' He rubbed his throat and coughed.

'If you're lying, I'll rip your fucking head off,' I threatened. My precarious grip on my temper had almost shredded again. I found myself wanting to be mad at Ellie. After all, she was the one who had lied to me for years. But Ellie I loved too much and Harry was actually here, and was guilty by association.

'I'm not lying,' he said weakly, finally lifting his head and looking at me. His eyes grew wide suddenly with terror, and he spun around and sprinted off into the darkness. I turned to see what had scared him off and walked right into a tree branch flying at my head.

I tried to duck, but it was way too late and the branch caught me high on my cheekbone, slamming my head to the side. My body followed, and I landed in a heap on the ground. My vision was grey and fuzzy, and the all-too-familiar taste of bile rose in my mouth. I looked up into bright torchlight and couldn't see much else beyond that. There was little doubt who was standing behind it, and when he spoke, all my hope evaporated.

'Ah, there you are Murray. I've been looking for you everywhere. I see your cowardly accomplice has deserted you in your hour of need. I guess you should have been nicer to the man.'

He must have crept up on us as I was trying to strangle the life out of Harry.

Robert moved the torch and I glared into his grey, soulless eyes, incredulous that I was once more at his mercy. And maybe he was right, I should have been kinder to

Harry. The sod had run off and left me to this crazy maniac. I couldn't exactly blame him – maybe I would have done the same. Warm blood oozed down my face.

'Get up, now, on your feet. And don't try anything stupid, Murray,' Robert ordered, brandishing the branch menacingly. I was convinced he'd just hit me again if I got up, but if I stayed on the ground, I was literally a sitting target. Up on my feet at least I had the option of running. So far, the taser hadn't come out, nor the knife.

I struggled up, my head floating half a metre off my shoulders and the side of my face starting to pound. Robert threw something in my direction, which I caught instinctively. Plastic cable ties, like the ones Harry cut off me in the van. Robert seemingly had an infinite supply.

'Round your wrists and pull them tight,' he barked, drill sergeant like.

I dropped them on the ground at my feet. I was fucked if I was going to help him. I shook my head gently, not trusting my voice.

Robert's eyes flared with brutal anger, and in the same instant the tree branch whistled through the air and I was back on the ground. Fuck, he moved fast. I was being an idiot. He could simply club me into unconsciousness or worse and then put the bloody plasti-cuff things on me himself. I should have run while I was on my feet.

I was still trying to clear my head when he kicked me, catching me under my diaphragm, forcing the air clean out of my lungs. I thrashed about in the dust trying to remember how to breathe and desperately trying not to vomit.

'Be sensible, Murray, and save yourself some pain. Don't you want to see your precious *Ellie* one last time before

I slit her worthless throat? I'll even let you watch as I hack your unborn child from her belly and stamp on its head. Or I can kill you now so you don't have to see it. The choice is yours.'

'I wouldn't help you find her even if I knew where she was,' I hissed through the pain, hopefully sounding more defiant than I felt. I was struggling to think coherently as the throbbing in my head and abdomen intensified.

'We'll get to that, Murray, but for now, be a good boy and put the cuffs on BEFORE I LOSE MY FUCKING PATIENCE.'

I pushed myself up into a sitting position, surprised my head didn't roll off my shoulders. Just as I slipped my right wrist through the stiff circle of plastic, Robert's tall body folded over, almost falling on top of me. Harry stood behind him with a farm instrument of some kind clutched in his hand – a silhouette in the light formed by the fallen torch. He'd managed to sneak up on Robert and hit him with all his strength.

Robert lay awkwardly on the ground, but he was already starting to groan and move. There was blood leaking from the back of his closely shaven skull. Harry hadn't laid him out, only knocked him off his feet.

'Come on, let's get out of here,' Harry yelled, grabbing my elbow.

Ignoring my hippocratic oath, I left Robert writhing on the ground, climbing unsteadily to my feet. I set off after Harry as fast as I could manage.

We sprinted back to the trees, took a left and headed roughly downhill towards where we'd escaped the van. All I could think about was putting as much distance as possible between me and the man who wanted mine and Ellie's lives. Adrenaline overrode my pain. I overtook

Harry and started leading the way.

CHAPTER 50

I ran as I'd never run before in my life. My head throbbed every time my feet hit the ground, but sheer desperation drove me down the hill in the direction of the distant lights. My chest was on fire and my pulse roared in my ears. I could feel the lactic acid burning in my quads but still I ran with Harry close on my heels. I could hear his ragged breathing above my own. Harry had left Robert stirring back in the barn and I knew he would come after us.

'For fuck's sake, Finn... stop!' Harry panted. 'We can't keep running blindly. We need to think.'

Desperate for a respite from the furious pace I'd set, I jogged to a stop in the darkness between the units of the industrial park. The place seemed deserted.

'I think we should find a place to rest up. At least until its light. We can't keep running in the dark,' Harry gasped, trying to catch his breath.

The rain had finally stopped, but the wind felt damp and cold. We were both shivering again, bathed in icy sweat.

'He could be right behind us, Harry. We have to keep moving. He's... he's going to kill Ellie and the baby. He said—'

'I know Finn, I know. And it scares me shitless too. But we have to make a plan. It's pitch dark and we're running blind.'

'But Ellie... He said—'

He put his hand on my arm, his voice remarkably calm. 'Ellie is safe, Finn. Robert doesn't know where she is, or he wouldn't be chasing us around the wilds of Hampshire.'

He had a good point.

'So what do we do?'

'We stay out of sight, wait for daylight and then make our way to Ellie.'

'Hang on, you said you didn't know where she was.' I took a step closer, anger rising in my gut like an old friend.

'Okay mate, here's the truth, but don't go all *Rambo* on me, okay? Ellie and I agree on most things, but not this. She wants to see you, and I'm cool with that, to a point. I'll take you to her, but I'm not telling you exactly where she is. It's just safer that way.'

'Safer? What the hell are you insinuating? I'd never betray Ellie.'

'I know mate, I know, but Robert can be pretty persuasive from what I hear.'

'And what makes you immune to his knife and fucked-up torture techniques? What says you won't tell him?' I growled in response.

'I would give my life to keep Ellie safe.' His reply was soft and adamant. His loyalty to Ellie was irrefutable. 'Look, we do it my way. Okay? We get to Ipswich, somehow, and then I'll take you to Ellie. But that's all you get. No address, no phone number. No debates.'

'*Ipswich*? Why Ipswich? Why is Ellie in Ipswich? It's clear across the country. It must be over 200 miles in the wrong fucking direction. And Robert has my car keys.' I only realised I was yelling when Harry shoved me in the chest.

'Keep your voice down, arsehole. Come on, we need to get out of sight. Let's find somewhere safe and then we'll carry on this conversation.'

He was right, again. In my defence, I had recently learnt that my dead wife was alive and about to give birth to our child, and I was standing in a grimy alley, literally lost in the dark and she was somewhere on the other side of the country. My head was all over the place.

'Fine, but we need to get to her soon. She's in danger. Did you hear what that bastard was threatening?' I was insistent, only just managing to keep my voice down to a low roar, unable to shift the images Robert had planted in my head.

'I know Finn, I know. But we won't get there in the dark. We'll move at first light. Listen, the petrol station will be closed but the car wash has a roof. We'll be out of the wind, we can rest, wait for daybreak and then we'll find a way to get to Ipswich. Deal?'

The petrol station's security lighting was dim, leaving plenty of dark, ominous corners. I kept looking back over my shoulder, checking for any sign of Robert following us. The car wash did have a high perspex roof, but it was open-sided and damp. We found a corner that was mostly dry and hunkered down amidst an array of hoses and buckets.

'Why Ipswich? Ellie's never even been there.' I started on him as soon as we sat down.

'She owns a house there.' He carried on quickly before I could interrupt, 'Oh don't worry, mate, her ownership of it can't be traced, not even by Robert. She's perfectly safe there.'

'A house?' I parroted stupidly, too numb to react. Of course Ellie owned a house that I knew nothing about. Along with 5.3 million pounds and maybe even a castle or two thrown in for good measure.

'Yeah, her mum left it to Ellie when she died. But she used a different lawyer. It's in the name of some shelf company or something, so it's completely unconnected and untraceable.'

'And when did Ellie know about the house?' I didn't even try to disguise the misery in my voice as I added another lie to Ellie's ever-growing list.

Harry answered, oblivious to my anguish, 'When we were released from care. We lived there for a while before she moved to Southampton for uni.'

'Why, Harry? Why didn't Ellie tell me any of this? I don't get it. You say she loves me, then why didn't she tell me?'

At last, a flicker of empathy showed in his eyes. 'Sorry mate, that's her story to tell. All I know is she lived afraid of Robert her whole life, and maybe keeping you in the dark was her way to protect you from him. But you need to ask her.' He yawned. 'And now, mate, I'm going to get some kip. We move as soon as this place starts opening up.'

He turned awkwardly on his side and yawned again loudly, leaving me to my demons. I was utterly exhausted but sleep was never going to happen.

I kicked out at him and he groaned before turning back

to face me.

'As soon as it's light, I'm going to the police. They are the only ones who can protect Ellie from Robert,' I declared confidently.

His bleary eyes stared at me for a moment before he spoke. Again, his voice was soft enough to make me lean closer. I was beginning to realise that when Harry was at his most serious, he spoke quietly.

'Then Ellie and the kid are both already dead,' he said.

I had more to say but the mention of my baby made me hesitate. Harry filled the void.

'You have to listen, mate. The police won't catch Robert. He was a serious special forces soldier or something back in the day. If we waste our time trying to convince the coppers that a madman's hunting your dead wife, then two things happen: one, we get sent to the loony bin, and two, Ellie dies. I'm not prepared to take that chance, are you?'

His argument was both compelling and terrifying, and then he sealed the deal: 'Ellie wants you there for the birth, so let's just get that done and then we think about contacting the police, okay? If Ellie agrees that is.'

'And how do we – the two of us on our own – how do we deal with Robert when he finds us? Especially if he's some bloody super-soldier. A doctor and a waiter? We have no chance.' I threw my hands up in the air in desperation.

'He won't find her, and we have a trick or two up our sleeve. Now for fuck's sake, let me get some sleep. We have a bloody long journey and need to be moving in a few hours. Once we get to Ellie, we'll decide how to handle Robert. Ellie will know what to do.'

He rolled over again and I left him in peace. There was no way I could sleep. Not while Robert was hunting my wife.

CHAPTER 51

Our first break came as a weak spring sun rose wearily over the horizon. Cars and trucks arrived at the petrol station almost as soon as it opened at six. Harry approached the driver of a large lorry filling up with diesel with a story of being mugged, and needing to get as far east as possible. I wasn't sure exactly what he told the man, or if he even believed our story, but he kindly offered us a lift anyway.

The cab was surprisingly warm and comfortable. The truck driver – a large, balding man with a small hoop earring in his right ear who was wearing a *Metallica* t-shirt that revealed most of his stomach – shared his slightly stale turkey sandwiches with a generosity that restored my faith in humanity. Although they didn't do much to ease the growling hunger in my stomach.

My face and head were still throbbing, but at least the bleeding had stopped. Despite the pain, the bone seemed like it was still intact, and the warmth and food had a hypnotic effect over my body. I drifted off leaving Harry to chat with our Guardian Angel. My last blurry thoughts revolved around Ellie; her lies, our love and our unborn baby.

The truck driver got us around the M25, but unfortunately he was only going as far as Chelmsford. Harry shook me awake. I felt sore, stiff and absolutely starving.

'Sorry gents, this is as far as I can take you. We're not actually allowed to give lifts to strangers,' he grinned, 'so I'll need to drop you here before I get any nearer my customer. Don't forget to report the assault.'

'Yeah, of course mate, we will and thanks for everything. This is perfect,' Harry waffled.

'Thanks so much,' I agreed, yawning.

We were somewhere along the A12 in a layby, and in the distance, a road sign showed an exit to Chelmsford. I could just about make out the outskirts of the sprawling city. The sun was overhead in a clear blue sky, with only a few fluffy clouds drifting aimlessly. My stomach agreed it must be lunchtime.

'Come on, Finn, we need to keep moving,' he said, marching off. 'We need to find another lift, there are at least another forty miles to go.'

'Or we could steal a car?' I suggested helpfully.

'And do *you* know how to boost a car, mate?' His tone was barely short of patronising, but he was right. I could restart a heart, re-inflate a collapsed lung and deal quite effectively with any manner of medical emergencies, but I didn't have a fucking clue how to steal a car.

'Let's carry on down to the services and see if we can hitch another lift,' he suggested, as I followed along behind him less enthusiastically. We were filthy, unshaven and our wrinkled clothes were covered in mud and blood. I didn't fancy our chances, but I was fresh out of alternatives.

We trudged five exhausting miles to the nearest roadside service station. It had a Little Chef, and the smell of fried onions made my mouth water and my stomach ache with hunger. Harry remained annoyingly upbeat.

We slipped into the washroom and made ourselves as presentable as possible. I cleaned the blood off my face, uncovering some angry bruising spreading from my swollen cheek. Harry all but washed his shirt, so now, instead of being dirty, it was stained, creased and damp. I just finger-combed my hair into some resemblance of neatness. I was willing to sell a kidney for a toothbrush.

It was hours before we found our next good Samaritan. His name was Gareth, he was Welsh and terribly proud of it.

It was my turn to sit up front and chat to our driver. I could hear Harry snoring in the back of the comfortable Volvo estate. I did my best to look awake and attentive, a skill I developed early as a junior doctor, but I only heard about one word in ten. He had a cool-sounding job, I think, driving around the countryside, discussing the merits of seeds and insecticides with farmers and agronomists for one of the big pharmaceutical companies. Harry had spun the same story of a mugging and needing a lift towards Ipswich. Gareth asked surprisingly few questions – I think he was just enjoying the company. When he realised we had no money, he stopped at a garage and bought us a ham sandwich and a coffee each. I could have kissed him.

Gareth kept up a running commentary about the complexities surrounding the responsible use of fungicides for the rest of the drive while I fought to stay awake.

Over an hour later, our new best friend dropped us on the outskirts of Ipswich. Heavy grey clouds formed as we neared the East coast, and the daylight was fading quickly. The journey – along with all our stops and searching for lifts – had taken the best part of a day.

As Gareth drove off, I turned on Harry. 'Please, I need to know where she is. I just can't take this not knowing. We're miles from Southampton and Robert. We're safe now, he can't find us. I deserve to know where my wife is.'

Harry scrubbed at his face, rubbing away his fatigue. He hesitated, too tired to argue anymore. 'You just never give up, do you mate? All right then, I guess we're so close now it makes no damn difference. But we walk and talk, okay? We're still a couple of hours away on foot and I'd like to get home before it starts chucking it down again.'

He let out a long sigh and set off, his pace brutal after the long day cooped up in cars. I was strolling on clouds, knowing I was within touching distance of Ellie. 'The address is 56 Crediton Close in Kesgrave, he said. 'It's a little village north of Ipswich town centre. It's a nice house in a great neighbourhood. Ellie and I were going to raise the child there, you know, if you didn't want her back.'

I pulled him to stop. 'If I didn't want her back? What the hell do you mean?'

'Ellie lied to you about everything, mate. Including dying for fuck's sake. We weren't sure how you would handle it or if you'd still be able to love her. We needed a contingency plan in case you wanted nothing more to do with her. We would bring the child up in her mum's house. Ellie keeps saying the schools in the area are good.' He turned and kept walking, leaving me standing still, lost for words.

So Ellie planned to shack up with Harry and bring up my

child with him because she thought I wouldn't love her anymore. In a moment of clarity, all her lies and deceit and the heartache of the last few months melted into nothing. How could I ever not love her? All she'd wanted was to protect our baby and me. If anything, I loved her more for it.

I caught up with Harry, my exhaustion and hunger forgotten.

'Let's go find Ellie,' I announced with a spring in my step. 'By the way, how does Rachel fit into all this? Or was that just another of Ellie's secrets?' I'd almost forgotten about Rachel and the information I'd uncovered with a few quick Google searches back in Southampton after I'd seen her get into that van.

'Who the fuck is Rachel? Was she the woman you were with in the café?'

The sound of an engine slowing directly behind us drowned out anything else Harry said.

CHAPTER 52

I turned my head and a set of bright headlights blinded me. I could just about make out a horribly familiar van pulling in behind us. The engine was still idling when the driver's door flew open and a tall man shot out.

He moved incredibly fast, covering the ground in two long strides. By the time my eyes adjusted to the brightness, Robert was standing with Harry's head tightly wedged in the crook of his arm. It would only take a tug of his wrist to snap Harry's neck. I stood still, dread keeping me frozen. How the hell had the sick fuck found us?

The traffic was speeding past too fast for any passing driver to notice us on the hard shoulder. We were fucked – again.

'Good to see you again, Murray.' Robert raised his voice above the roar of the cars. 'I'm not here to mess about. I know she's close.' Harry squirmed, but Robert only adjusted his hold, keeping Harry frozen in place. His neck was bent at a near-impossible angle. 'I just want to know where she is, Murray. No more games. Tell me where my daughter is.'

'Daughter? What the—'

'Tell me where she is! Or Grainger dies right here.' Robert's voice was flat and hard, and not for a moment did I think he wouldn't do it. 'Where is Eleanor?'

I stared at him, willing my brain for a workable solution. I couldn't lead him to Ellie – he wanted to kill and torture her, but could I watch him kill a man right in front of me to protect her? I had to do something, and I desperately hoped Harry would be on board with my decision. I kept my mouth shut and my eyes glued on Robert, willing him to ease his grip on Harry's neck.

'Do you want your friend to die?' Robert shouted, squeezing his arm tighter and making Harry cry out in a strangled whimper, feet stamping on the ground feebly.

My resolve wavered. Robert's sick, sociopathic logic had correctly gauged the fact that I couldn't simply stand there and let Harry die. I changed tack. I desperately needed time to think and had to keep him talking.

'How did you find us? We have no phones to trace, no credit cards. We've been hitching lifts.'

Robert laughed dryly. 'Finding people is my job, Murray. I tracked your phone to the mall but needed a more high-tech solution. Feel in the back pocket of your jeans. Right-hand side.'

I stared at him in total confusion. Then, with a sinking feeling, I stuck my hand in my pocket and pulled out a small, flat metal disk about the size of a twenty pence piece and about the same weight. It looked similar to the battery we used in our kitchen scales at home.

'Yeah, and what's this?' I asked, holding it up to the van's headlights. I'd already guessed the answer.

'It's a GPS tracker device. The latest military-grade model, in fact. Excellent range.' Robert spoke proudly as if lecturing a group of new recruits. He shifted emotional gears so fast it left my head spinning. 'I slipped it into your pocket back in the barn, before our friend here tried to crack my skull open. You've been relatively easy to follow ever since. I've been right behind you ever since you left Southampton. It took you two idiots all bloody day. I nearly gave up and offered you a lift myself just to speed things up, but I was keen to see how well the tracker worked in real time.'

I looked down at the little disk in my hand and a shiver flew down my spine. He'd been right there stalking us all day. We were a couple of incompetent fools believing we could ever outsmart him.

'So why grab us now? I can't imagine you wanted to save us the walk?' I was wasting time but I needed to get him riled up and a little distracted. I prayed my strategy wouldn't backfire. Harry's neck was literally on the line.

His lips twitched in a failed attempt at a smile. 'Unfortunately, the benefits of the tracker being so compact is that it has limited battery life. I didn't think it would take you this long. It's almost dead. I was about to lose you.' Lesson complete, he re-focussed. I still had no idea what I was going to do. 'So I'll ask one last time, Murray. Where is Eleanor?' To emphasise his question he tightened his grip around Harry's neck.

Harry's face turned a frightening shade of puce and his feet flailed desperately on the ground. I think he was trying to kick Robert, but he wasn't even getting close. Robert was over a head taller and was slowly forcing the life out of him. Time was running out.

I dropped his precious tracker on the ground. '*Shit!*' I exclaimed loudly, bending down quickly to retrieve it.

I scooped up a handful of gravel instead and flung it straight at Robert's eyes, hoping his height difference would keep most of it out of Harry's face. I quickly lowered into a half-crouch and lunged forward, my legs pumping frantically. I barrelled into the two men and we went down in the dirt at the side of the van in a tangle of limbs and escaping breath. I didn't know which body parts belonged to Robert and which to Harry, so I couldn't hit out but I couldn't stick around long enough to find out either.

I got to my feet, yelling, 'RUN HARRY, RUN!'

And that's precisely what I did myself. I ran. A metre from the van, the hard shoulder fell away sharply, and in the dark, I fell, skidded and finally rolled head over heels to the bottom. There was a small drainage ditch, a grass verge and a wooden rail fence. I don't remember getting up and scrambling over it, but soon I found myself running across a field in the darkness.

I thought I heard feet behind me and hoped with all my heart that it was Harry and not Robert. Perhaps it was the wind and the dying sound of the receding traffic.

CHAPTER 53

Rachel blew her nose and dabbed at her eyes with a soggy tissue. She couldn't stop crying. She'd been so stupid, so bloody stupid.

What started out as a bit of fun had quickly spiralled into a twisted conspiracy where people (herself included) were getting hurt and killed.

Growing up as an only child while her mother's mental issues intensified, raised mainly by her maternal grandmother, meant that Rachel had little family. Then one day, an advert in the dentist surgery caught her attention.

Send in a sample and receive your DNA databank matches today.

Reuniting families every day.

And she'd thought, why not? It couldn't do any harm, and just maybe she would find some long lost family out there somewhere. Rachel knew nothing about her father after all. She hadn't even known his name until her mother had made her watch that heart-wrenching video describing her ill-timed conception at the hands of an adulterous student who had then abandoned her pregnant mother in favour of his fiancé, amongst other things.

Finding out that her biological father and his entire family had been killed in a car accident had only increased her guilt at having never questioned the true extent of her family, so she swabbed her cheek and sent the sample.

Family had come calling... in the shape of Robert Hudson.

Rachel sat in her white BMW opposite the run down B&B in a forlorn seaside town on the Essex coast. She watched as the older couple crossed the road in front of her, hand in hand like young lovers, bent against the wind heading for the deserted beach and their regular evening stroll.

She didn't bother to follow them – this time. She had only been told to watch and report anything out of the ordinary. She didn't even know who they were or how they fitted into this nightmare narrative she'd become embroiled in. Instinctually, she reached for her phone but then thought better of it. They were only going for an evening walk and she knew they would be back. It was getting dark and the clouds were threatening yet another downpour. The couple had taken nothing with them, not even an umbrella.

Almost everything she had told Finn was true. Almost. She believed she was Eleanor's half-sister and that they shared a father. Her mother left Cambridge, pregnant and in disgrace after having an affair with a student. Rachel's childhood had been challenging, her mother suffering severe bouts of depression for as long as Rachel could remember; depression caused, she sincerely believed, by a broken heart at the hands of Thomas Hudson.

Meeting her uncle was thrilling at first. He bought her presents, took her to fancy London restaurants for dinner and even lent her rent money. They spoke for hours and he would describe how Thomas had used her mother and discarded her to marry his heiress, how he'd stolen Robert's inheritance and lied about his daughter's death.

Then Robert outlined his plan to put things right, but he needed her help and was willing to share the rewards.

Rachel had recently lost her job as a paralegal secretary, let go following the general post-Brexit financial downturn in the city. The monthly cost of her mum's private care home was threatening to drown her financially, and her meagre savings were already dwindling fast.

Robert's plan sounded so simple. She would infiltrate Finn's life and report back on his every move. She would also need to encourage him to find Eleanor, alerting Robert when she was found. The man was adamant his niece was alive, but Rachel was less so, having read up on the reports of her accident in the local press. But the task seemed simple enough in itself and would mean an end to her financial worries. So she had agreed.

Finn had proved a pushover, and Rachel's similarity to her half-sister had helped win over the hapless widower. He crumpled into a pathetic poodle just at the sight of her, barely questioning her story of birth certificates and emails and plans made to meet up with his late wife.

She felt sorry for the grieving man, so sad and pathetic in his misery, but Robert said he deserved it, insisting he had to be complicit in the plan to fake Eleanor's death and that he knew exactly where Eleanor was hiding, despite his outward show of anguish.

At Robert's insistence, Rachel went along with Finn's idiotic quest to find answers. Her real objective was never to find a half-sister – she was in it for the money. That had always been her only goal.

Robert had promised to give her half of the trust fund – a hundred thousand pounds, he'd said. That was a fortune in itself to her, but when she found out that the trust fund was actually worth over five million, she realised how she'd been misled. She was pretty sure he would kill her before she ever saw a penny. Robert had already shown what his temper could do.

He had visited late one night, just as she told Finn. By then she was having serious second thoughts and had pleaded to be released from her side of the deal. Robert only became incensed, shoving her violently up against a wall, his hand so tight around her neck she thought she would pass out. There had been nothing fake about the livid bruising he had left around her throat, and not only had he threatened her, but he had also threatened her mother by showing Rachel a photo of her mum outside her care home.

Rachel had never been so scared in her life, but Robert held all the cards, exerting total power over her.

To make matters worse, she'd already taken a down payment. In the early days, Robert had been extremely generous. Designer clothes, expensive jewellery, the latest iPhone and even the fancy new car she was driving, although now she knew it was all to fuel the illusion that she was a high-earning London lawyer so Finn wouldn't think she was just after his money. She didn't even think Finn noticed. He just missed his wife with a longing that

Rachel found genuine and disarming.

Robert dismissed her observations as totally irrelevant, of course, and he put even more pressure on her to push Finn into giving up his wife's hiding place. Petrified into submission, Rachel carried out her orders, telling Robert about their zoo visit, luring Finn into the alley near the butterfly house and even wasting time on the drive home so Robert could ransack Finn's house and take the Christmas presents she'd told him about. She'd even agreed to join Finn on his ridiculous road trip to Southampton, although by then she was more convinced than ever that Eleanor was really dead.

As they were setting out that Saturday morning, the nursing home called. Her mother had fallen overnight and was in hospital. She begged Robert to let her abandon the futile search. Between texts to the care home staff and pleading with Robert, she had barely registered what Finn was telling her. At last, Robert agreed to let her go, but only after she had enabled and hidden the *Find-a-Friend* app on Finn's phone so he could take over tracking Finn's progress.

Robert picked her up at the station and issued an ultimatum; she could visit her mother quickly but then he had another job for her. There was no negotiating with Robert. The closer he got to the prize of finding Eleanor and the money, the less he was able to hide his true psychotic nature. Rachel had come to realise that she was in league with a certifiable madman who wouldn't stop at bruising a neck if he ever did find Eleanor.

Rachel didn't stay long at the hospital. Her mum had broken her left hip and would be kept in for a few weeks before returning to the nursing home. She hadn't recognised her anyway. Once she knew she was going to be okay, she caught an Uber to Finn's house, picked up her car and drove out to the east coast of Essex as per Robert's explicit instructions.

Her task: to watch the unknown couple.

So here she sat, lamenting her poor choices. She had accepted Robert's offer of money and was now stuck in a vortex with a cruel, disturbed man and could see no way out of her awful predicament.

Rachel dabbed at her eyes, not knowing who she was crying for.

CHAPTER 54

More fences, more fields. My lungs were on fire, but I didn't slow down or look around. The uneven farmland would be treacherous enough in the light, and I found myself face down in the dirt more times than I could count. How I didn't roll an ankle, I'll never know. Entering a small group of trees next to a fast-flowing river, I slowed and stopped, entirely spent. I doubled over, hands on my knees, gulping in lungfuls of air.

That was when I realised Harry wasn't with me. Standing in the trees, I looked back the way I'd come over the fields. No Robert. No Harry. I was so sure I'd heard him following me from the road.

The fields remained dark and eerily quiet. I took another few seconds to rest but knew I needed to keep moving. Harry could have taken a different route, I argued with myself. The very idea of having left him to the mercies of Robert left a horribly unpleasant taste in my mouth. He'd come back to save me and I hadn't returned the favour.

A terrifying thought filled my head and panic ate at my insides. If Robert had Harry... I couldn't finish the sentence. Harry had made a big show of how he would never let Ellie down and would protect her with his life, but Robert would be just as determined to extract the information from him.

I shook my head to get the horrific images out of it. My first priority had to be Ellie. Ellie and my baby. I needed to find her and I needed to do it bloody quickly. Feeling guilty about Harry was only going to slow me down, and I knew he would agree. At least I hoped he would.

I set off in the general direction of the city lights, staying in the trees where I could, but eventually having to move out across open fields. The moon stayed hidden behind the threatening rain clouds for the most part, hopefully hiding me but also hiding Robert if he was still chasing me. There was no time to think about the mistakes I'd made or their consequences for Harry and inevitably perhaps for Ellie. I just put all my effort into running.

A couple of hours before dawn, I jogged across a small parade of shops surrounded by blocks of flats and rows of houses. They were closed for the night. I was lost and exhausted. I didn't want to stop – stopping meant not getting to Ellie – but I had no idea where Kesgrave was, and for all I knew, I was heading in the wrong direction. I needed a plan, some rest and a phone with Google Maps.

There were some homeless people sheltering in shop doorways, but otherwise the whole area was as quiet as a grave. A light drizzle fell softly, leaving me damp and shivering. There was nothing more I could do until it was daylight, so I joined the local down-and-outs and found myself a dry-ish doorway. It was maybe a degree warmer out of the wind. I hugged my arms around my knees, trying to warm up, and inevitably, my fatigued brain settled on Ellie.

It wasn't this new Ellie I thought about, not the one who owned houses and trust funds and a past I'd been completely excluded from; it was *my* Ellie, my real Ellie, who I loved with all my heart. My Ellie who drank milk from the bottle and giggled uncontrollably if I went anywhere near her toes and liked exactly three marshmallows in her hot chocolate. At some point, I drifted off.

Grating metal and voices drifted through my fatigue, and I struggled awake. The square looked grimy and tired in the early morning light. Shopkeepers were rolling up metal window covers and unlocking doors. It was time to get moving. I rose stiffly to my feet realising I couldn't remember the last time I hadn't ached from head to toe.

Opposite me, a newsagent was opening. I could steal a map and run like hell. Or... I spotted my victim. Baggy jeans, greasy hair and a straggly beard. It was hard to know if he was leaving home early or heading back late from a night on the town. I guessed the latter. Up close, he smelt of cigarette smoke and alcohol, but all I was interested in was the smartphone in his hand.

An earphone wire snaked up to his ear and he was speaking into the microphone bud on the cord. He carried the phone loosely in his left hand. I needed the phone unlocked and ready to use. He was young but looked a little pale and hungover. I would need to outrun him.

He was explaining to some guy named Toby how he'd scored with Maisie last night in graphic detail. I judged my approach to perfection, tore the phone out of his hand and sprinted for the nearest street, careful to keep the phone unlocked but disconnecting the call. I heard a commotion behind me, but little in the way of a concerted chase.

After I had run for about five minutes, taking a variety

of left and right turns, I found myself in a narrow alleyway. I stopped running. I couldn't see anyone chasing me, but knew I didn't have long before Baggy-jeans started tracking his phone or simply disconnected the SIM card. I brought up Google Maps and keyed in the address Harry had given me, praying to the god of desperation that he hadn't been fucking me over in a last-ditch attempt to protect Ellie.

Kesgrave turned out to be real, but bloody miles away; it was a residential suburb far to the northeast, way out of town. As I looked at how far away it looked on the phone's cracked screen, my heart sank. Before I walked off, I committed the route, several surrounding road names and landmarks to memory, then deleted the search and left the phone in a fairly obvious spot.

A couple of hours later, the heavens opened in earnest. The rain was now so heavy I could barely see my hand in front of my face. I was desperate to get to Ellie, but if I carried on walking in this downpour, I ran the risk of getting seriously lost. Under an overpass bridge, I found a dry patch of ground screened from the road by shrubs and I settled down as comfortably as I could on the hard, damp ground. The storm raged around me. I was cold, wet, hungry and miserable, but I was getting nearer to Ellie and that's all that mattered. I tried waiting for the rain to ease but I kept falling asleep, only to wake up with a jolt, imagining Robert in every noise.

I think around several hours passed. It was difficult keeping track of time. Eventually, the deluge dialled down enough for me to see where I was going. I seemed to take several wrong turns, but finally I stopped and stood admiring a sign that read:

Kesgrave welcomes careful drivers.

I'd drunk some foul-tasting water from some dubious sources en route to keep myself hydrated, promising myself a strong course of antibiotics when this was all over. Yesterday's ham sandwich was long gone, and my stomach growled incessantly. To add to my misery, I'd actually walked holes through the sides of my trainers so my socks were wet and blisters grew with every step.

It must have been late afternoon, although it was difficult to tell since the sky remained so overcast. I realised I didn't even know what day it was. I must have missed at least a couple of shifts at work. My arse was so fired, but right now all that mattered was that I was standing on the same road as Ellie.

Number 56 was a large detached house on a quiet leafy avenue in a pleasant neighbourhood. I walked past quickly on the other side of the road, head down, only looking at the house in my peripheral vision. There was no movement and the curtains were closed, but there was a car on the driveway.

I crossed the road and turned the corner, looking for a way into the back garden. Worst case scenario, I had to presume Robert was already waiting behind the front door. I wasn't about to walk up and knock, despite the desperation that squeezed my heart.

On the parallel road behind Crediton Close, roughly opposite where I judged number 56 to be, there was an empty house. I couldn't believe my luck. The grass was overgrown and I could see through the empty windows.

I clambered over the wooden fence at the bottom of the garden, hoping like hell I'd counted the houses properly and that this was, in fact, the back of number 56. The garden was filled with well-tended shrubs, flower beds and a neatly cut lawn. I wondered who had looked after the property while Ellie played house with me down in Berkshire. For all I knew she could have a whole other family living here – and another husband.

The curtains were open and electric lighting filtered out into the garden. Hugging the shrubbery, I edged close enough to peer in. And then my heart stopped.

Ellie was sitting on the couch flicking through a magazine, her legs curled up next to her, the way she always sat. I could imagine her beautiful eyes and her scar even though I couldn't see them at this angle, but it was her, and she was alive. Alive and very pregnant. She shifted her bulging belly uncomfortably as I watched. I stepped nearer and lifted my hand to knock on the window to get her attention.

I froze.

A man had walked into the room carrying a mug, and he handed it to my wife before gently kissing the top of her head. He was tall with ridiculously broad shoulders, his basketball shirt displaying his shredded biceps. His sun-bleached blond hair hung long down his neck. They talked for a few seconds before he left the room and she went back to her magazine, balancing the mug on her distended tummy.

Why the fuck hadn't Harry warned me?

I turned to leave, my ruined heart shattering once again into a million devastated pieces, but instead I walked straight into the business end of a spade flying at my head.

CHAPTER 55

A millisecond later and I would have been laid out, but I ducked just in time and the spade whistled over my head, skimming my hair. The blond man I'd seen inside reversed the spade's direction and whacked me hard on the opposite shoulder. My right arm fell and hung uselessly numb at my side. I swung with my left at his smug, wife-kissing mouth and felt a firm connection, but I couldn't follow it up. Blondie dropped the spade, stepped in and drove his fist straight into my mouth. My arms went up to protect my face but he jabbed underneath them and caught me square on my jaw. Flares of light flashed and dimmed, and the ground rushed up to grab me. There was no pain, no sense of anything. Just blackness.

The mind is both incredibly strong and easily deceived. I watched my wife's coffin being rolled into the flames at the crematorium, and I knew without a shadow of a doubt she was dead. Then a man I didn't know told me she was alive and living in Ipswich, so I hitched and walked halfway across the country on the off chance I'd misinterpreted reality.

Captured in a black sea of pain I heard her voice, and a celestial choir of angels couldn't have sounded more beautiful. Then I smelt her shampoo; grapefruit and mint. I was hallucinating. I even felt her hand on my cheek.

Words penetrated my groggy brain.

'Finn, FINN! Oh God please wake up. Finn! Ben, why did you hit him so bloody hard?'

Concern flooded Ellie's voice, and I desperately wanted to comfort her but I didn't want to open my eyes, too scared I'd lose the dream.

I raised an eyelid and glimpsed the fibres of an unfamiliar rug and the wooden legs of a couch. My stomach turned over and I vomited bile and filthy rainwater, adding to the pattern in the paisley design. I heard her voice again and I turned slowly towards it with trepidation.

'Finn, don't move. You're concussed and may have a serious head injury.' I spun my head regardless and looked into the gorgeous mismatched eyes of my dead wife.

'Ellie?' It didn't sound like my voice, but then nothing felt real at all.

Her arms flew around my neck and she hugged me. I closed my eyes and smelt her hair, felt her body and at last believed she was real. Ellie was alive and in my arms, and for a few seconds I just held on to her and this blissful moment.

Then I sensed the tall blond man standing to my left. Obviously my brain was still on a hiatus because my left arm shot out, swept at his legs and jerked him off his feet. He landed on the glass coffee table which smashed under his weight. He'd stolen Ellie from me and I was going to remove his balls or die trying.

Disengaging from Ellie's embrace, I scrambled awkwardly and painfully slowly to my feet, then promptly collapsed. Luckily I crashed into an armchair, but the world kept spinning furiously. Perhaps emasculating Blondie would have to wait.

I watched Ellie move over to the man, helping him to his feet. He seemed fine to me and close up he looked even bigger, but I didn't think Ellie went for steroid-induced gym bunnies. I wished I had his spade in my hands. Ellie was talking but I was having trouble concentrating. The man was answering her in an American accent. Jealousy and anger drove me back to my feet – no bloody yank was going to steal Ellie from me without a fight.

'Finn, for the love of God, sit down and let me explain,' Ellie implored, as the damn ugly rug rushed up again. My balance was shot. Blondie's strong hands caught me, gently lowering me back down onto the armchair.

Ellie knelt at my feet and looked into my eyes as I fought the vertigo.

'Finn, this is Benjamin, my brother. Stop trying to hit him. He's on the Canadian Olympic wrestling team, for God's sake.'

Blondie stuck his huge bear-sized hand in my face. 'Hey, buddy, call me Ben. Sorry I whacked you back there.' He grinned, and I could see that he even had great teeth.

I immaturely slapped his hand away. Ellie's brother? My head was clearing, but agonisingly slowly. Something kept nagging at me, some danger I needed to warn Ellie about, but it kept slipping away.

'You hit me with a spade,' I whined through my swelling mouth. Perhaps I'd mistaken the kiss for a platonic peck.

'Not really, I mainly missed. I did get you with my fist

though, and I'm really sorry about that.' He shrugged and shook his bruised hand without a shred of remorse. 'This whole place is rigged with CCTV and intruder alarms and shit, both inside and out. You set off the motion sensors in the garden when you fell over the fence. I couldn't take any chances, buddy.'

I still wanted to hit him. I was desperate to hit a lot of people these days. I wasn't sure where I'd lost my caring side.

Ellie pushed Ben out of the way, dispatching him to get warm water, towels and dry clothes. He also brought a surprisingly well-stocked, if slightly illegal first aid kit, and she gave me a thorough once over, checking my reflexes and the reaction times of my pupils.

'You're concussed and need to stay sitting for now, okay? Let's get you into dry clothes and then we can talk. I know I owe you lots of explanations, Finn. I hardly know where to start. But please don't ever think I stopped loving you. It's because I loved you so much that I had to go away. I was trying to keep you safe. I'm sorry it all turned out so badly.'

There were tears in her eyes and her scar was translucent with tension. In that moment I didn't care about any of it, I just melted into her arms. My hand hovered over her belly, not quite believing she was right there with me.

'Our baby, is it—?'

'Yes Finn, the baby's fine. I thought I was in labour a couple of days ago but it was a false alarm. It's not going to hang on much longer. I think it was just waiting for you to come find us,' she simpered, stroking my hair.

'You didn't make it easy, Ell,' I added softly. 'You broke my heart.' Reality was slowly seeping through my pounding headache. She took my hand, laying it softly on her extended tummy and I swear I could feel our child stirring under the pressure.

'I know, I'm so sorry, I had no choice. Robert—'

Something clicked, and I tried to stand again but Ellie shoved me back down. I'd remembered.

'Robert. He has Harry. I think. I had to leave him, I didn't mean to but I had to run. I'm so sorry Ellie, I know how close you two are. Robert will know about this house. He'll come here as soon as he makes Harry tell him. We have to go. He said something about you being his daughter...' I had to make her understand.

'Finn, slow down. Harry won't tell him anything. We need to think clearly. Now first let's get you out of these soaked clothes and then we'll talk.'

Olympic wrestler Ben handed me a towel and a pile of clothes. I was fucked if I was changing in front of him. Ellie helped me up since I still couldn't stand without toppling over. Thankfully Ben had the sense to shuffle off and check the perimeter or something. I longed for a shower, but I knew my legs wouldn't hold me yet.

'Ellie, please. You have to listen to me. Harry will *have* to tell Robert this address. He's persuasive, he won't have a choice.' God, it felt so long ago. So much had happened since then, but I could still remember my fear in that basement. 'He has a huge knife and God knows what else, and—'

'I know. Robert takes great pleasure in hurting people,' Ellie interrupted, her tone almost wistful, her fingers stroking her scar. 'That's why I had to *die*. I stupidly believed Robert would give up and that then you'd be able to safely come find me. But I know now he'll never stop. We're safe here for now though Finn. Harry won't tell him anything.'

Millions of questions buzzed in my head, but I was finding it hard to focus, mesmerised by Ellie's soft touch on my skin as she helped me out of my soaking wet clothes. Ben's were about fifty sizes too big and they had me questioning my sanity for even trying to take him down.

Ellie gave me an ice pack and forced some painkillers down my throat. I felt a guilty pang as I thought about how close I came to swallowing those pills as a way out only a few weeks ago, believing I'd lost everything.

'Ellie.' I took her hands and looked at the woman I loved. 'We need to talk and we need a plan. We need to end this madness with Robert. For Harry's sake, for ours and for our baby's.'

CHAPTER 56

I cringed with embarrassment as Ben cleaned up my vomit with a big friendly grin on his face. I think he was even whistling the Canadian national anthem as he scrubbed. I kept reminding them that Robert could be on his way, but Ellie remained adamant that Harry would stay strong.

Ellie fussed in the kitchen making me a ham sandwich – not the best idea for a mild concussion but I was starving and it actually stayed down. She also gave me a glass of the best tasting clean water I'd ever drunk. At last, she came and sat down opposite me on the couch.

She picked at her nails nervously, unsure where to start. Around a mouthful of wholemeal bread, I decided to help her out.

'Ellie, I never stopped loving you, even after I thought I'd lost you, even when I thought you'd left me for someone else...' My voice cracked and we both teared up. I took her hand, my sandwich forgotten, and finally she lifted her eyes to mine. Her voice, when she spoke, was barely above a whisper.

'I didn't want to disappear Finn, you have to believe me, but Robert found me. He attacked me in the car park when I was doing some Christmas shopping, and the only reason he didn't kill me was because of the baby and the fact that I offered to give him...' she hesitated, her face blushing with discomfort, '...I had some money that I was due to inherit. I haven't told you about it, I—'

I interrupted gently to put her out of her misery. 'I know about the trust fund Ell, and I know some other bits and pieces. Harry filled me in on some of it. We can talk about all that later. Just explain why you didn't tell me he'd threatened you. *We* could have gone to the police.'

Ellie let out a slow breath. Ben was still hovering so she suggested that he go make some tea.

'That's precisely why, Finn. Your first instinct would have been to tell the authorities and that would have gotten you killed. Robert would have lashed out. It's what he does. Getting Harry to help was the only option I had left.'

She squeezed my hand and we sat with our knees touching. I didn't want to let go, petrified she would disappear again.

'I lied to you, Finn. I lied to you about absolutely everything and I'm so *so* incredibly sorry. When I met you, I was completely entrenched in my fabricated life, but then I fell in love with you and I still didn't know how to tell you the truth. I was so afraid I'd lose you. Everything I've ever told you about me was a lie. And then I met your parents and they were so lovely and I just wanted that too. I just wanted normal – with you, but then Robert...' She couldn't finish the sentence. Her face had scrunched up in pain.

'Ellie?' I jumped up and managed to stay on my feet even as the room tilted.

'I'm fine, it's just a twinge. I don't think there's much room left in there.' Her hand rubbed her stomach protectively, and she breathed in and out slowly.

None of the lies and deceit mattered. All the unanswered questions could wait. Ellie was going to have our baby and I didn't care about anything else right now. She still loved me and wanted to be with me. We'd work the rest out. Right now it was time for *me* to take care of my family.

I sat Ellie and Ben down on the couch. Sitting next to each other you could see the sibling similarities. I laid out my plan, ignoring their objections. I'd had a shitty few days and was tired of being on the defensive. They weren't happy, but I pushed my arguments and they conceded we were out of options. Ben and I modified specifics as Ellie packed a bag for her with supplies for the baby, and then I made my first call on one of Ellie's endless supply of burner phones. It wasn't a term I'd ever envisaged using in real life, but this was my reality now. I had a second chance to protect my wife and child. I wasn't going to fuck it up.

My head was still throbbing but my arm was returning to normal, if a little heavy. I could walk without falling over which was a vast improvement, and my thought processes seemed as unscrambled as they were going to get. I dialled my parents.

I had a hard time making them understand that their daughter-in-law was in fact alive and that I wasn't in the throes of a complete mental breakdown. Once they had spoken to Ellie they slowly started to believe the impossible. My mum was the slightly less hysterical of the two, and when I explained that Ellie was actually pregnant and needed somewhere safe to stay and that she was only days away from giving birth to their grandchild, I immediately had her undivided attention.

After much debate, they reluctantly agreed to tell no one and to not go near a hospital unless Ellie's or the baby's life depended on it. I knew if it came to a home birth, Ellie would be in the best hands with my mum.

I kissed Ellie with all the passion I had in my being, running my thumb over her scar, committing every contour of her face to memory. I couldn't go through losing her again. I'd only just found her and we were having to say goodbye already.

I kissed her belly and whispered to my child telling them to wait to make their appearance until I could be there, if he/she could. My heart lodged firmly in my throat as I waved goodbye. Ben would drive Ellie down towards my parents and meet my dad halfway before hurrying back.

Knowing I'd have to face Robert before I saw Ellie again left my mouth dry and my heart beating ten to the dozen.

Upstairs in the en-suite bathroom was a large bath with jets and bubbles that I couldn't resist. I had some time to waste before Part B of our plan went into action. I hoped that the Dartford Crossing would remain clear for once, else we were completely screwed. I was going to need the big blond wrestler by my side if I was going to survive the night.

Lying in the hot soapy bathwater, I mulled over the new image of Ellie forming in my head, trying to assimilate our new reality from the limited information she'd had time to share.

Much of it echoed what Harry had told me. Ellie had been born to wealthy parents; Thomas and Elizabeth Hudson, and Benjamin, *call-me-Ben*, was her biological brother. Neither of them could remember the events that led to

Ben being sent, in secret, to distant maternal cousins in Canada, but it followed an incident where Robert threatened the lives of both children and left Ellie with her facial scar.

Ellie's parents impressed on the young child the complete need for secrecy before carrying out their joint suicide. Her life in foster care was hard, but she carried no bitterness about having been abandoned. She knew it was to save her from her deranged uncle. Bizarrely, Ellie said she always felt that her parents were still with her somehow, looking down from heaven, watching her every move.

When Robert found her, she turned to Harry to help her stage the accident. For the umpteenth time, I wondered where he was, desperately hoping he'd gotten away from Robert.

Ellie always knew her brother was alive, and not long after we got married she finally found him on Facebook. They met up a couple of times when Ben travelled to London to take part in international wrestling competitions. When Ellie had emailed him to warn that their uncle had resurfaced, Ben dropped everything and came to the UK. That was the effect Ellie had on the people who loved her. I only wished she'd had the same faith in me, but that was a discussion for a later date.

The water was lukewarm and the surface was covered in an unhealthy looking scum as I pulled myself reluctantly out of the bath and dressed in the smallest of Ben's clothes. It was time for my second phone call. It didn't go well.

I started off by asking nicely and then threatening, before changing tack and begging with all my heart. Police officers were seemingly not too keen on leaving their home jurisdictions. By the time I had hung up, I wasn't entirely sure we'd agreed on anything. My brilliant plan was beginning to unravel. But there was no turning back now.

My stomach was full and I was warm and dry. I could have slept for a week, but now I had another call to make, and for this one, I needed a clear head. I slugged down a can of Red Bull I had found in the fridge, and with trembling fingers dialled a number from memory. It rang a few times as my blood thundered in my veins. Everything depended on me getting this right.

'Hello?'

'Hi, Rachel? It's me, Finn.'

CHAPTER 57

'**R**achel, are you still there?'

'Finn, hi, yes… sorry I didn't recognise the number. Are you okay? I was so worried. I haven't heard from you for days. I tried your mobile over and over. I was worried that maybe Robert—'

In that moment, I almost blurted out that Robert, the sodding bastard, had my phone. Shit. I had to stay focused.

'He did grab me but I got away, but I never made it down to Kent and I've lost my phone. But I did find Harry and we followed some leads.' I stumbled through my words vaguely. 'It's the worst news. Oh Rachel. I don't know what to do.'

'Slow down Finn. You're not making any sense. You're with Harry Grainger? Have you found Eleanor? Is she alive?'

It was difficult to read what Rachel was thinking and which answer she really wanted to hear.

'I was with Harry and then we got separated, but not

before he told me where she was.' I paused for dramatic effect. 'Rachel, I found her. I found Ellie. She really is alive.' I let the words hang awhile in the silence. Thinking of Ellie and the baby made it easy to inject the emotion into my voice. 'I stole this phone so I could call you. I'm standing outside her house right now. She's alive, Rachel, it's actually her, but... I...' I paused again, turning my performance down a notch. If I overplayed this she'd see right through me. She was used to me sounding vague and I didn't want to give too much detail away.

'But what, Finn? But what? You're scaring me.'

'She's... she's with someone. She left me for another man. Fuck I'm such an idiot.' My voice caught. 'I should just walk away and go home. I can't face her. It's too much, I just—'

She interrupted almost immediately. 'No. Finn, you need to speak to her, get closure and find answers. If you don't, you'll never have peace. Would it help if I met you and we confronted her together? I would still like to meet my half-sister. I have a few questions of my own,' she added almost as an afterthought.

'Confront her? Er... oh God, Rachel... I'm not sure I can. I just don't think I can do it. I'm miles away from you anyway.'

'You need to Finn, for your own peace of mind. You have a right to know about the baby and the money. You'll need answers so that you can move on.' She was almost pleading now. 'Tell me where you are and I'll come straight away. We'll do this together and then it will all be over. You can go back and rebuild your life and I can be there for you,' she offered magnanimously – as if she could ever replace Ellie.

What I'd learnt on the internet back in Southampton had confirmed what I should have guessed all along. Rachel wasn't who she said she was. She wasn't a lawyer for a top London law firm but an unemployed legal secretary. Ellie knew nothing about her and had never emailed her. There was a good chance they were biological half-sisters, but for some reason, which I couldn't quite fathom, she was symbiotically connected to Robert.

And if I played it right, she would send him to me.

'Are you sure? Thanks so much, Rach, I couldn't do this without you.' I sniffed dramatically and gave her the address of the house in Kesgrave.

'Kesgrave? That's near Ipswich. I'm in Clacton! I'll be there in half an hour max,' she said, and hung up. I was caught off guard. I'd wrongly assumed she was still in London. What could I do? It was too late to uninvite her. She was my segway to getting Robert where I wanted him to be. Now I'd have to deal with her *and* Robert.

I altered the plan on the fly and went to find some coffee and Ellie's exceptionally well-equipped first aid kit.

There was a wooden bus shelter a little way down the road from Ellie's house that kept the wind out while I waited. The rain had finally stopped and the sky was clear with bright moonlight and a sprinkling of stars.

I hadn't been there long when Rachel pulled up in her expensive car. I guessed that was another prop of her bullshit story.

'Finn, I'm so sorry.' She ran up and hugged me, and I forced myself to relax into her embrace. If she had noticed my new set of bruises and thick lip in the street-light, she didn't comment.

'Thanks again for coming,' I started whimpering. 'I just can't believe Ellie did this to me. I loved her so much.' Her hand rubbed my back sympathetically.

'You need to have it out with her, find out why she left you. It's bloody outrageous that she went to such extremes to get away from you. It makes no sense, Finn. You need to confront her.' She took a breath, her hands firmly on her hips, and looked up and down the quiet suburban street. 'Let's get it over with. So which is her house?'

I hadn't told her the number of the house, just the road name. Most homes had lights on and cars parked outside. Families were settling in for the night. Number 56 had no cars but there was light escaping around the edges of the drawn curtains.

'You just missed them. They just left. Ellie and her new man... her *lover*.' I spat the word out, proud how I'd managed to combine disdain and misery so perfectly into one word. 'The bastard had a suitcase with him. I was hiding behind the wall and heard them talking. Sounded like she was dropping him off at Stansted Airport for some reason. That's at least a two hour round trip. She won't be back for ages.'

Rachel twirled her hair around her fingers, deep in thought. She wasn't getting there fast enough, so I helped her out.

'I had a bit of a look around while I waited for you. There's a way in around the back. There's a window which I think I can climb through.' I sighed with sadness. 'I wanted to see where she was living, you know?

Get a sense of why this life is so much better, why she left me. I chickened out though. Came out here to wait for you instead.' Real tears filled my eyes. I was getting far too good at this.

'Of course you want to know and you have a right to, Finn. What Eleanor put you through... it's disgusting. I mean, she faked her own death. How can someone even do that?' I just shook my head dejectedly. 'Let me grab a torch from my car and we'll go see what else she's been up to.'

I watched her walk away, her hand already reaching for the phone in her pocket. I crossed the road and waited by the side of number 56. Rachel joined me, mumbling something about flat batteries to explain why she hadn't actually got a torch. We climbed over the back gate into the neat rear garden and crept up to the window. I'd left some of the curtains open and light spilt out perfectly, showing the way. To Rachel, I hoped it looked like a house left in a hurry to get to the airport on time.

I should have picked an easier window. This one proved awkward to climb through. My right arm still felt like a dead weight and I bashed my still aching head on the window frame as I jumped down. Everything was laid out, and I grabbed what I needed before going to let Rachel in through the patio doors.

I could immediately see she was impressed. Her eyes had lit up with interest when she saw the quality of the furniture, the expensive-looking artwork and the immaculate decor. Obviously, in this life, Eleanor had money.

I hesitated, hoping I'd guessed right about where Rachel's allegiances lay. If I had it wrong, I would no doubt have a long time to reconsider the folly of my actions from inside a prison cell. I flipped the cap off the pre-filled syringe with my left thumb as I grabbed Rachel's arm with my right hand. I pressed the needle through her shirtsleeve, depressing the plunger as soon as I felt it slide into her muscle.

Rachel turned on me, eyes wide with shock, and then she snapped. She screamed and began to struggle like a wild animal, and it took all my strength to hold her as she kicked out and clawed at my face. She carried on yelling and screaming in a frenzy, but I reasoned the neighbours were far away enough to think it was only the TV. At last the Flunitrazepam, more commonly known as Rohypnol, began to work, and her frantic movements slowed. It was about ten times more effective than Valium and often used to subdue and sedate patients pre-operatively or during unpleasant procedures. It suited my purposes perfectly.

Rachel was beginning to calm down. Her muscles were growing floppy and her eyelids were starting to droop. Without the ability to coordinate her movements, she stopped fighting me. I led her down the hall, only just about stopping her from toppling over.

The kitchen was large and spacious, with lots of gleaming stainless steel appliances and fancy cabinets. It also had a big walk-in pantry which was about half the size of our entire kitchen back at home. I lay Rachel on the floor in the recovery position, her head on the flat pillow I'd left there earlier. Her eyes were droopy. I popped the lid off another prefilled syringe and added some midazolam to her bloodstream. That should keep her out of the way for a few hours.

I stepped out and locked the door, refusing to even think

about how or why Ellie had these kinds of drugs in her possession. I hid the key to the pantry in the tea caddy and waited.

I instinctively knew I wouldn't have to wait that long. Icy fear urged me to run like hell, and my palms were sweaty. The thought of facing Robert again was totally terrifying, but I'd had enough running.

The doorbell rang. It was showtime.

CHAPTER 58

I opened the door on the second ring.

The spade Ben had used on me was propped up against the wall, well within grabbing distance – but I didn't even get a chance. Harry fell heavily into my unsuspecting arms and I caught his dead weight. When I looked up, I saw Robert standing behind him. A wave of déjà vu washed over me, except this time instead of a taser, he was holding his ugly serrated knife threateningly close to Harry's kidneys.

'Move inside Murray, and don't drop your little friend, he's feeling a bit under the weather.' Robert laughed, his grey eyes as cold and vindictive as always. He grinned when he saw the spade and kicked it derisively away.

Harry groaned as I staggered back into the hallway, struggling under his weight. I wanted to put him down to assess his injuries, but Robert's knife encouraged moving through into the lounge.

I eased Harry onto the couch as gently as possible. He was still wearing the filthy remains of his waiter's uniform, only now the dirty white shirt was saturated with blood. I slipped a cushion under his head and he moaned weakly. His eyes were too swollen to open and his face was a mess, bruised, bleeding, cut into pieces – more raw meat than recognisable features. His pulse was thready, weak and fast, and he was clearly in a lot of pain and barely conscious. He needed proper medical attention. Even Ellie's first aid kit wouldn't cut it.

Anger rose in my gut as I tried to get him comfortable. I knew now how important he was to Ellie, and I wished for the hundredth time that I hadn't abandoned him at the side of the road with this armed maniac. Guilt and stupidity drove me to my feet. I swung at Robert, vaguely targeting his nose, putting all my strength behind the punch.

'YOU BASTARD!' I shouted. 'What have you done to him?'

Robert sidestepped with practised ease and drove his fist into my kidneys as I flew past. I landed roughly where the stain from my earlier vomit marked the carpet, and a wave of agony rattled through me. I was almost sick again. My stitches had burst open and blood was dripping down my arm.

I'd learnt a little from my brief tussle with Ben. I knew that the longer I stayed down, the more vulnerable I was. I stood up as quickly as I could, turned and threw another punch.

We were both taken by surprise at the speed of my counterattack. My fist connected with the side of his jaw. I definitely hit bone – the reverberating pain shot up my arm. Robert stepped back with one hand massaging his jaw and the other holding his back. He was standing awkwardly straight. I wondered in my never-off-duty doctor's head if he had an issue with his spine – an old injury perhaps. Before I knew it, Robert was coming at me again, and I didn't have time to worry about his prognosis. I hunkered down and took what he threw at me, as Ben had suggested. He made it sound so easy. It fucking wasn't.

Robert's punches rained down on me until I hit the carpet once more. He grabbed a handful of hair, yanking my head back and exposing my throat. I felt the sting of his knife and held my breath. If he killed me now he would go straight after Ellie and the baby.

'UP!' he barked. The serrated edge plucked at my skin.

With the knife at my neck, I scrambled to my feet, warm blood oozing down my skin. He turned me around and I felt the tip of the blade hovering around my lower back.

'Hands behind your back, Murray, or I'll gut you where you stand. I'll still find Eleanor without you, believe me. The choice is yours.'

I complied. This was so far off plan as to be ludicrous. How had I ever thought I would get the better of him?

His free hand fixed one of those nifty little cable ties around my wrists and used another to secure me to one of the dining room chairs. My brain was becoming fuzzy and I was bleeding all over Ben's clothing.

I was well and truly fucked.

'And here we are again, Murray,' said Robert, backing away slightly. 'The question remains the same. You told Rachel that Eleanor lives here, so where the fuck is she? And while we're talking of missing women, where is that stupid cow?'

I spat out some blood and part of a tooth, secretly pleased to see Robert's jaw reddening from my punch. It was a pathetically small victory, but I took what I could get.

With a sinking feeling, I realised I'd mistimed things badly. I knew my body couldn't take much more punishment at the hands of this sadist, so I needed to delay things. I started with the question that had been nagging at me for days:

'Why is Rachel helping you? Is she even Ellie's sister?'

Robert rocked back on his heels, debating whether to answer my question or keep beating me up. Thankfully, he started talking.

'Oh Rachel is Thomas's daughter all right. His illegitimate daughter that is,' he explained dismissively. 'He had an affair with her mother. It destroyed the woman's career. She was his lecturer at Cambridge. Terribly scandalous back in the day. And then he abandoned her and her unborn child. Rachel never knew her absentee father or any family, so she jumped at the chance to play-act the long lost sister. You were so easy to fool. I've promised her a tidy sum of money for helping me. I'm sure she'll enjoy watching Eleanor suffer as much as I will.'

He was beyond delusional but seemed in a talkative mood, so I pushed for more.

'Did you kill Cassie?'

'Cassie?' Robert actually had to work hard to remember, and when he did, he just sniggered. 'Oh you mean Grainger's whore? The little drugged up bitch? Yes, I remember now. She wouldn't tell me where he was. I had to get quite resourceful with her, but the stupid girl died before I got anything useful.'

A shudder flew down my spine as I thought of Cassie's last agonising moments. How was this psychopath even free to walk the streets? He was clearly certifiable. 'She didn't even know where Harry was. She couldn't have told you anything,' I argued softly.

He smiled at me manically with wide eyes. 'Perhaps, but we're wasting time. So...' his gaze drifted around the room, 'this is where Eleanor has been hiding out is it? And where exactly is she now? Rachel texted to say she was on her way to the airport but would be on her way back soon. Correct?' He looked around as if she could be hiding behind the curtains, and content she wasn't there, focussed back on me. His tone was conversational, but his words sent my blood thrumming through my veins. 'Now then Murray, you know the drill. Start giving me answers or I'm going to start carving you into little pieces. Why is she living all the way out here, for starters?'

I refused to let myself look at the knife in his hand. Forcing steadiness into my voice, I continued my interrogation. 'What about the poor sod you left in my shed? Was that you as well? Who was he? How did he fit into all this?'

Robert looked at me for a long time and I started to worry that I had overplayed my hand. He drew up a dining room chair and sat down gingerly, resting his back. Our knees were almost touching.

'Ah yes, the man in your shed. Quite clever really, it kept you busy with the police didn't it? He was just a lucky extra who came my way. My idiotic brother sent him to kill me, but then you know all about that don't you, given you're in cahoots with the whole family...'

I couldn't make sense of what I was hearing. I knew the man was a marshmallow short of a sundae, but did he honestly believe his brother was alive as well? The man had died over twenty years ago. I forced myself to refocus. Robert was still talking. I had to stay on point.

'...name was Adam something or the other. He was far too easy, he told me everything. No fun at all.'

'But you still killed him, before dumping his body I mean?'

'Well of course I killed him. I couldn't very well have him going back to tell Thomas he'd been rumbled.' He laughed loudly and looked genuinely pleased with himself. 'Now while we're on the topic of my brother, let's add him to the list of missing people you can tell me about. Now enough chatting, shall we get started?'

He got up stiffly and walked back into the hall, only to return with a brown gym bag. He dumped it at my feet. Dread and bile rose in my mouth. I spat out some more blood and pulled desperately at my wrists. I needed more time.

'She's not your daughter, you know. Ellie, she's not yours. You can tell by her eyes.'

Robert stopped and looked at me like he wanted to pull my insides out and set them alight, but I had his attention.

'*Go on.*'

My throat was bone dry. I knew what was coming but forced the words out of my mouth. 'Her type of heterochromia – it has to be inherited from a parent. You don't have it which proves she's not your daughter. Ellie says she inherited it from her father, Thomas. He had different coloured eyes too, right?' I apologised to my genetics professors for skewing the facts, but I was desperate to keep Robert talking instead of torturing me. 'So I guess you're actually nothing more than her uncle, right? And a pathetically jealous one at that. Ellie says your parents never loved you, is that why you're so—'

Robert's fist shot out, connecting with a solid punch. I felt my nose pop and blood gush over my mouth and chin. My vision blurred and the room spun wildly. A loud buzzing filled my ears. Fuck that hurt.

Through the confusion in my head, I heard the zipper open on the gym bag. A new fear and a wash of adrenaline chased away the pain. I'd gone too far. He'd lost interest in our conversation. A lump of solid ice settled in my heart. It was too late. He'd do things to me now – unimaginable things – until I told him everything, and none of it would save Ellie or the baby. I'd also added my parents and Harry to this psycho's list of victims and it was all my fault. I'd been so arrogant in thinking I could best him, no wonder Ellie hadn't trusted me to protect her against this madman.

I looked over at Harry who was still out for the count on the couch. We'd all sacrificed so much, and for nothing.

Robert grabbed my hair, twisting me to face him. The corner of his mouth lifted ever so slightly, perhaps in a smile – it was hard to tell – but his eyes remained stone cold. I threw a terrified glance at his other hand, expecting to see a bigger knife, or a hammer, or a wrench – something out of a torture scene in a horror film. But instead, he was holding a clear plastic freezer bag. I almost laughed with relief until I realised what he was going to do with it.

I fought the cable ties, shredding my wrists to the bone. With his hand still gripping my hair, Robert slipped the bag over my head, and in the same movement removed a long elastic band from his pocket. It landed tight around my neck, sealing the plastic.

I couldn't breathe.

In sheer panic, I used up what little oxygen there was inside the bag in seconds. The plastic flew into my mouth every time I gulped for air. Blackness gathered at the edges of my vision, and there was a humming in my ears. I was dying, and the only saving grace was that death prevented me from telling Robert about Ellie.

CHAPTER 59

'Thomas?'

'Eleanor?'

'Rachel?'

Robert was yelling at me ruthlessly.

He was fucking good at this. He was standing behind my chair, his hands on my shoulders, holding me down as my body writhed and jerked, desperate for even a molecule of oxygen. Just as the blackness began to obliterate the pain, he released the elastic band, and like a drowning man, I drank in sweet air. My vision cleared slightly but my head buzzed in agony. My heart was trying to thump its way out of my chest.

'So where shall we start?' he asked, and slapped my face hard. I was struggling to focus but he was back in front of me, looming nearer. 'With Eleanor I think.'

I wanted to ask him questions, keep him talking – anything to stall him, but I couldn't formulate the words.

When I didn't answer, he threaded his finger around the elastic band and twisted it. My air disappeared. I closed my mouth and tried to keep a trickle of oxygen in my lungs. When I couldn't stand it any longer, I opened my mouth to breathe – the bag was completely empty.

I was tumbling into a dark and terrifying pit, and I wondered if Ellie would catch me. No. She was gone. Not dead, but gone. Confusion weighed down on my hypoxic brain cells. Just as I reached the brink of no return, with practised timing, Robert allowed some air to dribble back into the bag.

'Where... is... Eleanor?'

This time he let me get a good few mouthfuls of oxygen, but I wasted them stupidly. 'Fuck off you cunt,' I gasped from inside the plastic.

He punched me in the stomach, forcing what little air I'd accumulated straight back out again before he immediately tightened the band. Grey drifted quickly to black. I couldn't even make sense of the pain anymore. I fought desperately to find any air, but I was slipping away fast.

Out of nowhere, a massive golden bear drove into Robert and knocked him flying. But it was too late for me. The bag was still too tight. I was already floating a long way down a dark curvy tunnel, but I could hear him and the bear struggling. Their voices were getting further away as I drifted off.

Claws scratched at my face, my lungs were on fire and white noise raged in my pounding skull. A hole appeared in the bag, a trickle of air and then another hole. The bag was slowly being torn from my face and delicious oxygen filtered slowly back into my lungs as the room swam.

Ben was back, not a bear with claws. He was fighting Robert while managing to tear the bag from my face.

He'd only turned his back to save my life. I could hear both men grunting and the sound of crashing furniture, and I felt desperate to help. I weakly tried to move, but I was still attached to the chair and groggy as hell.

'Ben, hit his lower back,' I urged in a rasping voice. I don't know if he heard me, my voice sounded pathetically weak and I didn't want to talk anymore. My throat was on fire. I think I heard the distorted sound of the door-bell over the sound of their fighting, and I pulled wearily at my restraints. My wrists were sticky with blood but there was no give. I needed to help Ben and get to Harry.

Then the room was an explosion of people, noise and chaos. Everyone was yelling. Nothing made sense. It felt as if I were submerged underwater – my senses were hazy and unreliable. Orders were being shouted, and I heard Ben's name in the din, someone telling Robert to keep still. And then Detective Renshaw's face floated into view. He still didn't look happy.

'I told you to wait until I arrived, Murray. This is a right cluster fuck you've engineered here.'

I don't think I'd ever been so happy to see a policeman before in my life, and my shoulders sagged with relief. It was over. It was finally over.

Renshaw had arrived mob-handed. I even spotted Constable Spike drifting about the crowded uniform-filled room. Paramedics were working on Harry, who didn't look good. Both Ben and Robert were in handcuffs, which worried me, until I saw the ridiculous grin on my newest brother-in-law's face.

Robert looked a mess. Whatever had happened between the two of them, the Olympian had thumped the older ex-army psychopath.

Renshaw cut my wrists free and immediately called for a paramedic. They were bleeding freely, and perhaps he was a little concerned about Ellie's expensive carpet.

'Right, whose house is this? And why the fuck is there is a drugged woman in the pantry?'

Oh God, this was going to be a long night.

'Actually, it's my wife's house.' It was agony to talk. I could barely get any sound past my inflamed throat, but I owed him answers. He had come to save us. 'Seemingly she isn't quite as dead as everyone thought she was.' I was trying to think of that famous Mark Twain quote about his death being exaggerated, but I couldn't forge the sentence coherently. Either way, Renshaw was not amused. Which reminded me, and ignoring the detective, I looked at Ben and asked the only question that mattered. 'Did you get her there okay? Is she alright?'

'Everything's okay Buddy, no sign of the baby yet but everything's under control. You're a mess dude! I told you to roll with the punches, not take the sick fuck on single-handed,' he admonished, but his tone was gentle. 'Ellie will kill me if anything happens to you.' The two uniformed policemen tightened their grip around his massive biceps at the mention of more killing.

Adrenaline dispersed, and my whole body began shaking furiously. Renshaw really didn't care, and even while the paramedic was bandaging my wrists and checking my slowly returning vitals, he demanded an explanation. But then I guess I had begged him to come here.

I refused to answer any questions until they had removed Ben's cuffs, and then I let him explain about the CCTV cameras. He took Renshaw up to one of the spare bedrooms and showed them the monitors and recording equipment.

The live feed had caught, on camera, Robert confessing to the torture and murder of two people, and it also showed him trying his best to make me his third victim. Even if this wasn't admissible in court, Robert was going to have a hard time convincing a jury he was innocent.

Robert, in the meantime, was making threats and screaming at everyone, using expletives that made Friday night in A&E sound like a Sunday school picnic.

I watched as the paramedics wheeled Harry out on a stretcher to the waiting ambulance, not liking the worried expressions on their faces. I wanted to go with him, make sure he was looked after properly. Renshaw refused.

'So, you say your wife's back in the land of the living?'

'She was never dead,' I corrected him. 'She faked her death because her life was in danger, hers and the baby's. Her sick fuck of an uncle wanted to torture and kill her and steal her inheritance. Harry—'

Despite his restraints, Robert managed to throw himself at me one last time, and we landed in a mess on the floor. Uniformed arms pulled him off me, none too gently, and dragged him outside where blue lights were whirling through the curtains.

Renshaw helped me up and it took a while for me to gather my breath before I continued. 'Ellie's with my parents in Kent, but she's going to give birth any day now. She won't go missing again. I promise. He can't be allowed to hurt either of them. Please, promise me that.'

Renshaw helped me move into the armchair. I felt like I was about ninety. The second ambulance crew were hovering, wanting to take me away to get properly checked over.

'And the woman in the pantry?'

'That's Rachel Bates. You remember her? Ellie's half-sister. She was helping Robert by keeping tabs on me, but only because he was threatening her and her mum, I think. She'll be fine in an hour or two.'

'Okay. And the half-dead man from the couch? The big blond American?'

'He's Canadian,' I warned, 'and they're both her brothers, sort of.'

'Oh for fuck's sake, Murray. You told me your wife was an orphan with no family. Now brothers and sisters and uncles are appearing all over the place.'

'It's a long story, so let me start at the beginning.' I arranged my aching body into the comfortable armchair and started. 'Ellie's real name is Eleanor Elizabeth Hudson...'

EPILOGUE

Six weeks later

The noise woke me from a deep and dreamless sleep. I struggled out of bed and over to the crib in the corner. For something that weighed less than three and a half kilograms, it made a helluva racket. Thankfully Ellie slept through it, or she was pretending to. We'd agreed that I'd do this feed to give her a rest.

I lifted my daughter, Chloe Elizabeth Murray, gently into my arms. My heart was so full of love and awe that I thought I could burst with pride. I carried her downstairs and she kept wailing as I warmed up the bottle of breast milk Ellie had expressed earlier.

In the breakfast nook of the large kitchen in the Kesgrave house was a rocking chair my parents had insisted on buying us. Chloe and I sat there watching the moonlight dance over the garden. Well, I watched and the baby gratefully guzzled her milk.

We were staying in Ipswich while things got sorted out. The first few days had been harrowing. The police arrested all of us, including Rachel, who gave Robert up immediately. He, on the other hand, was saying nothing.

They also wanted to incarcerate Ellie, but they hadn't counted on my mother. She enlisted the help of her local MP – a lady who she just happened to play mah-jong with every Tuesday – and Ellie was left in peace to give birth in my old bedroom at home. My only regret was not being there for the delivery of our daughter. But at least they were safe.

At first, they were hell-bent on prosecuting Ellie for faking her death and Harry for stealing and burning the Jane Doe's unclaimed body. Harry was still in intensive care at that point and couldn't answer for his actions. And Ben, well no one knew what to do with him – or me. My dad even cashed in some shares ready to pay for a defence attorney, but that was before everything took a wonderful turn for the better.

The army stepped in.

News of Robert's arrest filtered through to them and it turned out they had been hunting him since he'd gone AWOL following an in-depth inquiry into his clandestine actions.

Seemingly, there were several incidences of brutality and torture they wanted to question him about. Thankfully for us, because he'd served under the radar in the army, they preferred to keep things in-house so to speak, and were extremely keen to avoid the publicity that a civilian trial would generate.

To keep the whole mess out of the spotlight and after weeks of legal wrangling, charges against Ellie and Harry were thankfully dropped. They were both judged as having acted in self-defence. I got the feeling, however, that Renshaw was a sore loser and would be waiting to pounce if any one of us so much as got a parking ticket.

Harry walked stiffly into the kitchen. He'd come out of the hospital a few days ago but was having trouble sleeping. Robert had really worked him over and left him with a permanent limp and a few reconstruction procedures to look forward to. But the tough bugger never told Robert a thing – and for that, he had my unwavering respect, gratitude and love.

'Aloysius is awake again I see?' he grumbled good-naturedly. I doubted she would be rid of her silly nickname any time soon.

'Yep,' I replied, 'and hungry. Oh, and busy filling her nappy. Like her mother, she takes multi-tasking to a whole new level.'

Harry pulled a face. He wasn't overly taken with babies, but I knew he loved my daughter. He wandered off with a glass of water towards the lounge. He was staying with us until he was ready to be on his own – and until the money was sorted.

Ellie turned thirty in less than a month, and the trust fund would become legally hers. Well, hers and Ben's. We were still trying to get our heads around what to do with it. We were using a new lawyer and my dad was helping us plan. Her parents hadn't included Ben in the trust fund – another strange anomaly we would perhaps never fully understand, but there was plenty to go around and Ellie was happy to share.

She also wanted to give some to Rachel. She was thrilled to find she had a half-sister.

Once Rachel had calmed down about being drugged and locked in a pantry, the two of them had spent time getting to know each other. Although annoyingly, she insisted on calling her Eleanor. I think she did that just to piss me off. Rachel's childhood sounded almost as miserable as Ellie's, so they had a lot in common.

Robert had manipulated Rachel with promises of money when she was desperate, and then he had threatened her when she wanted out.

So the trust fund was being split between all the siblings which still left more than enough for Ellie, me and baby Chloe.

I think Ben's share would be used up quickly, on food mainly. The fridge heaved a sigh of relief when he returned to Canada and his interrupted preparations for the Olympics. He promised to return and spend Christmas with us.

Chloe gave a contented sigh and sagged, somewhat sated, into my arms. I loved Ellie with all my heart but it was nothing compared to the unconditional love I felt for our daughter. Ellie and I still had a way to go before we were completely back to normal. She was sharing more of her past with me every day, and it was helpful now that we had Harry around to fill in the details.

Should there be another crisis, I still wasn't convinced that I'd be the first person she'd turn to, but coming third behind Ben and Harry was enough – for now. We had our whole lives to get it sorted, whatever the future held for us.

I walked through to the lounge and found Harry watching reruns of Top Gear, flinching at every loud sound. I was concerned he had shades of PTSD from his gruelling experience with Robert.

I handed him my precious daughter, who he shovelled around like a basketball unsure which end was which. She grabbed his finger in her perfect miniature hand

and, opening her eyes wide, looked right into my soul. Although only just six weeks old, I could have sworn her left eye was changing from blue to a honey gold colour. She would have her mother's beautiful eyes.

'Cuddle your niece, Harry, and I'll make us a cup of tea. I remembered yesterday to pick up some milk.'

THE END

ACKNOWLEDGEMENT

To everyone who helped provide feedback and technical input, to everyone who read various drafts and to those who had to painstakingly listen to me talk about my book, sorry I can't mention you all by name. Still, you know who you are and how much you are appreciated.

Special thanks to my talented editor, Hollie Kingsland, for her incredible technical editorial input and continual support and encouragement to achieve my dream.

Printed in Great Britain
by Amazon